HIGH CRIMES

HIGH CRIMES

JOSEPH FINDER

AVON BOOKS
An Imprint of HarperCollinsPublishers

For Michele
and for Emma & her fan club

AVON BOOKS
An Imprint of HarperCollins*Publishers*
10 East 53rd Street
New York, New York 10022-5299

First Avon Books paperback printing: March 1999
First Avon Books special paperback printing: February 1998
First William Morrow hardcover printing: February 1998

10 9 8 7 6 5 4

ACKNOWLEDGMENTS

We should all have editors as dedicated as Henry Ferris. Just hours after his twin daughters were born, when most new fathers can't think straight, he was tirelessly exchanging faxes and FedEx packages from the hospital. I'm grateful for his sound judgment, his taste, and his determination. (If it were up to him, he'd have deleted this paragraph as needless excess in a section already too long.)

With each of my four novels, I've been privileged to have such superb and generous sources, above all my friend Jack McGeorge of the Public Safety Group in Woodbridge, Virginia, expert in security, munitions, terrorism, and just about everything else. The longer I know him, the more he seems to know. Once again I'm indebted to other friends who've given freely of their expertise, contacts, and advice: Paul McSweeney of Professional Management Specialists; H. Keith Melton, expert in (and world-class collector of) surveillance devices; Peter Crooks of the Association of Former Intelligence Officers; the remarkable Paul Redmond of the CIA; Thomas Powers, for his wise counsel; and Marty Peretz, for his generous and unflagging support from the very beginning of my writing career.

A number of experts in various fields provided valuable assistance: in voice and tape identification, Lonnie Smrkovski; on the military and its security procedures, Mickey Connolly; on the U.S. Marshals, Dick Bigelow; and on government secrecy, Steven Aftergood of the Federation of American Scientists. Carlos Salinas of Amnesty International furnished useful background on American involvement in El Salvador. In the Cambridge Police, I was helped by Kathy Murphy, Alisse Cline of the Identification Unit, and Detectives Lester J. Sullivan and John Lopes of the Criminal Investigation Section; and in the Massachusetts State Police, by Chris Dolan in Crime Scene Services. Tom Williams helped make the polygraph scenes as authentic as possible. At Quantico, Chief Warrant Officer Jim Hart granted me an enlightening tour of the brig. Carl M. Majeskey shared with me his unparalleled ballistics expertise. My brother and medical consultant, Dr. Jonathan Finder, was as usual supremely generous with expert medical advice, as well as with an unfortunately timed computer catastrophe.

Claire would have had an even rougher time of it without my team of Boston attorneys: Ralph D. Gants of Palmer & Dodge; Morris M. Goldings of Mahoney, Hawkes & Goldings; Charles W. Rankin of Rankin & Sultan; Nick Poser; and especially Harry Mezer; and in Washington, Joseph E. diGenova and Victoria Toensing. At Harvard Law School, Alan Dershowitz and particulary Martha Minow were extremely helpful, as was M. Tracey Maclin at the Boston University Law School.

The author Rodney Barker kindly provided entrée to the insular and highly specialized world of military law. Thanks to him I was able to assemble my own Dream Team of civilian attorneys specializing in courts-martial, including William J. Baker, Tom Folk, David Sheldon, and the estimable David L. Beck. Charles W. Gittins helped immensely in devising Claire's legal strategy, at a time when he was working round the clock to defend the Sergeant Major of the Army. And I can't say enough about the great Mike Powell, a civilian military attorney with the imagination of a novelist, who cheerfully served as my chief legal adviser and military consultant, and became a friend. If ever I were court-martialed, I'd hire him in an instant. The malevolent nature of Tom's court-martial is purely my own invention and not based on anything I ever saw in real life. None of the military judges I met were at all like my Warren Farrell. (What's *possible*, though, is another matter. . . .) Any procedural or legal errors are mine, or maybe Claire's.

At William Morrow I thank Paul Fedorko, Ann Treistman, and Fritz Metsch. I had a superb copy editor in Terry Zaroff-Evans. My wonderful and supremely able assistant, Kathy Economou, made my writing life a lot easier. My gratitude to my terrific literary agent and all-around consigliere, Molly Friedrich; her assistant, Paul Cirone; and Aaron Priest; and again I appreciate the enthusiasm of my foreign-rights agent, Danny Baror, and Richard Green and Howie Sanders of United Talent Agency. My parents, Morris and Natalie Finder, are outstanding unpaid freelance publicists and supporters. And of course my brother, Henry Finder, peerless editor/consultant, still sets aside time for me even as the demand on his time grows and the outside world gets wise to his talents. My wife, Michele Souda, not only helped give life to Claire but also recognized that in my fiction, men who cook are to be watched closely. She encouraged me from the start and continues to believe, and I'm grateful as always for her loving support.

He that has eyes to see and ears to hear may convince himself that no mortal can keep a secret. If his lips are silent, he chatters with his fingertips; betrayal oozes out of him at every pore.

—SIGMUND FREUD, *Dora*

PART ONE

1

At exactly nine o'clock in the morning, Claire Heller Chapman entered the cavernous old Harvard Law School lecture hall and found a small knot of reporters lying in wait for her. There were four or five of them, one a TV cameraman hefting a bulky videocam.

She'd expected this. Ever since the Lambert verdict was announced, two days ago, she'd been fielding calls from journalists. Most of them she'd managed to avoid. Now they stood at the front of the old classroom, by her lectern, and as she walked right by them they shouted questions at her.

Claire smiled blandly and could make out only fragments.

"—Lambert? Any comment to make?"

"—pleased with the verdict?"

"—Are you at all concerned about letting a rapist go free?"

A murmur of student voices went up. With the lectern giving her the advantage now of two feet of height, she addressed the reporters. "I'm afraid you're going to have to leave my classroom."

"A brief comment, Professor," said the TV reporter, a pretty blonde in a salmon suit with shoulder pads like a linebacker's.

"Nothing right now, I'm sorry," she said. "I have a class to teach."

Her criminal-law students sat in long arcs that radiated outward from the front of the room like the rings around Saturn. At Harvard Law School, the professor was construed as a deity. This morning the deity was being assaulted.

"But, Professor, a quick—"

"You're trespassing, folks. Out of here, please. *Out.*"

Muttering, they began turning around, straggling noisily up the creaky floor of the center aisle toward the exit.

She turned to the class and smiled. Claire Heller, as she was known professionally, was in her mid-thirties: small and slender, brown eyes and dimpled cheeks, with a tangle of coppery hair nuzzling a swan neck. She wore a tweedy but not unstylish chocolate-brown jacket over a cream silk shell.

"All right," Claire said to the class. "Last time someone asked me, 'Who's Regina? And who's Rex?' " She took a sip of water. There were a few chuckles. A few guffaws. Law-school humor: you laugh to show you get it, you're smart—not because it's funny.

"It's Latin, folks." Another sip of water. It's all in the timing.

A gradual crescendo of giggles. "English law. Regina is the queen. Rex is the king."

Loud, relieved laughter, from the slower ones who finally got it. The best comedy audience in the world.

The back door of the classroom banged shut as the

last cameraman left. "All right, *Terry* v. *Ohio*. One of the last Warren Court decisions. A real landmark in liberal jurisprudence." She cast her gaze around the classroom, a Jack Benny poker face. A few students chortled. They knew her politics.

She raised her voice a few decibels. "*Terry* v. *Ohio*. That great decision that permitted the police to shake people down for just about any reason whatsoever. Mr. Chief Justice Earl Warren giving one to the cops." She swiveled her body suddenly. "Ms. Harrington, what if the cops burst into your apartment one evening. Without a search warrant. And they find your stash of crack cocaine. Can you be prosecuted for possession?" A few titters: the humorless, studious Ms. Harrington, a very tall, pale young woman with long ash-blond hair parted in the middle, was not exactly the crack-smoking type.

"No way," said Ms. Harrington. "If they burst in without a warrant, that evidence can be excluded at trial. Because of the exclusionary rule."

"And where does that come from?" Claire asked.

"The Fourth Amendment," Ms. Harrington replied. The purple circles underneath her eyes advertised how little she'd slept her unhappy first year of law school. "It protects us from unreasonable government searches. So any evidence obtained in violation of the Fourth Amendment must be excluded from a criminal trial. It's called 'fruit of the poisoned tree.' "

"Like your vial of crack," said Claire.

Ms. Harrington peered gloomily at Claire through raccoon circles of purple and gave a grim half-smile. "Right."

The students, the smarter ones anyway, were beginning to sense the undertow: the good old liberal wisdom from Claire Heller, old Sixties Liberal, arrested during her student days at Madison, Power to the People, Fuck the Establishment. Time to whip-saw them.

"Okay, now will someone tell me where in the Fourth Amendment it says that evidence illegally obtained must be excluded from trial?" Claire asked.

Silence.

"Ms. Zelinski? Ms. Cartwright? Ms. Williams? Mr. Papoulis?"

She stepped off the rostrum, took an Oprah-like stroll down one of the creaky-floored aisles. "No-where, folks. Nowhere."

From the back of the room came the reedy bari-tone of Chadwick Lowell III, sandy-blond hair al-ready receding above round British National Health Plan wire-rim glasses, probably from his year as a Rhodes. "I take it you're no fan of the exclusionary rule."

"You got it," Claire said. "We never had such a thing apply to the States until maybe forty years ago—a hundred and seventy years after the Fourth Amendment was adopted."

"But the exclusionary rule," Mr. Lowell persisted disdainfully, "didn't exactly bother you at the Gary Lambert appeal, did it? You got his conviction over-turned by getting the search of his trash excluded, right? So I guess you're not so opposed to it, are you?"

There was a stunned silence. Claire slowly turned to face him. Secretly she was impressed. Mr. Lowell did not flinch. "In the classroom," she said, "we can talk about principle. In the courtroom, you put aside whatever the hell you believe in and fight with every goddamned scrap of ammunition you've got." She turned to her podium. "Now, let's get back to *Terry* v. *Ohio*."

* * *

"Still working on that?"

The waiter was tall and rail-thin, early twenties, insufferable. He looked like a Ralph Lauren model. His blond hair was cropped short; his sideburns were trimmed. His sandpiper legs were clad in black jeans and he wore a black linen T-shirt.

Claire, her husband, Tom, and her six-year-old daughter, Annie, were having dinner that evening at a family-friendly seafood restaurant in an upscale shopping mall in downtown Boston. "Family-friendly" usually meant helium balloons, crayons, and paper placemats. This place was a cut or two above that, and the food was decent.

Claire caught Tom's eye and smiled. Tom liked to make fun of that old standard waiter's line. They both did: since when was eating dinner supposed to be *work*?

"We're all set," Tom said pleasantly. Tom Chapman was a youthful mid-forties, trim and handsome in a navy Armani suit. He'd just come from work. His close-cropped hair was graying and receding slightly. His eyes, bracketed by deep-etched crow's feet, were gray-blue, more gray than blue, and almost twinkled with amusement.

Claire nodded agreement. "All done working," she said with a straight face.

"I'm all done, too," said Annie, her glossy brown hair in pigtails, wearing her favorite pale-pink cotton jumper.

"Annie-Banannie," Tom said, "you didn't even eat half your burger!"

"Was everything all right?" the waiter asked with concern.

"Very good, thanks," Tom said.

"But I ate the fries!"

"Can I tempt you with dessert?" asked the waiter. "The *marquise au chocolat* with pistachio sauce is fabulous. To *die* for. Or there's a warm molten chocolate cake that's really *sinful*."

"I want chocolate cake!" said Annie.

Tom looked at Claire. She shook her head. "Nothing for me," she said.

"Are you *sure*?" the waiter asked conspiratorially, wickedly. "How 'bout three forks?"

"No, thanks. Maybe just coffee. And no chocolate cake for her unless she finishes her hamburger."

"I'm *going* to finish it!" Annie protested, squirming in her seat.

"Very good," the waiter said. "Two coffees?"

"One," Claire said when Tom shook his head.

The waiter hesitated, cocking his head toward Claire. "Excuse me, are you Professor Heller?"

Claire nodded. "That's me."

The waiter smiled wide, as if he'd been let in on a state secret. "I've seen you on TV," he said as he turned away.

"You don't exist unless you've been on TV, you know," Tom said when the waiter had left. He squeezed her hand under the lacquered tabletop. "The burdens of fame."

"Not exactly."

"In Boston, anyway. How are your colleagues at the Law School going to deal with this?"

"As long as I meet my teaching obligations, they really don't care who I defend. I could represent Charles Manson; they'd probably whisper I'm a publicity whore, but they'd leave me alone." She placed a hand on one of his cheeks, then the other hand on his other, and planted a kiss on his mouth. "Thanks," she said. "Wonderful celebration."

"My pleasure."

Light glinted off Tom's forehead, his deeply furrowed brow. She admired the planes of his face, his high cheekbones, his square chin. Tom wore his hair short, almost military style, in order to de-emphasize the balding, but as a result he looked like an overgrown school kid, fresh-scrubbed and eager to please. His blue-gray eyes, this evening tending toward blue, were translucent and innocent. He caught her looking at him and smiled. "What?"

"Nothing. Just thinking."

"About?"

She shrugged.

"You seem a little subdued. Feeling funny about getting Lambert off?"

"Yeah, I guess so. I mean, it was the right thing to do, I think. A really important case. Evidence that clearly should have been suppressed, the whole issue of 'knowing and informed consent,' unlawful search and seizure, inevitable discovery. Important Fourth Amendment stuff."

"And yet you got a rapist off," he said gently. He knew how uneasy she was about having taken on the Lambert case. The famous heir to the Lambert fortune, thirty-year-old Gary Lambert, whose picture you couldn't help seeing in *People* magazine, usually in the arms of some supermodel, had been charged by the New York Police Department with the rape of a fifteen-year-old girl.

When Lambert's fancy trial lawyers asked Claire to handle the appeal, she didn't hesitate. She knew why she'd been hired: it wasn't simply because of her growing reputation as an appellate lawyer but, rather, because she was a professor at Harvard Law School. Her prominence in the legal profession might go a long way toward offsetting Gary Lambert's fairly squirrelly reputation. Yet she was fascinated by the legal issues involved, the police search of Lambert's penthouse apartment and his trash, which she knew wouldn't stand up. She never doubted she'd get his conviction overturned.

Suddenly, as a result of the case, Claire was on the cusp of minor celebrity. She was now a regular on Court TV and on Geraldo Rivera's legal talk-show. The *New York Times* had begun to quote her in articles on other trials and legal controversies. She certainly wasn't recognized walking down the street, but she was on the national media's radar screen.

"Look," Tom said, "you always say that the more despicable the person, the more he needs counsel. Right?"

"Yeah," she said without conviction. "In theory."

"Well, I think you did a great job, and I'm really proud of you."

"Maybe you can give my interviews to the *Globe*," she said.

"I'm all done now," Annie said, holding up a crust of bun. "Now I want dessert." She slipped out of her chair and crawled into Tom's lap.

He smiled, lifted his stepdaughter up in the air, and gave her a loud smacking kiss on the cheek. "I love you, pumpkin. My Annie-Banannie. It's coming soon, baby."

"I forgot to tell you," Claire said, "that *Boston* magazine wants to name us one of its Fifty Power Couples, or something like that."

"Mommy, can I get ice cream with it?" asked Annie.

"Let me guess," Tom said. "They just called because you got Gary Lambert off."

"Yes, sweetie, you can," said Claire. "Actually, they called a few days ago."

"Gee, I don't know about that, honey," Tom said. "We're not that kind of people."

She shrugged, smiled with embarrassment. "Says who? Anyway, it'd be good for your business, wouldn't it? Probably attract a lot of investors to Chapman & Company."

"I think it's a little tacky, honey, that's all. 'Power Couples' . . ." He shook his head. "You didn't say yes already, did you?"

"I didn't say anything yet."

"I just wish you wouldn't."

"Daddy," said Annie, one small arm curled around his neck, "when is the man bringing the cake?"

"Soon, babe."

"Do they have to *bake* it?"

"Sure seems like it," Tom said. "It's certainly taking long enough."

"Did I tell you the cops think they might have recovered one of the stolen paintings?" Claire said. They'd had a break-in a few days earlier, in which two of their paintings had been stolen—a Corot sketch of a nude woman that was a recent birthday gift to her from Tom, and a William Bailey still life in oil that Tom loved and she hated.

"Seriously? And I was all set to file the insurance claims. Which one'd they find?"

"Don't know. Of course, it wouldn't tear me apart if the Bailey's lost forever."

"I know," Tom said. "Too cold and precise and controlled, right? Well, I loved it. Anyway, honey, it's only stuff, you know? Objects, things. And no one got hurt; that's the important thing."

The waiter arrived with a tray. On it were the chocolate cake, a coffee cup, and two flutes of champagne. "Compliments of the house," the waiter said. "With our congratulations."

As they left the restaurant, Annie darted ahead into the mall's food court, shouting, "I wanna go play in the space ship!" The giant plastic space ship was located in Annie's favorite kiddie store nearby, in front of which stood giant resin statues of cartoon characters.

The food court was lined with upscale fast-food places and furnished with small round tables, wooden benches, and ficus trees in brass planters. The floor was tiled in highly polished marble. The big open space was three levels high and ringed with balconies that rose all the way up to a glass skylight illuminated by floodlights. At the far end of the atrium was an artificial waterfall that cascaded down a jagged granite wall.

"Slow down, Annie-Banannie," Tom called out, and Annie circled back, grabbed her father's hand, and tugged at it, at the same moment that two men in suits approached them.

One of them said, "Mr. Kubik, come with us, please. Let's make this simple."

Tom turned to the one on the left, puzzled. "Excuse me?"

"Ronald Kubik, federal agents. We have a warrant for your arrest."

Tom smiled, furrowed his brow. "You've got the wrong guy, buddy," he said, taking Claire's hand and striding quickly past them.

"Mr. Kubik, come along quietly and no one will get hurt."

Puzzled, Claire laughed at the absurdity of this. "Sorry, boys."

"You're making some kind of a mistake," Tom

said, raising his voice, no longer amused.

The man on the right abruptly grabbed Tom's arm, and Claire said, "Get your hands off my husband."

Suddenly Tom swung his briefcase to the right, slamming the man in the stomach, knocking him backward and to the floor, and then, in a flash, he'd sprung forward and was running away, into the food court, at astonishing speed.

Claire shouted after him, "Tom, where're you going?"

Annie screamed, "Daddy!"

A voice yelled: "*Freeze.*"

Claire stared in shock as the two men chased after Tom, and then from all around the atrium men began to move abruptly. Why was he running, if this was indeed a case of mistaken identity? On her left, a couple of short-haired men in their late twenties, who'd been sitting having coffee in front of the chocolate-chip-cookie place, jumped to their feet.

Claire shouted, "Tom!" But he was already most of the way across the court, still running.

One of the men, wearing a navy blazer and tie, had just left the line in front of the pizza place and began gesturing to the others. He was older and appeared to be their leader. "Hold it!" he shouted. "Hold fire!"

On her right, another short-haired man, who'd been loitering near Yogurt 'n Salad, whipped around and joined the pursuit. A pair of tourists with cameras around their necks who'd been inspecting the Williams-Sonoma window display suddenly turned and began running toward the far side of the atrium.

"Tom!" Claire screamed. What the hell was happening?

From every direction now men rose from tables,

emerged from nearby shops. Tourists and casual loiterers were suddenly moving quickly, smoothly, converging on Tom from every direction.

A loud, metallically amplified voice came over a bullhorn: *"Freeze! Federal agents!"*

The place was in an uproar. People were crowding at the glass balconies on the upper levels staring down at the scene in disbelief.

Claire stood still, frozen in terror, her mind racing. What was going on? Who were all these men chasing Tom? And why was he running?

"Mommy!" Annie whimpered. "Where's Daddy going?"

"Cover the emergency exits!" yelled the man in the blue blazer into the commotion.

Claire held her Annie tight, stroking her face. "It's okay, baby," she said. It was all she could think to say. *What was happening?* From all over, people streamed into the middle of the food court. A young boy clung to his father's leg, crying.

At the far end of the atrium she could see Tom, running even faster, knocking over chairs and benches as he went, suddenly swerve toward the white-tiled wall next to the Japanese take-out kiosk and grab a fire-alarm pull-box. A deafeningly loud bell began to clang. Screams now came from all directions. People were running everywhere, shouting to one another.

"Mommy!" Annie cried in terror. "What's going on?"

Hugging Annie even more tightly, Claire shouted, "Tom!," but her voice couldn't be heard above the incredible din, the clanging fire alarm, the screams from all around. She watched Tom sprint toward the bank of escalators that led up to the movie theater on the floor above.

One of the pursuers, a tall, lanky black man, managed to reach Tom and lunged for him. Claire let out an involuntary scream. Then, suddenly, Tom whirled around and slammed the flat of his hand against the black man's neck, grabbed the man's underarm with the other hand, and forced the guy to the floor. The man bellowed in pain and lay flat on the floor, eyes closed, legs twitching, apparently paralyzed.

Claire watched in speechless astonishment, a dull, almost vacant state of horror and disbelief. None of this made sense. All she could think was, *Tom doesn't know how to do any of these things.*

As Tom streaked past a stand marked PASTA PRIMO, another man lunged from behind the counter, and Tom tackled him to the ground, then sprang to his feet, weaving away from him. But the man managed to rise and kept coming at Tom, now pointing a gun. Tom grabbed a heavy-looking metal briefcase out of the hands of a horrified onlooker and flung it at his pursuer, knocking the gun out of his hands and sending it clattering to the floor.

Then he wheeled around and bounded toward the fake waterfall coursing down its granite wall at the end of the atrium, just as two other men emerged from an emergency door next to the Italian restaurant just a few feet away.

Tom scrambled up the rocks and boulders in front of the waterfall and in one great leap—Claire could barely believe what she was seeing—he began scaling the jagged stone wall, grabbing on to jutting edges of stone, using them as finger- and toeholds, pulling himself up with his hands, face-climbing up the wall like a skilled rock climber.

"Freeze!" one of the men shouted at him, pulling out a gun and aiming. He fired a shot, which pockmarked the granite very close to Tom's head.

She screamed, "Tom!" To the others, she yelled: "Stop it! What the hell are you doing?" She could barely believe what Tom, her husband of three years, the man she loved and knew so intimately, was doing. It was as if another man had taken his place, a man she didn't know, who could do things her Tom would never have dreamed of.

For an instant Tom actually stopped, and Claire wondered whether he really did intend to halt where he was, almost ten feet off the ground, clinging to the artificial rock face.

Another shot hit the glass wall of the balcony just above him, shattering it, and then Tom continued up the rock face with an awesome agility, and Claire stared in rapt amazement as he reached over to the brass guardrail around the balcony, grabbed hold, and deftly swung himself up into the gawking, frenzied crowd of people who'd been waiting to get into the movie theaters or were streaming out of them, and then at once he was gone.

"God*damn* it!" the leader shouted as he reached the escalators. He swept an index finger around at his men. "You two, to the parking garage! You, up this way, into the theater. Move it!" He whirled around and called to another of his men, "Damn it, we lost the fucker!" Then he pointed directly at Claire and Annie, jerking his thumb to one side. "I want *them*," he shouted. "*Now!*"

2

Claire and Annie were hustled off to a small, windowless room just off the atrium—a mall security station, by the look of it, and judging by the uniformed rent-a-cops standing guard outside, in light-blue shirts with dark-blue shoulder patches. Special Agent Howard Massie of the FBI, the man in the blue blazer, was beefy and crewcut, with small gray eyes and a pockmarked face. The other men were U.S. marshals.

As Annie squirmed in her arms, Claire said, "What the hell is this all about?" The knot of anxiety in her stomach had swollen; the underarms of her blouse were damp with perspiration.

Annie wriggled to the floor and held on to Claire's skirt. She whined, "Where's Daddy?"

"Mrs. Chapman," Agent Massie said, "I think it's better if we speak alone. Perhaps your daughter can wait outside, in the care of one of these fine gentlemen here." He leaned forward and gave Annie a brief pat on the head. Annie, in reply, frowned, twitched her head, and shrugged away from him.

"You get your hands off my child," Claire said.

17

"You are not touching her. She's staying here with me."

Massie nodded and managed to regain a semblance of a smile. "Ma'am, you're obviously upset—"

"Upset?" she gasped. "Ten minutes ago we were having dinner. Suddenly everyone in the world is chasing my husband, firing guns! You want to know *upset*? You're looking at a multimillion-dollar civil lawsuit for the unnecessary use of force by two government agencies, reckless pursuit, and reckless endangerment of the lives of innocent bystanders. You and your cowboys just stirred up a shitstorm, agent."

"Mrs. Chapman, we have a fully authorized warrant for your husband's arrest. As to the guns, we weren't authorized to kill, but we were permitted to wound if necessary, and we didn't even do that."

Claire shook her head, laughed, and pulled her cell phone out of her purse. She extended the antenna and began punching numbers. "You might want to have a better story prepared for the *Herald* and the *Globe*," she said. "You obviously have the wrong man, and you just screwed up royally."

"If we have the wrong man," Massie replied quietly, "why did he run?"

"Obviously because you guys were in hot pursuit. . . ." She faltered, depressed the END button. "All right, what's your point?"

"You see," Massie said, "you don't want to do that. You don't want to call the media."

"Oh, I don't, do I?"

"Once it's out of the bottle, you can't put it back in. You may not want this made public. We'll have any police report sealed, and we'll do our best to quash any media coverage. You'd better pray you weren't recognized."

"Mommy," Annie said in a high, frightened voice, "I want to go home."

"Just a couple of minutes, sweetie," Claire said, reaching around to give Annie a quick one-armed hug. To Massie, she snapped: "What exactly are you referring to?"

"Your husband, Ronald Kubik, is wanted for murder."

For a long moment Claire was speechless. "Now I *know* you have the wrong man," she said at last. She smiled in relief. "My husband is Tom Chapman."

"That's not his real name," Massie said. He pointed to a cheap-looking white conference table. "Why don't we sit down?"

Claire took a seat across the table from Massie. Annie at first sat in a chair next to Claire's, then slid off it onto the floor and began inspecting the underside of the table.

"And even if you do mean my husband, Tom," Claire said, "who's he supposed to have murdered?"

"I'm sorry, we're not authorized to say. Mrs. Chapman, or should I say Professor Heller, believe me, we know who you are. We're aware of your reputation. We're being extremely careful here. But what do you know about your husband's background? What has he told you?"

"I know everything," she said. "You've got the wrong guy."

Massie nodded and smiled sympathetically. "What you know is his legend, his created biography. Happy childhood in southern California, Claremont College, worked as a broker, moved to Boston, started his own investment firm here. Right?"

She narrowed her eyes, nodded. " 'Legend?' "

"You ever check with Claremont College?" he asked.

She shook her head. "What are you implying?"

"I'm not *implying* anything. And, frankly, I can't tell you much at all. But your husband, Ron Kubik, has been a fugitive from justice for thirteen years."

"That's the name you guys called him out there," she said thickly, her heart thudding. "I've never heard it before."

"He hasn't told you anything about his past?"

"Either this is some colossal mistake, or you guys are framing him. I know how you guys work. Tom is not a murderer."

"Three days ago you had a burglary at your home in Cambridge," the FBI man said. "The local police ran all the fingerprints in your house, which is standard procedure these days, put them into AFIS, the computerized Automated Fingerprint Identification System, and your husband's prints came up flagged. They've been on the system for years, waiting for him to commit some crime, or get fingerprinted for some other reason. Bad break for your husband. Lucky for us the Cambridge police were so thorough."

She shook her head. "My husband wasn't even *home* at the time," she said. "He didn't give the cops his prints."

"The police ran all the fingerprints in the house in order to eliminate everyone who wasn't the suspect. Naturally your husband's prints turned up," Massie said. "We came close this time. Unfortunately, a few minutes ago, we lost him somewhere in the parking garage. Your husband has disappeared before, and he'll try it again. But this time it won't work. We've got him."

Her mouth went dry. She felt her heartbeat accelerate. "You don't know who you're messing with," she said with a small, hollow laugh.

"He'll get in touch with you," Massie said. "He needs you. And when he does, we'll be watching."

3

C laire found the car in the mall parking garage, just where she'd left it, almost expecting to find Tom crouched in the back seat, or at least something there, some sort of sign from him. A note on the dashboard, or slipped under the windshield-wiper blade. But nothing. Their Volvo station wagon was empty.

For a few minutes, she sat still, breathing heavily, trying to regain control. The reality of what had just happened—or, rather, the *unreality* of it—was just beginning to sink in. While Annie sat in the back seat, licking at an ice-cream cone, her fright apparently having subsided, Claire's thoughts were in turmoil. What had she just witnessed? If Massie was lying to her, as she assumed, then why *had* Tom run away? And where had he learned to do such things?

There was a car phone in the Volvo, and as she drove out of the parking garage toward Cambridge, she half expected it to ring, but nothing.

Where had he gone? Was he all right?

Their house was an enormous Georgian, saved from grandeur only by an unruly ramblingness, a series of additions slapped on by a succession of previous owners. It was on Gray Gardens East, in the toniest part of Cambridge. Even a good distance away, as soon as she had turned the corner, Claire could see the stroboscopic flash of blue light, the unaccustomed buzz of late-night activity that she realized was coming from their driveway. She felt her stomach twist and turn over.

The front door was open.

Looking closer, she saw that it had actually been taken off its hinges. Dread roiled her stomach. She parked the car, grabbed Annie, and ran toward the door.

Inside the house men were everywhere, opening drawers and carting off cardboard boxes of papers. Some wore suits and trench coats; others were in dark-blue FBI windbreakers.

Annie burst into tears and choked out, "Why are these men in here?"

Claire stroked her back as they entered the foyer. "Nothing to worry about, my baby." Then she yelled out, "All right, who's in charge here?"

A man in a gray suit and trench coat emerged from the kitchen: tall, with a thatch of brown hair that was obviously colored, a few shades too dark, and a matching brown mustache. He held out a leather ID wallet. "Special Agent Crawford, FBI," he said.

"Where's your search warrant?" she demanded.

He glowered at her, then reluctantly reached into the breast pocket of his suit and pulled out a few sheets of paper, which he handed to her.

She looked them over. The first one, the authorization to search their house, seemed to be in order. It not only gave the correct address but described the appearance of the house. It also gave a ridiculously long list of items they were looking for, a laundry list so long, detailed, and comprehensive that it couldn't possibly leave out a thing. Telephone records, airline tickets, bus or train tickets, any notes concerning times of flights and train departures, out-of-state newspapers, advertisements, any notes pertaining to such that might be found in the trash, in Tom's files, among his personal possessions . . . It went on and on.

Claire looked up at Crawford. "Where's the warrant affidavit?" she asked.

"It's sealed."

"Where is it?"

He shrugged. "Probably in the chambers of the federal magistrate. I really don't know. Anyway, the warrant's valid."

He was right, of course. "I want a complete inventory of everything that's taken," she said.

"Certainly, ma'am."

She looked at the second warrant, the arrest warrant, which listed that same strange name, Ronald Kubik. The FBI agent saw what she was examining and said, "It also gives his assumed name, Thomas Chapman, ma'am. Everything's in order."

She heard the team spreading throughout the house, heard the scrape of furniture against the wooden floor in Tom's study immediately above, heard shouts back and forth. The sound of glass breaking. She cringed involuntarily. Everything felt unreal to her, terrifying and quietly menacing and unreal.

"They broke something!" Annie said, looking at her mother aghast.

"I know, honey," she said.

"Mommy, I want these guys to leave."

"Me too, baby."

"Mrs.—Uh, Professor Heller," Agent Crawford said, "if you have any knowledge whatsoever about your husband's whereabouts and you do not reveal them to us, you can be charged as an accessory after the fact, which in this case would be a felony. And obstructing justice, which is another felony."

"Try it," she said. "Go ahead, charge me. Really, I'd welcome that."

Crawford scowled. "You have a vacation home?"

"We've got a house in Truro, on Cape Cod. You're welcome to send your boys out there—I can't stop you—but do you seriously think that, if he's really on the run for some reason, he'd hide out in such an obvious place? Get real."

"Friends, relatives he might try to approach?"

"What do you think's going on?" She shook her head.

"You understand, Mrs. Chapman, that we'll be watching your every move in case he tries to contact you, or you try to contact him."

"I'm quite aware," Claire said, "of what sort of shit the government is capable of when they decide to come down on you."

Crawford nodded, half smiling.

"And you can bet my husband is aware of that, too. Now, if you don't mind, I'd like to put my daughter to bed."

4

Claire's sister, Jackie, arrived half an hour after Annie went to bed. She was taller than Claire, skinnier, but not as pretty, with long streaked blond hair. She was two years younger but looked older. Jackie wore black jeans and a black T-shirt under her scruffy denim jacket. Her fingernails were painted, not black, but a sort of eggplant, a Chanel Vamp color.

They sat on the glassed-in sun porch. The stuffy, overheated room was like a greenhouse. Its floor-to-ceiling glass walls were steamy; its outside surface was running with condensation.

"They really tore the house up, didn't they?" Jackie said in her husky, smoker's voice. She ate sesame chicken with chopsticks out of a white paper carton.

Claire nodded.

"Can't you sue for that? Destruction of property, or whatever?"

Claire shook her head slowly. "We got bigger problems, kid."

"What do you think's going on?"

"I don't know," she admitted, her voice quavering.

Jackie took a swig of her Diet Pepsi, then fished out a cigarette from the pack of Salems. "Mind if I smoke?"

"Yes."

Jackie flicked the plastic lighter anyway. The tip of the cigarette flared orange. She sucked in and spoke muzzily through a mouthful of smoke. "They want him for murder? That's got to be bullshit. Pope Tom?"

"Pope?"

"Good Catholic and Mr. Perfect."

"Very funny, Jackie. You don't get it, do you? You're making jokes."

"Sorry. Did the arrest warrant say what he did?"

Claire shook her head again. "Sealed."

"Can they do that?"

"You don't know the government. You wouldn't *believe* the shit they can get away with."

"What's with the name? Rubik or whatever."

"Kubik. Ronald Kubik. I have no idea, Jacks."

"Can that be right?"

"What do I know anymore? They seem so sure of it."

"They *say* they're sure of it. Who knows what the real story is."

"Good point. I'll have one of those. I *need* one."

"Uh-oh."

"You're a bad influence." She took a cigarette and the lighter from Jackie. She lighted it, inhaled, and coughed. "It's been a couple of years."

"Like riding a bicycle," Jackie said.

"Ooh, menthol," Claire said. "Yuck. Almost as bad as clove cigarettes. Tastes like Vicks Vapo-Rub."

Jackie looked through the steamy glass at the perfectly landscaped backyard. "So where *is* he?"

Claire shook her head, exhaled a cloud of smoke. The room was hazy with cigarette smoke. "They say they lost him in the parking garage."

"Doesn't that tell you he's guilty of something?"

"Oh, come on!" Claire snapped. "That's such bullshit. Tom's not guilty of a goddamned thing."

"So what are you going to do?"

"Do? They're right, he'll get in touch with me. Or he'll come back. And he'll explain what's going on."

"And if he really is guilty of murder?"

"You know him, Jackie," Claire said, low and intense and angry. "What do you think?"

"You're right. He's not a murderer. But he did run. And you gotta wonder why."

Claire scowled, shook her head as if to dispel the thought. "You know," she said after a while, "when all those guys were chasing him down, one of them reached him, and I thought it was all over. But suddenly Tom had him down on the ground. Disabled him with his bare hands. Crippled him or knocked him out—maybe killed him, I don't know."

"Jesus."

"It's as if—Well, I've never seen him do anything like that. I had no idea he could do something like that. It was scary. And the way he scaled that wall, the waterfall. It's like a different Tom took over."

"I had no idea he knew how to rock-climb."

"I didn't either!"

They sat for a minute in silence.

"Think there'll be something in the papers about this?" Jackie asked.

"I haven't gotten any calls yet. I don't think anyone recognized me, except the waiter, who probably didn't see the incident."

Jackie exhaled a plume of smoke through her

nose, her chin jutting forward. "Tom'll be back. He'll explain all this shit."

Claire nodded.

"He's a great stepdad. Annie adores him. Daddy's little girl."

"Yeah." She felt a swelling in her chest. She missed him already, and she was frightened for him.

"Annie told me he came into her school for Mom's Day last week."

Claire winced. "I was all set to, but I was in New York, meeting with Lambert's attorneys, and I couldn't get a flight back in time."

"Ouch. She must have loved that."

"I felt horrible."

"How come he's able to just take off time in the middle of the day like that to go to her school? I thought he's one of those obsessive-compulsive Type A types"

"He let his chief trader, Jeff, man the trading desk, I guess. I don't know. Lot of guys wouldn't do that."

"At least he doesn't call her Princess. That would be gross."

"I get a feeling Annie thinks *I'm* the stepparent."

"She was, what, like two when you guys got married? She doesn't even remember when he wasn't her daddy."

"Still," Claire said sulkily, "I *am* the birth mother."

"You guys got any vodka?" Jackie asked.

Claire was convinced that happy marriages were only really appreciated by those who'd been married, badly, already. She'd met Jay, her first husband, at Yale Law School, and at the time he'd seemed such a good match. He was good-looking, seemingly easy-going (though in reality wound tighter than a clock spring), tall and blond and slim. He'd paid her the kind of attention no man had really paid her before, and that alone—for an insecure young woman whose father had abandoned the family when she was nine (she'd been in therapy; she recognized the issues)—was almost mesmerizing. Jay was as career-oriented, as hardworking as she was, which she'd mistakenly thought made them compatible. After her clerkships, when she was hired to teach at Harvard Law School, he'd moved to Boston to take a job at a high-powered downtown firm, and also to be with her. They were married. They worked, and talked about work. On the weekends Jay would unwind by getting roaring drunk. He also became abusive. He was, it turned out, a deeply unhappy man.

Though she was about to turn thirty, neither one of them was ready to start a family. Only later did Claire realize that her reluctance was an early-warning signal of a bad marriage. When she'd gotten pregnant by accident, Jay started drinking regularly, on weekdays, then at lunchtime, then pretty much all the time. His work suffered, of course. He didn't make partner. He was told to begin looking at other firms.

He didn't want a child, he said. He wasn't even sure he wanted to be married to her. He admitted he was threatened by this high-powered woman he'd married. By the time Annie was born, Jay had moved in with his parents in Austin, Texas.

Here she was, a young star on the Harvard Law School faculty, a great success by most conventional measures, and her personal life was a train wreck. Without the help of her sister, Jackie, she didn't know how she'd have made it.

Jackie, and a guy named Tom Chapman, the investment adviser Jay had chosen to manage their small but growing portfolio of stocks. Tom became a friend, a support, a shoulder to cry on. When Annie was six months old, Jay, the daddy she'd never known, was killed in a car accident. Drunk, naturally. And Tom Chapman had been there, at Claire's house, almost nightly, helping her through it, helping make funeral arrangements, counseling her.

Five months later, Claire and Tom started seeing each other. He'd nursed her back to emotional health, forced her to go out to Red Sox games at Fenway Park and Celtics games at the old Boston Garden. He explained to her the mysteries of basketball, the fast break and the pick-and-roll. When she was morose he wheedled her with jokes, mostly bad ones, until she laughed at their badness. They'd go for picnics in Lincoln, and once, when they were rained out, he set it up on the carpet of the front room of his South End apartment, with picnic baskets stuffed with sandwiches and macaroni salad and potato chips. Tom was as emotionally attentive as Jay had been unavailable, distant. He was gentle and caring, yet at the same time fun-loving, with a mischievous streak she adored.

And he loved Annie. Was in fact crazy about her. He would spend hours playing with Annie, building castles out of blocks, playing with the big wooden dollhouse he'd made for her. When Claire needed to work, Tom would take Annie to the playground or the pet shop or just walking around Harvard Square. Annie, who didn't understand what had happened to her real father, was at once drawn to him and instinctively resentful of him, but by the time Claire had fallen in love with Tom, Annie had too. A year and a half later Claire and Tom were married. Finally she'd found a man to build a life with.

All right, so the first husband had been a mistake. There was an old Russian proverb Claire had read once and never forgotten: The first pancake is always a lump.

She brushed her teeth twice with a new baking-soda-and-peroxide toothpaste, but her mouth still tasted like an ashtray. How come it never used to bother her when she smoked a pack a day? Tom hated it when she smoked and had gotten her to quit.

A little woozy from the vodka she and Jackie had drunk, she settled into bed and thought.

Where could he be right now? Where could he have gone?

And why?

She picked up the phone to call Ray Devereaux, the private investigator she often used. The dial tone stuttered, indicating that there were messages on their voice mail.

Nothing unusual about that, but maybe Tom had left a message. It made a certain sense: only the two of them knew the secret code to access their voice mail.

Then again, if the FBI was really monitoring their phones, they'd hear anything she did.

She speed-dialed voice mail.

"Please dial your password," invited the friendly-efficient female automaton voice.

She punched the digits.

"You have two messages. Main menu: To hear your messages, press one. To send a message—"

She punched one.

"First message. Received today, at six-fifteen P.M." Then a woman's voice: "Hey, Claire, long time no speak. It's Jen." Jennifer Evans was one of her oldest and closest friends, but she liked to gab, and Claire had no time for it now. She punched the number one to get rid of the voice, but instead it started the message from the beginning. Frustrated, she sat there listening but not listening to Jen's long and involved message, until finally Jen wound it up, and then the friendly female automaton gave her the option of replaying or erasing or forwarding a message, and she erased it, and the next one came on.

"Received today, at seven-twenty-seven P.M." Then a male voice, Tom's, and her heart jumped.

"Claire . . . honey . . ." He was calling from someplace out of doors, the sound of traffic roaring in the background. "I don't know when you're going to get this, but I don't want you to worry about anything. I'm fine. I'm . . . I had to leave." A long pause. The throaty snarl of a motorcycle. "I—I don't know how much to trust the security of this voice mail, darling. I don't want to say too much, but don't believe anything you're being told. I'll be in touch with you one way or another, very soon. I love you, babe. And I'm so, so sorry. And please give my little dolly a great big hug for me. Tell her Daddy had to go away on business for a little while, and he's sorry he couldn't kiss her goodbye, but he'll see her soon. I love you, honey."

And the message was over. She played it again, then saved it by pressing two, then hung up.

Alone in their bed, she began to cry.

5

She woke up, reached for Tom, and remembered.
A bit hungover from the booze, she made breakfast for Annie and herself, a four-egg omelet, nothing else in it or on it, but it came out okay, which was nearly a miracle. Tom was the family's master chef, and eggs were pretty much the outer limit of her culinary ability. She flipped it onto Annie's favorite plate, then cut it neatly in two, taking half for herself.

"I don't want it," Annie said when Claire set it in front of her. She was still in her pajamas, having refused to get dressed. "I don't like eggs like this."

"It's an omelet, honey," Claire said.

"I don't care. I don't like it. I like it the way Daddy makes it."

Claire inhaled slowly. "Try it, honey."

"I don't want to try it. I don't want it."

"We're going to share it, you and me." Claire pointed to the omelet half on her own plate. "You see?"

"I hate it. I want it like Daddy makes it."

Claire sat down in the chair next to Annie's,

stroked her incredibly soft cheek. Annie turned her head away sharply. "Babe, we don't have any more eggs left, so I can't make you scrambled eggs like Daddy does."

"I want Daddy to make it."

"Oh, sweetie, I told you, Daddy had to go away on business for a while."

Annie's face sagged. "What's 'a while'?"

"A couple of days, babe. Maybe longer. But it's very, very important business, and Daddy wouldn't leave you unless it was *very* important. You know that."

"But why did he run away from me?"

So that was it. "He didn't run away from *you*, sweetheart. He . . . well, he had to get away from some bad men."

"Who?"

A good question. "I don't know."

"Why?"

"Why what? Why did he have to get away?"

Annie nodded, watching intently, hanging on her words.

"I don't know yet."

"Is he coming back?"

"Of course he is. In just a couple of days."

"I want him to come back today."

"So do I, baby. So do I. But he can't, because he has some very important business meetings."

Annie's face was blank. For a moment it appeared as if the storm had passed, as if her concerns had been allayed.

But suddenly Annie thrust out both hands and shoved her plate off the table, onto the tiled floor. The plate shattered with a loud crash, sending shards everywhere. The yellow half-moon of omelet

quivered on the floor, festooned with jagged slashes
of crockery.

"*Annie!*" Claire gasped.

Annie stared back with defiance and triumph.

Claire sank slowly to the floor, burying her face
in her hands. She could not move. She could no
longer cope.

Her eyes pooling with tears, Claire looked up at
her daughter. Annie stared in shocked silence.

In a small voice, Annie said, "Mommy?"

"It's all right, baby."

"Mommy, I'm sorry."

"It's okay. It's not that, baby—"

The front door opened. A jingling of keys, then a
cough announced Rosa's arrival.

"Is that Daddy?"

"It's Rosa. I told you, your daddy's going to be
away for a while."

"Mrs. Chapman!" exclaimed Rosa, rushing over to
Claire and helping her slowly to her feet. "Are you
a'right?"

"I'm okay, Rosa, thanks. I'm fine."

Rosa gave a quick, worried glance at Claire, then
kissed Annie on the cheek, which she sat still for.
"*Querida.*"

Claire brushed back her hair, nervously adjusted
her blouse. Knew she was a mess. "Rosa," she said,
"I've got to be at work. Can you make her breakfast
and walk her to school?"

"Of course, Mrs. Chapman. You want French
toast, *querida*?"

"Yes," Annie said sullenly. She slid her eyes furtively toward her mother, then back to Rosa.

"We're out of eggs, Rosa. I just used the last this
morning. On that." Claire gestured vaguely toward
the mess on the floor.

"Then I want toaster waffles," Annie said.

Rosa knelt on the floor, gingerly picking up shards of china and putting them into a paper Bread & Circus grocery bag. "Okay," Rosa said. "We have waffles."

"Give me a kiss, baby," Claire said, leaning over to kiss Annie.

Annie sat still, then kissed her mother back.

On the way out of the house, Claire picked up the kitchen phone and listened for the broken dial tone that might indicate a new voice-mail message.

There was none.

6

"*It's bad*," moaned Connie Gamache, her longtime secretary. "The phone hasn't stopped ringing in two days. The voice-mail thingo is full, can't take any more messages. People are getting *mean*. There's a lady and several *gentlemen* here to see you." She lowered her voice. "I use the term loosely."

" 'Morning, Connie," Claire said, turning to look. The waiting area, two hard couches and a couple of side chairs, normally empty, or maybe occupied by a lone student or two, bustled with reporters. Two of them she recognized: the *New York Times* Boston bureau chief, and a TV reporter from Channel 4 News she liked. Claire raised her chin in a silent greeting to the two of them. The last thing she wanted was to talk about the Lambert case to a bunch of indignant journalists.

"*I* need to hire an assistant," Connie went on without pause. "All of a sudden you're Miss Popular."

"I've got a faculty meeting in half an hour or so," Claire said, unlocking her office door—CLAIRE M. HELLER engraved on a brass plaque, her professional name—and removing her coat at the same time.

Connie followed her into her office, switched on the overhead light. She was broad-shouldered, large-bottomed, white-haired; decades ago, she'd been beautiful. She looked much older than her fifty years. "You've got a lot of reporters who want interviews," she warned. "Want me to send them all away, or what?"

Claire began unpacking her briefcase into neat piles on the long cherrywood desk. She exhaled a long sigh of frustration. "Ask what's-her-name from Channel Four—Novak, Nowicki, whatever it is—how long she needs. Ask the *Times* guy if he can come back later on, maybe this afternoon."

Connie shook her head in grave disapproval. She was good at handling the media but considered them all leeches to be plucked off the instant they'd affixed themselves. Claire was grateful, actually, for her secretary's concern, since she was usually right—reporters tended to sensationalize, exaggerate, and fuck you over if they possibly could. And usually they got their stories wrong. In a minute Connie returned. "Now I've got them mad. Carol Novak says she just needs five or ten minutes."

"Okay," Claire said. Carol Novak, that was her name, had been good to her—smart, reasonably accurate, with less of the animus toward Harvard than the other local reporters tended to exhibit. "Give me a couple of minutes to check my e-mail, then send Carol Novak in."

Carol Novak of Channel 4 entered with a cameraman who quickly set up lights, rearranged a desk lamp, moved a couple of chairs, and positioned himself facing Claire's desk. Meanwhile, the reporter, a small, pert redhead—very pretty, but overly made up, as TV reporters tend to be on the job—made small talk. Her lips were lined perfectly, Claire noticed, and her eyebrows were plucked into perfect slim arches. She asked about Annie; both of them had six-year-olds. She gossiped a bit about another, far more famous member of the Law School faculty. They shared a joke. Carol dispensed some praise and put her hand on Claire's, woman friend to woman friend. She didn't seem to know anything about the incident at the mall. The cameraman asked if Claire could move her chair away from the window and against the floor-to-ceiling bookshelves. Then, when the cameraman was ready, Carol sat at a chair next to Claire's, in the same frame, and hunched forward with an expression of deep concern.

"You've been criticized a lot recently for taking on the Gary Lambert case," the reporter said. Her voice had suddenly become deeper yet breathy, ripe with solicitude.

"For winning it, you mean," Claire said.

Carol Novak smiled, a killer's smile. "Well, for allowing a convicted rapist to go free on a technicality."

Claire matched smile for smile. "I don't think the Fourth Amendment is a 'technicality.' The fact is, his civil liberties were violated in the search of his apartment. My job was to defend his rights."

"Even if it meant a *convicted rapist* is free to rape again?"

Claire shook her head. "Lambert was convicted, but the trial was flawed. Our successful appeal proved that."

"Are you saying he *didn't* do it?"

"I'm saying the process was flawed. If we allow flawed trials to take place, then we're all at risk." How often she'd said this; did she always sound as hollow, as unpersuasive as she felt right now?

Carol Novak sat back in her chair. She stared into Claire's eyes with a fierceness that was startling. "As a woman, how do you feel about getting a rapist off?"

Claire responded quickly, unwilling to allow a pause that might be mistaken for misgivings. "As I said, that isn't the issue—"

"Claire," Carol Novak said with the deeply felt sorrow, the stricken intensity, the appalled concern of a daytime talk-show host interviewing a trailer-park denizen who was sleeping with the child he'd fathered by his own daughter, "do you ever feel, sometimes—*right here*"—she tapped her chest—"that what you're doing is wrong?"

"If I ever felt that," Claire said with great certainty and a dramatic pause, "I wouldn't do it," and she gave a smile that said, *We're all done now*, a smile with which, she knew, Channel 4 would end the interview.

Ray Devereaux stood in her office doorway. The private investigator was almost as big as the door, a good three hundred and fifty pounds, but he didn't appear fat. He was, instead, massive. His head seemed small, out of proportion to the immense trunk below, although that may have been an optical illusion, given his height.

Devereaux had a gift for the dramatic gesture. He didn't enter a room, he made an entrance. Now he had positioned himself at the threshold, arms folded atop his girth, and waited for her cue.

"Thanks for coming, Ray," Claire said.

"You're welcome," he said grimly, as if he had performed for her a great Herculean feat. "Where the hell do you park around here?"

"I park in the faculty garage. But there should have been plenty of spaces on Mass. Ave."

He scowled. "I had to park at a hydrant. Left my blank ticket book on the dash." He hadn't been on the police force for some twelve years already, but he still used all the tricks and appurtenances, the perks of being on the job. His blank book of parking tickets was no doubt more than a decade old by now, but the meter maids would still observe the shibboleth and spare him a fifty-dollar ticket. "Congratulations, by the way."

"For what?"

"For winning the Publishers Clearing House Sweepstakes, what the hell you think? For Lambert."

"Thanks."

"You realize you're total an-thee-ma to your fellow women now." He meant "anathema." "They're never going to let you into NOW."

"I never thought much about joining. Come in, make yourself at home. Have a seat."

He entered her office tentatively, ill-at-ease. Devereaux never liked meeting with her at her office, her turf. He preferred to meet at his lair, a fake-wood-paneled office suite in South Boston adorned with framed diplomas and certificates, where he was czar. He stopped before one of the visitor chairs and glowered down at it as if unsure what it was. The chair suddenly looked dainty next to him. He pointed straight down at it and grinned. When he smiled, he was a ten-year-old boy, not a forty-seven-year-old private investigator.

"You got something I won't break?"

"Take mine." Claire got up from her high-backed leather desk chair and switched places with Devereaux. He took her seat without objection, now comfortably enthroned behind her desk. A fillip of authority symbolism, she figured, would put him at ease.

"So, you rang," Devereaux said. He leaned way back in her chair and folded his arms across his belly. The chair creaked ominously.

"I called you, but I didn't leave a message," she said, confused.

"Caller ID. Recognized your number on the box. So what's this about, Lambert again? I thought you were done with that sleazeball."

"It's something else, Ray. I need your help." She told him about last night: the mall, the agents pursuing Tom, his disappearance, the search of their house.

Slowly Ray leaned forward until both of his feet were on the ground. "You're shittin me," he said.

She shook her head.

He pursed his lips, jutted them out like a blowfish. He closed his eyes. A long, dramatic pause. He was said to be excellent at interrogations. "I know a guy," he said at last. "Knew him from my FBI days. Probably looking to get out. Maybe I'll offer him a job with me."

"You're going to hire someone?"

"I said *offer*."

"Well, be discreet. Fly below the radar, you know? Don't let them know why you're interested."

Devereaux scowled. "Now you're going to tell me how to do my job? I don't tell you about torts—or whatever the hell it is you teach."

"Point taken. Sorry. But could this whole thing be a mistake, a misunderstanding?"

Devereaux stared at the ceiling for a long moment, for maximum dramatic effect. "It's unlikely," he said. "Count on the fact they've got your phones bugged. And a trap-and-trace on Tom's office, your home—"

"My office, here, too?"

"Why not, sure."

"I want you to sweep my phones."

Devereaux gave a sardonic smile. " 'Sweep' your phones? If they're doing this outa the central office, which I'm sure they are, I'm not going to find anything. I'll sweep if you want, but don't expect anything. Anyway, even if I did find something, I can't remove it if it's legal."

"Does that mean, if he calls me to check in, they can trace the call and find out where he is?"

"I'm sure that's what they want. But it's gotten a lot harder these days. You just buy one of those prepaid phone cards, and in effect the service is making the call for you, so it's impossible to trace."

"He left me a voice-mail message."

"Where? Here or at home?"

"Home."

"They can access that, no problem. Don't need any secret code. If they've got a warrant, NYNEX is going to let them listen to any voice-mail messages left there."

"So they heard the message Tom left?"

"Count on it. But he probably counted on that, too."

"And they're probably going to get all phone records, at home and at Tom's office, right? So they can see who he might have tried to reach."

"You got it."

"But only long-distance, right?"

"Wrong. The phone company keeps a log of every single local phone call that's made—phone number dialed, duration of call, all that. That's how they do billing for people who don't have unlimited calling plans." Claire nodded. "But they don't preserve the records beyond one billing cycle, which means roughly a month."

"So is there any way Tom can contact me without them knowing?"

Devereaux was silent for a moment. He cupped a hand over his mouth. "Probably."

"How?"

"I'd have to think on that. 'Course, Tom's probably already thought about that. Also, we have to assume that they've bugged this office, too."

"You gotta find out what's going on, Ray."

"I'll see what I can dig up." He grasped the arms of the chair and fixed her with a stagy glare. "Will that be all, Professor?"

7

"*I* want to eat while I'm watching *Beauty and the Beast*," Annie chanted.

"You'll eat at the table," Claire said as sternly as she could. Jackie served Claire and herself salad from an immense rustic Tuscan bowl. Salads were one of her specialties. Jackie was a vegetarian these days, having gone through vegan and macrobiotic phases, all the while smoking heavily.

"No. I want to eat while I'm watching *Beauty and the Beast*. I want to eat macaroni-and-cheese on the couch while I'm watching *Beauty and the Beast*."

At one end of the spacious kitchen was a corner where Annie stashed her vast collection of toys, which included a ragged Elmo, a torn Kermit the Frog puppet, a battle-scarred Mr. Potato Head. There were dozens of others that Annie hadn't touched or even noticed in months. A large television set faced a tattered, slipcovered sofa stained with a thousand microwaved frozen macaroni-and-cheeses, a thousand sippy-cups of grape juice, a thousand red popsicles (no flavor known to man, just red).

"Come on, kiddo," Jackie said, "come eat with your mommy and me."

"No."

"We're a family," Claire said, exasperated. "We eat together. And you're not having macaroni-and-cheese. Jackie made some delicious chicken."

Annie ran over to the sofa and defiantly popped the *Beauty and the Beast* video into the VCR. "I want macaroni-and-cheese," she said.

"Not on the menu tonight, kiddo," Jackie said. "Sorry." To Claire, she said: "You poor thing. What would you do without me?"

"I don't know," Claire acknowledged, and said, louder: "Okay, listen, Annie. Come over here."

Her daughter obediently returned, stood erect in front of Claire as if at an army inspection. She knew she had maneuvered herself onto the shoals of big trouble.

"If you'll eat the chicken Jackie made, you can watch *Beauty and the Beast.* On the couch."

"*Okay!*" Annie said, running back to the couch. "Excellent!" She pressed the VCR's play button, and dove onto the couch to enjoy the lengthy previews for other Disney videos and the ad for Disney World.

"That's laying down the law," Jackie muttered. "You disciplinarian, you."

"But just this once!" Claire called out lamely. She dished out roast chicken and mashed potatoes on a plate and brought it over to Annie, with a small fork and a napkin. As she turned back to the kitchen table, she noticed something outside the window, a dark shape visible through the lilac bushes.

A dark-blue government car: a Crown Victoria. Jackie saw Claire staring out the window and said, "Aren't these goons outside driving you crazy?"

"You have no idea," Claire said. "One followed me to and from work today."

"You can't do anything about it?"

"Well, they're on public property. They're respecting the curtilage."

"The who?"

"Curtilage. The area of privacy around a dwelling. They're not trespassing. They have the right to be there."

"What about your freedom of—I don't know, freedom not to be molested by goons?"

Claire half smiled. "Of course, maybe I could go to court to get a 209-A restraining order against them. Make 'em stay a hundred yards away from me."

"Yeah," Jackie said, "I bet that would go over big, trying to get some local judge to order the federal government to back off. I don't *think* so."

"I called Tom's office," Claire said. She returned to the table and, stomach tight, tried to regain an appetite for the dinner Jackie had cooked. "Apparently Tom left e-mail messages for his chief trader, Jeff Rosenthal, and his assistant, Vivian, telling them he had to make a sudden, very hush-hush business trip out of the country. Said he'd be gone for a week, maybe longer. They were wondering what's going on, because everyone at Chapman & Company was questioned at home by FBI agents asking lots of questions about Tom and his whereabouts."

"That must've made 'em suspicious."

"To say the least. Tom told them in his e-mail that the FBI might be questioning them in connection with a security clearance. I don't think they were convinced."

"No," Jackie said, "I bet not. They've got to be wondering, just like we are."

* * *

Annie went to bed without any trouble, and Claire and Jackie sat in the enclosed sun porch, both smoking. Jackie sipped at a tumbler of Famous Grouse; Claire, in an oversized Gap T-shirt and sweatpants, drank seltzer.

"Well, Annie seems to be holding up okay with Daddy gone," Jackie said, exhaling a lungful of smoke through her nostrils. "She's had her difficult moments," Claire said.

"You're not surprised she's difficult sometimes, are you? Don't forget, you did read *Rosemary's Baby* while you were pregnant. What if she's really the spawn of Satan?"

Claire smiled pallidly.

"You holding up okay?" Jackie asked.

Claire nodded. "I don't know what to think. I asked Ray Devereaux to look into it, see what he came up with."

"They're telling you he used to have a different *name*, a different identity—you think they might be telling you the truth?"

"You *know* him, Jackie," Claire said. "You know he's not a murderer." Claire put her cigarette down in the ashtray.

"I don't know him," Jackie replied. "Obviously you don't know him either."

"Oh, come *on!*" Claire cried. "You have good character judgment—so do I. Look how much time we've both spent with Tom in the last three years. How can you say you don't know him?"

"Or is it Ron?"

"Fuck you."

"Look, we know he can get pretty angry. He's got a temper. We've all seen it. You remember when we were driving down to the Cape and this car cut in front of us, cut us off, and Tom just about lost it?"

"He didn't lose it."

"Oh, come on, his face got red, he cursed the guy out, took off after him. It was terrifying! You were yelling at him to calm down, and finally he did, but . . . Remember?"

"Yeah," Claire said wearily. "So what? He's got a temper. Does that make him a murderer? Okay, he lied to me about his past—but does *that* make him a murderer either?"

"Jesus, Claire, how much do you really know about him? I mean, you've never met his family, right?"

"Not true. I met his father, Nelson, at the wedding and once after that, when we visited him at his condo on Jupiter Island, Florida. But, look, I think I met Jay's parents only once."

"And you've hardly met any friends of his."

"Friends? Guys in their forties rarely have more than a couple of friends, haven't you ever noticed that? Men aren't like women. They get married and get buried in their jobs and sort of fall off the face of the earth. Every guy considers every other guy a potential rival. Men his age have colleagues, they have contacts. Maybe they have guys they play sports with or watch basketball or football with. I mean, Tom has plenty of casual friends—everyone likes him. But no *old* friends, as far as I can tell. Then again, Jay didn't have any old friends either."

"Claire, you never met any boyhood friends of his, any college friends. Or anyone who knew him before he moved to Boston. Am I wrong?"

Claire sighed. She traced her index finger down the sweat on the outside of her glass tumbler. "Once in a while he'd get phone calls from an old college friend. Once I remember him getting a phone call from a friend of his in California. No, he didn't seem to be in touch with any old friends, not on any regular basis. But, Jackie, you don't seem to be listening to me. There was nothing out of the ordinary about that. Why in the world would I assume he was lying to me?"

"So where is he, do you think? Where do you think he's gone?"

Claire shook her head. "I have no idea."

A long silence passed between them.

"Do you remember what Dad looked like?" Claire asked suddenly. "I don't."

"Yeah, well, I do. I wish I could forget. He was an asshole."

"Remember how he smelled—his aftershave?"

"I remember he reeked like a French whore."

"I loved the way he smelled. Old Spice. Whenever I smell it, it takes me right back."

"Right back to your happy childhood and our loving dad," Jackie muttered. "I hope Tom doesn't wear Old Spice."

"Dad was a troubled guy."

"He was a selfish loser. You know what smell I associate with him?" Jackie said. "Seriously. The smell of gasoline when a car's starting up. You know, partially combusted gas? I remember standing outside the house on the gravel driveway saying goodbye to him, watching him drive off, smelling that smell. I loved that smell. I mean, it's a bittersweet smell to me, 'cause I never knew if he'd be coming back. I never knew if he was going away for good."

Claire nodded. They sat in silence again. Jackie snubbed out another cigarette, finished her scotch. "Can you hand me that bottle?" She poured out the rest of the Famous Grouse.

"He's my husband, and I love him," Claire said very quietly. "He's a great father and a great husband and I love him."

"Hey, I kinda like the lug myself. Is this the end of the scotch?"

8

*F*rom the street, the Dunkin' Donuts in Central Square looked like some high-priced gourmet shop in Concord, the kind that sells forty types of balsamic vinegar and no iceberg lettuce. Its hunter-green façade, with a grid of tiny window panes, had recently been renovated in one of the spasms of gentrification that overcame Central Square every few years. But it would recede, like all the others, leaving the fundamental seediness of the place untouched. Unlovely Central Square, land of a thousand Indian restaurants, home of ninety-nine-cent stores and store-front lawyers and discount jewelry exchanges, would never lose its genuine decrepit proletarian soul.

Ray Devereaux had called her early in the morning and asked her to meet him after she dropped off Annie at school. Claire had an hour to spare before she had to be at Harvard to lecture. She refused to cancel her classes. She was keeping up with all appointments, all classes, all meetings—keeping up appearances, even though she could barely concentrate on anything but Tom. Ray was already sitting at a tiny magenta modular table, his immense girth spilling awkwardly over the narrow rail-back chair attached. An empty baby stroller crowded him. The baby, whose mother sat indifferently nearby with an immense crinkling plastic shopping bag in her lap, toddled around the seating area in a red bunny suit tied at the neck with a pink bow. The mother, a large dark-haired woman, was having a heated conversation in Greek with a silver-haired, large-nosed old man in a black leather jacket. Soft rock blared over the speakers (Rod Stewart rasping "Reason to Believe"), competing with the almost deafening white noise of the exhaust system.

Ray was fastidiously tucking into a chocolate cruller and taking sips from a refillable plastic commuter mug. He was a regular.

"You've got company," he said nonchalantly.

"Hmm?"

"You've grown a tail."

Claire turned back toward the plate-glass front of the shop. A dark-blue Crown Vic was just pulling away from the curb.

"Oh, that," she said. "Yeah, they've been tailing me all over the place. To and from work. They're just trying to bust my balls."

"They probably think you got balls, honey." He chuckled. "But they're gone now. They can't double-park here, not in the middle of traffic."

He took another large bite of the cruller, wiped his hands with the little napkins to remove the sticky stuff. "So I put out some lines to my friends in the Cambridge PD," he said. "The good news is they got the guy did the B & E. Your paintings will be harder to find."

"Ray, you didn't ask me to come to Central Square just to tell me—"

"Cool your jets, honey."

He fixed her with a glare until she appeased him: "Go ahead."

"Anyways, so I call up the National Association of Securities Dealers, the folks who regulate brokers and money managers and what have you, and they faxed me down the résumé Tom has on file with them. I look at it. Born Hawthorne, California, graduated Hawthorne High School. Graduated Claremont Men's College, 1973. So I call Claremont, the Alumni Association, and I'm trying to get in touch with Tom Chapman, old college buddy, do they know where this guy is, what he's doing now. You'd be amazed at how much the alumni associations of these colleges keep on file. Real treasure trove."

"Okay," she said, keeping her voice neutral. The air was overheated; she took off her coat and her blazer.

"Bad news is, your FBI friends are right. There's no record of a Thomas Chapman at Claremont Men's College. Which has since been renamed, by the way."

An old Chinese woman a few tables over was clipping her fingernails. The dark-haired mother scooped up her baby, now screaming, and put her in the carriage.

"So that set me digging," Devereaux said. "Find out what's really going on with your husband. And I found some really interesting stuff on him."

"Like?"

"Well, so I check with Social Security, see if there's any irregularities. Strangest thing—everything's hunky-dory, everything's copacetic, but there's no Social Security payments before 1985. Nothing. Well, that's a little bit strange for a guy who's, what, forty-six or so? Unless the guy just never worked before he was thirty or whatever, which I guess is possible. And then I check with TRW, the credit people, and everything's fine, no delinquencies—but he also has no credit history before 1985. Also bizarre."

Claire felt her stomach tighten. She shifted her feet, which had adhered to a sticky coffee spill on the gray-and-magenta-tiled floor.

Now Steely Dan was playing on the radio. What was it, "Katie Lied?" "Katie Died?" Something like that. A smarmy saxophone solo competed with the insistent bleating of a microwave, then a lushly harmonized chorus: "...Deacon Blue...*Deacon Blue*..."

"His résumé lists several jobs after college. Good, respectable jobs with companies, brokerages and the like. So I'm asking myself, why is there no record of Social Security payments if the guy was working all that time? So I make some calls, and another strange thing—all the companies he's ever worked for before he started his own firm have gone under."

"Maybe he's a black cat," Claire murmured.

"I mean, one maybe. But *three*? Three investment firms and brokerage houses he used to work for that don't exist anymore. Which means there's no records available. Nothing to check up on."

Claire listened in stricken silence. She watched an anxious, short-haired, bespectacled woman with two handbags slung over her shoulder stride in, clutching a Filofax, and order a large coffee, light, two sugars.

"So, what does this mean?" Devereaux said. "Before 1985—when he was, what, over thirty—he had no credit cards, no AmEx, no Visa, no MasterCard. And I check some more—the IRS has no returns on file for him before then either. So he lists all these jobs with companies that no longer exist, and he paid no Social Security and filed no tax returns."

"What am I supposed to make of all this?" Claire said. She could not think. She stared. She felt vertiginous.

"Well, I have a buddy works out of L.A., and I asked him to take a little trip down to Hawthorne. Right near L.A.X.—"

"And he didn't go to Hawthorne High," Claire interrupted. "You don't have to tell me this. I've figured it out."

"There's no record at the high school. None of the teachers, the old-timers, remember him. No one in the Class of '73 remembers him. He's not in the yearbook. Plus, going back in the old phone directories, there's no record his parents ever lived there. No Nelson Chapman ever lived there. Now, I'm not saying the FBI isn't full of shit. I'm not saying your husband committed any crime. I'm just telling you that Tom Chapman doesn't exist, Claire. Whoever your husband really is, *whatever* he really is—he's not who you think he is."

After class, Claire returned to her office, met with a few frantic students—the semester was almost over, and final exams were imminent—then checked her e-mail.

Unfortunately, the dean had only recently discovered e-mail and had started using it to send every notice, in addition to any stray thought that crossed his mind. He'd left several pointless memos. There were a couple of press queries—attempts to get to her through the back door—but she knew how to deal with them: complete and utter silence. No answer. And a long-winded, chatty message from a friend in Paris.

And a message whose return address she didn't

recognize, in Finland. It was addressed to Professor Chapman, which was strange, because almost everyone knew her as Professor Heller. She read it, then read it again, and her heart began to thud.

Dear Professor Chapman,

I am interested in having you represent me in a matter of great urgency and utmost personal concern. Although circumstances prevent me from meeting with you in person, I will be in touch directly soon. Telephone, including voice mail, insufficiently private. Please do not believe the incorrect impressions about my case that you may have been given. When we meet I will explain all.
Fondest regards to you and your offspring.

R. LENEHAN.

R. Lenehan, she knew at once, referred to their favorite small restaurant in Boston's South End, a place called Rose Lenehan's, where they'd had their first date.

She clicked the reply icon and quickly typed out:

Very eager for meeting soonest.

9

In the middle of the night Claire sat up suddenly, drenched in sweat. Her heart racing, she walked around the darkened bedroom, the only illumination coming from a streetlight outside, until she found the drawer where they kept the family photos. The FBI search team had left it more or less alone. They were interested in more revealing, more immediate things—itineraries, travel times, flight numbers, that sort of thing.

There were countless pictures of Annie, album after album of photos from her birth to her last school picture. She had to be one of the most fully documented children in the history of the world. There was an album of pictures of herself, a bunch of baby pictures: Claire with Jackie, Jackie tagging along behind Claire and Claire looking aggrieved. A number of pictures of the family, Claire, Jackie, and their mother, who always seemed to look tired. A lot of pictures of Claire on a vacation in Wyoming with some college friends. Shots of her college graduation (she'd had a miserable outbreak of acne and had gained a lot of weight during spring semester senior year, and so never allowed herself to look at these pictures).

And Tom's photos?

One baby picture, a small black-and-white with a scalloped border. It might have been any generic baby; it looked nothing like the adult Tom, but baby pictures often bear no resemblance to the adult.

And photos of him as a boy? None.

High school? Nothing.

College, too. Nothing.

There were no pictures of Tom except that one generic baby picture. No high-school yearbook with pages defaced by long goodbye notes in loopy handwriting from girls who had unrequited crushes on Tom.

What kind of person had *no* pictures of himself growing up?

Why had she never wondered where all his photographs were?

Returning from class late that morning, trailing two insistent students who'd attached themselves to her like limpets, Claire gracefully asked them to return later in the day. She had a meeting, she told them. They were nervous about finals; she'd be happy to spend time with them later on.

Connie was at her desk doing correspondence. She looked up, started to say something.

Claire smiled, gave a nice-to-see-you-but-I'm-too-rushed-to-stop-and-talk-just-now wave, went into her office, and shut the door behind her.

Ray Devereaux was sitting in her chair.

"The shit has hit the fan," he said. He was dressed in a gray suit, surprisingly well cut, a white shirt, a pale-turquoise tie.

"Tell me about it."

She sat down in one of the visitor chairs, dropped her briefcase to the floor. "Your sources are good?"

"Not especially. I've been calling around, but everyone's awful tight-lipped. This isn't a rinky-dink operation. This is big stuff."

"How big are we talking?"

Devereaux leaned back in the chair, which creaked alarmingly. She half expected him to topple over backward. "They've accelerated the surveillance. They know he left a voice-mail message for you at home, and they're approved to get your office voice mail at Harvard. They have no idea where he is, but they're waiting for him to contact you. They have people outside his office downtown. A couple of guys outside this building. Everywhere you drive, they'll follow you, in case you might be driving to meet him somewhere."

"Like that song by the Police, right?" Claire smiled grimly. " 'Every Step You Take.' "

Devereaux looked blank. "Let's take a walk," he said.

They went for a stroll through the Law School quadrangle. She noticed the two plainclothesmen following at a not-so-discreet distance.

"Nice day, huh?" Devereaux said. "Real late-spring day."

"Ray—"

"Not yet, honey. I've always thought those long-range directional microphones they got are overrated, particularly on a crowded street. But I don't want to take a chance. I mean, we could walk along Mass. Ave. and drive them crazy trying to pick out our voices from a hundred other babblers, but why chance it? Let's take a ride in my car. I just picked it up this morning, and I know I wasn't followed, so it's not likely they put a bug in it. Yet."

Devereaux's car was a new Lincoln. One of his clients ran an auto-leasing agency and let him lease cars for free, as compensation. She sank back in the comfortable, well-cushioned leather seat while he drove around aimlessly.

"You mentioned his father," Devereaux said. "Nelson Chapman. You said he lives in Florida."

"You talked to him?"

Devereaux shook his head slowly. "No such person."

"I've *met* him. We visited him at his condo on Jupiter Island."

"You've met a man who called himself Nelson Chapman. The condo you said you visited is owned by someone who's never heard of any Nelson Chapman. Neighbors there, even longtime neighbors, have never heard of him. You don't believe me, call if you want."

"Are you saying Tom arranged for someone to play the *role* of his father?"

"That's what it looks like. It's real compartmented, this operation." He steered with one index finger. "Real tough to get anything. My contacts don't know shit, and those that know anything are shut up tight. But this much I learned: they're saying Tom used to be a covert operative for the Pentagon."

"Oh, come *on*!" she scoffed.

"Why is that so hard to believe?"

"He's a money guy."

"Now. But I'm told that he was in the military and disappeared, went AWOL, like more than a decade ago, that he's escaping something really nasty, real serious. Some bad kind of shit."

"What are you telling me?"

"They're saying he's wanted for murder."

"So they tell me."

"That he was some kind of clandestine operative for the U.S. government who committed some horrible crime and then went on the lam."

She shook her head, chewed on a fingernail. An old law-school habit she thought she'd stopped. "That's not possible."

"You're married to him," Devereaux said equably. "You'd know." He turned to look at her, then turned back to the road.

Claire smiled, a strange bitter smile. "How well do you ever know the person you married?"

"Hey, don't ask me. I didn't know when I married Margaret that she was a bitch, but that's what she turned out to be. Is it possible that Tom could have worked for the government, for some clandestine branch of the military? Sure. Fact is, he made up a history, a biography. The college thing was just the tip of the iceberg. He's covering something up, escaping *something*. That much I'd say for sure."

"But couldn't there be a—benign explanation?"

"Like he ran up a lot of parking tickets in Dubuque? Doubtful."

Claire did not smile.

"But I'll tell you the truth," Devereaux said somberly. "I always thought Tom was a little too smooth for his own good, but he's your husband, so I gotta side with him. When the government starts gathering its forces to go after one guy, you gotta believe they're trying to hide something, too."

That evening, as she was trying to convince Annie that it was bedtime, the phone rang.

She recognized the voice right away: Julia Margolis, the wife of her closest friend on the Harvard faculty, Abe Margolis, who taught constitutional law. "Claire?" she said in her big contralto. "Where are you? You're an hour and a half late—is everything all right?"

"An hour—Oh my God. You invited us for dinner tonight. Oh, shit, Julia. I'm so sorry, I totally forgot about it."

"Are you sure you're all right? That's not like you at all." Julia Margolis was a large and still very beautiful brunette in her late fifties, a great cook and an even greater hostess.

"I've been insanely busy," Claire said, then revised that: "Tom had to go out of town on business suddenly, and I feel like everything's falling down around me."

"Well, I've had the swordfish marinating for something like two days, and I really hate to waste it. Why don't you come over now?"

"I'm sorry, Julia. I really am. Rosa's gone home, and I don't have a sitter, and I'm just frantic. Please forgive me."

"Of course, dear. But when things settle down, will you call me? We'd love to see you two."

10

Later that evening Claire and Jackie sat in the downstairs study, in paired, slightly weathered French leather club chairs. Tom had spent two months searching for the perfect chairs for Claire's office, because she'd once admired them in a Ralph Lauren ad. Finally he'd located a dealer in New York who imported them from the Paris flea market. They'd gone from a Paris nightclub in the twenties to Cambridge in the late nineties, and they were still magnificently comfortable.

Jackie again wore black jeans and a black T-shirt. Paint spatters freckled her shirt and arms: she was a painter who earned her living as a technical writer. Claire was still wearing her blue suit, a Chanel knockoff but a nice one, because she hadn't had a minute to change. She was exhausted and her head ached and her neck and shoulders felt stiff. All she wanted to do right now was run a nice hot bath and soak in it for an hour.

The room glowed amber as the sun set.

"Ray Devereaux says Tom used to be some kind of clandestine army operative who got entangled in something," she said. "Jesus. You think Ray's information is good?"

"He's usually reliable. Always has been."

"So what do you think, he did something for the government, the Pentagon, something undercover, and maybe he got into trouble? And . . . and he goes AWOL, just takes off, and he goes into hiding and changes his name, and then he moves to Boston and goes into business and hopes he never gets caught? And then, one day, by coincidence, your house is broken into and the cops run his prints, and bingo, the Pentagon's found him? Is that how it goes?"

"Basically, yeah." Claire turned to see whether Jackie was being ironic, or simply skeptical, but she wasn't. She was thinking out loud, as she so often did.

"Hard to get a job with a firm if you have no references for them to check into," Jackie went on, "so he starts his own business, and that way he doesn't have people checking too deeply into his background."

Claire closed her eyes again, nodded.

"So everything you know about Tom is a lie," Jackie suggested gently.

"Maybe not everything. A lot. An enormous amount."

Very softly, Jackie said, "But you feel betrayed. It's, like, custom-made to rip your heart out."

Tears came to Claire's eyes, tears of frustration and exhaustion rather than of sadness. "Is it a betrayal if he's escaping, hiding?"

"He lied to you, Claire. He never told you about it. He's not who he told you he was. A man who can lie about his life, create a whole fake background, is a man who can lie about anything."

"He contacted me again, Jacks."

"How?"

"We don't know if there are bugs here," Claire said, pointing at the ceiling, although who knew where listening devices might be planted?

"Well, what are you going to do?" Jackie asked, but then the doorbell rang. They looked at each other. Now who could it be? Claire got up reluctantly and went to the front door.

It was a young guy in his early twenties, with a scuzzy goatee and a brass stud earring in his left ear, wearing bicycle shorts and a leather jacket. "Boston Messengers," he announced.

Claire looked past him to see two Crown Victorias parked at the curb in front of their house. Passengers in both vehicles were staring at the visitor.

"Are you Claire Chapman?"

Claire nodded, alert.

"Jesus, lady, those guys out there stopped me and asked me a million questions, who am I and what am I doing here—you got something going on in here? You in some sort of trouble? 'Cause I don't want trouble."

"What are you doing here?" Claire demanded.

"I got a package for Claire Chapman. I just need to see some kind of ID."

"Hold on," Claire said. She closed the door, retrieved her purse from the hall table, and removed her driver's license from her wallet.

She opened the door again and handed him the license.

The kid inspected it, comparing the picture to her face. He nodded. "I gotta ask for your Harvard faculty card, too."

"Who's the package from?"

"I dunno." He looked at it. "Something Lenahan."

Claire was immediately flooded with relief, then

excitement. "Here," she said, handing him her faculty ID card.

He looked at it, once again comparing the photos. "Okay," he said warily. "Sign here."

She signed, took the package—a flat, rigid cardboard envelope about nine by twelve inches—tipped him, and closed the door.

"Who's it from?" Jackie asked.

Claire smiled and didn't answer. Tom knew the phones were tapped, which meant that voice mail and the fax machine weren't safe. He knew they'd be monitoring the mail. The sudden appearance of a courier might work just once, but without a court order they couldn't intercept the package.

Inside was a handwritten letter, which brought tears to her eyes—and a plan, which for the first time brought her hope.

11

A *full* moon. A warm night. The watchers at their
stations in their government-issue sedans lulled
by the tedium. It was barely half an hour later. The
doorbell rang, and Claire answered it. She wasn't at
all surprised to see the two FBI agents, Howard Massie and John Crawford, standing there in almost
identical trench coats. No doubt they'd been sum-
moned by the watchers and had rushed over.

Massie spoke first as they entered. "Where's the
envelope?" he demanded. He was a large man,
larger than she'd remembered from the nightmarish
scene at the mall and the "conversation" that followed.

"First we talk," Claire said, leading them into the
sitting area just off the foyer, a sofa and a couple of
comfortable upholstered chairs on a sisal carpet,
around a tufted, tapestry-covered ottoman neatly
stacked with old *New Yorker*s. It was a part of the
house they rarely used, and it looked that way, sterile, like a display in a furniture store.

Crawford began, menacingly: "If you plan on hiding something from us—"

Massie interrupted, "We need your cooperation, and if your husband has tried to arrange a meeting—"

"How can you prove to me the man you're looking for, this Ronald Kubik, really is the same man as my husband, Tom Chapman?" Claire said abruptly.

Massie looked at Crawford, who said: "It's the prints, ma'am. The fingerprints don't lie. We can show you photographs, but his face is different."

Claire's stomach felt as if it had flipped over. "What does that mean, his face is different?"

"There's only a slight, passing resemblance between the photos we have of your husband and those of Ronald Kubik," Massie explained. "Photo superimposition demonstrates beyond question that they're the same person, but you'd never think they were the same person, not after the amount of plastic surgery he's had. Sergeant Kubik's an extremely bright man, extremely resourceful. If it weren't for your burglary, and the thoroughness of the Cambridge police, running all the prints and all, he might never have been caught."

"Sergeant?"

"Yes, ma'am," Crawford said. "We're only the contact agency. We're really working on behalf of the U.S. Army CID. Criminal Investigation Division." Massie watched her with heavy-lidded interest.

"What the hell is the army investigative service interested in Tom for?"

"I know you're a professor of law at Harvard," Massie said, "but I don't know how much you know about the military. Your husband, Ronald Kubik, is facing a number of charges under the Uniform Code of Military Justice, including Article 85, desertion, and Article 118, murder with premeditation."

"Who'd he kill? Allegedly?"

"We don't have that information," Crawford replied quickly.

Claire looked at Massie, who shook his head, then said: "We know you've been contacted by your husband. We need to know his whereabouts. We'd like to examine the package."

"That's what I called you to discuss," Claire said.

"I understand," said Massie. His eyes were keen.

"You and I want two different things," she said. "I only want what's best for him. Now, whatever he's done, I know it's not going to be cleared up by running. Sooner or later the Department of Injustice will catch up with him."

"We thought you'd see the light sooner or later," Crawford said.

Claire gave him a look of withering contempt, then said: "I don't want a perp walk. No showy arrests in a public place, no leading away in handcuffs, no guns drawn, no manacles or shackles."

"That shouldn't be a problem."

"Since he's arranged to meet me at Logan Airport, the surrender will take place in the parking lot at Logan across the street from the terminal. I'll make sure either he's unarmed, or he throws away his weapon, and you'll be able to confirm it."

Massie nodded.

"Now, before the surrender, I'll want time alone with him first—a minimum of one hour." Massie raised his eyebrows. "In private, so we can talk. Your guys can keep a close watch, so you can make sure he's not going to run, but I want privacy."

"That may be a problem," Crawford said.

"If it is, you can forget taking him in. Or seeing his letter."

"I think," Massie said, "we may be able to arrange it."

"Good. Next, I want assurances from you that you will not freeze his assets."

"Professor," Crawford said, "I don't think that's—"

"Make it happen, gentlemen. It's nonnegotiable."

"We'll have to talk to Washington."

"And I don't want the FBI charging him with violating the False Identity Act. In fact, I'll want all civilian charges dropped."

Crawford glanced at Massie in astonishment.

"And I'll want all of these assurances in writing, signed by an assistant director of the Bureau. No one lower. I want complete accountability. No one's going to try to wriggle out of this by claiming they didn't have the proper authority."

"I think we may be able to arrange this," Massie said. "But it's going to take some time."

"You take too much time, the window of opportunity slams shut on your fingers," Claire said. "I'll want signed documents by noon tomorrow. Our rendezvous is early evening."

"Noon tomorrow?" Crawford said. "That's— that's impossible!"

Claire shrugged. "Do your best. Once we come to terms, you can read Tom's letter. And then you can take him into custody."

Claire left the house early the next morning wearing a bright royal-blue coat she'd bought once at Filene's Basement in a fit of fashion dementia. She took Annie to school, walked her into the building and to her classroom, then returned to her Volvo and drove to her office. Two Crown Victorias followed like faithful sheepdogs.

At eleven-forty-five in the morning, a package arrived by courier from the Federal Bureau of Investigation, Boston field office. It contained the letter she had requested, signed by an assistant director of the FBI, whose signature was an indecipherable jagged up-and-down EKG.

Half an hour later a messenger came by to pick up a sheet of paper and take it to Massie at the FBI office downtown.

When Connie went off for lunch a little after one, Claire gave her a shopping bag, which contained the bright-blue coat, neatly folded, and asked her to leave it with the waiter at the bustling fern bar/restaurant where Connie invariably ate lunch with her regular luncheon companions, two other Harvard Law administrative assistants.

Claire then taught a class, and canceled several afternoon meetings.

At four-thirty she packed up her briefcase, closed her office, said good night to Connie, and walked to the elevator. If a watcher was lingering in the waiting area on her floor, she didn't notice. She took the elevator to the basement and wandered through the tunnels beneath the Law School campus for a while until she was certain no one was following her. They knew the tricks of their trade, they knew surveillance and patterns of pursuit, but she knew the entrails of the Law School.

At precisely five o'clock, just as Claire had promised the FBI agents, her Volvo pulled slowly out of the faculty parking garage. As she passed on foot, from a good distance away, Claire could see the dark-haired driver in a royal-blue coat and oversized sunglasses, a pretty fair approximation of Claire, or at least as close as Jackie could pull off, with the assistance of a wig she had hastily purchased downtown. The Volvo took a right into rush-hour traffic on Mass. Ave., followed closely behind by an unmarked Crown Victoria, and then pulled out of sight. Jackie would drive to Logan—a nasty, traffic-choked route at this time of day—and go from terminal to terminal as if confused about which one she was supposed to go to, and they would no doubt follow.

The letter Claire had couriered to Massie—single-spaced, printed on the LaserWriter in Tom's home office on letter-size twenty-pound Hammermill CopyPlus Bright White paper, taken from a sealed ream and therefore without fingerprints, and unsigned—had instructed her to meet him at the Delta terminal at Logan, where he'd be arriving at five-thirty on the New York shuttle. There would be watchers waiting at the arrival gate, but, because they were suspicious, they would naturally follow her Volvo, to make sure she was going where she said she would.

Then Claire took a leisurely stroll to Oxford Street, behind the Law School, and located Tom's Lexus at a metered parking space. It had been a few hours since Jackie had parked it there, and the meter had long ago expired, so Claire wasn't at all surprised to find a Day-Glo–orange parking ticket tucked under the windshield-wiper blade.

Take the FM radio from the bedroom, Tom had instructed in the letter he'd sent her, not the one she'd drafted for the FBI's eyes. Tune it to a station high on the dial, around 108 megahertz. Make sure the signal comes in loud and clear. Now take it out to the garage, and bring the antenna as close as you can to every surface on the car.

Listen for interference. Listen for a squawking

noise. Listen for the abrupt change in the quality of reception.

If you detect the presence of a transmitter somewhere in the car, or you're not sure, don't go anywhere.

If the car is clean, go.

But wait for rush-hour traffic. Drive in rush-hour traffic, because they'll find it hard to follow you when the traffic is dense. Drive at nightfall, when tailing is harder, because lights are visible for a long distance.

Take a circuitous route, he had instructed, which was easier said than done. If you're being followed, nothing is really circuitous. Before you get on the Massachusetts Turnpike, drive around the city. Make four right turns, one right after another, to flush out any followers, because anyone still behind you has to be following you.

Make plenty of left turns, because left turns are harder to shadow unnoticed. Go through yellow lights whenever possible. Come as close to running reds as you can without getting killed.

They will not follow directly behind if they're attempting covert surveillance. They will follow one or two cars behind. There may be as many as four vehicles following you. Or there may be none.

Watch the right rear of the car, the blind spot that followers favor.

Drive at inconsistent speeds. Speed up, then slow down. Drive very slowly, excruciatingly slowly, forcing everyone to pass you. Stop at a rest stop and park in the back. Have dinner. Kill a couple of hours. Take some hard object and smash out your rear right taillight. Then return to the pike.

At least once, make a U-turn on the pike, wherever there's a turnoff.

Once you've passed Exit 9 on the turnpike—out beyond Sturbridge, in the far-western part of the state—begin to drive slowly, in the right lane, with your flashers on.

At first she had marveled at Tom's expertise at tradecraft, at the techniques of surveillance. It was a side of him she'd never seen.

Then she remembered who they said he'd been, and she knew that at least part of it was true.

At just past ten o'clock at night, when it was too late to call Annie even if she dared, which she didn't, she was driving along a stretch of the turnpike in the Berkshires near Lee, Massachusetts, where the road was lightly trafficked. She thought about Annie, asleep in bed, with Jackie downstairs, smoking.

The road became hilly out here. It cut through ravines, then out into the open, up a steep grade to the top of a hill. She drove slowly, in the breakdown lane, hazard lights flashing. No one was following her, that she felt sure of. As she began her descent down the steep gradient, she noticed, in her rearview mirror, a car pull out of a wooded turnoff, lights dark, and accelerate until it was just behind her. The car flashed its high-beams twice.

She pulled off the road into the next turnoff, which was shrouded by a dense copse, and switched off her lights.

Her heart hammered.

She stared straight ahead, not daring to turn her head to look.

The other car pulled up just behind her and coasted to a stop. She heard the car door open, heard footsteps on the pavement.

Now she turned to look out of her rolled-up window and saw Tom, a few days' growth of beard like charcoal smudge on his face, binoculars hanging from a strap around his neck, smiling down at her, and she smiled back.

Tears flooded her eyes, and she threw her arms around him.

12

❖

She followed him in the Lexus along a meandering route, off the turnpike, onto local roads that became country roads, until she had no idea where they were. Tom was driving an old black Jeep Wrangler, though where he'd gotten it he hadn't explained. They passed through a small town that seemed frozen in the nineteen-fifties. She glimpsed an old orange Rexall Drug sign, a Woolworth that had to be fifty years old, an antique round Gulf sign. The town was dark and shuttered. Along an unlit country road past a low modern brick elementary school, through a railroad crossing, and then nothing for a very long time. Then Tom signaled her to stop.

She parked the Lexus and joined him in the Jeep. "Where are we going?" she asked.

He nodded. "I'll tell you everything. Soon." He took an abrupt, unmarked turnoff into a dense forest, the road degenerating in abrupt phases from macadam to hard-packed gravel, on which her wheels crunched for a good five minutes, to rutted earth for even longer, until it dead-ended at a shelf of rock, jutting shale and schist and irregular boulders. He switched off the lights, then the engine, and let the Jeep coast to a stop. Then took a large black Maglite from the floor and motioned for her to get out with him.

By the flashlight's powerful concentrated beam they entered a cluster of large misshapen firs, starved of sunlight in the dense forestation that crowded the shore of a small lake. He navigated a jagged course along a path that was barely a path, a lightly trodden trace of dirt between the towering trees. Claire followed him, losing her footing several times. She was wearing her dress shoes: no traction. Outside the cone of light that shone from Tom's flashlight, she could see nothing. All was blackness. There didn't seem to be a moon in the sky.

"Stay close," Tom said. "Careful."

"Why?"

"Stay close," he repeated.

Finally he stopped at a small, crude wooden house along the bank—a shack, really—with a steeply sloping, asphalt-shingled roof that here and there was missing its shingles. The shack was in rough shape. There was a small window, but a yellowed paper shade pulled all the way down hid the interior. The roof came down low enough that Claire could touch the eave. The shack appeared to have been painted white once, probably decades ago; now the remaining splinters of white paint looked like tiny snowdrifts on the weathered clapboard siding.

"Welcome," Tom said.

"What is this?" But Claire knew her question was all but unanswerable: what is what, precisely? That it was an all-but-abandoned shack on the shore of a deserted lake in western Massachusetts was obvious.

That it was a hiding place Tom had somehow found, a bolt hole, was equally obvious.

She came closer. Tom had not shaven in a few days. There were dark circles under his eyes. The lines on his forehead seemed even more deeply etched. He looked exhausted, bone-tired.

He smiled, a lopsided, bashful smile. "I'm a crazy poet from New York who needs a little solitude for a few weeks. Place belongs to the fellow who owns the Gulf station in town. Used to belong to his father, who passed away twenty years ago, but his family won't go near it. I scoped the place out a few years ago in case I ever needed a quickie escape hatch. When I called him a few days ago, he was more than happy to take fifty bucks a week for it."

"A few years ago? You've been expecting this day?"

"Yes and no. Part of me thought this would never happen, but another part of me's always been ready for it."

"And what did you think was going to happen to Annie and me if this happened?"

"Claire, if I'd had any idea this was really going to happen, I would have taken off right away. Believe me." He opened the heavy door, which screeched on its hinges. There was no lock. "Enter."

Inside, the wide pine floorboards were rough and worn and looked dangerously splintery. There was a wood-burning stove, on top of which was a box of Ohio Blue Tip strike-anywhere kitchen matches. The air smelled smoky, pleasantly, like wood fire. He appeared to have made a home. A small cot stood against one wall, made up with an ancient-looking dark-green woolen blanket. On a tiny, rickety wooden table were piled foodstuffs: a carton of eggs, a half-gone loaf of bread, a few cans of tuna fish.

Next to them was a small pile of things, mechanical-looking objects she didn't recognize. She picked up one of them, a light-brown oblong box the size of a pair of binoculars with a viewfinder at one end.

"What's this?" she asked.

"A toy. One of the things I picked up at an army-surplus store."

"What is it?"

"Protection. Insurance."

She didn't pursue it.

The sound of a small plane high above broke the silence.

"Remind me not to buy property on this lake," Claire said.

"There's some private airport nearby. I think we're on its flight path. So . . ." He put his arms around her and gave her an embrace so powerful it almost hurt. Once again she was reminded of the great strength in those lithe limbs.

He murmured, "Thanks for coming," and kissed her full on the mouth.

She pulled away. "Who are you, Tom?" she asked quietly, venomously. "Or is it Ron? Which is it?"

"I haven't been Ron in so long . . ." he said. "I was never happy when I was Ron. With you I've always been Tom. Call me Tom."

"So, Tom." Disgust now seeped into her voice. "Who are you, really? Because I really have no idea how much of you is left after all the lies are removed. Is it true, what they're saying?"

"Is what true? I don't know what they're telling you."

She raised her voice. "You don't know . . . What they're telling me, *Tom*, is more than you ever told me."

"Claire—"

"So why don't you finally tell me the fucking truth."

"I was protecting you, Claire."

She gave a bitter laugh that sounded like a hoarse bark. "Oh, that's a good one. You lied from the first goddamned second we met, and you were protecting *me*. Of course, why didn't I see that? What a gentleman you are, what a chivalrous guy. What a protector. Thank you for protecting me, me and my daughter, with three years of lies—no, what, *five* years of lies. Thank you!"

"Claire, babe," Tom said, reaching for her again with his arms, and as his arms began to encircle her shoulders she swiftly kneed him, neatly and to great effect, in the groin.

"When I first met you, I was lonely and depressed and making a decent living managing other people's money. I had to run my own show, my own business, because anyone who checked out my employment history too carefully would have found everyone I'd ever worked for had gone out of business. Who wants to hire a black cat?" He smiled sadly. "By then it was already six years or so since I'd disappeared, become Tom Chapman, and I was still looking around me whenever I walked down the street. I was still convinced they were going to track me down, because they're good, Claire. They're really good. They're ruthless and they're killers and they're really, really good."

"Who are 'they'?"

"I worked for a supersecret clandestine unit of the Pentagon. A black OPSEC support group. A detachment of the Special Forces."

"Translation, please."

"An operational-security group—a group of

twelve highly skilled, highly trained Special Forces who served as covert operatives the Pentagon could send out wherever they wanted to assist secret, often illegal, covert operations anywhere in the world where the Pentagon or the CIA or the State Department didn't want anyone to know they were messing around."

Tom was sitting on the edge of the cot. Next to him, Claire sat cross-legged. "Tom, you've got to slow down."

But Tom seemed not to want to slow down. He kept talking, in an oddly intense monotone. "Officially the group didn't exist. It wasn't on any flow charts or directories. No record of its existence anywhere public. But we were extremely well funded out of the Pentagon's black budget, their massive slush fund. We were officially named Detachment 27, but we sometimes called ourselves Burning Tree. Headed by a real zealot, a corrupt guy, Colonel Bill Marks. William O. Marks."

"Name sounds familiar, I think." She was overwhelmed. Her head spun.

Tom snorted in disgust. "He's now the general in charge of the army. A member of the Joint Chiefs of Staff. In 1984, when the Reagan administration was fighting a covert war in Central America—"

"Tom, you've got to rewind. Start at the beginning. This is too abrupt, too bizarre to make sense to me. Tell me what's true, what's not. You did or you didn't go to college, work for a series of brokerages . . . ? Is that all a fiction?"

He nodded. "The story I told you about Claremont College—there was some truth in that. Only I was born and raised in a suburb north of Chicago. But it's true about my parents divorcing, about my dad refusing to pay for college. And this was 1969, remember. If you weren't married or in school or had some disability, you were drafted and sent over to Vietnam. So I was drafted. But for some reason I got plucked out for the Special Forces, and after my Vietnam tour was done they brought me down to Fort Bragg, and I was inducted into Burning Tree. I was good at it, and—I'm ashamed to admit it now— I believed in it. There was a real bond there, a shared zealotry. We all believed we were doing the dirty work that America needed done but its weak-kneed government was afraid to do openly."

She looked at him curiously, and he smiled. "Or so I believed at the time. By the nineteen-eighties, the CIA and the Defense Department were up to their knees in it in Central America. The CIA was printing up training manuals teaching its agents down there how to use torture."

She nodded; the CIA training manuals had become common knowledge.

"The Reagan administration was insane about routing the Communists down there. But Congress hadn't declared war, so officially we weren't supposed to be involved in combat there. Just 'advising.' So our unit was sent, wearing sanitized fatigues—so in case we ever got caught we couldn't be identified—to help train the Nicaraguan guerrillas in Honduras and help out the government in El Salvador. Reagan's State Department took the really clever, legalistic position that they didn't have to notify Congress that the CIA and the Pentagon had secret units down there because the War Powers Act didn't cover antiterrorist units. Which was us.

"So one day—June 19, 1985—in this nice part of San Salvador called the Pink Zone, the Zona Rosa, a bunch of American marines, off-duty and out of uniform, were eating dinner at this row of sidewalk restaurants. Suddenly a pickup truck pulled up and a bunch of guys jumped out with semi-automatic weapons and opened fire. These urban commandos—leftist, antigovernment guerrillas—managed to kill four marines and two American businessmen and seven Salvadorans in their ambush before they went speeding off. A real bloody massacre. Unbelievable.

"And the Reagan White House went apeshit. We had an agreement that the leftist guerrillas in Salvador wouldn't target Americans, and now this. There was a ceremony at Andrews Air Force Base, where the bodies of the four marines were flown back. Reagan was furious. He vowed that we'd move any mountain and ford any river—you remember how he talked, that phony poetry—to find these jackals and bring them to justice."

Claire nodded, eyes closed.

"Only what he didn't say was that the orders had been passed down already. Get the fuckers. Get the guys who did this. 'Total closure,' they said—which everyone knew meant kill everyone remotely involved. So Burning Tree went out to find the murderers. We had an intelligence lead that the commandos, a splinter group of the leftist organization called FMLN, were based in this village outside San Salvador. A tiny village, I mean grass huts and stuff like that, Claire. The lead was wrong. There weren't any commandos there. There were civilians, there were old men and women and children and babies, and it was obvious right away that this was no hideout for urban commandos, but, you see, we were out for blood."

Now Claire stared at him, looked piercingly, fiercely into his eyes.

"This was the middle of the night. June 22. The entire village was sleeping, but we were ordered to awaken the entire village and drag them out of their beds, out of their huts, and search for weapons. I was checking for hidden caches of ammo on the far side of the village when I heard gunfire."

And now tears streamed down Tom's cheeks, and his head was bowed, his fists clenched.

"Tom," Claire said, her stare unwavering.

"And by the time I got there, they were all dead."

" 'They'?"

"Women and children and old men . . ."

"How were they killed?"

"Machine guns . . ." Head still bowed. His face was contorted, ugly, and his eyes were closed, but tears continued to drip down from them onto the rough blanket. "Bodies sprawled, bloodied . . ."

"Who did it?"

"I . . . I don't know. Nobody would talk."

"How many were killed, Tom?" she asked softly.

"Eighty-seven," he choked out.

Now Claire closed her eyes. "Oh, Jesus," she whispered. She rocked back and forth in silence, murmuring, "Oh, Jesus. Oh, Jesus."

Tom, clenched and red-faced like an infant, sobbed silently.

13

A long silence passed.

At last he spoke again. "The unit was recalled to Fort Bragg for debriefing. The word had gotten out. There had to be sanctions." He wiped his face with his hand, squeezing his eyes hard with his thumb and forefinger. "The colonel denied he gave the order, and he made his men say the same thing when they were interviewed by CID, the army's Criminal Investigation Division. They pinned the blame on me. They said I'd lost it. I'd flipped out. I'd killed all these people. Colonel Marks was afraid that, since I wasn't there and I refused to lie for him, I'd be the weak link who'd tell the truth. So he turned the tables. Had them all blame me. I was naïve. I had no idea what was going on."

"What do you mean?"

"Marks was spared. I was targeted for prosecution—for first-degree murder. Eighty-seven counts. And the ones who wouldn't cooperate in the cover-up, one by one each of them died—committed suicide in their cells, died in car crashes, you name it. And I knew I was next. Because the Pentagon wanted the entire incident covered up. You know the drill—any one of them could have tried to blackmail the Pentagon leadership, because they knew the command was complicit in the massacre."

"So you escaped."

"It wasn't complicated. I slipped a bribe to one of the MPs, the military policemen watching me—asked him to step out and get me a Coke—and I disappeared."

"Disappeared how?"

"God, Claire, we'd been *trained* in this stuff. Some of the same tricks they use in the Federal Witness Security Program. I took a bus to Montana, got a Social Security card, which is ridiculously easy to do once you get access to birth and death records—which are public. And from there you get all the other identity cards, and you start a credit record. I did my own witness-protection program. Made myself disappear and then reappear as a whole new person. But believe me, I was terrified the whole time. I worked at shitty jobs, washing dishes, short-order cook, auto mechanic, you name it. And I had plastic surgery done. The shape of my nose and chin altered, implants put in my cheeks. They can't give you a whole new face, but they can change the old one so much that you're virtually unrecognizable. And slowly and carefully I began to put together a false résumé. Fake medical records are the simplest—you just hand them to whoever your doctor is, no one questions anything. School and college records are the toughest—the U.S. government usually gets an administrator to plant fake school records, for the good of the country and all that, but I didn't have the resources to do that. Still, my new identity had to be really solid, because I heard after a while that there was a price on my head of two million dollars."

"Offered by whom—the Pentagon?"

"No, not like that. At least not officially. By the other members of Burning Tree, the surviving ones."

"Including Colonel Bill Marks?"

"Now General Marks," he said with a nod. "A four-star general. I'm the only one out there who knows about the massacre. If word ever gets out—"

"If it does, then what? That was, what, thirteen years ago."

"—that the current chief of staff of the army, a member of the Joint Chiefs of Staff, led a massacre of eighty-seven Salvadoran civilians, men, women, and children, and then covered it up?"

She nodded.

"That's why my fingerprints were on the national crime database. So that, if I ever turned up anywhere, arrested for anything, even just fingerprinted for anything, they'd have me. The local police didn't know what they were doing when they ran my prints, but once they did, that was it. The Pentagon was alerted, and they sent the FBI and the U.S. Marshals. If I'd known they'd lifted my prints, I'd have fled to protect you and Annie. The Pentagon wants me locked up forever, I'm sure, and a lot of other people want me dead."

"So who was Nelson Chapman?"

"A friend. Really, the father of an old army buddy. I saved his son's life once. He was willing to help me out. He was also willing to lend me some money to start up my investment firm. I doubled his seed money in four months."

"How long do you think you can hide out here?"

"Don't know. Not long, before I attract suspicion."

"I wasn't followed here, as far as I can tell."

"You did a great job evading them. Almost like a pro."

"I followed your instructions, that's all. What about the e-mail message you sent me—can they trace that?"

"No way. I sent it through an anonymous remailer in Finland. I have an e-mail account, one of those small independent service providers, which I pay for with money orders. I linked into it through a laptop I bought around here, secondhand, and a public phone and an acoustic coupler. The courier trick would only work once, I knew. . . ."

His voice faded away, and Claire turned slightly and put her hands on his knees and once again stared into his eyes. "Tom, you've lied to me for six years or more. I really don't know what to believe anymore."

"Why the hell do you think I lied to you, Claire?" he said, eyes flashing. "What do you expect, that I could have told you the truth? 'Oh, by the way, Claire, I'm not really Tom Chapman from California, I'm Ron Kubik from Illinois, and, oh yes, I also haven't really been a money manager all these years, I was actually a covert operative, and now I'm on the run. And, oh yes, another thing, I've had plastic surgery, so this face you're looking at isn't really the face I was born with.' Is *that* what you honestly expected me to say? And *you* of course would say, 'I see, that's interesting, and what time's dinner?'"

"Not at the beginning, maybe, but sometime after we got married, maybe you could have opened up to me, been honest."

"And maybe I would have!" he almost shouted. "Maybe I would have. How do I know? We'd been married three years, baby. In the scheme of things, that's not a long time! Probably I would have told you, when the time was right. But I looked at you and your little daughter—my daughter—and thought, The most important thing I can do in the world right now is to make their world safe. Is to protect them. Because I knew that, if I told you, you'd immediately be put into danger. You'd know, and once you know, you're vulnerable. Things happen, people talk, word gets out. And I wasn't going to do that to you. My job was to protect you!"

He encircled her with his arms, and moved to kiss her, but she turned away.

"What was I supposed to do?" he said.

"I don't know what to say."

He slipped one hand into her blouse and cupped her left breast, and she shook her head.

"Honey," he said plaintively, withdrawing his hand.

She was torn by emotions, wholly confused. She could barely resist him, yet at the same time she desperately wanted to resist him. Finally, she closed her eyes and kissed him, and then he gently began kissing the nape of her neck, the swell at the top of her breasts, her nipples, the underside of her breasts.

She said, "I'm starved. I didn't eat dinner."

Naked, the two of them were entwined on the narrow cot.

He looked at his watch. "It's three in the morning. Care for an early breakfast?"

"I'd love it."

Another plane roared by overhead.

She said, "Three guesses why this lake is deserted."

"After a while you don't even notice the planes,"

he said. He stood up, walked over to the stove. "We've got eggs and toast."

"Brioche?"

"Sorry. Wonder Bread." He knelt down, lit the wood stove, watched until it had caught fire. "Gotta catch sometime," he said. "Ah, here it goes." He smiled in satisfaction. "And that takes care of *that*."

"It's cold here," she said. She got up from the cot and put on one of his plaid flannel shirts.

"Good idea," he said, and slipped into his jeans and a T-shirt. He returned to the stove, put four slices of bread on the toasting rack and a chunk of butter into the hot frying pan, and cracked several eggs over it. The eggs crackled and sizzled and filled the shack with the most wonderful smells.

"Where do you bathe around here?"

"Guess."

"That freezing lake?"

He nodded. Then, suddenly, he turned his head. "Claire."

"What?"

"Do you hear something?"

"Don't tell me you have animals out here, too."

"Shh. Listen."

"What are you doing?" she whispered as he walked to the door and began slowly to open it. "Tom?"

"Shh." He looked out the door, looked around in all directions. He shook his head. "I thought I heard something."

He slipped on a battered pair of Reeboks she'd never seen before and stepped outside. She followed him.

He stopped and looked up at the sky. Now Claire could just make out a noise from above that didn't sound like an ordinary plane: a drone, high-pitched and insistent, that grew louder. As it did, another sound distinguished itself: the thwack-thwack of helicopter blades. Tom kept looking up.

"There must have been a transmitter in the Lexus," he said.

"But I did the check you told me to do!"

He shook his head. "I shouldn't have let you drive here. Even stopping the Lexus a few miles away. Those transmitters have gotten more sophisticated since my time in the military—you couldn't have found it. Those planes we heard, must have been small single-engine fixed-wing—"

Suddenly, from somewhere on the ground, came a series of sharp explosions that sounded like fire-crackers going off.

"Oh, God, Tom, what is it?"

"My booby traps. Get back inside!"

"What?"

The thwack-thwack of helicopter blades grew louder as the helicopter approached and then hov-ered directly overhead, and suddenly a blindingly bright light came from the sky. She looked up. Bright lights shone down from the helicopter, illuminating the whole area. She blinked, her eyes trying to adjust to the sudden brightness.

"Go!" he shouted, and she turned swiftly and ran back to the shack, with Tom right behind.

He shut the door, grabbed her. "Get down on the floor."

"Tom—?"

"Now!"

She dropped and flattened herself on the rough wooden floor.

"I strung up booby-trap devices all around. Trip wires nailed to the trees. They never expected it. My primitive burglar-alarm system."

Before she could say anything, a loud, amplified voice from out of the sky boomed: *"Federal agents! Come out and drop all weapons!"*

"Tom, what are we going to do?" she cried, her voice muffled by the floorboards.

He didn't reply. He was searching for something. "Tom?"

"They're not going to rush us, not with you in here," he said. "Also, they don't know what I've got in here. Now, they've got us surrounded, but they're not going to move any closer."

"What are we going to do?" she said desperately.

"Let me do it, Claire."

She turned to watch him looking out the window through the viewfinder of the brown oblong box she'd seen earlier. He seemed to be pointing it up at the sky.

"Tom, what are you doing?"

"It's a laser range-finder from a tank," he said. "Old Special Forces trick."

"Where the hell did you get that?" She turned her head so she could see out one of the windows.

The amplified voice boomed: *"We are the U.S. Marshals Service. We have a warrant for your arrest. Come out peacefully and no one will be hurt."*

"Army surplus in Albany," Tom said. "Thousand bucks. Use the laser to temporarily blind the pilot, zap him in the eyes. Old trick. We have no choice. That's their surveillance post in the sky. Take care of that first."

"Come out with your hands up."

He pressed a button on the box, said, "Got him."

She looked out at the helicopter, heard the racket suddenly get louder. The helicopter seemed to be tipping, banking to one side. Then, just as suddenly, it flew off, taking with it the bright lights.

The shack returned to darkness, the noise diminished almost to silence.

"Got the pilot with the laser. Pilot couldn't see, probably freaked out. Copilot probably took over. They're not idiots; they're not coming back. That leaves our friends out there, but they're going to be a little freaked out themselves.

"Looks like they're fifty yards away," he said.

Now another voice came from out in front of the shack, also amplified, flat and mechanical sounding: *"We've got you surrounded. Come out with your hands up."*

"Stay down there, Claire."

She turned her head to look up. He was standing in the shadows, peering out the open window.

"Now what?" she said.

"I'll take care of it. Their standard operating procedure now is to negotiate. We let them talk."

"You've got ten seconds," said the voice, loud and slow and deliberate. *"Come out peacefully and no one gets hurt. You have no choice. We have you surrounded. You have six seconds."*

"Jesus, Tom, what are we doing?"

"They're not going to fire on us, babe."

"Three seconds. Come out now *or we commence firing."*

"Tom!"

"They're bluffing."

And suddenly there was a series of muffled shots, a *phump-phump-phump.* Terrified, Claire scrambled off the floor, crouched, peered out one of the open windows, and saw that several objects had been fired at them—

"Grenades," Tom said quietly.

"Oh my God!" she screamed.

Each grenade, she saw, was emitting a thin cloud of white smoke.

"Gas," Tom said. "Not explosives. Incapacitant gas. Shit."

And suddenly Claire felt drowsy, uncontrollably, deeply tired, and then everything went black.

PART TWO

14

❖

Quantico Marine Base, Quantico, Virginia

*T*he gate, made of steel bars painted institutional
gray, slid open slowly, electronically. A marine
guard stood at attention. The floors were pale-green
linoleum atop concrete; the corridor echoed as she
walked. The gate slid shut behind her, filling her
with dread. A red sign on the wall said B-WING. The
cinderblock walls in this section of the Quantico
brig, Special Quarters One, were painted white. In
this wing violent rapists and murderers were incar-
cerated. Security cameras were everywhere. Her escort, the duty brig commander, led her to a door
marked CELL BLOCK B and held it open. It was eight-
thirty in the morning.

Another guard snapped to attention. She was
taken to a windowed visitors' room just off the cell
block, shown to a blue chair at a wooden conference
table. She sat and waited in the cold.

A few minutes later a rattling and clanking of
chains announced his arrival.

Flanked by two large guards, Tom stood before

her naked, except for gray military-issue under-shorts. He was in handcuffs, leg irons, and a con-necting waist chain. His head had been shaved. He was shivering.

Tears sprang to her eyes.

He said, "Thanks for coming."

She began to weep.

She got to her feet. "What the hell is this?" she shouted at one of the guards, who looked at her im-passively. "Where are his clothes?"

"Suicide watch, ma'am," one of the guards said.

"I want clothes on him right now!"

"That request has to go through the duty com-mander, ma'am," the other guard said.

"You go talk to him now. This man has rights," Claire said.

They brought Tom back, dressed in a light-blue prison jumpsuit. He was still in restraints, which forced him to take small, mincing, jangling steps to-ward her. Still weeping, she embraced him. His hands still cuffed, he could not hug her back.

"I want the cuffs off," she said.

"Only one hand can come out of the cuffs, ma'am," a guard said. "Duty commander's order."

Tom sat at the conference table across from Claire. A guard stood watch just outside. A security camera was mounted in one corner of the room, where the wall met the ceiling. Guards watched them through one glass wall.

They sat for a moment in silence. He wore a tan ID badge with a tiny smudged black-and-white photo, his name—Ronald M. Kubik—his Social Se-curity number, and the date of the confinement, which was today. A black strip on it said DETAINED.

A red strip said MAX, for maximum-security confinement.

"This is all my fault," Claire said.

"What is?"

"This." She waved her hand around. "All this. You know—the car."

"You'd never have found the transmitter. I blame myself. I shouldn't have let you drive it anywhere near the lake."

"They don't fuck around," Claire said.

He nodded.

"You're in the army now," she said.

He nodded again. He reached his free hand across the table and held hers.

"No joke," she said. "You've been joined to a headquarters-and-service company, on paper anyway. After thirteen years they've got you back on active-duty status. The good news is, you start drawing pay again." She flashed a fake smile.

"How's my little girl?" he asked.

"She's okay. She misses you. I kissed her goodbye this morning. Jackie took her to school. It's her last day. End of the school year."

"Early in the morning for Jackie, isn't it?" He gave a rueful smile.

"She's a trouper. I got the first flight out of Logan. I'm basically running on fumes."

"Are you going back to Boston today?"

"Probably not."

"Where are you staying?"

"For now, some Quality Inn right outside the Quantico gates."

"What am I charged with?"

It occurred to her for the first time that Tom had been kept entirely in the dark. They'd flown him directly to the marine base at Quantico on one of the

U.S. Marshals Service DC-9s—"Con Air," they called their fleet of planes—and trundled him into a holding cell, stripped him, confiscated all his possessions, printed him, photographed him, gave him a regulation haircut. Thrown him into Cell 3, Cell Block B, wearing nothing but army-issue shorts. Told him nothing. All the U.S. Marshals had told her was that they had been subjected to a sophisticated new incapacitating agent, a formula that had been developed after the FBI's fiascos at Waco and Ruby Ridge. The grenades burned a formula that contained a built-in antidote, so that, as soon as the two of them were knocked out, a chemical immediately started waking them up. Within an hour both of them were awake, though groggy and nauseated.

They'd threatened her with all kinds of charges: they were furious at her evasion and at first refused to allow her to see Tom. In the end, though, the FBI men had backed down. Legally, they couldn't do anything to her. She had a right to meet with her husband; it was as simple as that. The next day she flew to Washington's National Airport, rented a car, and drove to Quantico, Virginia.

"I don't know," Claire said. "Officially you haven't been charged. They don't have to do that yet. Some system they got here."

"They made me sign a confinement order."

She scowled. "Don't sign anything."

"It was just to acknowledge that I'd read it."

"What did it say?"

"Just the 'nature of the offense.'"

"Which is?"

"Desertion. Nothing else. Article 85 of the Uniform Code of Military Justice. I guess they drew up those charges years ago, after I disappeared."

She nodded. "And more to come. Did they read you your rights?"

"Yep."

"Damn. Now we need to find you an attorney."

"What about you?"

"Me? What the hell do I know about military justice?"

"They'll assign me a military attorney automatically. He'll know all the military stuff."

She shook her head slowly. "We have to find you an outside attorney who really knows what he's doing. In addition to whoever they assign to you."

"How?"

"I'll find someone. Don't worry about it."

"Claire, don't you realize what's going on here? Don't you know what they're planning to do to me? They're going to put on a court-martial. A fucking kangaroo court. They'll probably do it in secrecy. They'll find me guilty, and then they'll lock me away in Leavenworth, or maybe some special Pentagon facility no one's ever heard of, for the rest of my life. Which won't be long, because soon they'll 'discover' me dead in my cell, presumably a suicide."

There was a knock on the door.

"Have you seen my cell, Claire? You can see it from here—look."

The guard entered. "Time," he said.

"We're not finished yet," Claire said.

"Sorry," the guard said. "Commander's orders."

Tom pointed with his free hand. Through the open door she could see his cell, just a green mattress on a metal shelf and a steel toilet-sink unit.

"Claire," Tom said, "I need you."

15

Despairing and angry and, above all, confused, Claire sat in the rental car for a long time after leaving the brig. She felt lost and powerless and didn't know whom to turn to for help, and finally she took out her cell phone and called an old friend.

Arthur Iselin, a prominent Washington attorney who was her old boss and a trusted friend, agreed to meet her for an early lunch at the Hay-Adams. Iselin was a partner at one of the biggest and most powerful law firms in Washington. Fresh out of law school, she had clerked for him when he was solicitor general. He was then, and remained, one of the wisest men she knew.

Without asking, the waiter brought him his regular, the farmer's omelet with piping-hot biscuits, which he slathered with plenty of butter. No health fanatic, he. Nearby sat the White House chief of staff with a Republican senator; Iselin, who knew them both, nodded at them.

"You know, there's an old saying," he said. He had widely spaced gray eyes, under which were deep circles, and a large mouth with large lips, the bottom one appearing to be split. "Military justice is to justice as—"

"As military music is to music," Claire finished. "I know, I know. But I thought they'd gotten a lot better since Vietnam."

"Since the Calley court-martial, actually. When I was in the army everyone used to tell me the military system is far superior to our civilian one because at least they take it seriously. But I never believed it. Still don't. I think, if the military wants to lock someone away and throw away the key, they can do it. And I have no doubt they want to lock your husband away."

"Probably true," Claire conceded.

"And if you tell me he's innocent, he's innocent."

"Thank you."

"Of course, that's easy for me to say. After lunch I go back to my office and my stack of briefs. Your life will never be the same."

"Right." She nibbled on a bite of salad. Since the arrest she'd had no appetite.

"The first decision you'll have to make, and it's a big one, is whether to make this public. Tom's story itself is a headline maker. If the Pentagon goes ahead and prosecutes, that makes it front-page stuff."

"Why wouldn't I publicize it?"

"Because that's your ace in the hole. The Pentagon is terrified of public scrutiny these days. Going public is a potent threat. Use it when you have to. For now, I'd keep all this absolutely secret."

She nodded.

"Tell you something else. If you leak it, even if he's acquitted, he'll always be known as a mass murderer. Your family will be destroyed. I wouldn't do it, given the choice."

"Makes sense to me."

"Sounds like you've already decided not to get involved as an attorney of record."

She shrugged.

"I'd reconsider. You're the last one they want trying this case. To the military, civilian lawyers are wild cards. Get them involved, next thing you know you got what the military calls a CONGRINT, a congressional inquiry. And you most of all—Claire Heller Chapman, big scary Harvard Law School celeb—you'll scare 'em to death. They'll piss their pants. You really should do it." He looked at her, assessed her dour expression, then chomped down blithely on a biscuit. "Failing that, there's this." He slid a typed sheet of paper across the table.

"Your list of civilian lawyers who do military law."

"Correct. You'll notice it's not a very long list. Good civilian criminal lawyers who don't just practice military law but actually specialize in it, there's maybe a handful of them around the country. You'll want someone who lives and works in the Virginia area, ideally, so that narrows it down even further. Every one of these was once a JAG officer in one of the service branches of the military. Judge Advocate General Corps."

"I know what 'JAG' is."

"This is good. You'll see, the military speaks a different language, and the sooner you learn it the better. Not that many decent civilian military lawyers in the area. Slim pickings."

She looked the list over with dismay.

"It's a tough way to earn a living," Iselin went on. "In the old days when we had a draft, there were rich kids whose daddies were willing to pay the big bucks for a civilian attorney. In the new military, not too many can scrape the money together. If it were me, I'd pick this guy Grimes. In solo practice in Manassas."

"Why?"

"He's smart as hell, and he knows the ins and outs of military justice as well as anyone. But most of all he hates the military with a vengeance. You want someone like that, someone with fire in the belly. Because you've got a really tough case, and you need a fighter."

She looked at Grimes's entry. "He's a former army JAG and he hates the military? Why?"

"Oh, they forced him into retirement five or six years ago."

"Over what?"

"I don't know. Some scandal or something. He's black, and I think it was racism. Ask him. Thing is, he's a scrapper and a street fighter, and he's obsessed with beating them at their own game."

"But there must be some hotshot partner in a Washington firm who was an army JAG."

"Sure. There's a partner in one of the big firms, but you don't want him."

"I don't?"

"Nah. He's like me—full plate, stretched way too thin, hands everything off to his associate. You want Bernie the Attorney, you want someone who knows the system inside and out and still has lots of time available for this case, because it's going to be a huge time-consumer. They'll have him up on murder charges, count on it. Mass murder, whatever the military calls it." He peered at her over his coffee cup. "Though I thought they were in the mass-murder business."

"You know anyone who has a house to rent?"

"A house?"

"Preferably furnished. This is going to be a long haul."

When she returned to her room at the Quality Inn, across from the Quantico gates, she was surprised to find her bed unmade. When she called down to Housekeeping to ask about it, she was told that a DO NOT DISTURB sign had been hung from her doorknob for most of the afternoon. She knew she hadn't put the sign up. This prompted her to check her suitcase; sure enough, the zipper was aligned differently from the way she had left it.

She sank onto the unmade bed and, more depressed than frightened, began to make telephone calls.

16

◆—◆

"*Boy, it's* a real honor to meet you, ma'am," the young man said. His name was Captain Terrence Embry, he was twenty-seven years old, and he was the military defense counsel assigned to Tom. (Claire still could not get herself to call her husband Ronald, to think of him as anyone except Tom.)

She smiled, nodded politely, stirred nondairy creamer into her coffee. It was early in the morning and they were meeting for breakfast at the McDonald's on the base. His invitation: he'd called the Quality Inn the night before, told her he'd just been detailed to the case, and would she like to get together?

"I mean, we studied your book *Crime and the Law* in my criminal-law class," he went on. "I'm just sorry about the circumstances and all. . . ." His voice trailed off, and he looked down at his Egg Mc-Muffin. His face reddened.

Terry Embry had reddish hair, cut short in what she was beginning to recognize as an army regulation haircut, large prominent ears, nervous watery blue eyes. He blushed easily. He had long slender

fingers and a dry, firm handshake. On his left hand
was a large, perfectly shiny gold wedding band, obviously brand-new. On his right hand was a heavy
West Point ring, on top of which was mounted a
synthetic black star sapphire. He was a West Point
graduate, he said, sent by the army to the University
of Virginia Law School and then the Judge Advocate
General school there, in Charlottesville. He was a
smart young man, Claire saw at once, and almost
totally inexperienced.

Her appetite still hadn't returned. She took a sip
of her coffee. "Do you mind if I smoke, Captain Embry?" she asked.

Embry's eyes widened and he looked around anxiously. "No, ma'am, I . . ."

"Don't worry, we're in the smoking section," she
said, as she unwrapped a pack of Camel Lights,
pulled one out, and lighted it with a plastic Bic
lighter. She despised herself for smoking again—actually buying a pack, and not just bumming from
Jackie, was serious—but she couldn't help it.

She exhaled. There were few things more disgust-
ing than smoking a cigarette at breakfast. "Tell me
something, Captain—"

"Terry."

"Okay, then. Terry. Tell me something. Have you
ever tried a case?"

His face reddened. She had her answer. "Well,
ma'am, I've done a number of plea bargains, mostly
for drugs, unauthorized absences, that sort of
stuff—"

"But you've never actually done a trial."

"No, ma'am," he said quietly.

"I see. And have they assigned a prosecutor yet?
Or is it still too early for that?"

"Well, it's really early, but they've already detailed someone, which tells me they're probably planning on a court-martial."

She smiled grimly. "What a surprise. And who have they assigned?"

"Major Waldron, ma'am. Major Lucas Waldron." He took a healthy bite of his Egg McMuffin.

"Is he any good, do you know?"

His eyes widened. He accelerated his chewing, then tried to speak through a mouthful of food, but settled for vigorous nodding. Then he said, "Pardon me, ma'am. Major Waldron—yes, ma'am, he's good. He's real good. He's probably the best they've got."

"Is that right?" she said, unsurprised.

"Well, he's a bit of a hardass, ma'am, if you don't mind my saying. He's the most experienced trial counsel in the JAG Corps. Really aggressive. And he has a perfect win-loss record. No one's ever been acquitted at a trial he's prosecuted."

"I don't suppose that means he only takes the easy cases, in order to maintain his perfect record, does it?"

"Not that I've heard, ma'am. He's just really good."

"My husband is being scapegoated."

"Yes, ma'am," he said politely.

"When you read whatever files they give you, you'll see that. It's a conspiracy. Can you deal with that?"

"If it's true, yes, ma'am, I can."

"It won't be good for your career, Terry, going after a cover-up within the military, will it?"

"Ma'am, I don't know what's best for my career."

"Enough with the 'ma'am,' okay?"

"Sorry."

"Terry, you should know I'll be hiring civilian counsel."

He examined his Egg McMuffin. "That's certainly your right, uh, Claire. Would you like me to excuse myself from the case?"

"No."

"Well, one of us will have to be associate counsel," he said. When Claire didn't answer, he said, "I suppose it'll be me. That's certainly fine."

"Tell me something, Terry. Why do you suppose you, a complete rookie, were assigned to this case, against Major Waldron, the best the army has? Any idea, Terry?"

"I have no idea," he admitted with a candor she found disarming, "but it doesn't look good for us, does it?"

She gave a soft snort. "You didn't choose this assignment, did you?"

"That's not the way it works in the military. You go where they tell you."

"Wouldn't you rather be prosecuting it?"

"This case?" He reddened. "Just from the way it looks, this is a slow soft pitch right across the plate, just hanging there, waiting to be hit out of the ballpark."

"By the prosecution."

"Just from what I've heard, but I haven't dug into it yet."

"Did you choose to go into defense, Terry, or did they just put you there?"

"I was assigned. I mean, everyone in JAG school wants to prosecute, not defend, you know? Defending bad guys is not exactly a career-enhancing billet."

Claire's eyes flashed. "I want you to know something, Terry," she said coolly. She exhaled a plume of smoke like some kind of dragon, or perhaps a femme fatale. "My husband is not a bad guy."

"Well, so, anyway, I think you should look at this." He withdrew some papers from a folder and, without even looking at them, handed her a stapled sheaf.

"What's this?" Claire asked.

"The charge sheet. They work fast. Article 85, desertion. Article 90, assaulting or willfully disobeying superior commissioned officer. Article 118, murder in the first degree. *Eighty-seven specifications.*" He looked up at Claire, shook his head.

For the first time, the seriousness, the finality of it all struck her. They were really going after Tom. He could in fact be executed. The military still had the death penalty.

She had to do it.

"I think I've just changed my mind," she said, steely. "How the hell do I sign up to help represent my husband?"

17

Twenty minutes from Quantico, along the two-lane Dumfries Road in Manassas, Virginia, Claire pulled the sleek rented Oldsmobile over onto the shoulder and once again inspected the street number. This was the correct number, it had to be. It was precisely the same address that appeared on the short list Arthur Iselin had given her, and neither Arthur nor his secretary made mistakes. And she had talked to the lawyer on the phone and had taken down the street number he told her. So it was impossible that she'd gotten the address wrong.

But this could not be the office.

This was a tiny yellow clapboard house, almost a dollhouse. It was a house, not an office building, and it was a house out of *Tobacco Road*; all that was missing was a turnip truck and maybe a car chassis up on cinderblocks. This could not be the office of Charles O. Grimes III.

When she'd driven past the house three or four times, she finally pulled into the driveway and got out and rang the doorbell.

After a few long minutes the door opened. A

handsome black man in his late forties, with graying hair, a gray-flecked mustache, and large amused eyes, stared at her for a disconcertingly long time. "You get lost, Professor? I saw you pass by here, must have been four times."

"Thought I might have had the wrong address."

"Come on in. I'm Charles." He extended a hand.

"Claire."

"Let me guess," he said, guiding her through a tiny cluttered living room dominated by an immense TV, "you're asking yourself, why does this guy work out of the same little shitbox he lives in, right?" Claire, following him through a doorway into a fake-wood-paneled study, didn't answer. "Well, you see, Professor, I had a wife who wasn't too happy when I started boinking my secretary, who was never much of a secretary anyway, and isn't my secretary anymore. In fact, I don't even know where she is. So the wife dumps me, holds me up for child support, takes all my money, and now look at me. I used to have a Jag. JAG with a Jag. Now I've got a thirdhand rustbucket Mercedes." He sank down into a cheap orange-vinyl-cushioned desk chair and interlaced his hands behind his head. "Have a seat. Welcome to Grimes & Associates."

She lifted a stack of papers off the only other chair and sat down. This was the tackiest office she'd ever seen. The floor was covered in hideous wall-to-wall orange shag carpeting. Piles of papers were everywhere, some in cardboard boxes, some in precarious towers on the floor or heaped on top of the flimsy-looking tan four-drawer filing cabinets. In one corner of the room a portable fan stood on the floor next to a red-and-black shoe polisher. There were a few diplomas on the wall she couldn't make out. Atop one of the file cabinets was a cluster of bowling trophies. A fake-antique wooden sign hung on one wall announcing, in olde lettering, "DULY QUALIFIED HONEST COUNTRY LAWYER *at your service*—Wills— Deeds filed—Disputes settled—Bondsman—Patents review'd—Consultations from 25¢—*Your lawyer is your friend.*" Hanging from the bottom of the sign was another sign, a wooden rectangle: "C. O. GRIMES III, ESQ."

"Grimes & Associates?" Claire asked. "You have associates?"

"Planning on it. A man can dream, can't he?" A powerful mothball odor wafted from his seventies-style polyester pullover sweater, a psychedelic riot of brown, orange, and yellow.

"Look," she said. "Don't take this the wrong way. You come highly recommended. By, of all people, Arthur Iselin."

"How is Artie?"

"He's fine. He says you're a star of the civilian military-law field. I assume that means you win a lot of cases. You're successful. Now, in my world, if you're a big star—"

"—a big swinging dick, you have a corner office in a skyscraper, am I reading you right?"

"Yeah."

"Well, some of the guys in my business do, but mostly they practice other kinds of law, too. Like corporate, or big-deal criminal, or whatever. You can't get rich on military law. Myself, I supplement my military practice with personal-injury and insurance work. No, I'm not a big Harvard Law School celebrity like you-all. But you wouldn't even be here if you hadn't talked to some other civilian military lawyers and checked out my record, and if you have, you know I like to win cases. I don't always, but I try . . . *real hard.*"

"Why'd you leave the military?"

Grimes hesitated a split second. "Retired."

"Why?"

"I was tired of it."

"Something happen?"

"I got tired of it," he said, a note of irritation entering his voice. "That's what happened. You mind if I ask *you* a couple questions?"

"Go ahead."

"Arthur called me. I got the background. Sounds like you're in some kind of deep doodoo. He been charged yet?"

She handed Grimes the charge sheet. He looked it over, raised his brows here and there, hummed. By the second page his humming got louder and went up an octave. "Someone's been a bad boy," he said.

"You better be joking."

"Of course he didn't do it," Grimes said, a twinkle in his eye. "I like to tell people all my clients are innocent. They're always innocent—or else they won't plead guilty."

Claire suppressed her annoyance. "Is he a deserter? No question about it. But he's no mass murderer. They tried to set him up to take the fall for this massacre thirteen years ago, and he was smart enough to escape their clutches. General William Marks—that's right, *the* four-star General Marks, the chief of staff of the army—commanded the platoon in 1985, when he was a colonel. The Special Forces detachment that was sent down to El Salvador to take revenge for the killing of some American marines. General Marks himself ordered them to kill eighty-seven civilians for one reason alone: cold-blooded revenge. Tom didn't take part in it—he wasn't even there."

Grimes nodded, watching her steadily.

"General Marks initiated and supervised a cover-up thirteen years ago and tried to nail my husband with responsibility for it. So whoever takes this case is going to flush him out and expose his attempted cover-up. Because I'm going to go after the whole corrupt system. The whole goddamned military system—"

"Oh, no, you're not," Grimes interrupted. "No fucking way. Bad mistake. Get that out your head, sister. You're going to play by the rules. Play hard, play aggressive, but it's their game—hell, it's their fucking *stadium*. Their fucking ball club. Lady, let me tell you something. Every civilian who's ever gone into a military general court-martial and tried to attack the foundations of the military has lost his case. No exceptions. The military is a tight, closed fraternity. They take it real serious. Military justice is a deadly-serious business. You'd be surprised how much it's like the civilian justice system—it was made that way. Modeled on the U.S. criminal-justice system. Lot of the same rights. You want to defend your husband, you go after the charges and prove they haven't made their case, just like you'd do in a regular courtroom. You think there was a cover-up, go ahead and go after General Marks. Go after General Patton, General Douglas fucking MacArthur, General Dwight fucking *Eisenhower* if you want. But you don't attack the system. Now, you know I'm hungry for this case, but I'm not going to lie to you. If you hire me, you're hiring someone who plays by their rules. I play nasty, but I play their game. I just play it better than them."

Claire nodded, smiled.

"They hook you up with a detailed defense counsel yet?" Grimes asked.

"Yes. Some kid named Terry Embry, fresh out of law school."

"Hmph. Never heard of him. He any good?"

"He's totally green. Smart. Well meaning, I think. Nice kid. But strictly junior-varsity."

"We all got to start somewhere. Why should the Pentagon give you their best? How about trial counsel? That's what the military calls the prosecutor. He assigned yet?"

"Lucas Waldron."

Grimes leaned back in his chair and laughed. He laughed so loud, so hard, that he had a coughing fit. "Lucas Waldron?" he choked out.

"You've heard of him, I take it."

When he finally stopped coughing, Grimes said, "Oh, I heard of him, all right. He's a totally ruthless son of a bitch."

"You ever come up against him?"

"A couple times. Got some light jury sentences off him, but never won a case against him. But what I don't get is why they're even putting your husband on trial."

"What else could they have done? Legally, I mean."

"Oh, man, they could have done much worse if they wanted to. They could have had three army shrinks declare him crazy and lock him up in some government mental institution, some federal facility, and throw away the key. I really don't get why they want to go the court-martial route."

"Probably because of me. Do everything by the book."

He nodded slowly. "Maybe. Still doesn't make sense."

"You'd be second chair, you know. If I hire you."

"Second to the fetus?"

"Second to me. He'd be third chair. If I even keep him on. I don't know if I can trust someone from the army."

"Nah, you want to hold on to the assigned co-counsel. He's got the power to order military witnesses to appear for an interview; we don't. Plus, you need him around to cut through all the administrative bullshit. I'm telling you, the army has a reg—a regulation—for everything, including how to wipe your ass."

"Okay."

"No offense, Professor—you want to be lead counsel on this, go right ahead, it's your money, your husband, your case. You're the boss. But I don't get the feeling you know too much about court-martials."

"You just said it follows civilian law pretty closely."

"You want to be gettin your training wheels when your husband is facing the death penalty?"

"I'd expect you to do a lot of backseat driving."

He shrugged. "Hey, you're Claire Heller Chapman. You want to do it that way, fine with me. You got clearance?"

"Why?"

"I promise you, they're going to close this courtroom, shut it tight as a drum. Plus most of the statements and evidence will be classified top secret. That's how they're going to play this."

"I'll get clearance. You think that'll be a problem?"

"Shouldn't be. You'll have to fill out a bunch of paper. Standard form 86. They'll do an NAC, that's a national agency check. Background check by FBI and the Defense Investigative Services. Clear you up to 'secret.'"

"And if they don't give me clearance?"

"They have to. Now that you're counsel. They have to give counsel clearance, otherwise your husband doesn't have to talk."

"How fast can I get it?"

"They can grant it overnight if they want. Now, we're going to need a good investigator."

"I know a really good one."

"Army background? CID?"

"Boston PD and FBI."

"Good enough for me."

"He's in Boston, but he's worth the added expense. Really good investigators are rare."

"Tell me about it. In this case, they'll be vital. This case is going to be brutal. So what's the deal here? Am I hired or not?"

18

❖

On the way from the airport, Claire stopped first at Arthur Iselin's law firm, just off Dupont Circle, to pick up the keys. Annie and Jackie waited in the rented Olds. The house was on Thirty-fourth Street, near Massachusetts Avenue, a very short walk to the Naval Observatory. It was a Federal-style town house, cream-painted brick front with black shutters, quite handsome. It belonged to one of the senior partners in Iselin's firm, who had recently retired and moved to Tuscany for six months. He was asking a lot for the short-term rental, but Claire decided, as she walked up the front steps, that it was worth it.

"Do I get my own room?" Annie asked.

"I'm sure you do," Claire replied.

"How 'bout me?" Jackie asked.

"Hey, you get your own *wing*," Claire said.

As soon as Claire had the door unlocked, Annie bolted ahead into the house. She squealed as she ran, "Mommy, this is *so cool!*"

Claire took in the spacious and elegant foyer, the beautiful old Persian rugs, the antique furnishings, the linen-white wainscoted walls. "We're in trouble," she said to Jackie. "She's going to destroy this." The air was musty—the house smelled as if it had been empty for months—yet laced with furniture polish. Someone came in and cleaned once a week or so, she decided.

Jackie set her duffel bag down and looked around, eyeing the graceful staircase that wound around upward from the left of the foyer in a fan of white balusters. "Cool," she said. "You did good."

She'd taught her last class and instructed Connie to turn away all requests from potential clients. There would be final exams, but she'd have the completed exams FedExed down to her here. She told her students she was available by telephone and gave her number in Washington. Two of her pending cases she turned over to a friend at a downtown Boston firm. That left her with one appeal before the Supreme Judicial Court, which would involve a quick flight to Boston and back. Their house would stand empty, but Rosa—who had kids of her own and certainly couldn't come down to Washington to work—would stop in every couple of days to make sure everything was all right. Jackie, who paid the rent doing what she called "boring fucking technical writing," could do her work down here and was willing, saint that she was, to take care of Annie.

She placed a couple of calls to friends in Boston, told them she'd be in Washington for a while, perhaps even several months, working on a case she wasn't supposed to talk about. A few hours later, while Claire and Jackie were still unpacking and settling in and Annie was discovering new rooms and new hiding places, the doorbell rang.

An army courier, a young black man wearing a

name tag that said "Lee," was carrying a large carton. "I need your signature on some forms, ma'am, but first I'm going to need to see a driver's license."

She signed with a sense of anticipation and anxiety far different from her customary feelings about documents provided her during litigation. These were documents about Tom and his life before he met her, his concealed life.

They were copies of his enlisted-evaluation reports—DA Form 2166-6, photocopies of what she imagined were old, yellowed pieces of paper from deep in files somewhere in North Carolina (Special Forces trained at Fort Bragg). They were stamped FOR OFFICIAL USE ONLY and included ADMINISTRATIVE DATA and PERFORMANCE EVALUATION—PROFESSIONALISM and PERFORMANCE AND POTENTIAL EVALUATION. She settled down in the room that she'd chosen as her office—a comfortable library on the first floor, far removed from the living quarters—and examined copies of Tom's service-records books. Most of them were boring and anodyne, but she forced herself to read closely. She discovered his file photo, attached to a copy of his personnel file, taken when he was sent to Vietnam. He was almost thirty years younger. A kid of nineteen. Younger, yes, but also a very different face—a different nose, more bulbous; hollow cheeks; a receding chin. If she hadn't known it was Tom, she wouldn't have recognized the photo. It surprised her that the plastic surgery that had altered his appearance so dramatically had also improved his looks considerably.

Then she read something that made her blood run cold.

Charles Grimes met her at the entrance to the Quantico brig. This time he was wearing an ill-fitting jacket and tie. In addition to his briefcase, he was carrying a large portable radio.

"What's that for?" Claire asked.

"Tunes," Grimes said and didn't elaborate. "Bad news."

"What," she said vaguely. Nothing surprised her anymore. They stopped at the sentry and opened their briefcases.

"The battalion commander's ordered the Article 32 investigation and hearing," Grimes said. "Docketed for a week from now. They normally take thirty days between preferring charges and the Article 32 hearing, but they're really moving this one along."

"English, please."

"It's the pretrial investigation. Required by Article 32 of the Uniform Code of Military Justice. To weigh all the facts, the issues raised in the charges. And decide whether to go ahead with the court-martial."

"Sort of like the grand-jury investigation in the real world."

"But better. We get to be there. Question witnesses, impeach stuff. No jury, and it's run by an investigating officer, not a judge. It's a good discovery opportunity—see what evidence they got, what kind of case they got."

"But they're not going to really drop the charges, are they? They're going ahead with the court-martial."

"Look, we got the right to waive the hearing. But we want it. We want to scope out their case."

"The hearing's in a week?"

He nodded as they walked along the echoey corridor, accompanied by an escort. "Not much time for us. They've had years to put this together. You get the documents?"

"I read them."

They talked briefly. Grimes told Claire about his brief meeting with Tom in the brig yesterday. Tom had approved of hiring Grimes.

They stopped at the long conference room before the entrance to Cell Block B. "We're going to meet here," Grimes said to the escort. "Can you get the prisoner now?" He turned back to her, told her he'd spent hours going over Tom's case file. "Your husband's had quite a life. Interesting experiences."

She didn't answer. She didn't know what to say. Instead, she talked about the Article 32 hearing. Concentrate on the legal proceedings, she told herself. This you can do. "You want to try to get the court-martial knocked out?" she asked.

"Do I want to?" He put the radio down outside the conference-room door and switched it on to some rap station. "Notorious B.I.G.," he said. "*Life After Death*. I hate this shit. Yeah, sure I want to. Ain't gonna happen, but I'm willing to try. Long as you're paying me."

"You were serious about tunes, weren't you?"

He smiled. He had an endearing smile, perfect white teeth. "No, it's to keep 'em from listening in. Old Quantico brig trick." He entered, set down his briefcase, took a seat at the head of the long Formica-topped table. She looked around the long, narrow room, noticed there was no camera in here. "See," Grimes said, "I told you they'd give you clearance. I'm surprised you accepted the conditions, though."

"Why?"

"Famous civil-liberties lawyer like you, I woulda thought you'd refuse. They investigate you, you had to sign that gag order, now you can't speak out about the classified evidence in the case. Kinda like selling your soul."

He was right. "I didn't have a choice," she said.

"Not if I wanted to defend Tom." She sat down next to him.

"True, but still. You call him Tom, huh? His assumed name?"

"That's how I know him. I don't know him as Ron."

"You still think he's innocent, huh? After what we both read?"

She turned to him angrily, but before she could reply, the door opened. Tom, in his blue jumpsuit, stood there in his restraints, flanked by guards. She noticed he was wearing black boots.

"All right, I want these off," Grimes told the guards, waving at Tom. "All of 'em. And not just one cuff either. You tell your CO we want all these off or we're going to file complaints with every single goddamned member of the Senate Armed Services Committee plus the senators from Massachusetts *and* Virginia, and then we're going to initiate a CONGRINT and your CO's going to go blind with paperwork." Tom remained standing at attention, looking at Grimes curiously.

"Yes, sir," one of the guards said. They turned and escorted Tom off.

Grimes laughed, almost a cackle. "I love threatening these guys," he said. "I mean, Christ's sakes, where the hell is this guy going to go anyway? They think he's going to escape from a conference room *inside* the fucking brig, with steel bars everywhere?"

They brought Tom back a few minutes later with all his restraints gone. Claire kissed and hugged him, and for the first time he could hug her back. He looked gaunt and haggard. "Charlie Grimes," she said. "Your new lawyer. You've already met."

"Charles," Grimes corrected, and shook Tom's hand.

"Where's the kid?" Tom asked as he and Claire sat down. "What's his name, Embryo?"

"We're meeting without him this morning," Grimes said.

"How are you?" she asked.

"Mostly bored," he said. His voice was hoarse, as if he hadn't spoken in a long time. "New-prisoner indoctrination. They bring around a library cart with a shitty selection of paperbacks. TV call for an hour three times a week, but there's nothing I want to watch. I get 'sunshine call' an hour a day, outside in this awful little cement courtyard. In full restraints. By myself."

"They didn't give you the tour of the health club?" Grimes asked. "Sauna, steam, Nautilus, pretty girls giving massages? No?"

"Missed it," Tom said. "Yeah, I can't complain, I guess." To Claire he added, "But I miss you."

"I miss you. We all do. You can call us, you know."

"I just figured that out. They bring the phone around on this wooden cart and plug it in. Collect calls, thirty minutes max."

"Yeah," Grimes said, "and they monitor the calls, so be discreet."

"I'm representing you, too, Tom," she said. "I've signed on. Did an appearance letter. It's official."

"Thank God," Tom said.

"Thank her," Grimes said. "Bet she figures she'll save you guys money that way."

"You know this is a death-penalty case," she said, ignoring him. "And I haven't done a full-blown criminal trial in years. I'm rusty on trial law. That doesn't make you nervous?"

"You?" Tom said. "No way. Thank you, honey."

"Can I smoke?" she asked Grimes.

"Nonsmoking facility," Grimes said with a firm shake of the head.

"How politically correct," she said. "Tom, we're going to have to know everything. No more holding back—*anything*. You understand that?"

He nodded.

Grimes spoke up. "It may not be pleasant for you. But if you start holding back, we're going to get tripped up. They're coming at you with all the ammo they got, and if you leave out a detail, *especially* something that's unflattering to you, we're all screwed, dig?"

"I dig," Tom said.

"All right, cool," Grimes said.

"Tom," Claire said, "you didn't tell us about your tour in Vietnam."

"I told you I went to—"

"That's not what I'm referring to. You know damned well what I'm referring to. You never told me you were part of the Turncoat Elimination Program."

"What are you talking about?" Tom said.

"What are we talking about?" Grimes said angrily. "U.S.-government hit squads, that's what we're talking about. Special hunter-killer operations, teams of U.S. Army and Marine snipers sent deep into enemy territory to assassinate *Americans*. To eliminate American 'traitors,' deserters. Officially sanctioned assassination of American soldiers. You were on one of those recon-combat patrols. You were a hired killer for the U.S. government, Tom. A little something you forgot to mention."

"That's *bullshit*!" Tom exploded. "They're making that up!"

"It's in your file," Claire said, desperately hoping he was telling the truth. "Says you volunteered for this mission. That you were one of their top snipers, with deadly accuracy. That's why you were accepted into the program, even though you were so young."

"It's a *lie!*" he said. "I did a normal tour of duty, then I was sent to Special Forces training at Fort Bragg. I heard of those teams—everyone heard rumors about them over there—but I had nothing to do with it. I didn't eliminate American soldiers. They've forged records or something, trying to make me look like a cold-blooded killer. You can't possibly believe this, Claire!"

"I don't know what to believe anymore."

"You can't believe this, Claire!"

"We can get it excluded," Grimes said. "It doesn't have to come up at court-martial."

"But it's a goddamned despicable lie! Look, those assassination patrols were such a goddamned closely guarded secret, nobody knew about it. If there's anything on paper about it, wouldn't it be top secret or something? It wouldn't be in my unclassified files!"

Claire sighed in frustration. "That's true. It would be in the classified stuff."

She looked at Grimes, who shrugged. "Whatever. We'll get it excluded. Of course they won't want that on the record anyway—it's a government scandal, one of the most shameful secrets of the Vietnam War."

"What are they telling you about what happened in Salvador?" Tom asked.

"We haven't seen the records yet," Claire said. "But Charles tells me discovery starts now, so we'll see it soon."

"The good news for you," Grimes said, "is that we'll be going to trial soon. The military has a speedy-trial provision. They've got to start the court-martial within a hundred twenty days of the time you were locked up here."

"But we don't want a speedy trial," Claire said. "We need as much time as we can get to comb through the evidence, interview the witnesses. Raise reasonable doubt. We don't want to try this case half-assed. They've been putting this sham together for years, I'll bet."

"Hey, you're in the army now," Grimes said. "They got the right to force us to trial if they want, when they want. The good news for you, Tom-or-Ron, is that in less than four months you'll either be out of here or—"

"Or in Leavenworth," Tom said mordantly. "Or executed."

"Right," Grimes agreed with a blitheness that seemed inappropriate. "So the clock's ticking."

19

The military policeman stood straight and tall and perfectly dressed in a perfectly creased uniform. He had whitewalls behind his ears. His shoes appeared to be spit-shined to a mirror gleam. He looked like he'd just stepped out of an inspection box. He was "strac," Grimes marveled. "Strac," he said, was army lingo for spiffy, impeccably attired, and groomed in the very best, strictest army manner.

He stood guard before a windowless room in the basement of a building at Quantico called Hockmuth Hall, where all classified materials in the Ronald Kubik matter were stored under conditions of the highest security. Outside the room Claire waited with Embry and Grimes.

"This is what we call a SCIF," Captain Embry told Claire. He pronounced it "skiff."

"Another new word," Claire said dryly. "Meaning?"

Embry hesitated.

"Special Compartmental Information Facility," Grimes said. "Something like that."

"I think it's Sensitive Compartmental Information Facility," Embry said.

"Whatever," Grimes said.

"I requested a continuance on the 32," Embry said. "But the investigating officer turned us down."

"What a surprise," Grimes said. "Who is he, by the way?"

"Lieutenant Colonel Robert Holt. Nice guy."

"They're all nice guys," Grimes said. "Watch out for nice guys in the military."

Embry ignored him. "He instructed me that this is a case with national security implications, and any conversations regarding it must be conducted in the SCIF."

"Whatever that stands for," Claire said. Grimes caught her eye, which she took to mean, Pay no attention to their instructions.

"Next time we talk to your husband," Grimes said, "I want to do it outside the brig. I don't trust these guys. Who knows who might be listening in?"

"They're not allowed to listen in on conversations between attorney and client," Embry said.

"Oh, *I* see," Grimes said. "You want to tell 'em that, or should I?"

Grimes and Embry had just met this morning, and already Grimes was testing Embry's patience. But Embry was too polite to rise to the bait. In any case, before Embry had the chance to say anything now, the door to the SCIF was opened by a security officer.

It was just a room, linoleum floors with government-issue green metal tables and gray metal chairs. There were, however, a number of large safes, Sargent & Greenleaf brand, officially approved government safes, that opened with combination locks. Inside were separately locked drawers, each with its own combination lock. Each of them was given a drawer where he or she was to lock up any notes taken. No notes were to be removed from the room. They'd brought yellow legal pads—Grimes had told her not to bother bringing a laptop computer—but even their own handwritten notes had to stay there in the locked drawers. All notes on classified files would become part of an official government file, kept under government control.

Claire found this alarming, even a little ominous. They couldn't take notes out with them? How could they work anywhere outside this awful little room? The official headquarters of the Ronald Kubik defense was the library at her rented Thirty-fourth Street house, where all their files were kept; how could they work there without notes on the classified files? She was given no satisfactory answer. Neither Embry nor Grimes seemed perturbed by this ridiculous precaution.

She was shown a procedure designed to ensure that no one else looked at her notes. Any papers she chose to leave here would be placed inside a manila envelope, sealed with two-and-a-half-inch brown paper tape, the kind you moisten with a little sponge. The security officer would seal it for her, after which she would sign her initials over the tape's seal line. That went into another manila envelope, which was then sealed with the same tape and then initialed. That envelope was marked SECRET-SENSITIVE PROPRIETARY and then placed into yet another envelope marked PRIVATE FOR _____.

The whole ritual was designed to set the notetaker's mind at ease, and, indeed, it appeared to be awfully hard for anyone to get to her private notes without being detected, but she put nothing past these people. Anyone who came up with such elaborate and lurid precautions probably had figured out how to penetrate them.

"Jesus," Grimes exclaimed from his seat at an adjoining table. "Either your husband is really some kind of sick fuck or they got some fine creative minds over at the JAG Corps."

"What are you talking about?" asked Claire.

Grimes waved a sheaf of papers. "CID statement taken in, what, August of 1984. Sergeant Kubik was stationed at Fort Bragg for training, living off-base in Fayetteville at the time. Neighbor, a civilian, lodges a complaint against him."

Claire approached, tried to read over Grimes's shoulder.

"Seems the neighbor's dog kept pissing on Kubik's rosebushes, Kubik complained a number of times, and then one morning he grabbed the dog, slit its throat, and hung it by its hind feet from the neighbor's mailbox. Hoo-boy."

Claire, speechless, shook her head. "That's . . . that's impossible. That's not—Tom."

"Man," Grimes said. Embry looked over nervously, then returned to whatever he was reading. "Hoo-boy. Avon calling. No welcome wagon for this bad boy."

"It's got to be a forgery," Claire said. "Can't they make these things up? I mean, look at it, it's a couple of crappy typed pages."

"The CID agent's name who took the complaint is down there. Neighbor's name, too. Roswell something."

She shook her head again. "That's not Tom," she repeated.

"No, Professor," came a voice from the entrance to the room. "That's Ronald Kubik. And I'm Major Waldron."

Major Lucas Waldron was a tall, lean, brown-haired man in his late thirties whose predominant

feature was his aquiline nose. He was neither handsome nor plain—he had a fine, strong brow, and a
thin, weak mouth—but he was unmistakably intense. He did not smile as he shook hands. Claire
felt her stomach clench, as it did whenever she met
a powerful adversary.

"Maybe you're beginning to understand, Professor, why so many people consider your husband a
stain on the army's reputation," Waldron said.

Claire looked at him for a moment. "Are you
proud of prosecuting this farce?"

Waldron gave a glacial smile. "Given who your
husband is—*what* your husband is—I personally
don't think he's even worthy of a trial—"

"The charade of a trial, you mean," Claire inter-
jected. "I'm surprised you were willing to accept this
assignment. You might spoil your perfect win-loss
record."

"Let me tell you something, Professor," Waldron
said. "This is not a case the army's going to lose.
When you get a look at the evidence we have here,
you'll understand. I can only assume that you don't
have any *idea* what kind of monster this man is, what
kind of monster you married."

"You've got to be awfully naïve if you believe the
stuff they're handing you," she said. "If you can't
smell a cover-up."

"All you have to do is check out the evidence."

"Believe me, I plan to."

"Just check it out. You'll see. And as for my perfect win-loss record, well, part of that's because I'm
lucky. And I'm thorough. But the main reason is, the
people I prosecute happen to be guilty."

"I'm sure you're good, too," Claire said. "Anyone
can convict a guilty man, but it takes a really good
prosecutor to convict the innocent."

"My father was a POW in Vietnam," Waldron said. "I'm an army officer and I happen to be proud of it. I plan to spend my whole career in the army. But if I had to destroy my career to get a sicko like your husband convicted, I'd do it. And gladly. Nice to meet you, Professor."

And he turned and left the room.

"Nice guy, huh?" Grimes said.

"Over here, guys," Embry called out. "CID's got seven statements here, from seven members of Kubik's unit in Salvador, Special Forces Detachment 27. Taken on 27 June 1985. Five days after the 22 June incident, in debriefings back at Fort Bragg. They're almost identical. And they're devastating." Embry looked at Claire anxiously, almost wincing. He licked his lips.

Grimes bolted from his seat. "They're only calling one eyewitness at the 32 investigation. A Colonel Jimmy Hernandez, now a senior administrative officer based in the Pentagon. Now, he wouldn't happen to be one of the seven, by any stretch of the imagination, would he?"

Embry flipped through the pile in front of him. "Major James Hernandez, the XO. The executive officer. Yep, he's here."

Claire felt her stomach constrict. "Let me see it," she said.

Embry handed it to her with an involuntary wince.

Her heart thrumming, she at first skimmed it, then began to read through it very slowly. Her mouth was dry. She felt sick.

The top page was a cover sheet from the Criminal Investigation Division of the United States Army. Statement taken at Fort Bragg, 27 June 1985. The time. HERNANDEZ, James Jerome. His Social Se-

curity number. His grade. Then several long blocks
of text, each initialed by Hernandez at the beginning
and the end of each paragraph. Then several pages
of questions and answers.

"I, Major James J. HERNANDEZ," it began,

make the following free and voluntary statement to JOHN F. DAWKINS, whom I know to
be a Criminal Investigator for the United States
Armed Forces. I make this statement of my own
free will and without any threat or promises extended to me.

On 22JUN85 my unit, Detachment 27 of the
Special Forces, a top-secret combat unit, was
based at Ilopango, El Salvador. I am the unit's
XO. Our mission was to conduct operations regarding the antigovernment forces in El Salvador. Our CO, Colonel William MARKS, received
intelligence from a reliable source that a splinter
group of the leftist, antigovernment guerrilla organization FMLN, which had killed four off-
duty marines and two American businessmen
several days before at the Zona Rosa in San Salvador, had gone to ground in a tiny village outside San Salvador. The village, which was called
La Colina, was the birthplace of several of the
guerrillas. They were said to be in hiding there.

In the middle of the night, early on 22JUN85,
we located the village. The unit split in half to
approach the village from two directions. We
had silencers on our weapons to prolong the element of surprise, to shoot dogs or geese or
whatever animals we might encounter. Both
teams moved in and took control of the village,
going from house to house, waking inhabitants
and rousting them from their huts. We took this

approach to ensure that the inhabitants had no firearms.

All of the inhabitants, who numbered eighty-seven individuals, were assembled in an open area that was presumably the town square. They were all civilians, old men and women and children and infants. They were interrogated in Spanish but claimed no knowledge of the whereabouts of the guerrillas. Col MARKS, who remainded behind at headquarters, was informed by radio our determination that the intelligence lead was wrong and there were no commandos in hiding in La Colina at that present time. Col MARKS then directed us to leave. There was an exchange between several of the villagers and Sgt KUBIK. Suddenly Sgt KUBIK leveled his M-60 machine gun at the villagers. I noticed he had linked two ammo belts together on his shoulder so he had two hundred rounds. Sgt KUBIK began firing directly at the inhabitants and in a few minutes he had killed them all.

The following questions were asked by J. F. DAWKINS and answered by myself.

Q: Was an attempt made to restrain KUBIK?

A: Yes, but no one could approach him, because he was firing wildly.

Q: Were the civilians checked for weapons?

A: No, because Col MARKS thought we had lost control of the situation and ordered us to move out of there immediately.

Q: Did Sgt KUBIK have any comment after he finished killing the eighty-seven civilians?

A: No, he just said, "Well, now, that takes care of *that*."

Claire put down the page she was reading and felt lightheaded. She excused herself and located the women's room in the corridor outside. The "head." She staggered to a stall and was sick. Then she washed her face at the sink with a brown block of army-issue soap.

20

◆

*A*s *she* waited to be admitted to the brig, she
found herself lost in thought.

It is shortly after their wedding, on their honeymoon, in fact. They are checking into the Hotel Hass-
ler in Rome, at the head of the Spanish Steps, on the
Piazza Trinità dei Monte. She'd wanted to stay at a
more modest *pensione* nearby, the Scalinata di
Spagna, but Tom insisted they treat themselves to
some serious luxury. The reservation, however, has
been lost. A screwup. The suite he'd reserved is no
longer available. The most they can offer, with deepest apologies, is a "junior suite." Tom flushes, slams
his fist down on the counter. *"We made a reservation,
goddamn it,"* he thunders. Everyone in the lobby
turns, appalled and fascinated. The reservation clerk
is all apologies, flustered, humiliated. He almost
dances before them. Tom glowers terribly, but then,
just as quickly as he ignited, he cools. He nods. "See
what you can do," he says.

There are other times, she now remembers.

The time when his assistant at Chapman & Company confused the date of a lunch meeting with a

big-time potential investor so that Tom missed the appointment. He flew into a rage, became abusive, and fired her, but then relented a few hours later and hired her back.

The time when a neighbor accidentally swerved his Range Rover into their lawn and gouged out a rut. Tom came storming out of the house, face dark with fury, but by the time he reached the neighbor's car he seemed to have cooled down.

The time when, as he was walking with Annie in Harvard Square, she reached out to pet a dog, and the dog growled and snapped at her, and Tom grabbed the dog by the scruff of the neck until it yelped. The owner protested angrily; Tom set the dog back down, and it slunk away, tail between its legs. "Don't you worry about anything," he said to Annie.

There were dozens of such incidents, but what did they mean? A man who didn't want his perfect honeymoon spoiled. An overly exacting boss. A meticulous homeowner. An overprotective father. In the course of marriage—even a relatively brief one, as theirs had so far been—you witness anger and sadness. You see the best in your spouse, and you see the worst. Tom had a quick temper, but he'd never directed it at her, never at Annie, and he'd always managed to contain it.

And then there was the way he had paralyzed the U.S. Marshals agent who had pursued him at the shopping mall. No doubt it was his Special Forces training. Had he really been unnecessarily brutal? They were trying to imprison him for a crime he insisted he hadn't committed. He hadn't killed the man.

Even the ruthless way he'd fought off the marshals at the lakeside cabin in the Berkshires—but was that anything more than self-protection, the survival instinct?

Did all these things really make him a killer?

"Hey, where's the rest of my team?" Tom asked. He'd begun to exhibit the occasional flash of joviality, which for some reason irritated Claire. They met in the small glass-walled room that adjoined his cell. This time they had removed all restraints, presumably as a sign of respect to her.

"Just me right now," Claire said quietly. "I want to know about La Colina. What really happened."

He cocked his head, squinted. "I told you—"

"I've just read seven statements. They're all substantially the same—"

"They're probably *identical*. The military can be clumsy in their forgeries."

"Who's Jimmy Hernandez?"

"Hernandez? The executive officer of my detachment. Marks's number two. Kid from Florida, son of Cuban immigrants—"

"Is he honest? A truth-teller?"

"Claire," Tom said with exasperation. "Honesty is a relative concept to these people. Their CO tells them to fart, they fart. And if he tells them it's gardenias, they'll say it's gardenias. Hernandez is Marks's asshole buddy. He'll say whatever Marks tells him to say."

"Well, the prosecution is calling Hernandez as an eyewitness to the atrocity you allegedly committed. If he's as believable as his CID statement, we're in trouble." She adopted a carefully neutral, professional tone.

"And what, he says I did it? I was some kind of mass murderer of eighty-seven civilians?"

"Yeah."

"I told you, Colonel Marks gave the order to waste the whole village. 'To teach 'em a lesson,' he said. Hernandez was the XO, Marks's loyal number two—it wouldn't surprise me if he was one of the shooters. I wouldn't participate in the cover-up, so they turned the tables and blamed me. That's what this is all about. It was thirteen years ago, for God's sake, I don't know why they don't just let it go away."

"The Criminal Investigation Division interviewed the entire unit. They must have interviewed you, too."

"Sure they did. They interrogated me at length, and I told them the truth. Obviously I didn't do a statement for them."

"And you didn't report this to anyone? The truth, I mean?"

"Report to who? You don't know the military. You keep your mouth shut and your head down and hope for the best."

"But some of the guys in the unit must have seen you on the other side of the village. Some of them must know you weren't there."

"You're not going to get anyone to testify to that. Either they took part in the massacre, or they're part of the cover-up. They probably all have deals, immunity, whatever. You can find that out in discovery, can't you?"

"They're required to tell me. You didn't have any friends in the unit? Any guys who might have refused to deal, but agreed to keep silent? Who might be willing to help you out now?"

"I liked maybe three guys in the unit. One or two of them I'd call friends. You know I don't make close friends easily. Anyway, how do I know they didn't fire at the villagers."

"Tom," she began. "Ron."

"You can call me Ron, if you want," Tom said softly. "If you'd feel more comfortable."

"I know you as Tom. But that's made up, isn't it?"

"It's the name I chose, not the one my parents gave me. I became Tom with you. I sort of like being Tom."

"Tom, why should I believe you? Really. You've lied to me for six years, as long as I've known you. Really."

"I lied about my past. To protect you from the kind of crazies who don't fuck around. Who if they heard the slightest whisper that I was alive and living in Boston would have tracked me down and killed me and everyone around me. I should never have fallen in love with you, Claire. I should never have ruined your perfect life, me, with my horrible background—"

"You didn't ruin my life." Tears misted her eyes. She exhaled slowly.

"Claire, I've been thinking a lot about who might know the truth. About what really happened. There is a guy." He bit his lower lip. "Someone who knows about what really happened. He'll have the proof. He knows the Pentagon's trying to cover this up. I'll bet he can turn up the documents for you."

"Who?"

He took her pencil and scribbled a note on one of her legal pads. He whispered: "Keep this name locked up. Destroy this paper. I mean, flush it down the toilet."

She glanced at it. Her eyebrows shot up.

"Tom," she said, "I have to ask you something else." She told him about the grisly incident with the neighbor's dog and the mailbox back in Fayetteville, North Carolina.

Tom closed his eyes, shook his head slowly. "Come on. I did live off-base, they got the right address, but I bet, if you try to track this supposed 'neighbor' down, you'll find he doesn't exist." His eyes were moist. "Claire, we need to talk."

"Okay," she said guardedly.

"Listen to me. You are my rock right now. When Jay took off, I was there for you because I valued you as a friend. I've tried to be a rock for you, because I love you. But now I need you. I can't tell you how hurtful it is that the person I love most in all the world doubts me."

"Tom—"

"Let me finish. I'm utterly alone here. Totally alone. And if it wasn't for you, your faith in me, I don't think I'd make it. I really wouldn't."

"What does that mean?" she asked softly.

"Just that I don't think I'd live through it if I thought you didn't believe in me. I need you. I love you, you know that. Deeply. When this is over, if I pull through this okay, we're going to get our life back. I need you, honey."

She felt the tears spring to her eyes, and she hugged him, hard. She felt the sweat rising hotly from his shoulders.

"I love you, too, Tom," was all she could say.

21

❖

The library in the rented house was the real thing, an old-house, old-money library. Linen-white-painted bookshelves that held not just the requisite leather-bound antiquarian volumes in sets of ten and twenty and fifty, but real books as well, recent and not-so-recent hardcover editions, mostly politics and history, no fiction in sight. The sort of books that the owner of the house, right now perhaps drinking *un caffè macchiato* at a café in Siena, probably actually read. His library was the century-old prototype of Claire and Tom's modern study back in Cambridge.

Captain Embry, dressed in civilian clothes (brand-new deep-indigo jeans and a short-sleeved shirt, both neatly pressed), sat on a hard chair at a side table, taking notes with a chewed Bic pen on a legal pad. Grimes (once again in his nineteen-seventies orange Day-Glo sweater) was sunk deep in a floral-upholstered wing chair, legs splayed.

Claire sat, smoking, at the immense oak library table, surrounded by law books: *Military Rules of Evidence Manual, Military Criminal Justice: Practice and Procedure, Manual for Courts-Martial: United States.*

"So all the prosecution is planning to present at the 32 hearing"—already she spoke like an old hand—"are those seven CID statements and one so-called eyewitness, this Jimmy Hernandez guy, to corroborate? That all?"

"Yeah," Grimes said. "The government doesn't have to present everything they got. Just enough. Remember, all they got to do is demonstrate there's enough probable cause to go on to a court-martial. It would be dumb for them to present more than the bare minimum."

Embry put in: "The idea is, we're supposed to try to knock it out."

"Which ain't gonna happen," Grimes said. "No matter how hard we try. So consider the 32 as the government's tryout, their audition. We get the chance to scope out their case in advance, see what they put on the table. Cross-examine to point out all the weaknesses."

"What about the other six members of Burning Tree who gave statements?" asked Claire. "Why aren't they being called as witnesses?"

"One, they don't have to," Grimes replied. "Any witnesses who are 'legally unavailable,' meaning more than a hundred miles away, don't have to appear. Two, the government doesn't need 'em."

Claire nodded. "Can they surprise us? Pop something on us at the hearing?"

Embry said, "Normally they give you the evidence as soon as they get it."

"Yeah," Grimes said, inspecting the ornate detail on the vaulted ceiling, "or they might give it to us a day or two before. But I doubt they're going to surprise us at the hearing. They want to be able to say they gave us everything in advance."

"Anyway," Embry said, "if they do drop something on us, we ask for a continuance, that's all."

"Same as a civilian court," Claire said. "But what about Article 46 of the code? The equal-access clause?"

Grimes lowered his head and turned slowly to regard her. "Someone's got the UCMJ on her bedside table."

"We get 'equal opportunity to obtain witnesses and other evidence' blah blah blah, right?" Claire said.

"Right," Grimes said, "but it doesn't say equal *time*, does it?"

"Mommy?" came Annie's voice, high and sweet and tentative. She was wearing blue-jeans overalls and pigtails. She stood at the open door, curiously stealing a glance at the two men.

"Yes, honey?"

"Mommy, Jackie's making dinner. It's going to be ready soon."

"Okay, honey. We'll be done very soon, too. Now, let us work, babe, okay?"

"Okay." She looked around shyly. "Hi."

"Hi," both men called out.

"Why are you smoking, Mommy?"

"Come on," Claire said, "out of here. I'll see you at supper."

"But I want to play here," Annie said with a pout.

"Not now, sweetie."

"Why not?"

"Because Mommy's working."

"You're *always* working!" Annie said, stalking off.

"Man," Grimes said, "you got a serious case of that nasty habit. I thought no one in Cambridge is allowed to smoke, some zoning law or something."

"Yeah, well, I'm going to quit when this is over,"

she said. "I *was* going to invite you guys to stay for dinner, but—"

"Invitation accepted," Grimes said. "I can smell it from here. Someone around here knows how to cook. I love garlic."

"Terry?" she said.

"I can't," Embry said. He reddened immediately. "I'm sorry, I've—I've got to meet someone."

"Cheating on the wife already?" Grimes said.

Embry smiled bashfully, shook his head.

"All right, now," Claire said, "I want to find out whatever we can on Hernandez. Terry, I want you to start a file on every witness or potential witness, starting with Hernandez and the other six who gave statements against Tom. I want their, what do you call them, fitness reports, service records, the works. Then I want to interview Hernandez."

"Uh, you better leave the interviewing on this guy to me or Embry here," Grimes said.

"Why?"

"Because we're both army guys. I've done my time in the service. We know how the shit works."

"Fine, but I want to be there. I want to see his face."

"Of course," Grimes said.

"I also want to find out if this guy's been offered anything in exchange for testifying. Like immunity. Same for anyone else they might call at the trial itself."

"We get that in discovery," Embry said. "The general-discovery request."

"Well, no we don't, necessarily," Grimes said. "You got to put in a specific request. Demand the government state with specificity which witnesses are claiming privilege and why. Tell 'em you want a copy of all grants of immunity given to any witness. Or any promises of leniency. We want a copy of all informants' agreements, including any records of monetary and property remunerations."

"All right," Claire said, lighting a fresh cigarette. "I want the names of all members of this unit, their current names and addresses and phone numbers. I'm going to have Ray Devereaux track them all down."

"You won't find 'em all," Grimes said. "These guys disappear, sometimes."

"Ray's good," she said.

"They're better."

"You think we can trust them in the discovery process?" Claire asked. "To give us everything we ask for?"

Embry hesitated. Grimes said, "Can you ever trust your opponent in discovery? In the real world, I mean?"

"Not always," she admitted. "It's always a question."

"There you go," Grimes said.

"But the *Brady* rule requires them to give us all exculpatory evidence, anything that might indicate Tom's innocence," she said.

Grimes chuckled.

"You don't trust them," Claire said.

"It's why I have a job, baby," Grimes said. "It's what keeps the big bucks rolling in."

"If we don't get everything the prosecution has," Claire said, "we got ourselves a mistrial."

"If we can prove it," Grimes said.

"Terry," she went on, "I want you to do a complete search through the Iran-Contra hearings and the United Nations reports on abuses in Central America in the nineteen-eighties. See if there's any mention of the massacre at La Colina."

Embry jotted a note.

"All right," she said, "we're going to request that all charges be dismissed. We're going to argue that the government has no jurisdiction, since we were in an area we weren't supposed to be in. The government, in effect, has unclean hands."

"But what about the desertion charges?" Embry said. "You're not going to contest those, are you? I mean, he destroyed his military uniform and his IDs—he obviously had no intent to return."

"Least of our problems," she replied. "Our defense is duress."

"Duress?"

"Desertion is a specific-intent offense. That means his intent counts, right? Well, he feared he'd be killed—whether he would have been killed or not, it's a valid defense, as long as we can show the defendant had a good-faith *belief* he'd be killed. Maybe we can get it dropped to 'unauthorized absence.' "

"It's not the 'defendant,' it's the 'accused,' " Grimes said. "It's not the 'prosecutor,' it's the 'trial counsel.' You'll get the hang of the lingo."

Claire flashed Grimes a sulfurous look of annoyance. "Thanks. Basically, we'll prove that the U.S. government is trying to make Tom the fall guy for a gruesome government-sanctioned massacre."

"Baby, you can argue all you want," Grimes began, back to inspecting the ceiling.

"You say the 32 hearing is for scoping out the government's case," Claire said. "Well, here's how *we're* going to use it. To let them see we know how to play the hard way, that we *intend* to play the hard way. That, if they go ahead with this kangaroo court-martial, we're going to bring out the shit they *never* want out. We plan to embarrass the hell out of them. We're going to graymail them. Bring out operational info, stuff they don't want out in the day-light."

"It's a closed proceeding," Embry objected. "Both this hearing and the court-martial that may or may not follow. Totally sealed."

"Closed?" Claire said. "We leak. No such thing as an airtight trial."

Grimes chuckled dryly.

"Leak?" Embry asked, horrified. "But we signed a nondisclosure agreement. If we leak, they'll do an investigation, and we'll all be up on charges—"

"Hey, you wanted the case, right?"

"Well, no, ma'am, as I told you—"

"Claire."

"Ma'am?"

"Call me Claire. And don't sweat it. Leaks are al-most impossible to prove, as long as you're careful about where you call from. And if they can't prove it, it goes nowhere. Anyway, then we're going to argue against this closed-courtroom bullshit. We're going to argue Tom's Sixth Amendment right to a public trial, and the public's right to a public trial."

"And they're going to argue national security," Grimes said, now sitting up, drawn into the game.

"So we file an extraordinary writ for an open trial. We go to the federal district court."

"They'll say, We're not going to intervene in a mil-itary matter," Grimes said.

"So we file an extraordinary writ for an open trial with the Army Court of Criminal Appeals. And the Court of Appeals for the Armed Forces. And then the goddamned Supreme Court. And let them try to argue national security—I'm going to argue that the operation is no longer ongoing, hasn't been for years. That they're just trying to protect the reputa-tion of the Pentagon. Where's the national-security interest? They want to have it both ways—protect the national security, yet prosecute my client."

Grimes nodded slowly, rhythmically. A smile crept across his face. Embry watched her, panic-stricken.

"And you see if the government really wants to go ahead with this court-martial," Claire said. "I'll bet they lose their enthusiasm."

"Claire," Grimes said, "do you really want this trial open?"

She considered for a long moment. "I don't, do I? In a sense, we're trapped. I don't want Tom's name smeared. Once the charges are out in public, that's it. They're accepted as true." She nodded. "You may have a point, Grimes. But I'll tell you something else. We're going to call General Marks to testify."

Grimes brayed a laugh, his ha-*ha*. "I want some of whatever you're smoking," he said.

"Camel Lights," she said. "I'm goddamned serious. If he refuses, I'll subpoena him."

"The lady's kickin butt and takin *names*," Grimes said.

"Claire, ma'am," Embry said desperately, "General William Marks is the chief of staff of the army. He's a four-star general. You can't make him testify."

"Who says? Where does it say that? I didn't read anything like that in the Uniform Code of Military Justice."

"I like it," Grimes said. "You got balls."

"Thank you," Claire said, then added, "That *is* a compliment, right?"

22

After dinner Jackie told Claire, "You got a call from a reporter at the *Washington Post*. Style section, I think. They heard you've rented a house in D.C. and want to know why. Like it's their fucking business."

"What did you tell them?"

"I said I had no idea. They wanted to know if you're doing some big-deal case here, or if you're teaching here, or what."

"No comment," Claire said.

"I figured."

"How about we go get a drink," Grimes said.

"We've got booze here," Claire said.

"I got a place I want to show you. In Southeast."

"Can you wait till I tuck my little girl in?"

"I'll wait in the library. File a motion or something."

Later, Grimes drove them in his beat-up old silver Mercedes. He circled the block where the bar was three times, but no parking space opened up. Finally he saw a large open space right in front of the bar, but before he got there a Volkswagen Jetta zipped

into it. Grimes pulled the Mercedes up alongside the
Jetta, beeped the horn, and electrically lowered his
window. "Uh, excuse me," he shouted. "Excuse
me."

"Come on, Grimes," Claire said. "She got there
first."

"Excuse me," Grimes shouted again.

The woman driver leaned over, cranked down her
passenger-side window, and said warily, "What do
you want?"

"Hey, none of my business, but you don't want to
park there. That's valet parking, and believe me,
they tow, night and day."

"Valet parking?" the woman said, confused. "But
there's no sign!"

"The sign's down, but that's not going to stop 'em.
Ten minutes after you park there, your car's going
to be towed to some part of the city you ain't never
been to before and you don't *ever* wanna go to
again."

"Jeez, thank you!" the woman said. She cranked
the window back up and pulled out of the space and
into traffic.

"Hey, Grimes," Claire said, "forgive me. That was
mighty nice of you."

He laughed, ha-*ha*, as he backed into the space.
"Always works," he said.

She shook her head in disgust but couldn't sup-
press a smile. "Valet parking," she said, disapprov-
ingly. "I like that."

The bar was a dive, dark and dingy and reeking
of spilled beer. The creaky wooden floor was sticky.
The music—an old song by Parliament/Funkadelic
on the jukebox—blasted. "This is it?" she said.

"Authentic, huh?"

"Funky," she said without much enthusiasm.

Once a plastic pitcher of sudsy beer from the tap had been placed in front of them, along with two large plastic tumblers and a dish of pretzels, Grimes said, "Now, one thing I have to tell you. In the interests of honesty and full disclosure."

"Yes?"

"You want me to be second chair, fine. But you want me to stand up and cross-examine a witness while you're sitting there—one of the best in the biz? I don't *think* so."

She laughed. "My cross-examination skills are rusty. Anyway, what do you know about me?"

He took a long swig of beer. "After you graduated from Yale Law School, you did a pair of clerkships. Two years for Arthur Iselin in the D.C. Circuit Court, Court of Appeals. There you worked on opinions, did speeches. You did an insanity case, some busing, some ineffective-assistance-of-counsel cases. Then you clerked for one year for Justice Marshall at the Supreme Court, where you read applications for certiorari."

"Very impressive," she said. "Did you do some sort of Nexis search for interviews with me?"

He took another swig. "Truth is, I read every article, every interview with you. Even before we met. I think you're pretty cool." He smiled, embarrassed, and hastily added, "What was Justice Marshall like? Cool guy?"

"Very," she said. "Extremely funny. And a really nice guy, definitely the nicest guy on the Court. He was the only one there who actually hung out with the clerks. One of his favorite TV shows was *People's Court*, you know, that one with Judge Wapner."

Grimes exploded with laughter. "No way."

"True story. Now, let me ask *you* something. Why'd you leave the army?"

He studied his beer, took a sip. "Retired, like I said."

"Voluntarily."

"Hell, yeah," he said, annoyed.

"No offense intended. I thought you were sort of forced out."

"What did Iselin tell you?"

"Just that there was some sort of, I don't know, scandal."

"Oh, yeah? Scandal, is that what he said?"

"Something like that."

He shook his head, drank again. A long silence passed.

"So, what was it, Grimes?"

"You do your twenty years as a lawyer in the army, it makes sense to take retirement. You run the numbers."

"You weren't forced out?"

"You don't stop, do you?" Grimes looked up at her with a hostility that seemed tinged with desperation.

"I'm sorry," she said quickly. "But I need to know your background."

He set his beer down, tented his fingers. "Look. I joined the Army as an enlisted man, went to Vietnam, and lived. Okay? I came back, did night school for years, got my bachelor's and my law degree, got my commission. I'm a lawyer by the time I'm thirty-one. Army's always telling you they're the only real equal-opportunity employer, blacks get treated same as whites, and for a while I begin to believe that. I never get beyond major, but that's 'cause I started late. Fine." Grimes hunched forward. "Okay, so there's this brother down in South Carolina. Fort Jackson. Black guy, PFC—that's private first class— accused of armed robbery on a white guy at the base. I get the case probably for no other reason than I'm black. I fly down there, talk to the kid. Kid never done anything wrong in his life, okay? I mean, National Honor Society in high school, athlete, never been in trouble, army's gonna send him to college, which is why he enlisted, 'cause his family's poor. Okay, so what does the prosecution have? This totally weak ID—the victim couldn't tell one black from another. Meanwhile, I've got this case sewed up. So happens that, at the time the robbery went down, this kid's at home, two hundred miles away, on a weekend pass. Not only that, but I got every fucking *second* of his time that weekend accounted for. Seven different alibi witnesses, none of them with criminal records or anything. I had neighbors testifying to his good character. When I say 'altar boy,' I'm not bullshitting. But the prosecution brings the kid into the courtroom in manacles, which you're not supposed to do, and they didn't even need to do that, 'cause the all-white military jury was in and out in five minutes. They didn't even have time to do a secret written ballot. Gave him ten years in Leavenworth." Grimes finally looked up. His eyes, blazing, glistened with tears. His expression was fierce. "They gave this fucking altar boy, who joined the army so he could go to college, ten years in Leavenworth for armed robbery. Well, I knew this couldn't stand up, but I'm a lawyer, see? I was gonna fight this thing up to the Supreme Court. Meanwhile, his whole unit knows he's innocent, and after the sentencing, they give him fifteen days deferment of confinement so he can go home and say goodbye to his mamma and his brothers and sisters." Grimes clenched a fist and gently pounded it on the table. "I wish to hell they'd put him in the brig." He shook his head.

Claire, moved to tears, said, "Why?"

"They put you in the brig, they take away your gun, put you on suicide watch. He never could have done it. This kid killed himself. Blew his brains out with his pistol. And the next day, I put in my letter."

"Jesus, Grimes."

Very quietly he said: "So you see, kid, you don't need to convince me what shit a military jury's capable of, okay?" There was a long, uncomfortable silence, and then Grimes's voice became louder, his tone belligerent. "So let me ask you a personal question. Do you really think your husband is innocent? Not that it matters to our case, of course."

"Of course I do," she said. "I wouldn't take this on if I didn't."

"Well, you *are* married to him."

"Grimes, if I thought he was guilty, I'd hire someone else. I wouldn't do it myself, not if I thought he was really the sort of monster they're trying to make him out to be."

He gazed at her levelly. His eyes were bloodshot. " 'Course, you represented Gary Lambert, didn't you?"

"This is different, Grimes," she said, exasperated. "He's my husband."

"You think this whole thing is a frame-up."

"Of course it is. Colonel Bill Marks comes back to the States after the massacre that he ordered, and realizes he'd better cover his ass, and so he blames it on the one guy in the unit who refused to lie, to cover up. The one who could destroy his career. Here he is, thirteen years later, chief of staff of the army, soon to be chairman of the Joint Chiefs, and he figures he got away with it. Well, the fucker's wrong. He didn't count on me."

"What am I, chopped liver?" Grimes said.

"Nah, you're pâté. Hey," she exclaimed suddenly, "why not polygraph him? And introduce the results at the 32 hearing? That'll get the court-martial thrown out faster than anything."

"No way. Don't go there. Get that nasty idea out your head. Anyway, polygraphs aren't admissible."

"Oh, they're admissible, all right. You don't keep up on this?"

"Rule 707 of the Military Rules of Evidence says no. In the annotated cases. Based on a 1989 decision of the Army Court of Criminal Appeals. Flat-out no."

"Grimes, it didn't use to be admissible, but now it can be. It's up to the judge. *U.S.* v. *Scheffer*, 1996, decided by the Court of Appeals for the Armed Forces. If it's exculpatory and the accused's counsel can lay foundation for it, it may be admissible."

"And what if you're wrong? What if he really is guilty?"

"He's not."

"You're gonna take that chance? Plus, he could be innocent and fail because he's nervous. Then we're screwed, because people talk, you know. Word gets around. The jurors at the court-martial hear the wa-ter-cooler gossip. Everyone'll know he failed. These guys, these examiners, are Chatty Cathys."

"Not if he's hired by us. That makes him an adviser to defense counsel. Falls under attorney work product, brings him within lawyer-client privilege. I'll see what Tom thinks, but you know a good examiner?"

He sighed with resignation. "I know one. Does a lot of work for the military. You want another pitcher?"

"I couldn't. Not a third. You shouldn't either, if you're driving."

* * *

As they left, Grimes wove his way unsteadily between the bar and the tables. Claire made a mental note to insist upon driving him home. She could pick him up in the morning, but she wouldn't let him drive now. They passed a large round table near the entrance where they heard a sudden burst of laughter. She reflexively turned to look and saw Embry surrounded by a bunch of other short-haired men, some in civilian togs, some in army fatigues.

"Grimes," she said.

He turned with a beer-addled grin, saw where she was looking, who was sitting next to Embry. "Well, how do you do. Our own Captain Terry Embryo. Hoisting a few with our very own trial counsel, Major Lucas Waldron. Well, hell-o."

PART THREE

23

◆━━━◆

*N*ot *even* four in the morning, and the sky was indigo-black with just a trace of pink on the horizon. Dew on the grass on the forlorn little hillock in front of the "defense shop," the low white temporary-looking structure that served as Judge Advocate General defense offices at Quantico. It looked like a dressed-up Quonset hut.

Grimes had arrived first, in jeans, a sweatshirt, a black leather jacket out of *Shaft*. Claire wore jeans and a green shetland sweater and a suede jacket. They stood in silence. A pair of guys in identical gray sweats and army T-shirts jogged by, huffing in rhythm. A car pulled up, a dark-gray Honda Civic. Captain Terry Embry's car. Grimes and Claire looked at each other. They hadn't seen him since that night at the bar; they hadn't said anything to him either.

Embry got out and sprinted over. "Sorry," he said.

"No problem," Claire said. "No one else's here yet."

"Morning," he said with a nod to Grimes. He was wearing his uniform, neatly pressed as always. His

165

complexion was clear with a ruddy flush. She could smell his mouthwash when he talked. "Claire, ma'am, bad news on the general. His office finally got back to me on our request and said the general won't be able to testify or even give a deposition. There's been a change in his schedule. He has to fly to CINCPAC, Camp Smith, Hawaii. So he's going to be totally out of reach from now through the 32 hearing."

"Ask for a continuance until he gets back."

"Yeah," Grimes said, "but you won't get it." He grunted. "Asshole."

"The good news is, I reached Hernandez for you, and he's all set for an interview with us."

"Thanks, Terry," Claire said.

"But . . ." Embry faltered. "You remember he works in the Pentagon?"

"Yeah?"

Embry unlocked the front door and switched on the lights.

"Well, he's the senior administrative officer to General Marks."

"What?" Claire said.

"Yeah. Turns out Hernandez is, like, the general's aide de camp. His XO, his executive officer. Handles personal business, scheduling, all that. He's followed General Marks around everywhere since '85. Totally loyal."

"I'm sure *he's* gonna tell the truth," Grimes said sardonically. "*He* won't cover for the general, oh no, not *Hernandez*."

They followed Embry to a conference room, where he also switched on the lights there. "Want me to stay for this, or no?" Embry asked.

"Best if you don't," Claire said.

"Okay, then, if you guys don't mind, I'd like to get back to my office at Fort Belvoir."

"That's fine," Claire said. "Thanks."

The polygrapher arrived fifteen minutes later, a stout, squat, bearded man in his late fifties wearing aviator horn-rimmed glasses. He carried a silvery metal briefcase. While he set up the instruments, he chatted. His name was Richard Givens. He had a deep, soothing voice. He spoke slowly, carefully, as if to a child, and in a soft-edged Southern accent. He was from Raleigh, North Carolina. He had attended polygraph school during his service with the Naval Investigative Service and had been an examiner with the navy at Newport, Rhode Island, and San Diego.

"Do you think there might be some more comfortable chairs anywhere around?" he asked. "Comfortable chairs would be a very good idea, if you have them."

Grimes went out into the hallway and returned a minute later with a chair under each arm. "These okay?"

"Those would be great," Givens said. He bustled around for a while. "I use a five-channel instrument," he explained. "That means five pens moving on this spool of paper here. There's three parameters—the pneumo, the cardio, and the galvanic. The pulse rate, the breathing pattern, and the galvanic skin response."

"Can we stay in the room?" Grimes asked.

"If you want to," he said. "But you'll have to stand behind the prisoner. Out of his line of sight."

"Fine," Grimes said.

"The test I give," Givens said, now stopped before Grimes, his short arms swaying awkwardly at his side, "is highly structured, very pure. Very dogmatic. First I will meet with the prisoner and talk until we feel comfortable with each other. I'll go over the questions with him in advance, several times. He will know every question in advance. There will be no surprises. When I feel the test is complete, I will send both you and the prisoner out. Then I'll go over the charts. Then I will call you back in first."

Claire nodded. She sat in one of the comfortable chairs.

"If I find that deception is indicated—if he's lying, in my opinion—I will tell you that. Please understand that my product remains confidential.

"Then I will call the prisoner in and give him a report as well. If he has failed the test, what I'll tell him is that the test is not going to help him in any way. Then, if you want, I'll begin the interrogation process. To elicit a confession."

"We'll let you know what we want when the time comes," Claire said.

Givens looked at his watch. "The prisoner isn't arriving for half an hour, is that right? Not till oh-five?"

"Right."

"Good. Now I need to find out from you the exact parameters you're interested in finding out about."

Claire and Grimes watched Tom—he was still Tom to her, whatever his official name—arrive in a white panel van. Wearing a khaki uniform and full restraints, he was escorted out of the van by several armed brig guards. They took him, jingling loudly, down the hall. One guard stationed himself outside the window of the conference room. Another stood in the hallway outside the door. Still another removed Tom's restraints and then joined the one standing outside the door.

"Tom, this is Richard Givens," Claire said, introducing the two as if at a cocktail party. "Richard this is—Ronald Kubik." They were about to go through a truth-telling examination. She would use his true name. It had the unintended side effect, however, of making him seem a different person.

"How do you do, Ronald," Givens said as they shook hands. He sat down in one of the comfortable chairs and gestured for Tom to do the same. They conversed for a long while. Givens had suddenly become warm and convivial, no longer didactic. The shift was startling. Tom had begun their talk wary, but after a while his reserve had melted and he was his usual amiable self.

"Ronald, have you ever been polygraphed before?" Givens asked.

"Yes, I have," Tom said.

"When was that?"

"At several points before and during my service with Detachment 27."

"Then you were given the test the army uses. It's called the Zone of Comparison Test. It's a very simple test, a very good test. That's the test I'm going to give you this morning. I don't know how the examiner who gave you the test worked, but when I give the polygraph, there are no surprises. No surprise questions. In fact, you and I are going to draw up a list of questions, and then we're going to go over it, okay?"

"Okay."

"No surprises. No ambushes. All very friendly, okay?"

"Okay. Sounds good to me."

"Now, Professor Heller, Mr. Grimes, could you come around here? I need you to stand out of Ronald's sight. No distractions, please."

They both moved around to where Givens was standing. Claire's pulse quickened—a sympathetic reaction to what her husband was experiencing?

"Is your name Ronald Kubik?" Givens asked. His voice had become once again slow and deliberate and monotonous.

"Yes." Tom's voice was clear and strong.

There was a long silence. Claire counted at least fifteen seconds. Had Givens forgotten what came next?

"Regarding your presence at the incident at La Colina on 22 June 1985, will you answer my questions truthfully?"

"Yes."

Another long pause. Grimes looked at Claire.

"Are you convinced I will not ask a surprise question on this test?" Givens asked.

"Yes."

Claire counted fifteen seconds again. The long silence was intentional.

"Before your enlistment in the army, did you ever deliberately injure anyone?"

"No."

"Did you actively participate in the death of anyone during the 22 June 1985 shootings?" Claire held her breath. She felt everything inside freeze. Even her heart seemed to stop beating.

"No." Tom's reply was loud and clear and strong. She exhaled silently. She squinted, trying to make sense of the pen-scratchings on the unspooling paper, but couldn't.

"Following your desertion from the army in 1985, did you ever deliberately commit bodily harm to anyone?"

"No."

Eighteen seconds this time.

"Did you take part in the shootings on 22 June 1985 in the village of La Colina, El Salvador?"

Tom's reply came more quickly this time. "No."

Sixteen seconds. Claire found herself following the jerky little movement of the second hand on her watch.

"Is there something else you're afraid I'll ask you a question about, even though I told you I would not?"

"No."

Fifteen seconds precisely.

"Have you ever threatened a loved one with bodily harm?"

"No." Seventeen seconds of silence.

"Did you see any civilians die on 22 June 1985 in the village of La Colina?"

"No."

Fifteen seconds, then twenty. The longest pause yet. "Thank you, Ronald," Givens said. "We're done now."

Grimes knocked on the door. It was opened, and the two guards came in. They put the restraints back on Tom. They took him out into the hallway, and Claire and Grimes followed. Grimes and Claire sat in front of the stenographers' office. Tom stood with his guards on either side. They all waited in silence, five minutes, which seemed forever.

Givens opened the door. "Professor Heller, Mr. Grimes, could I talk to you, please?"

They entered the room. Her heart thudded. She felt prickly perspiration under her ears.

He waited until they had both sat down. He didn't seem to be interested in generating suspense; he seemed to be following some script, moving through it with plodding deliberateness.

"Well," Grimes said, "is he a lying mother-fucker?"

Claire wanted to throttle him.

Givens did not smile.

"In my opinion, he is telling the truth. My report will state NDI. No deception indicated."

"Aha," Claire said, calm and professional on the surface. Inside she was elated. Not since Annie's birth had she actually experienced such a physical, biological sensation of elation: a great swelling inside her rib cage, the feeling that her organs, her heart and lungs, had lifted several inches. At the same time she felt an immediate easing of tension. "Thank you," she said. "When can we expect your report?"

24

The courtroom where the hearing was to take place was a windowless underground chamber, newly constructed, beneath the basement level of one of the buildings on the Quantico grounds not far from the FBI Academy. It had been specially built for security-classified meetings, courts-martial, and other proceedings, and was intended for the use of all four branches of military service. Two MPs stood guard before the steel stairway that descended to the steel double doors that locked by means of electronic cipher locks. It was extremely secure.

Shortly before nine in the morning—0900 hours—Claire and Grimes met in front of the red-brick building. She wore a navy suit, conservative—nothing too stylish or flashy. Grimes, she was pleased to see, was in a suit as well: double-breasted, pin-striped, elegant.

"I don't want Embry speaking," she said.

"I don't either."

"And I want you to start off with the first witness. I'll observe."

"Fine."

"You look good."

"Surprised, huh?"

"Yeah. Let's go." They entered the building and descended to the basement, then waited for the steel doors to the subbasement to be unlocked. The sleek, modern room was low-ceilinged, about twenty by thirty feet. The floors were gray linoleum over concrete; the walls were poured concrete as well. Otherwise, it looked exactly like every other courtroom in the world, with raised judge's bench and witness chair, a jury box (ten seats instead of twelve, but empty, because there would be no jury at this hearing), a long table for defense and one for prosecution. The furniture—the witness and jury chairs, the spectators' chairs, the tables—was modern and tasteful, blond wood and gray upholstering. An American flag hung from a pole next to the bench, on which was mounted a brass armed-forces seal. On the wall in back of the jury box was a large clock. The quality of sound in here was curiously deadened: the chamber was, of course, soundproofed.

Claire was surprised to see four or five unsmiling spectators already in place, uniformed men wearing security badges on white plastic-beaded chains around their necks. None of them she recognized. Why were they here, and how were they allowed in such a secret proceeding?

"I thought this was a closed hearing," Claire muttered to Grimes.

"Spectators are allowed if they have top-secret clearance."

"Who are they?"

Grimes shrugged. "Lot of people in the Pentagon are watching this case closely."

Claire, who'd done hundreds of trials and observed even more, couldn't help feeling nervous.

Her throat was parched. She looked around for some water. Sure enough, a glass pitcher was already in place on the defense table. She poured some water for herself and Grimes, then set down her briefcase and opened it to remove her carefully indexed file folders. Stuffed inside was a honey-colored, fuzzy Winnie-the-Pooh doll, a little gift, a message from Annie. She smiled, almost laughed out loud with pleasure.

A few minutes later Major Lucas Waldron entered, tall and lanky and dour, accompanied by his associate trial counsel, whose name, she'd been told, was Captain Philip Hogan. They were both uniformed and carrying identical bulky leather briefcases. Waldron saw Claire and Grimes and nodded at them as he and Hogan approached the prosecution's table.

"The gang's almost all here," Grimes said. "Where's the man?"

"He should be here any second," Claire said. She saw the steel doors open and, sure enough, Tom entered, flanked by two guards. He wore a sharp, dress-green uniform. She was stunned to see him in it: it fit him perfectly, he seemed a natural in it. His ankle restraints, handcuffs, and chain belt looked like some strange funky jewelry. His shirt was immaculately pressed but was noticeably too large at the neck. He'd lost weight. He looked pale.

He looked around the room anxiously until he saw Claire, then smiled. Claire gave him a wave. He was ushered to the vacant chair between Claire and Grimes.

At three minutes before nine, Embry entered, in his dress-green uniform, and rushed over to them. "Sorry," he said, as he sat next to Grimes.

"Late night?" Grimes said.

Embry shook his head, smiled pleasantly. "Car trouble."

"You friendly with the prosecution?" Grimes asked suddenly. Claire winced. She'd asked him not to confront Embry, not yet.

"Not especially. Why?"

"Because, if I learn that you've leaked anything to them, and I mean *anything*, no matter how trivial or stupid, I'll have you disbarred, and then I'll have your testicles marinating in a pickle jar in my office, next to my bowling trophies."

"What's all this about?" Embry said, hurt.

Grimes looked over, saw the investigating officer enter the courtroom from his chambers. "We can talk about it later. It's show time."

"This Article 32 hearing will come to order. I am Lieutenant Colonel Robert T. Holt. As you know, I have been appointed as the investigating officer under Article 32 of the Uniform Code of Military Justice." Lieutenant Colonel Holt was a career army man of around fifty, a JAG officer with clearance. Even from his seat on the bench he appeared tall; he was thin, with receding black hair, a high forehead crowning a long, narrow, pinched face. He wore squarish wire-rim glasses. His voice was husky, high, his cadences matter-of-fact. In front of him, at a low table, sat the court reporter, a stout middle-aged woman, whispering into a black rubber steno mask.

"The purpose of this investigation is to inquire into the truth and form of the charges sworn against Sergeant First Class Ronald M. Kubik, United States Armed Forces. Copies of these charges—and the order appointing this investigation—have been provided to the accused, counsel for the accused, counsel for the United States, and reporter. Sergeant First Class Kubik, have you seen these charges against you?"

He sat between Claire and Grimes at the defense table. His shackles had been removed. "Yes, sir, I have."

"You understand you have been charged with eighty-seven specifications of murder, which is a capital crime."

"I do."

"You are advised you have the right to cross-examine any witnesses produced against you at this hearing. All right, now to the first order of business. Have the nondisclosure statements been signed by both trial counsel and defense counsel?"

"Yes, they have," Waldron said.

"They have," Grimes said.

"You all understand that anything that is said in this hearing, anything that happens here, may not be divulged outside this room."

"We do," Waldron said.

Grimes got to his feet. "Yes, sir, we do, but we want to assert that, by signing the statement of nondisclosure, we are in no way waiving our right to a public trial as guaranteed by the Sixth Amendment. The government has made no showing whatsoever as to why these proceedings should be classified."

Lieutenant Colonel Holt peered at him for a few seconds and cleared his throat. "Your assertion has been noted for the record."

Now Major Waldron rose. "Mr. Investigating Officer, the accused doesn't need a public proceeding to get a fair hearing. As long as the defense has a full and complete opportunity to hear all the evidence, the public doesn't have to know about it."

"Thank you, Major," Holt said.

Waldron remained standing. "Sir, moreover, this is a CIPA case"—he referred to the Classified Information Procedures Act—"involving national security and classified information."

"*Moreover*," Grimes mocked in a priggish whisper.

"Yet the government has reason to believe that the defense may attempt to 'graymail' the government," Waldron continued, "by threatening to leak classified information, in order to obtain an unfair advantage in this court. Or they may even be planning to selectively leak information to try to sway public opinion in their favor—which would be a total violation of the nondisclosure forms they have signed. I'd like to request that, in the interest of the fairness of this proceeding, you order the defense counsel not to make any leaks to the press."

Claire and Grimes stared at each other, astonished. How much did Waldron know about their intentions—and was it Embry who had told them? Who else could it be?

"Uh, yes," Colonel Holt said. "Counsel, you are reminded that this is a classified proceeding and you are counseled not to make any statements to the press."

Claire stood up. "Sir, I appreciate your admonition, but as you well know, my cocounsel Mr. Grimes and I, as civilians, are not subject to your orders. I'm sure my military cocounsel, Captain Embry, will abide by your orders. But we have all signed a nondisclosure-of-classified-information form, and we intend to abide by that agreement. Anything else concerning this matter that you choose to instruct us with, sir, we will take for informational purposes only."

The investigating officer glowered at her. After a significant pause, he muttered, "So noted. Does government counsel have, at this time, a list of prospective witnesses they intend to call?"

Captain Phil Hogan replied, "Mr. Investigating Officer, at this point the government anticipates calling Colonel James Hernandez and Chief Warrant Officer Four Stanley Oshman."

"Who's that last one?" Claire whispered to Grimes.

Grimes shrugged. "No idea," he said.

"Okay, Captain Hogan, Major Waldron, would you like to begin your case in chief?"

Waldron stood. "Sir, the government offers Investigative Exhibits 2 through 21, copies of which have been provided to defense counsel for inspection and possible objection, and requests that they be considered by the investigating officer."

"Defense counsel?" Colonel Holt asked.

"Uh, yes, sir," Grimes said. "We object to the admission of Investigative Exhibit 3, a CID statement regarding my client's alleged misconduct involving a neighbor in North Carolina in 1984."

"On what grounds?"

"On the grounds that it deals with uncharged misconduct that's not relevant to this case. It's also improper character evidence. No charge was ever filed over this alleged incident—which we dispute anyway—and the statute of limitations has expired. Therefore, we object under Military Rule of Evidence 404(b) and 403. This uncharged misconduct has no relevance whatsoever on whether my client murdered eighty-seven civilians in El Salvador. The government is simply and obviously attempting to admit this phony evidence for the sole purpose of impugning my client's reputation at this hearing."

"Trial counsel, how is this relevant?" Holt asked.

"Sir," Waldron replied, "we're offering this other

act of killing, the killing of a dog, not to show the accused's propensity—"

"Hold on," Holt said. "The killing of a *dog*?"

"*Alleged*," Tom whispered. Indeed, Devereaux had been unable to get any information on the incident, or on the alleged neighbor.

"Yes, sir," Waldron continued. "Not to show the accused's propensity to commit murder, but that the accused is able to form a premeditated design to kill."

Whatever that means, Claire thought.

There was a long silence.

"I'm going to agree with defense counsel," Holt said at last. "This is an extrinsic act of misconduct that's not relevant to any of the elements of the charged offense, and I am not going to consider them. Trial counsel, you may not present that evidence."

"Yes, sir," Waldron said neutrally, betraying no disappointment.

Grimes smiled. "We also object to Investigative Exhibits 6 through 11," he said. "The sworn CID statements allegedly given by six other members of my client's Special Forces unit, Detachment 27. It ain't easy to cross-examine pieces of paper. Where are these other six men?"

"Trial counsel?" Holt said.

"Sir, several of these men are deceased. As for the others, we are only required to produce witnesses who are 'reasonably available,' that is, located within one hundred miles of the site of the hearing. The others are at the moment unavailable under Rules of Courts-Martial four oh five golf one alpha."

Holt hesitated. "All right. I'm willing to consider these sworn statements alone. If there are no further objections, trial counsel, you may call your first witness."

Waldron called out—sang out, really: "The government calls Colonel James Hernandez."

25

*C*olonel *James* Hernandez, the general's aide de camp, was short but powerfully built, with short curly black hair, a thin mustache, and swarthy skin. Under his right eye was a scar. He had the slightest trace of a Cuban accent. As he spoke, he gripped the railing in front of the witness stand.

"They begged for mercy," he said. "They said they weren't rebels."

"And what did Sergeant Kubik do while he was machine-gunning them down?" Waldron asked.

"What did he do?"

"Did he react in any way?"

"Well, he smiled, sort of."

"Smiled? As if he were enjoying himself?"

"Objection!" Claire called out. She felt Grimes's restraining hand on her arm. "This witness can't possibly testify as to whether Sergeant Kubik was enjoying himself—"

"Uh, Ms. Chapman," Colonel Holt said, "this isn't a regular court-martial. This is an Article 32 hearing. That means that none of the rules of evidence apply here. The only thing we go by are the military rules of procedure for Article 32 pretrial investigations."

"Your Honor—"

"And I'm not Your Honor, much as I'd like to be. You can call me "Sir," or "Mr. Investigating Officer," but I'm not Your Honor. Now, are you going to be cross-examining this witness, when the time comes?"

"I am, sir," said Grimes.

"Well, then, counsel, I don't see why you're objecting anyway. Mr. Grimes here should be the one objecting. We have a rule here—one counsel, one witness. No tag teams. Understood?"

"Understood," said Claire with a half-smile. She whispered to Grimes, "Sorry."

"I have nothing further," Waldron said.

Grimes got to his feet. Standing just in front of the defense table, he said: "Colonel Hernandez, when you were contacted in regard to this 32 hearing, were you threatened with charges if you didn't cooperate?"

"No," Hernandez said.

"You weren't coerced in any way?"

"No, I was not." He gave Grimes a direct, confrontational stare.

"I *see*," Grimes said, as if he clearly didn't believe him. "And when you were interviewed by the CID in 1985, in regard to this incident at La Colina, were you pressured in any way by CID?"

"Back in 1985?"

"Right."

"No, I was not."

"No one threatened you with charges if you didn't cooperate—complicity, involvement in the alleged crimes, conspiracy to commit murder, even murder?"

"No one."

"No threats whatsoever?"

"None." He jutted his chin as if to say, So there.

"So this was a completely voluntary statement?"

"Correct."

"Now, you work for General William Marks, the chief of staff of the army, is that right?"

"Yes. I'm his executive officer."

"Did he ask you to give a statement?"

"No. I did it on my own."

"He didn't coerce you in any way?"

"No, sir."

"You're not afraid of harming your career if you say anything critical of the general?"

Hernandez hesitated. "If I had anything critical to say, I'm required to say it. I'm under oath. But he did nothing wrong."

"*Aha.* Now, tell me something, Colonel. When you saw Sergeant Kubik discharge his weapon at the civilians, did you *personally* try to stop him?"

Now Hernandez eyed him suspiciously. Was this a lawyer trick? "No," he finally said.

"You didn't?"

"No."

"Who did try to stop him?"

Hernandez hesitated again. He sat forward in his seat. He looked over at Waldron and company. "I don't know. I didn't see anyone try to stop him."

"Hmm," Grimes said. He took a few steps closer. He shrugged and said conversationally, "So you didn't actually see *anyone* try to stop him?"

"No, I did not."

"And, Colonel, since General Marks—then *Colonel* Marks—was back at headquarters at this time, you were in charge, is that right?"

"Yes."

"Colonel Hernandez, how long have you worked for General Marks?"

"Since 1985."

"That's quite some time. He must trust you enormously."

"I hope so, sir."

"You'd take a bullet for the general."

"If given the chance, yes, sir, I would."

"You'd lie for him, too, wouldn't you?"

"Objection!" Waldron shouted.

"Withdrawn," Grimes said. "Okay, now, Colonel Hernandez, I'm going to take you step by step through this incident. We're going to very slowly explore every single detail, just so's I don't miss anything, okay?"

Hernandez shrugged.

In mind-numbing detail, for two hundred questions or more, Grimes took the witness through every point he could think of. It was like watching a movie frame by frame. Where was he standing? What did Sergeant Major so-and-so say?

Then, suddenly, Grimes seemed to veer off course. "Colonel Hernandez, did you consider yourself a friend of Ronald Kubik's?"

Hernandez's eyes snaked over to Waldron for a moment. He looked sullen. He opened his mouth, then closed it.

"You can tell us the truth," Grimes prompted, walking away from the witness stand, back toward the defense table.

"No, I did not."

"You didn't much like him, did you?"

"I thought he was twisted."

Grimes stopped and whirled around. "Twisted?"

"That's what I said."

"Twisted like sick-twisted?"

"Yeah. Sick."

"Oh?" Grimes looked curious. "And how was he sick?"

"He was a sadist. He loved to kill."

"In combat, you mean."

Hernandez looked confused. "Yeah, when else?"

"You didn't kill people outside of combat, did you?"

"No. Outside of a designated operation, which wasn't necessarily combat."

"I see. So, during a designated operation, he loved to kill."

"That's right."

"Which was his job—*your* job."

"Only part of the time—"

"Part of the time it was your job to kill people."

"Right."

"And he was good at it. In fact, he loved it."

"Correct."

"Would you say Ronald Kubik was a good soldier?"

"What he did was illegal—"

"I'm not asking about what happened on June 22, 1985. I'm asking you, up until that point, up until that night, would you say Ron Kubik was a credit to the Special Forces?"

Hernandez looked trapped and resentful. "Yes."

"He was really good."

"Yeah," Hernandez conceded. "He was so fearless it was scary. He was one of the best guys we had."

"That's all I've got for this witness," Grimes said.

"As it's lunchtime," Colonel Holt announced, "we will recess for an hour and a half, until fourteen hundred hours." A rustle, oddly dampened by the soundproofing, arose, along with a flat babble of excited voices. The few spectators got to their feet.

Waldron headed for the exit; Hogan, his cocounsel, lagged behind, doing something at the prosecution table. The steel doors opened.

Tom gave Claire a hug and said, "We're doing great, don't you think?"

"We're doing okay," Claire said. "I think. What do I know?"

At that moment, Hogan brushed by the defense table. When he was next to Tom, he whispered: "You know we'll get you, you sick fuck, one way or another. In court or out."

Tom's eyes widened, but he said nothing. Claire, who had overheard the remark, felt a surge of adrenaline, but then she too said nothing.

Tom held out his wrists for cuffing. The restraints were put back on him and he was led away, back to the brig for a meal in his cell.

Embry came around the table and reached to shake Grimes's hand in congratulation. Grimes didn't meet it. He leaned over and spoke to Embry in a low, menacing voice. "What the fuck did you tell them about leaking to the press?"

Embry's hand dropped slowly to his side. His face darkened almost to purple.

"We saw you, Embry. We saw you having beers with Waldron and company."

"Yeah? Well, that's all it was. Beers. I work with these guys, you know. They're colleagues. I have to live with them, work with them, long after you guys are gone."

"And that's why you feel free to divulge confidences to them?" Claire asked.

"Now he's got you thinking this way? I didn't tell them a thing, Claire. Not a thing. I never would. It's unprofessional and it would just get me in trouble. Plus it would make me look like a chump. Anyway, why should I tell them I was party to a conspiracy to violate nondisclosure? That would just get me in a heap of trouble."

He turned, looking wounded, and walked off.

"You believe him?" Grimes asked.

"I don't know who to believe anymore," Claire said. "Let's get lunch. My car is parked really close. There's a McDonald's nearby."

"I'd go for McDonald's."

"Is there a McDonald's on every army base in the world?"

"Or Burger King."

On the way to the car, when she was satisfied no one was within earshot, Claire said: "I don't understand why you didn't trap him, Grimes. In his statement he says something like, We all tried to stop him. But on the stand he backed down from that. That's a major contradiction! Why didn't you bring out that inconsistency?"

"Because that's not the point of this proceeding," Grimes said. "We're looking to lock the witness into his story. Get it on paper. We're not trying to impeach him here."

"Explain."

"Don't blow your wad at the 32. We're going to trial, we both know that. So hold our ammo in reserve to blow holes in him at the trial. We treat this hearing like a discovery deposition. Don't confront the witness with his inconsistencies. Not here. Maybe we'll point them out at the closing, but I'd rather we didn't do it even then. Save the big guns for the trial."

She shook her head at the curiousness of the military system.

"Look," Grimes explained, "it's like those different kinds of mousetraps, okay? There's them sticky-glue traps where the mouse gets stuck to it and keeps wriggling around, alive, and you got to pick it up and throw it away. And then there's the old-fashioned snap-trap that crushes the little bugger in half a second—breaks his back. A 32 is like a glue trap. You get the witness to poke his little paws in the glue so he's stuck there, wriggling but alive. You don't crush the fuckers yet."

"Yeah, well, I wanted to crush the fucker."

"Because you're defending your husband. That's not the way the system works. That would have been ill-advised."

She flushed hotly, realizing that he was right. She wasn't being objective. How could her feelings for Tom not hinder the way she tried this case?

She unlocked the passenger side of the rented car first, and they both got in. The instant she switched on the ignition, they were engulfed by an enormously loud sound, the blare of the car radio, turned up all the way.

"Man, you trying to kill me?" Grimes shouted. "I just sustained permanent hearing loss. I didn't know you were the musical type."

She switched it off. "Jesus, what was that?"

"Marilyn Manson, I think. I don't know. I don't listen to that shit either, don't ask me."

"I didn't put that on," she said. "I never listen to the radio."

"Maybe you brushed it on by accident or something."

"I would have heard it go on. Believe me, I didn't put the radio on. Someone else did."

"A warning," Grimes said. "Telling you they can get into your car or your home, anytime they want, so watch it."

"Subtle," she said.

26

❖

"*Your last* witness, trial counsel?" Holt said.

"Mr. Investigating Officer," Waldron said, "I have some testimony that's not relevant now, which I've prepared in response to what I anticipate the defense will put on." Grimes looked at Claire, puzzled. "So, rather than keep Chief Warrant Officer Four Stanley Oshman around for another day and a half, I'd like to put him on now."

"Defense, do you have any objections?" asked Holt.

Claire whispered to Grimes, "You didn't find out who this guy is?"

"No luck," Grimes whispered back. "It's okay, we'll get to cross him, help us put on our case." Aloud, he said, "We have no objection."

"I call as my next witness Chief Warrant Officer Oshman," Waldron announced, "a polygraph examiner assigned to Fort Bragg."

The courtroom stirred.

"What the hell is this?" Grimes said aloud. He looked at Claire and then at Embry. "What the *hell* is this?"

Chief Warrant Officer Stanley Oshman, slight and owlish in thick glasses, with receding blond hair, in his early forties, got up from one of the spectator seats. He had been there all along, observing. He made his way to the witness stand and was sworn in. Waldron moved swiftly through the preliminaries while Claire and Grimes watched in dull horror.

"Chief Warrant Officer Oshman," Waldron asked, "in addition to your day-to-day responsibilities, what do you do with the Special Forces units you work with at Fort Bragg?"

"I teach them to beat the box," Oshman said.

"Beat the box? What does that mean?"

"I teach them techniques—tricks, if you will—that enable them to beat a polygraph, in case they're captured and interrogated behind enemy lines."

Aloud, but ostensibly to himself, Grimes said, "Wait one goddamned second."

"So it's your testimony here today," Waldron continued, "that certain Special Forces officers, like Ronald Kubik, can beat the polygraph."

"That's correct. He certainly can."

"That, if he's given a polygraph, he knows how to give the answers he wishes to, whether truthful or not, and yet most polygraph examiners will conclude that no deception is indicated."

"That's correct."

Too loudly, Grimes said, "Jesus fucking Christ. Our guy can just goddamn well go home now."

"Are you accusing me of leaking again?" Embry asked after the hearing was over. "Is that what you're implying?"

"I'm not implying, I'm saying," Grimes fulminated. "You got another explanation how Waldron knew we were going to call our polygrapher, introduce the results of the polygraph? You got another explanation, dude?"

"I have no explanation." Even Embry's ears were flushed. "I was just as shocked as you—"

"Oh, were you, really?" Grimes said.

"Give him a chance to talk," Claire said.

"For what?" Grimes said bitterly. "So he can stand here and bullshit us? The prosecution just successfully knocked out our ace. You think anyone's going to pay attention to an exculpatory polygraph taken by a guy trained to beat the box?"

Claire instinctively turned to Tom, then remembered he'd just been taken back to the brig.

"Fine," Embry said. "I see where this is going. I can see you don't really care what I have to say. So I'm going to make it easy for you. I'm withdrawing."

He turned and began striding away.

"You're still subject to attorney-client confidentiality, you asshole," Grimes called after him. He muttered, "Not like it ever stopped you, sorry-ass motherfucker."

Embry joined the exodus of spectators and lawyers from the courtroom. From a distance, Waldron approached the defense table. Claire wondered how much he had overheard. It wouldn't take particularly sensitive ears to hear the heated exchange.

When he was a few feet away, Waldron spoke directly to Claire. "Captain Embry didn't tell me anything. You owe him an apology. This is a small world, and things get around."

Claire chose not to give him the satisfaction of pursuing the matter. Instead she said, sweetly, "Maybe you can enlighten me about something. What's the point of conducting a trial if it's going to be held behind closed doors? I mean, I've always taught that a trial is held for the purposes of demonstrating to the public that justice is being done. So where's the public? Five anonymous guys with top-secret clearances?"

"Take it up with the secretary of the army," Waldron said.

"I just may," Claire replied. "But it's clear to me that the only justification for keeping this whole business so top secret is to keep certain persons from being embarrassed. There's clearly no real national-security justification, given that the events we're talking about are thirteen years old."

"The national security—" Waldron began.

"It's just us here talking," Claire said. "No investigating officer to play to. Just us. So we can be honest. You see, I really don't quite get the point of putting my husband through a court-martial. Why didn't you guys just lock him away in a loony bin?"

"That's actually where he belongs," Waldron shot back. "Your husband is a sociopath, a twisted, sick bastard. He demonstrated that as an assassin in Vietnam. He was a legend, a sicko legend in that covert world. But he was brilliant, he spoke a bunch of different languages and dialects perfectly, and he had no compunction about killing his fellow human beings. He was perfect for the military's purposes. Just like the U.S. government hired those Nazis at the end of World War Two. Only the Pentagon thought they could control Kubik. But he lost it."

"Ask yourself what the brass really want," Claire said. "Say whatever lies you want about my husband, the folks at the top really just want to keep all this buried. They want to make sure the fact of a U.S. massacre in El Salvador never becomes public. And we're prepared to agree to that. You drop the charges now, and we'll agree to complete secrecy. In writing if you want. Nothing will ever come out. But if you let this go to court-martial, you'll destroy the chief of staff of the army. This I promise you. And I'll go public with the story—the whole world will know. You've gotta ask yourself, do you really want that? He goes down, you do too."

Waldron smiled. It was an unpleasant, feral smile, the smile of someone who rarely did. "I really don't give a shit who wants to cover their ass. Or who goes down. My job here is to prosecute a mass murderer, to get him put in Leavenworth for the rest of his pointless life. And preferably executed. That's my job. And I'll do it happily. I'll see you at trial."

27

❖

Cleaning up the kitchen after dinner, Claire and Jackie talked. Annie was getting ready for bed, brushing her teeth. Claire, exhausted and ruminative, rinsed off the dishes while Jackie loaded the dishwasher.

"Will someone please explain to me what the deal is with Eeyore?" Jackie said. "I mean, give the poor donkey some Prozac, you know?"

Claire nodded, smiled.

"And this Kubik thing. I can't call him Ron," Jackie said. "That's fucked up."

"I can't either. I don't know what to call him, and there's something kind of symbolic about that. It's as if he's a different person, only I don't know who or what he is. I see him for five minutes before the hearing starts, we talk business. It's all business. He says I did a good job, or he asks me something procedural. I go to visit him in the brig, and we talk about the case. All business."

"Isn't that the way it should be? You're defending him, you're his lawyer, his life is on the line."

"Yes, you're right. But he's not *there* somehow."

"Anyone would be scared out of their mind. You mind if I ask something—did you get the polygraph results admitted?"

"Yeah, sure. But it was damaged goods. If I were the investigating officer, I'd think he beat the box because he was trained to do it."

"And what do you think? I hate this dishwasher."

"About what?"

"About whether he 'beat the box'—whether he pulled one over on the examiner?"

"How can I answer that? He could have—I mean, he apparently knows how to. Yet I don't think he'd have to—he's innocent."

"Okay," Jackie said guardedly.

"It's maddening. I've defended enough cases against the government where the government persecuted someone or scapegoated someone—a whistle-blower, whatever—so I know how they can do these things. How corrupt they can be. I once defended this guy who was fired from the EPA for whistle-blowing, basically, about this toxic-waste site. And it turned out his supervisor had forged and backdated personnel records, evaluations, to make it look like the guy'd had a drinking problem. When in fact he'd been a model employee. So I've *seen* this stuff happen."

Jackie turned over one of the hand-painted ceramic dinner plates. "These are cool," she said. "I'm surprised they're letting us use them. You think they're supposed to go in the dishwasher?"

"They didn't say not to."

"Can I be straight with you?"

"What?"

"Look, two months ago we both basically thought Tom Chapman was just this great guy—macho, good-looking, great at everything. Real *guy* guy.

Good provider, great dad, great husband, right?"

"Yeah? So?"

"So now we know he was hiding from us. He's got a different name, he has this creepy secret past—"

"Jackie—"

"No, wait. Whatever the truth is about these murderers. He was a member of this top-secret military unit that parachutes into places or whatever, into some foreign country where they're not supposed to be, carrying false ID, shoots the place up, then pulls out. I mean, you want to talk about symbolic? He parachutes into your life out of nowhere, takes it over, carrying false ID—"

"Very clever." Claire began scrubbing, with deep concentration, the detritus of Annie's Alpha-Bits cereal encrusted on a bowl.

"And we don't really know who he is."

"Whatever they throw at him, he's still the man I fell in love with."

Jackie stopped and turned to look directly at Claire. "But *you don't know who that man is*. He's not the man you thought he was—he's not the man you loved."

"Oh, now, what does that mean, really? When you come right down to it? I wasn't being fatuous or naïve when I said he's the man I fell in love with. Whoever he is, I got to know him as he was, for what he was. I loved him—*love* him—for who he is, who I know him to be. Everyone has a past, everyone conceals something. No one's ever totally open about their past, whether they're hiding stuff intentionally or not, whether it's their sexuality or—"

"And there you go, rationalizing it." Jackie raised her voice. "You don't know, bottom line, who he is and whether he did what they say he did—"

"I *know* he didn't do what they're charging!"

"You don't *know* anything about him, Claire. If he could lie to you about his family, his parents, his childhood, his college, practically his whole fucking life, do you *really* think he couldn't lie to you about this?"

Annie was standing at the entrance to the kitchen in her Pooh pajamas, sucking her thumb for the first time in years.

"Annie!" Claire said.

Annie removed her thumb with a liquid pop. She looked sullenly, suspiciously at her mother. "Why are you and Aunt Jackie fighting?"

"We're not fighting, baby. We're talking. We're discussing."

Accusingly, Annie said: "You sound like you're fighting."

"We're just talking, kiddo," Jackie said. To Claire she added: "I'm going to smoke a cigarette."

"Outside, please," Claire said. "I may well join you after Annie goes to bed."

"I've created a monster," Jackie said.

"No, you're not tucking me in," Annie told her mother. "Jackie is."

"Oh, but can I? I hardly ever see you anymore—I *miss* you!"

"*No,*" Annie said loudly. "I don't *want* you to tuck me in. I want Jackie to."

Jackie turned back. "Kiddo, let your mommy tuck you in."

Claire added, "Sweetie, your mommy—"

"*No!* You go work! Jackie will do it! Go *away!*" She ran out of the kitchen, her feet pounding up the staircase to the second floor.

Claire looked at Jackie, who shrugged.

"Go for it," Jackie said. "You can't blame the kid."

Annie's temporary bedroom was a guest room whose only personalizing touch was the toys she'd scattered about the floor.

Annie had already climbed into bed, looking at *Madeline and the Bad Hat*, sucking her thumb furiously. "Go away," she said when Claire entered.

"Honey," Claire said softly, approaching the bed and kneeling next to it.

Annie pulled out her thumb. "Go *away*! Go work!"

"Can I read to you? I'd really love to."

"Well, I don't want you to, so you can just go away."

She replaced her thumb in her mouth, staring balefully at the book.

"Can I talk to you?"

Annie ignored her.

"Please, baby. I want to talk to you."

Annie's eyes didn't leave the book.

"I know you're upset with me. I haven't been a good mommy at all, I know that. I'm so sorry."

Annie's eyes seemed to soften for an instant; then she lowered her brows, frowned. Still she said nothing. Claire had told her that her daddy was on trial, but how much did she really understand?

"I've been so busy trying to get Daddy out. I'm out of the house early, and I come home late, and I'm exhausted, and we haven't done any of the things we always do. And I want you to know that I love you so much. More than anyone in the world. I do. And when this is all over, we're just going to play together a lot, and go to the zoo, and get ice cream, and mostly just be together like we used to."

Annie pulled the blankets up to her chin. Without moving her eyes from the book, she said sullenly, almost demanding: "When's Daddy coming home?"

"Soon, I think. I hope."

A pause; then Annie said grudgingly, "Jackie says he's in jail."

Claire hesitated. She was loath to lie to her anymore, and right now Annie, ferociously observant like all small children, appeared almost to be daring Claire to tell the truth.

"He is, but it's a mistake."

Annie frowned again. "What's jail like?" She seemed to be demanding the details, as proof of Claire's credibility.

"Well, they keep him in a room, and they give him his supper there, and they give him books."

"Isn't there bars and locks and everything?" Annie asked warily.

"Yes, there are bars."

"Is he sad?"

"He's sad he can't be with you."

"Can I go see him?"

"No, babe, I'm sorry."

"Why not?"

Why not, indeed. "They don't allow kids there," Claire lied. Probably kids were allowed in the visiting room.

Annie seemed to accept this. "Is he scared?"

"At first he was, but now he's not. He knows they're going to let him out soon, and then we'll be a family again. Let's read some books."

"No, I don't want to," Annie said. Claire couldn't tell if Annie was mollified or not. "I'm tired." She turned over. " 'Night, Mommy," she said.

Claire fell asleep on the sofa in the sitting room, surrounded by case books on military law and packets of nonclassified discovery materials.

At around nine she was jolted awake by the doorbell. She ran to get it, before he rang again and woke Annie up.

Grimes's face was solemn.

"The decision's back, isn't it?"

Grimes nodded.

"When are we going to trial?"

"Can I come in? Or do I got to stand out here on the porch?"

"Sorry."

"The arraignment's in six days," he said, removing his fern-green overcoat and hanging it on the hall coat tree. "That means we got to have all our motions in by then, or we should, anyway. We probably go to trial in a month."

"Why did I even allow myself to think otherwise?"

"Because, underneath all your been-there, done-that, cynical worldliness, you're an optimist. A cock-eyed optimist."

"Maybe," Claire said dubiously. "You want coffee or something?"

"Naw. Not at night."

"So this is it," Claire said when they were seated at their usual places in the library-office. "We lose this, we're fucked."

"I don't believe I'm hearing this from the appellate queen of Cambridge. It's like baseball. Motions is your first base. Trial is second base. Then you got the Army Court of Criminal Appeals. Then Court of Appeals for the Armed Forces. They get a single, the game ain't over."

"So now who's the cockeyed optimist?"

"I'm just talking how the game is played. Lot of innings."

"But this whole charade is ridiculous. The investigating officer's finding tells any officer who might be on the jury that their commanding officer thinks Tom's guilty. They're not going to acquit after that! What's that?" She noticed a piece of paper in Grimes's hands.

"The convening order," he said, standing up and handing it to her. "Take a look. You see who's ordering the court-martial?" Grimes studied a fragile-looking porcelain urn on a white-painted wooden columnar pedestal next to the desk.

The letterhead said SECRETARY OF THE ARMY. The letter was signed by the secretary of the army himself.

"I don't get it," she said. "Why is the secretary convening it? I thought it was done by someone lower down on the food chain, like the commander of Quantico or something."

"Usually is. That's what's interesting. It's like they're ordering this from the very top to send a message—you know, We're not fucking around, this is serious shit."

"No," Claire said.

"No what?"

"That's not the reason. There's a legal reason, I'll bet. A really interesting one."

"Tell me."

"It's because General Marks, the chief of staff of the army, is involved in this. Legally, that makes him an accuser against Tom. And according to Article 1 of the Uniform Code of Military Justice and Rule of Court-Martial 504(c)(2), a court-martial can't be convened by anyone junior to an accuser. The only one senior to the general—"

"Is the secretary. Right." He traced a pattern on the urn, nodded. "Right."

"And what's this list?" Claire said, still looking at the letter. "Is this the jury?"

"Yeah, only in a military court they're called the 'members.' "

"I want all these guys checked out for any glitches. Any biases. Anything we can use for voir dire. How come all these guys are commissioned officers? Tom was a noncommissioned officer, that's lower rank. Don't we want some senior NCOs on the panel?"

"If we want senior NCOs, we can request it. But I think we'll get a fairer shake if we stick with officers. They're more inclined to look at the evidence, in my experience."

"I assume the most senior guy in rank automatically becomes the jury foreman."

"You're catching on. Everything is rank."

"And how do we know these guys haven't all been selected for their willingness to convict?"

"We don't. Officially it's unlawful command influence to try to stack the court, but good luck proving it. You can't."

The doorbell rang. "Shit," Claire said. "That's going to wake Annie up. She was just drifting off to sleep."

"Expecting someone?"

"Ray Devereaux. My PI. Excuse me for a minute."

Ray stood at the door like an immense statue with an improbably small head. He wore one of his good suits.

"Good evening," he said with exaggerated courtliness.

"Hey, Ray," Claire said. She went to hug him and ended up squeezing his stomach. He entered and looked around.

"I like this," Devereaux said. "You're living in the goddamned Taj Mahal and I'm staying in a roach motel."

"It's not a roach motel, Ray, it's—"

"Fuggedaboudit, I'm making a joke. What happened to your sense of humor?"

In the library he was introduced to Grimes and refused to sit down. "I wanna know why you guys don't drop a dime to the *Post* or the *Washington Times*," Devereaux said. "Only thing that'll derail this express train. Open the door and let in the light of day."

"No," Claire said urgently, shaking her head. "Then Tom becomes William Calley. No matter if we get him off or not. For the rest of his life, he's a mass murderer, and my daughter has to live with that."

"But if you change your mind," Grimes said, "just don't use your phone. Don't even talk about it on your phone."

"You think they've got an illegal tap on my phones?"

Devereaux laughed the laugh of the man who's seen it all.

"Lady," Grimes said, "I put nothing past 'em."

"Okay. Field report," Devereaux announced. "Of the men in Detachment 27 I've been able to locate, there's Hernandez, who probably salutes General Marks's bowel movements. Two are in the private sector. Two I can't find. That's all of them."

"Including Tom, that's six," Grimes said. "There were twelve in the unit. Where's the other six?"

"Dead."

"That's what Tom told me," Claire said.

"There seems to be a high mortality rate in that unit, wouldn't you say? Six of the men have died since 1985."

"How?" Claire asked.

"Two in combat, but there's nothing available

about the circumstances of their deaths. Three dead in car accidents. One, who lived in New York City and never owned a car or had a driver's license, died of a heart attack."

"Because they couldn't plausibly engineer a car accident for the guy," Grimes said, nodding. "But heart attacks can be faked, with the right chemicals."

"Tom was right," Claire said. "He said they were going to go after him, too."

"They didn't figure on losing him the way they did," Devereaux said.

Claire heard a small noise at the doorway and saw Annie standing there, thumb in her mouth, dragging her blanket behind her. Another regression. "What are you doing up?"

"The doorbell woke me up," Annie said in a small voice. She looked around the library, blinking.

"Annie!" Devereaux sang out. He strode over to her and put his arms out. "Want an elevator ride?"

"Yeah!" Annie said, reaching up.

Devereaux lifted her up almost to the ceiling. "Tenth floor! Going down." Lowering her in stages, he said, "Eighth floor! Sixth floor! Third floor! Lobby!" She screamed with delight. Then, catapulting her upward, he said, "Whoops! Going up! Tenth floor!" And, plunging her to the floor: "Going down! Express! Basement!"

"Ray!" Claire scolded. "This little girl has to go to sleep, and you're getting her all riled up."

Annie giggled. "More!"

"No more," Devereaux said. "Your mommy says it's sleepytime."

"Can I play in here for a little while?"

"It's bedtime, babe," Claire said.

"But I don't have school."

Claire hesitated but a moment. "All right, for a

little while. Do you guys mind? She never sees me these days."

"Is she bound by attorney-client confidentiality?" Grimes asked.

"You've got to be real quiet, okay?" Claire said.

"Okay."

Annie began walking around the library, inspecting the objects, playing with a paperweight.

"We're going to have to replace Embry," Grimes said. "Or they'll replace him, more likely. But we definitely need someone inside the system."

"You really think he leaked our plans about the polygraph?" Claire asked.

"You got any other candidates?"

"No. But, just judging by his character—I find it hard to accept."

Annie had both of her hands around the porcelain urn.

"Be careful," Claire said to Annie. "This isn't our house." But Annie didn't remove her hands. She stared at her mother with defiance.

"You're such a good judge of character?" Devereaux gibed.

"It's a different world, the military," Grimes said. "Different rules. Different loyalties. Different values. Different morality. He may be a moral guy, but his loyalty is to the system, to protecting the military. Not to us."

"If you really believe that," Claire said, "why not try to get him disbarred? Annie, honey, I mean it. I want you to go to bed now."

"Ah, I was just talking trash. How am I going to prove it? Never happen."

There was a sudden movement, and the urn toppled to the hardwood floor with a sickening crash.

"Annie!" Claire shouted.

Annie gave Claire a ferocious look and stared at what she'd done. The urn had smashed into tiny pieces, scattered far and wide over the polished floor.

"Oh, God," Claire said, jumping up. "Annie! All right, you, back to bed."

"No, I don't want to go to bed!"

"Bedtime, miss." Claire lifted her up.

Annie wriggled, swung her body to either side, protesting angrily, *"I'm . . . not . . . going . . . to bed!"*

"Hey," Devereaux said.

"What?" Claire said as Annie managed to free herself from Claire's arms and landed neatly on the floor. She ran out of the room. "Annie, come back here, baby!"

"Check this out." He pointed at the shards of porcelain scattered on the hardwood floor.

Claire and Grimes approached. "What you talking about?" Grimes asked.

"This," Devereaux said.

"Oh, man," Grimes said.

"What is it?" Claire asked. She stared at a tiny black object she'd never seen before.

Devereaux picked it up. It was oblong, no more than an inch long, half an inch wide, trailing a long thin wire.

"Transmitter," Grimes said, his voice hushed.

"Oh my God," Claire said in a high-pitched whisper.

"Man oh man," Grimes said.

Claire suddenly grabbed a ceramic foo dog on the cluttered table next to Grimes's chair and flung it to the ground. It shattered, another small black transmitter among its shards. "Oh my God," she repeated.

"Claire," Grimes called warningly.

She lifted the spherical black lamp from the library table she used as a desk and hurled that, too, to the floor. It split jaggedly in half, revealing another black transmitter.

"Cool it, Claire," Grimes said. "You're going to have to pay for all this shit."

"Enough, Claire," Devereaux said. "You don't have to do that. I'll locate the rest of them."

"This place is loaded with them!" Claire gasped.

"I told you," Grimes said, grabbing her arms to restrain her, "I put nothing past them. Now you see what I'm talking about."

28

❖

The house crawled with FBI agents—crime-scene
investigators, fingerprint and forensic people.
They'd arrived with astonishing speed after Ray
Devereaux, one of their own, had put in the call the
following morning. He'd done so after he'd finished
his own cursory inspection, which turned up a
dozen more miniature transmitters, in the library, in
Claire's bedroom, in the kitchen. And more to come,
no doubt. In the ceiling of an empty guest-room
closet one floor above the library Devereaux had located a large black box, which he said was used to
gather the signals, amplify them, and broadcast
them for miles to whoever was listening.

A meeting was scheduled for one o'clock that day
with the military judge who'd just been detailed to
the Ronald Kubik court-martial. As she drove to
Quantico, Grimes said, "Well, your complaint certainly sped things along." He was referring to the
complaint she'd filed with the U.S. attorney for the
Eastern District of Virginia, who took things like unlawful surveillance devices and interference with attorney-client privilege with the gravest concern.

"That's one way to get the military judge named—they wanted to have a judge named to deal with the bugging complaint. Problem is, now we're fucked."

"Why?" she said, and glanced at him to see whether he was being ironic.

"We're fucked because our judge is Warren Farrell, who happens to be a Nazi."

"How so?" Claire asked.

"He's what you call a real iron colonel."

"Huh?"

"That's what you call a full-bird colonel who's at his terminal rank, meaning he's not far from retirement and can't be threatened. So he can be as outrageous as he wants and piss all over us, which he likes to do to defense lawyers, particularly civilians. He certainly doesn't give a shit about a reversal down the line."

"I take it you've tried cases before him."

"Never had the pleasure. Heard a lot, though. He don't much like dark-green army boys like me." Grimes paused to take a sip of his take-out coffee. "Great circumstances to be meeting the judge for the first time."

"What are you talking about? It's great. Puts them on the defensive, makes us look good by contrast."

"You don't know Judge Farrell."

"What, he's going to be prejudiced against us because we had the misfortune to have our workspace illegally bugged by the government?"

"It wasn't necessarily the prosecution," Grimes said.

"Oh? You got any other candidates?"

"Hell, it could be the Pentagon. Defense Intelligence. Defense Humint Service, or one of those creepy military-intelligence groups they keep locked up in the basement of the Pentagon. Might even be some private organization of old Special Forces alumni who don't want shit like this coming out. Or want to make sure we lose."

"Maybe some friends of the general's," Claire said. "But FBI's not going to find fingerprints on anything, are they? The culprits aren't going to be that sloppy."

Grimes nodded slowly in distracted agreement. "This kind of shit happens all the time."

"In the military?"

"Oh, yeah. When I was with the Judge Advocates Corps, prosecuting, I heard all the time about how they'd plant bugs on civilian lawyers. Military doesn't like civilian lawyers playing in their sand lot, I told you."

"Bullshit, Grimes. Don't tell me the prosecution used information they picked up from bugs."

"Oh, they'd launder it first. Always happens. You find an independent source, attribute it to them. You think I'm kidding?"

"No, I don't. I just don't want to think you're right."

The meeting with the military judge was held *in camera*, in the high-security subbasement courtroom. Waldron was already seated, fuming, when they arrived. He shuffled papers as Captain Hogan talked to him. A court reporter was placing tapes in the Lanier recording machine and testing her equipment. The jury box was empty. Tom was seated at the end of the defense table in his uniform.

In time the bailiff entered the courtroom from the judge's chambers and called out, "All rise!"

A large, beefy, big-shouldered man, with a shock of white hair, entered. Under his black robe he wore a dress uniform. He was carrying a leather portfolio in one hand and a Pepsi in the other. He looked dyspeptic. Claire was sure he was scowling. Leisurely, he made his way to the bench and flicked a finger against the microphone. Satisfied by the amplified thump, he spoke in a gruff and gravelly voice: "This Article 39(a) session is called to order. Be seated."

When the defense and prosecution lawyers had sat down, he said, "I'm Judge Farrell." He put on a pair of black-rimmed half-glasses and consulted some papers on his podium. He ran through a few minutes of preliminaries.

Claire's heart sank. She'd heard voices like this in Charlestown, in all-white neighborhoods of Boston—self-assured, bigoted, thuggish, clannish. For all she knew he would turn out to be a fair man of judicial temperament, but her instinct told her he was a schoolyard bully.

He spoke as if he was already fed up with the trial, even before it had begun, even before the arraignment. "Now, as you all know, the purpose of this pretrial session is to address a complaint lodged by defense counsel regarding alleged bugs or transmitters or whatnot allegedly found on her premises, within her office." Warren Farrell's luxuriant thatch of white hair contrasted with his ruddy face, which was spiderwebbed with the broken veins of a serious drinker. He was a former Golden Gloves boxer, Grimes had said, which would account for his broken-looking nose. Farrell had attended night law school.

"Defense counsel," he growled, "you have somethin to say?"

Claire rose. "Your Honor, I'm Claire Heller Chapman. I'm the lead defense counsel." She held up a Ziploc plastic evidence bag, clearly marked "FBI" and "EVIDENCE," containing one of the tiny black transmitters. Very buglike indeed, with its slender black body and long filament tail. The FBI had reluctantly loaned it to her, after great pressure from Ray Devereaux.

"Your Honor," she went on, "I've received technical assistance from the FBI, which is investigating this matter right now, and which confirms that my office has been bugged by parties unknown." She spoke guardedly for the record, careful not to overstep. "I have reason to believe the government is involved. I would like to move for appropriate relief for disclosure of all intercepted conversations collected from my office. I would respectfully request that you direct the government to disclose any and all information regarding wiretaps, overhears, et cetera, and disclose copies of any and all transcripts or tapes made."

"Trial counsel?" the judge said wearily.

Waldron vaulted to his feet. "Your Honor, we find these allegations outrageous and clearly intended to prejudice Your Honor against the government. There is no evidence whatsoever that we had anything to do with such an egregious penetration of attorney-client privilege, and, frankly, we resent the accusation."

Waldron spoke so heatedly, with such righteous indignation, that for a moment Claire actually believed him. Certainly it was possible he knew nothing about the whole sordid business. If Grimes was right that information illegally obtained could be laundered through independent sources, wouldn't they—whoever "they" were—want to keep Waldron in the dark about where the juicy stuff came from?

"You're tellin me you had nothing to do with

this," Farrell said, fixing Waldron with a beady-eyed glare.

"Your Honor, not only did we have nothing whatsoever to do with this," Waldron replied in high dudgeon, "but I am personally outraged that—"

"Yeah, yeah," Farrell said, interrupting Waldron's tirade as if he were already tired of him, too. "All right, look, I'm going to make this short and sweet. Trial counsel, I'm going to issue an order for the government to show cause that defense counsel's allegations are untrue, and that the government has had no responsibility for these bugs. Now, in the event that the prosecution has had any involvement in this, I'm requiring you to produce forthwith copies of all transcripts or tapes of conversations intercepted, and to show cause why your conduct is not in violation of the law. And on a personal note, I wanna tell you that, if I find the slightest evidence of any monkey business on *either* side, there's goin to be hell to pay." He slammed down his gavel. "That's all."

Waldron passed by the defense table on his way out of the courtroom, and before he had a chance to say anything, Claire looked up at his thin-lipped face. "You should know I'm going to move to dismiss for outrageous government conduct," she told him. "You just blew it, Major. Violating attorney-client privilege is a mammoth violation of due process." She pursed her lips in disgust. "That was really pathetic. Amateur hour."

Waldron stared back with his lucid blue-gray eyes. "I hope you don't seriously think we even *need* to bug your offices." He shook his head and gave one of his feral smiles. "You really have no idea, do you?"

29

❖

The man whose first name and phone number Tom had scrawled on a scrap of paper in the brig met Claire at a yuppie bar in Georgetown—his choice, although as soon as he arrived he announced he hated it. Too many antiquarian Italian advertising posters, too many twenty-somethings smoking cigars. But neither one of them made a move to go someplace else.

He was short and trim, athletic-looking, about fifty. He was also entirely bald, shiny-bald, as if he waxed his head, which Claire had heard some men did. Upon closer examination she saw he shaved the hair at the sides of his head, probably daily. He had heavy dark eyebrows and would have looked sinister were it not for his morose demeanor. He made Claire ill-at-ease.

"I'm Dennis," he said without offering his hand. She did not expect a Dennis; a Dennis did not have a bullet head.

"Claire," she said, and didn't offer hers. For several evenings in a row she'd called the phone number Tom had written down for her, but it never answered. It was the man's home phone number, and he had neither an answering machine nor voice mail. It just rang and rang, until last night he'd finally answered.

"Who knows you're here?" Dennis asked. He wore a decent gray suit and an expensive-looking white shirt with a silvery tie and large gold cuff links.

"Why? Are you going to kill me?"

He wasn't amused. "You tell any of your cocounsel, any of the military guys?"

"No." She planned to tell Grimes later, but saw no need to get into that now.

"You don't have a tape recorder on you, I assume."

"No, I do not."

"I'll take you at your word. I could get into a fair amount of difficulty, so, please, no records of our meetings, don't tell anyone. You know the drill."

She nodded. "Do you have a last name, Dennis?"

"Let's leave it at that for now."

"How do you know Ronald Kubik?"

"I know him."

"Vietnam?"

"Rather not get into it."

"Do you mind if I smoke?"

"I'd rather you didn't." He flashed a genial smile, although his eyes did not participate.

"Well," she said. "I'm glad all *that's* cleared up. Where do you work?"

"Langley," he said, his face a blank.

"Ah, the Agency. I might have guessed. I don't imagine you want to tell me which division you're in at the Agency."

He shrugged and smiled. It just missed being a charming, boyish smile. "Can we get down to business?" His gray suit was wrinkled at the armpits, as if he'd been in it all day. This was not a man who worked in shirtsleeves. She guessed he was a fairly senior-ranking official at the CIA. "I assume you don't know much about how the military works," he said.

"I'm learning."

He smiled again. "Like what you see?"

"I'm not planning on enlisting, if that's what you mean."

"Well, when a combat unit comes back to base after field action, it's standard for the CO, the commanding officer, to file an incident report. In the army it's called an After Action Report. So tell me something: I'm sure you guys have filed discovery and all that—did you get a copy of the After Action Report that Colonel Marks filed after the La Colina atrocity?"

"No. We've gotten boxes and boxes of papers, but that's not in there."

"And it won't be. It doesn't exist. I was just curious as to whether they faked something up. The point is this: when Detachment 27 returned to their hooch, Colonel Marks—now General Marks—filed what's called an MFR. That's a memorandum for the record. To tell his side of the story, his version of what happened. Three or four lines, handwritten. See, Marks is the sort of guy puts 'take a dump' on a list, okay? He maps out everything. There's a saying in the army—MFR equals CYA. You know the expression CYA?"

"Yeah, we even cover our asses at Harvard Law School."

He didn't smile. "You want to get that MFR."

"How?"

"Specify it in your discovery request."

"You think we'll get it?"

"Hard to say. Pentagon's good at 'misplacing' things. Congress tried to get the Pentagon's files on Guatemala, took 'em five *years*. Pentagon said they'd misplaced them."

"Right. So we're not going to get the MFR. What good's it going to do us, anyhow? It's just going to give the same old bullshit line about Tom—er, Ron—massacring a bunch of innocent people."

"Maybe."

Claire's scotch-and-soda was just arriving, but Dennis was already slipping his olive trench coat back on.

"You must have a copy somewhere," Claire said.

He flashed another orthodontically perfect smile. "Well, as a matter of fact, we might. But you wouldn't believe what a mess our records are in. I could have one of my girls look. I'll let you know if she turns anything up."

"And what's it going to prove?"

"It may or may not prove Marks is a liar. Look, no one's going to testify against General Marks. But now maybe you won't need that."

Jackie was still up when Claire returned. They went into the small "rec room" off the laundry room for scotch and cigarettes. So much for her no-smoking-in-the-house rule. Civilization was crumbling.

"Ooh, spy stuff," Jackie said. "Cool. This guy sounds like what's-his-name, G. Gordon Liddy. You know, the Watergate guy who used to hold his finger over a lit candle to show how macho he was?"

"I think all bald spooks want to be G. Gordon Liddy."

"Why's he helping you?"

"That's the big question. I guess it's because he's a friend of Tom's."

"From where?"

"He wouldn't say."

"You think he's telling you the truth?"

"We'll see if he produces anything."

"But it makes you all the more sure Tom's telling you the truth."

"There's something about Tom's intensity that tells me that. Independently. It's the sound of truth spoken by a desperate guy. And he hasn't lost his faith. You know, last time I visited him at the brig he told me he wanted to go to Mass, but they wouldn't let him leave his cell. So they brought the chaplain to him."

"Home delivery. Can't beat it. You gonna put him on the stand?"

"I don't know," Claire said with heavy irony. "Plastic surgery, name change, false identity—I'm sure he'd make a great witness."

"Oh, right."

"Not just that. Fact is, I think he'd do well on the stand. I *know* he would. But if we put him on, all sorts of background stuff, bio stuff, becomes admissible. Stuff they cooked up, though we can't prove it. What he did in Vietnam, was he a sort of government assassin who killed American deserters. Did he do sicko stuff to dogs."

"Dogs?"

Claire lighted another cigarette. "Funny, isn't it, how we're more revolted by killing dogs than human beings?

"I figure U.S. soldiers in Vietnam were up to no good. Dogs are innocent." She exhaled a plume of smoke through her nostrils. "Your secretary from

Cambridge called. Connie. There's a long list of people who want to hire you."

"She told them no, I assume."

Jackie nodded. "The *Post* called again. I think they're really getting pissed off you won't talk to them."

"I don't have to talk to a newspaper reporter."

"They think they have a moral, God-given right to talk to you."

A long silence passed.

"Claire," Jackie said at last.

"Yeah?"

"If there's a chance—even the remotest chance— that he's guilty, that he's the monster the prosecution says he is, do you really want him around Annie?"

"If he were guilty, of course not."

"That's good to hear," Jackie said darkly. "Because for the last few weeks I've been under the impression that you're a wife first and a mom second. Like, *way* second. Look at Annie, how's she's reacting. Look how you've been ignoring her."

Claire looked at Jackie, saw the fury in her face. She'd never seen her sister so angry before. Then again, Jackie was fiercely protective of her niece. "I'm doing the best I can," Claire said in a subdued tone. "I'm working night and day—"

"Oh, come on," Jackie said brusquely. "You used to dote on her. Before all this happened. Now you barely talk to her. Jesus fucking Christ, Claire, you're the only parent that girl has! She needs you really badly. More than your husband does. Your husband can get another lawyer. Annie can't get another mommy."

Claire stared in dull shock, unable to reply.

*   *   *

As she lay in bed for hours, Claire's mind raced, in a disorganized, useless way. She cried for Annie, for the way she'd neglected her daughter. She didn't get to sleep until well after two.

At three-thirty-seven in the morning the phone rang.

She jolted awake, fumbled for the phone, heart hammering. "Yes?" She stared at the red digital numbers on the bedside clock.

Complete dead silence on the phone. She was about to hang it up when a voice came on.

An odd, metallic voice, metallic and hollow. Synthesized. "You should ask yourself who really wants him put away."

The voice was low-pitched and electronically altered.

"Who is this?" Claire demanded.

"Waldron's only the point man," the voice said. Then dead, flat silence.

"Who is this?" Claire repeated.

And the call was disconnected.

She was unable to go back to sleep for more than an hour.

30

In his baby-blue prison jumpsuit and manacles, Tom looked peculiarly vulnerable. His chasers, the two beefy brig guards, stood by, warily watching him examine a machine gun. They stood in a large empty room off one of the armories at Quantico.

The weapon, an M-60, was forty-four inches long and was sealed in a long plastic bag and tagged as evidence. Allegedly it was Tom's gun, the one he'd used while serving with Detachment 27, the one he'd allegedly used to slaughter eighty-seven civilians. To Claire it was just a machine gun; she'd never seen one up close before.

She and Grimes waited in a couple of metal chairs in the armory while he turned it over and scrutinized it.

"Do you know," Grimes said, "they call Quantico Camp Sleepy Hollow?"

"Why's that?" Claire said without bothering to feign interest.

"Since it's so quiet and wooded."

"And so peaceful," Claire said mordantly. "I want Embry back."

"What?"

"You hear me. I want Embry back on the team."

"What makes you think he'll come back?"

"Because they've probably got him doing drug busts and drunk-driving stuff. He'll jump at the chance."

"He quit, don't forget. We didn't fire him."

"We shamed him into quitting. We also wronged him. We accused him of leaking, when now we know they had the office bugged. We need him. We need an insider, you said so yourself. We need someone to interview and develop witnesses, do all the scut work that you and I don't have time for."

"Hey, you don't have to convince me. Talk to him. I sure as hell won't." In a louder voice he called out to Tom: "That look familiar?"

"What can I say?" Tom said. "I mean, how do I know it's mine? Seriously. I mean, it's an M-60. We used M-60s."

"Obviously we'll have our independent examiner look at it, and the bullets and shell casings," Claire said. "I don't trust them."

"I wonder why," Grimes said. "There's a serial number on there. Stamped on the receiver. Look familiar?"

"Grimes," Tom said, "you don't really think I can remember the gun's serial number after all these years?"

"Just trying to help. I thought you covert-action boys file down the serial numbers so they never get identified in case they're found."

"Old wives' tale," Tom said. "We were part of the army—we need serial numbers just like everyone else to keep track of weapons. We were just fancy about it. We used sterile weapons—new guns purchased by the Panamanian or Honduran governments, so there's no chain of custody."

"Shouldn't it be a simple matter to figure out whether this was the gun used to kill all those people?" Claire asked.

"Sure," Grimes replied. "Run the ballistics, compare the shell casings and the bullets to the barrel of the machine gun, see if you got a match."

"And if there's a match?" Claire asked. "How can they prove Tom fired it?"

"If there's a match," Tom said wearily, "then it wasn't my gun." All of a sudden he sounded defeated.

"But were there records of who got which gun?"

He shrugged, studied the floor. "Yeah," he said slowly. "Each one of us was issued one machine gun, one rifle, one pistol. We used the same one every time. You had to sign it out."

"So there's records," Claire said.

"Armory records," Grimes said.

"But we don't have them."

"Haven't come in yet. Maybe they don't have them either."

"If it's exculpatory," she said, "I bet they 'lose' them. Without the armory records, they don't have a case."

"It may be my weapon," Tom said, even more slowly, covering his eyes with a hand, "but if it is . . . it wasn't the one that fired the rounds. And if it's the one that fired the rounds . . ." He made a sudden hiccuping sound. "Claire?"

She looked at him sharply. It was a sob, which he'd tried to stifle. He was weeping. The suddenness of it frightened her.

He lurched forward toward her. His chasers vaulted forward and grabbed him, threw him down on the floor. There was a loud crack: his skull hitting the floor. The guards seemed to take some satisfaction in it. He howled in pain.

"Jesus," Grimes said.

"What are you doing?" Claire shouted.

"She's my wife, for Christ's sake!" Tom said. "I don't have the right to touch her?" The guards were silent.

"Claire, I want to talk to you! Alone!"

"We can't allow that, ma'am," one of them said.

"This is a legal visit," she said. "We have the right to talk without you present."

They moved Tom to the defense shop and waited outside one of the empty offices with Grimes while Claire and Tom talked.

By now Tom seemed to have regained his composure. "I'm sorry about that. It's just that it's sinking in."

"What is?"

"What's happening to me. *United States* v. *Ronald Kubik*. I think maybe I was in a state of denial. But this is real. This is happening. They're never going to let me go. I realize that now. This is real."

"I know what you're feeling," she said softly. Her chest felt tight. She wanted to cry on his shoulder but knew she mustn't lose it; he needed to see strength and confidence, whether she felt it or not. "It's a nightmare, a nightmare for all of us. But you've got to keep the faith. Grimes and I are doing all we can. We're not going to let them get away with anything. I promise you."

"Embry," she said when he answered the phone. "Terry."

"Ms.—Claire. Hi." He seemed glad to hear her voice. "How's it going?"

"Same old same old," she said. "We need you back."

A long, long pause. "You figured out I wasn't the leak."

"I never thought you were."

"Does Grimes want me back? Or is it just you?"

"Yes, he does too. Definitely."

"But aren't you guys always going to be suspicious? I mean, don't you want me to take the polygraph?"

"How do we know you weren't trained to beat it?" she said with a laugh.

31

❖

Waldron was waiting not far from Claire, Grimes, and Embry in front of the secure-courtroom door at fifteen minutes before nine in the morning. When Claire arrived he pounced.

"Ms. Chapman."

"Major," she said blandly.

"Are you ready to deal?"

Claire tried to conceal her astonishment. "Hadn't given it a thought."

"I wish I could believe that. I've been instructed to make you an offer. Personally, I oppose any kind of deal—I think you know that. I'm prepared to go for the death penalty, and I'm highly confident we can get it, in the current climate. But I've been asked to make an offer."

"We're listening."

Embry and Grimes gathered around.

"We're willing to drop to voluntary manslaughter—Article 119."

"How many specifications?" Grimes demanded.

"One," Waldron said. Grimes raised his brows. "Not eighty-seven. Same course of conduct."

"Voluntary manslaughter's fifteen years," Embry put in.

"Here's the crux of the deal," Waldron said. "We'd insist on total nondisclosure. In writing, of course. If the government of El Salvador gets wind of this, there'll be a major international incident. Sergeant Kubik will speak of the circumstances to no one, including the terms of this agreement and everything connected with these negotiations. No books, magazine articles, letters to the editor. No publicity whatsoever. No private conversations to anyone about the incident either."

Embry and Grimes nodded. Claire simply watched Waldron, blank-faced.

"All attorneys and support and investigative personnel would also be required to sign nondisclosure agreements," Waldron continued. "You also waive appellate review. Kubik gets dishonorable discharge, forfeiture of all pays and allowances."

"What about time?" Grimes said.

"He serves five years," Waldron said. "But all confinement in excess of five years will be suspended for fifteen years from the date of trial. His nondisclosure will be part of the good-conduct clause. He violates nondisclosure, we vacate the agreement, and he's back in Leavenworth."

Grimes turned to Claire.

Waldron said grimly, "Not bad, huh? Five years for killing eighty-seven people? You'll never beat a deal like this."

"Why are you suddenly so interested in making a deal?" Claire asked.

"Because this is a long and arduous and expensive process, and we think it's best for all concerned to come to a settlement now."

"When do you want to know?"

"Now."

"Now? You're crazy. I'll have to talk to my husband."

"He'll be here in a minute or two. I should warn you, the deal's off the table once he's arraigned."

"We've got three weeks before trial," Claire said. "What's the rush?"

"Just let me know your decision before arraignment. Which is in about five minutes."

When Claire told Tom the deal, as his restraints were being removed inside the courtroom, he shook his head.

"Why not?" Claire said. "The nondisclosure's no big deal—you've kept mum about it for thirteen years! And five years at Leavenworth—well, I won't minimize how tough any prison time is, but that looks awfully attractive, given the alternative."

"Claire, I'm an innocent man," Tom said. "I'm not doing five years for a crime I didn't commit. Anyway, I wouldn't survive Leavenworth. They'd have me killed. If they're offering to deal, that tells us they're scared. They're scared of what we might bring out at trial. Scared of what might become public. Don't you smell blood, too?"

"You're being awfully brave for a man who faces the possibility of execution. It's a gamble, Tom. A huge gamble."

"Everything I've done is a gamble," he said.

Grimes stared in disbelief and whispered to Tom, "Did I hear wrong, or did you just turn down Waldron's offer?"

"*I won't do time for a crime I didn't commit!*" Tom whispered back emphatically.

Grimes turned to Claire. "You didn't *make* him take it?"

"I can't make him take a deal," she whispered back.

"This man's gonna sue you later for ineffective assistance of counsel," he said, disgusted.

Claire approached the prosecution table and tapped Waldron on the shoulder. "We're passing," she said.

"Kubik heard the terms, and he's not jumping at this?" Waldron said. "You serious?"

"Drop the five years, and you've got a deal."

"Not negotiable."

"Then we're going to trial."

Waldron gave a gladiatorial smile. "You'll wish you'd taken it."

"Maybe so."

"Believe me. You don't know what's in store."

"Nor do you," she said.

PART FOUR

32

❖

"*All rise,*" the bailiff called out.

Judge Farrell, wearing a black robe over his dress greens, entered the courtroom and mounted the bench. He sat in his high-backed leather chair. In his rumbling voice he spoke into the microphone. "Please be seated. This Article 39(a) hearing is called to order."

Waldron remained standing. "This court-martial is convened by the secretary of the army, by convening order number 16-98," Waldron said. In military court-martials, the trial counsel also served as the court clerk. "*United States* versus *Sergeant First Class Ronald M. Kubik*. The accused is charged with violation of Article 85, desertion, and violation of Article 118, premeditated murder, eighty-seven specifications." And he continued reading a litany of preliminaries.

In front of the judge's bench sat the court reporter, the same middle-aged blond-haired woman who'd been at the last court session, at a small table, wearing headphones. The LED lights on the tape deck before her flashed, emerald-green lines jumping and sinking.

233

"All right, I am Colonel Warren Farrell, U.S. Army," the judge recited. "I've been detailed to this court-martial by the circuit military judge. I'm qualified in accordance with Article 26(a) of the Uniform Code of Military Justice. Would any counsel like to voir dire the military judge?" He referred to the seldom-used right to question, even to challenge, the judge's right to try the case.

Waldron stood. "No, Your Honor."

Claire stood next. "Yes, Your Honor. We would."

Grimes slapped his forehead with a large hand. The sound was audible as far as the prosecution table, where Captain Hogan regarded Grimes with a smirk. He'd tried to talk her out of this last night, but Claire was determined.

"All right, Ms. Chapman," Judge Farrell said in an attempt at bluff good humor.

"Your Honor," she asked, "do you know why you were assigned to this case?"

Farrell jutted his chin and regarded her with veiled eyes. He took a sip of his coffee. "I assume I was assigned because of my experience with national-security cases."

Claire considered this for a moment and decided to move on. "Can you please state for the record any conversations you've had with any member of the Office of the Judge Advocate General regarding this case."

Farrell's eyes flickered almost imperceptibly. But he remained game. "To the best of my recollection, counsel, I had one or two conversations that were purely administrative in nature."

"I see. And can you please state for the record any conversations you may have had with any member of the personal staffs of the secretary of the army or the chief of staff of the army." Here was the interesting question, and Claire wondered how honest he would be, whether he'd risk trying to cover his tracks.

But the judge was too clever. He took another sip of his coffee and glanced up at the low ceiling as if trying to recall a dim, distant memory. "Well, counsel, I can only recall one conversation I might have had that related to this case, with a member of the chief of staff's office a few days ago."

"Can you state for the record what you recall of that conversation?"

His eyes were dead. "Oh, we talked only generally about scheduling matters and such."

But why was someone from General Marks's office talking to the judge about scheduling matters? It made no sense.

"With whom did you talk, sir?"

"With Colonel Hernandez."

From behind her, she heard Grimes exclaim, "What?"

Straining not to show her astonishment, Claire asked, "Is Colonel Hernandez in your chain of command, Your Honor?"

"No, he's not." The judge's patience was visibly wearing thin.

"And, Your Honor, has Colonel Hernandez ever called you before about the scheduling of a case?"

Now he sounded dismissive. "I don't believe so, no."

"He's never had any other conversations with you regarding any other court-martial scheduling?"

"As I said, I don't recall any others."

"Now, Your Honor, could you be more specific about what precisely you talked about with Colonel Hernandez?"

But Judge Farrell had had enough. "Counsel, I'm

a busy man," he said flintily. "My days are scheduled to the minute. I have conversations with dozens of people every day about hundreds of things. Unfortunately, I'm not always able to recollect every word that was exchanged. Now, do you or trial counsel have challenge for cause against the military judge?"

Waldron stood. "We most certainly do *not* have a challenge, Your Honor."

"Your Honor, we need a brief recess to talk among counsel about whether we have a challenge," Claire said.

"This court is in recess for ten minutes," Judge Farrell said, and pounded his gavel.

Grimes reached out a hand and grabbed Claire's shoulder as she sat down. "I have one simple question for you. Are you out of your fucking mind, or have you just been smoking too much weed? You're not seriously going to challenge him for cause, are you? Because we don't *have* cause."

"No," she admitted. "He's stonewalling, unfortunately, and there's nothing there we can use."

"All right, he talked to Hernandez. Surprise, surprise. So is it just your intention to piss this asshole off?"

"Grimes, I want him to know we're watching him, and that he'd better be on his best behavior."

When court resumed, Claire said: "We have no challenge for cause at this time, Your Honor."

Judge Farrell seemed to be suppressing a smile. "All right, then, will the accused please rise."

Tom got slowly to his feet. He'd been briefed on what to say.

"Sergeant Kubik, by what form do you wish to be tried?"

Tom knew the answer. "A court-martial with officer members, sir." The members of the jury were selected by the convening authority. It was illegal to stack the court, though it was known to happen from time to time. Members were also supposed to be free to vote their conscience, without guidance from above, or "command influence." Generally, members were supposed to be senior in rank to the accused. If the accused was an enlisted man, not an officer, he had the right to request that at least a third of the jury members be enlisted; but Grimes had urged Tom to choose all officers, who tended to be more reliable, more trustworthy, and less likely to act rashly. Or so Grimes told him.

"By whom do you wish to be represented?" asked the judge.

"By Ms. Chapman, Mr. Grimes, and Captain Embry, sir."

"That request is approved. The accused will now be arraigned. Does the defense request the charges and specifications be read to the accused?"

"We waive a reading, Your Honor," Claire said.

"Sergeant First Class Kubik, I now ask you how do you plead, but before I ask you, I advise you that any motions to dismiss, or for other relief, must be made at this time."

"Your Honor, defense has a number of motions," Claire said.

There was a glint in the judge's eye. The motions weren't a surprise, since he'd demanded they get their motions in three days before the arraignment and present them in a hearing before the judge without the jury present. The whole procedure was a formality, a highly scripted ritual, a Kabuki dance. "Sergeant Kubik," he said, "you may be seated."

Tom returned to his seat in a crisp military maneuver. This was the only time he would ever be required to speak in court, and he was done.

And the Kabuki dance began. Claire presented and argued her motions, one after another, and Waldron stood to knock them down as best he could. There were quite a few motions. Move to dismiss the entire court-martial on the grounds of insufficient evidence. Motion *in limine* to exclude the record of Tom's service in Vietnam, which Tom continued to insist was cooked up, on grounds that it wasn't relevant to the charges.

And on and on and on. Judge Farrell scribbled furiously while Claire spoke, as she produced her appellate exhibits. And for several hours this went on.

Until at last Claire was finished, and Judge Farrell began, "Counsel, I've considered your motion to dismiss, as well as the testimony and evidence produced in support of the motion, and the evidence produced by the government, and it is denied. My findings of fact and conclusions of law will be appended to the record of trial, prior to authentication."

No surprise, but Claire stood to preserve the record. "Objection to your ruling, Your Honor."

"Your objection is overruled.

"Next, counsel, I've considered your motion for appropriate relief for admission of an expert witness to testify on an exculpatory polygraph, as well as the testimony of your expert witness, as well as the testimony produced by the government, and your motion is denied. My findings of fact and conclusions of law will be appended to the record of trial, prior to authentication."

This was a major loss, and Claire jumped up. "Objection to your ruling, Your Honor."

"Your objection is overruled."

And so it went. One after another.

Each motion, so artfully presented, so cogently argued—denied. Each time Claire popped up like a child's jack-in-the-box and preserved her objection for the record, but there it was. Denied. Overruled. Finally Judge Farrell said, with a glint of triumph, "Any further motions, counsel?"

Grimes shook his head, scowling. Tom stared straight ahead in numb disbelief. Embry looked distant, troubled.

"Yes, Your Honor," Claire said, getting wearily to her feet. "Defense once again challenges the closed nature of these proceedings. The accused, as we continue to maintain, has a right to a public trial, guaranteed to him in the First and Sixth Amendments, which we respectfully—"

"No," Judge Farrell snapped.

"Your Honor?"

"We've been through all that, so forget it."

"Your Honor, the defense respectfully maintains that such a trial—"

"Sit down. I said, forget it. I don't want to hear it again." The judge's ruddy face reddened further. "The government has already made a persuasive case that the accused's rights are not in fact compromised by holding this trial *in camera*. That there are valid national-security concerns. This is all covered under Military Rule of Evidence 505. I've made my rulings. Were you paying attention in court?"

From her seat at the defense table, Claire said: "Your Honor—"

"Let me tell you something, Ms. Chapman. Loud and clear. I don't want to hear it again. And if you bring this up in front of the panel, I'll hold you in contempt of court, you hear me?"

"Yes, sir," Claire said. Under her breath she muttered to Grimes, "I'm in contempt of this court most of the time."

"You say somethin?" Judge Farrell barked.

"No, sir."

"Good. Now, I'm dead serious about this. You raise this issue in front of the members—that's the jury, by the way, since you don't seem quite familiar with the rules of our court-martial system—you're gonna spend time in the Quantico brig yourself. And I don't know how these things work in *Cambridge*, Professor, but in these parts, warning is not mandatory. And you got no right of appeal. You hear me?"

Claire stood. "You can't enforce that. I'm a civilian, which means I'm not subject to your jurisdiction. And you certainly can't throw me in a military brig."

"You wanna try me?"

Claire and the judge stared at each other for several long seconds, and then Claire sat.

Grimes covered his eyes with his hand and sank down in his seat.

"Now," Judge Farrell said, "are you prepared to enter pleas on behalf of your client?"

"Yes, sir," Claire said with crisp disdain, rising. "We are."

"Accused, please rise." Tom got to his feet.

"Your Honor," Claire said, "through counsel, Sergeant First Class Ronald M. Kubik pleads, to all charges and specifications, not guilty."

"Very well. I understand your pleas, and you may be seated."

They sat. Claire clasped Tom's hand and gave it a firm squeeze. Tom gave a squeeze in reply. She whispered, "All right, we're done here."

"Some rough going, huh?" he whispered back.

"Worse than I expected. This judge just doesn't give a shit."

"Counsel," Judge Farrell called out, "are you prepared to conduct voir dire?"

"*What?*" Claire exclaimed.

"I said, are you ready to bring in the members?"

Claire turned to Grimes, who was as astonished as she was.

Tom blurted out, too loud: "The trial's not supposed to start for another three weeks!"

"Yes, sir," Waldron said, "we're ready."

Claire leaped to her feet. "No, Your Honor, we most certainly are not. It was our understanding that this trial was not to begin for another three weeks. This is a capital-murder trial, the charges are extremely serious in nature, and defense is not prepared to cross-examine witnesses. We're still in the midst of our investigation."

"What are you sayin, it was your 'understanding'?" Farrell shot back with narrowed eyes.

Grimes stood. "We were told that, informally, by the Staff Judge Advocate's Office, Your Honor." Claire had never before heard such anxiety, such timorousness, in his voice.

"Yeah, well, you may have that agreement with the Staff Judge Advocate's Office," Judge Farrell said, "but I'm the military judge, and I control the docket."

"Your Honor," Claire said, "we've just had a motion session this morning. We obviously couldn't prepare our case without knowing what your rulings would be on our evidence. Your rulings on the admissibility or nonadmissibility of certain evidence sculpt our case. There are certain witnesses we haven't had an opportunity to question at all. Other witnesses, we need more investigation to corroborate or contradict their testimony."

"Counsel," Judge Farrell said frostily, "you've had plenty of time to prepare."

It took all of her restraint not to lash out at the judge. "Your Honor, the defense has not been dilatory. We have planned our case based on the scheduling that was informally decided—that is, three weeks between arraignment and trial. I will say, too, that we've tried repeatedly to question the primary witness against my client, the chief of staff of the army, and he has repeatedly refused our requests. Therefore, we are absolutely not prepared to present our case today, and we are not prepared to question witnesses. We would in fact request a month in which to prepare for this trial."

"Your request is denied," Judge Farrell said flatly.

Waldron stood and said, "Your Honor, the Staff Judge Advocate has communicated to us that General William Marks has decided to make himself available to defense counsel for an interview."

Claire looked at Grimes. This was a thunderbolt. She got up. "In which case, Your Honor, we respectfully request two weeks to prepare for and conduct this interview before trial begins."

"Denied," Judge Farrell said.

"Your Honor," Grimes put in, "defense will accept the delay in speedy trial. The accused has been arraigned, so speedy trial is no longer a consideration. All that's at issue now is whether our client gets a fair trial, and he's not gonna *get* a fair trial if counsel's not prepared."

"Well, counsel," Judge Farrell said, "defense counsel *shoulda* been prepared, and if you're not, it's not this court's fault. This case is going to trial to-day."

Grimes sank into his chair, stunned. Tom turned to him wide-eyed, and whispered, "Is he serious?"

"This is a military court," Grimes muttered. "They got the right. Only in a military court."

"Son of a buck!" Embry whispered in disbelief.

"Your Honor," Claire said, still standing, "once again we object to proceeding today."

"Your objection is noted and overruled, counsel. Are you prepared for voir dire?"

"We are, Your Honor," Waldron called out.

"Your Honor," Claire said, "we've already made our position known on whether we are prepared. We are not. We are absolutely not prepared, because of assurances given us that this trial would not begin for another three weeks."

Farrell jabbed a stubby index finger at her. "I said, are you prepared for voir dire?"

"If you're going to force us to proceed," Claire said acidly, "we will conduct voir dire to the best of our ability."

"All right," Farrell said. "I will give you two hours to frame your questions for the members. As the lunch hour is almost upon us, this would be an appropriate time to take that break."

And he slammed down his gavel.

33

❖

"Is the government prepared to make an opening statement?" Judge Farrell asked.

Waldron stood. "Yes, sir."

This came after several hours of voir dire of the panel members. The jury. After several challenges for cause on both sides, and two peremptory challenges, it came down to two women and four men who would decide Tom's fate. The most senior member, a lieutenant colonel, became the president of the jury, equivalent to the foreman. He was a light-skinned black man with steel-rimmed aviator glasses. He sat in the center of the front row of the jury box, the next most senior to his right, the second most senior to his left, and so on. They were an unremarkable group, and they watched the proceedings with rapt attention. Each of them had top-secret clearance, and could be relied upon to maintain absolute secrecy.

Waldron started softly, his voice almost incantatory. Claire had expected a booming, stentorian beginning. Waldron, however, was too clever.

"On 22 June 1985, in the tiny village of La Colina, not far from San Salvador, eighty-seven people were awakened from their sleep and slaughtered like farm animals."

He had the jury members' complete attention. They wrote nothing: the judge had instructed them that opening statements weren't evidence and they shouldn't take notes. They watched Waldron slowly approach the jury box and stand still in front of them.

"These eighty-seven people were not soldiers. They were not combatants. They were not rebels. They had nothing to do with the battles then raging in the country. They were men, women, and children—innocent civilians.

"And these innocent civilians were massacred not by some warring faction, not by soldiers of the El Salvador government, or by rebels or guerrillas.

"They were slaughtered by one American soldier.

"You heard me right: by one American soldier.

"One.

"And not in the heat of battle. Not by accident. But for the thrill of it."

Claire looked at Grimes, who shook his head. Don't object as to motive, he was saying. Not now. Don't call attention to it. Not yet.

"How could this possibly have happened?" Waldron bowed his head as if in deep thought. He bit his upper lip. "Several hours earlier, a top-secret unit of the U.S. Army Special Forces, Detachment 27, was ordered to secure this village and determine whether the intelligence reports they had received were right—to see whether there were antigovernment rebels in hiding there.

"In fact, there were none. The intelligence, as often happens in wartime, was wrong."

He shrugged.

"And Detachment 27, under the able leadership of Colonel William Marks—now chief of staff of the army—made this determination. They prepared to return to their base at Ilopango.

"And then, suddenly, without warning, someone began to fire his weapon. A machine gun. An M-60. To fire this machine gun on the innocent villagers."

Claire turned to whisper to Tom and saw tears streaming down his face. She took his hand and squeezed it tight.

"You will hear from two members of the unit, Colonel James Hernandez, the executive officer, and Staff Sergeant Henry Abbott, who saw *this* man." Waldron turned slowly and walked to the defense table. He pointed directly at Tom. "Sergeant First Class Ronald M. Kubik. They saw him raise his machine gun and point it at the eighty-seven villagers, who were lined up in four rows, and begin mowing them down.

"They saw the villagers, who had no weapons, beg for mercy. They saw them scream.

"And they saw Sergeant First Class Kubik, while machine-gunning these eighty-seven civilians, smile."

Waldron turned back to the jury, a puzzled expression on his face. "He smiled."

Tom shook his head. He was still weeping silently. He whispered to Claire: "How can he lie like that?"

"The commanding officer, General William Marks, was unable, despite his best efforts, to stop this atrocity."

The panel members did not move. They watched in fascination. One of them had placed her index finger on her lips. The court reporter, a weary-looking middle-aged black woman with a floral shawl over her shoulders, softly ticked away at her machine.

"Two members of that unit will tell us about this horrible night. So will the commanding officer.

"But we will not stop with eyewitness testimony. We have hard evidence as well. We will present ballistic evidence: some of the bullets used to kill these civilians, and some of the shell casings ejected during this rampage. And we will demonstrate beyond any doubt that these bullets came from Sergeant First Class Kubik's own gun. There will be no doubt, no ambiguity, not a shred of uncertainty. We have eyewitnesses, and we have forensic evidence.

"Yet there's still more.

"After this nightmarish incident, members of Detachment 27 were recalled to Special Forces headquarters at Fort Bragg to be debriefed about what happened. Seven soldiers offered sworn statements. But what did Sergeant Kubik do? Sergeant Kubik was questioned at length but refused to give a sworn statement.

"And then he engineered an escape from custody.

"He escaped. He deserted the army.

"He fled across the country. He created a false identity using cleverly forged documents. He assumed a false name, even a false biography. And then he underwent extensive plastic surgery to drastically alter his appearance.

"Eventually Sergeant First Class Kubik, having assumed the name Thomas Chapman, moved to Boston, where he lived as a fugitive under a false name, with a new face. For thirteen years he had escaped his crime.

"Until a few weeks ago, when a lucky tip led us to him, and he was apprehended by federal marshals.

"This, ladies and gentlemen, is not the behavior of an innocent man. This is the behavior of a very clever, very calculating man who knew he was liable to be prosecuted for committing cold-blooded murder.

"We have rules, ladies and gentlemen. We have laws. Even in wartime—especially in wartime, some would argue—our conduct is governed by strict, honorable laws. And we do not slaughter innocent civilians for the demented pleasure of it. That way madness lies.

"The evidence you will hear in this trial will shock you and horrify you. All I ask is that it move you— to demonstrate that we Americans must never do such horrific things. And that you find Sergeant First Class Ronald Kubik guilty of murder in the first degree.

"Justice demands it."

Quietly, he returned to his table.

There was a long, shocked silence.

Judge Farrell cleared his throat. "Defense Counsel, do you have an opening statement, or do you wish to reserve?"

"I'm going to reserve, Your Honor."

"Very well. Then we will recess for the weekend. On Monday at oh-nine-thirty we will resume with the prosecution's case in chief."

Claire sank into her chair, drained.

34

Two grease-spattered cardboard pizza boxes sat on the library desk, empty Coke cans resting on top of them. It was late Friday night. Between Waldron's opening statement that morning, and the meeting with General Marks in the afternoon after court, it had been a long day. It had been barely a week since the Article 32 hearing, yet it felt like months.

Grimes and Embry sprawled in their usual chairs. Ray Devereaux was sweeping the room for bugs, going through the frequencies of an RF frequency-finder, which looked like a radio with a long antenna. Claire paced.

"What if we'd never brought it up with the general?" she said. "What if he'd never boasted he had immunity? When was the prosecution planning on telling us?"

Grimes and Embry said nothing.

"Aren't they required to notify the defense of any grant of immunity," she went on, "and serve us a copy of it before the arraignment?"

"Actually," Grimes said wearily, "it says 'Or within a reasonable time before the witness testifies,' something like that."

"Which means whenever the fuck they feel like it."

"Basically."

"It's clean," Devereaux announced. "You can talk freely."

"Bugs never stopped her before," Grimes said.

"I wonder if we should raise this issue with the judge," Claire said.

Embry shook his head slowly but said nothing.

"Claire," Grimes said, "let me tell you something. When you decided to voir dire the judge, when you went after him, you pissed him off royally. You questioned his integrity. Now I think it's time for you to cool it, lay off the guy. Stop pissing him off."

"I don't intend to stop pissing him off," she replied. "Here we are, we have no witnesses to corroborate Tom's account, and if we ask for a continuance, Farrell will laugh. The sworn statements from the other members of his unit are suspiciously identical—"

"You think they were coached?" Embry asked.

"They have to be."

"How can we ferret that out?"

"The only way," she said, "is from the witnesses. To try to get the unit members still living to repudiate the statements they made to CID thirteen years ago. So who do we have?"

Ray Devereaux spoke up. "The two Waldron mentioned as being the ones who saw Tom fire his machine gun are Hernandez and a guy named Henry Abbott. Hernandez you've already talked to."

"He's the general's boy," Grimes said. "He'll never back down. Though I may be able to trap him, corner him, if I'm lucky. Who's Abbott?"

"Staff Sergeant Henry Abbott left the army in

1985. Went into the private sector. Defense-contractor work, specifically."

"Why am I not surprised?" Grimes said.

"He's in 'government liaison' at one of those big scary defense corporations. That means he sells to the Pentagon. So somehow I don't think he's going to turn state's evidence for you. The Pentagon's got him by the proverbial short hairs."

"He's on the prosecution's witness list," Embry said. "But we don't know when he's being called."

"He's in Washington," Devereaux said, always the master of timing. "At the Madison Hotel."

"Let's see him," Claire said.

"I've set up a breakfast for you guys," Devereaux said. "Tomorrow morning at seven."

"What?" Claire said. "Thanks for telling us—"

"Seven?" Grimes moaned.

"I just set it up," Devereaux said. He turned to Grimes. "He's an early riser."

"Or he's just busting our balls," Grimes said. "Who does that leave us?"

"Two others," Devereaux said. "Robert Lentini and Mark Fahey. Fahey I finally located. He's in real estate in Pepper Pike, Ohio. Wherever the hell that is. I talked to him. He might be worth talking to— it's hard to say. He seems sort of embittered about his army experience. Not exactly gung-ho."

"Our kind of guy," Claire said.

"Then there's Lentini," Devereaux went on. "The mystery man. All I can turn up is his enlistment photo, which I put in a request for; they ought to dig it up in a few days, but it's not going to do us any good. After that, nothing. No files on him. No record of where he ended up. I checked the U.S. Army Reserve Personnel Center in St. Louis, which keeps the records of all personnel who've left the army. And the U.S. Total Army Command, in Virginia, where they keep the active army files. Zippo. And there's no record of his death anywhere.''

"That's impossible," Claire said. "If he's alive, he's either in the army or out of it. Can't be neither. Make sure there isn't some dumb glitch, like a wrong middle initial or a spelling error or something.''

Devereaux glared at her. "Do I *look* like an idiot?''

"Don't answer that," Grimes said.

"All right," Claire said. "Ray, I need whatever you got on Abbott, right now. You guys can stay up if you like, but it's almost two A.M., and I've got to get some sleep if I'm going to be coherent with Abbott tomorrow morning.''

35

There was the light tap of a car horn, and Claire opened her front door. Grimes's rusty silver Mercedes was sitting in her driveway. Saturday morning at six-thirty, and Thirty-fourth Street was deserted. The early-morning sunlight was pastel. A bird trilled musically, regular as a metronome. Her head ached and thudded at the temples. The daylight pierced her eyes.

"Rise and shine," Grimes said, sardonic.

"I read over the Abbott stuff until almost four. I need coffee."

"We'll grab some on the way."

In the lobby of the Madison Hotel they were joined by Ray Devereaux. He handed Claire a small Motorola cellular phone, spoke for a few minutes, and returned to the street.

They met Henry Abbott in the Madison restaurant. He was tanned and prosperous-looking, handsome in a vaguely sinister way. His silver hair was combed straight back from his square forehead. He wore gold wire-rim glasses. He was dressed in a gray suit, white shirt, elegant blue foulard tie.

He looked at his watch, a slim gold Patek Philippe, as they joined him at the small table. "You've got twenty minutes," he said.

Grimes rolled his eyes but said nothing.

"Good morning to you, too," Claire said, setting down her cell phone on the table in front of her. Caffeine and a fresh application of lipstick had made her feel marginally human. She introduced herself and Grimes.

"I have nothing to say to you," he said. "No law says I have to talk to military investigators."

"Then why'd you agree to meet us?" Claire asked.

"Curiosity. I wanted to see what you look like. I've read about you."

"Well, now you know," she said.

"She normally looks better," Grimes apologized, "but she's operating on less than three hours' sleep."

"We've got a couple of questions for you," she said.

"Why the fuck should I talk to you? I've got a reputation to protect."

I'll bet, Claire thought. "Your CID statement is quite specific," she said. "I'm sure they've provided you with a copy to refresh your memory."

"I didn't see what Kubik is supposed to have done anyway."

"That's not what your sworn statement says," Grimes put in.

"Yeah, well," Abbott said, and took a sip of coffee. A waiter came by and poured coffee all around. Claire took a grateful sip. The caffeine had an immediate effect, accelerating her heartbeat, causing prickles of sweat to break out at her temples.

"We know the real story," she said. "All your statements are exactly the same, all you guys in Detachment 27. Which is too cute by half. As this case goes on, you run the risk of being locked into your statement, the one that was coerced out of you thirteen years ago. You don't want that."

"Are you tape-recording this?" Abbott asked.

"No, I'm not," she said.

He dabbed at his mouth with a white linen napkin. "If, theoretically, I were to change my story, they'd charge me with lying under oath to the CID."

So that was it. "They can't," she said. "You have no criminal liability in the military anymore, now that you're discharged."

"Says who?"

"The Supreme Court," Grimes said. "Decades ago. You want to be the first guy who comes clean. You don't want to be the last guy holding out, telling the lie."

"And if I don't?" He was exploring his options now, looking for wiggle room.

"Simple," Claire said. "If you perjure yourself, you can be tried in federal district court for perjury. Under 18 U.S.C., you can get five years in prison. And when you get out, say goodbye to all those lucrative government contracts. They dry up right away."

"Look," Abbott said, exasperated. "You want a witness, I'm not your guy. I didn't see him shoot— I was on the other side of that fucking shit-hole village manning the radio."

"Yet you testified you saw him shoot."

"Are you really that fucking naïve, or are you just pretending to be?" he snapped.

"What's that supposed to mean?" she asked.

"Are we off the record here?"

"If you insist."

"Well, I do insist. This is off the record. Don't tell me you don't know how the system works. The sys-

tem works in favor of guys like Colonel Marks—
excuse me, *General* fucking Marks. The system wants
somebody to blame it on. Right after we got back to
Fort Bragg, Marks called each of us in, before our
interviews with CID, and says, 'I'm preparing my
statement and I want to make sure I have my facts
straight. What is your recollection of what happened?' And I say, you know, 'I don't recall one way
or the other, sir.' I was a good soldier. I knew what
to say. But he wanted more than that. He says,
'Didn't you see Kubik suddenly raise his weapon
and begin to shoot?' I say, 'No, sir, I didn't.' I mean,
this was night, and I was like two hundred yards
away. I saw someone fire. How the hell do I know
who it was? He says, 'Are you sure you didn't see
Kubik suddenly go crazy and start firing? Be sure
about this, Sergeant. This'll make or break your career. Kubik has violent tendencies. If you search
your memory, I'm sure you'll recall Kubik suddenly
taking out his weapon and firing.' Well, I wasn't
born yesterday, and I say, 'Yes, sir, of course, that
was it. That's what he did, sir, you're absolutely correct, sir.' And that's all it takes."

Claire nodded as if he were simply confirming
something she already knew.

"And let me tell you, I'll deny all this on the stand.
I've got to deal with the Pentagon every day. They
buy billions of dollars of equipment from my company. And they don't like snitches and turncoats. I
got a meeting." He stood up. "Was all that true, in
the *Post*?"

"I didn't see the *Post* yet this morning," Grimes
said. "What are you talking about?"

"You," Abbott said to Claire. "You really do that?
You probably don't want to talk about it, do you?"

"Shit," she said. "The *Post* found out why I'm in Washington, didn't they?"

He looked puzzled. "You read it, didn't you?" He popped open his metal briefcase, reached in, and pulled out a neatly folded copy of the *Washington Post*, which he dropped on the table in front of her.

She saw her photograph, small and below the fold, and the headline—A HARVARD PROFESSOR'S TAINTED PAST—and she felt the blood rush to her head.

36

❖

Claire smoked.
Annie danced around the kitchen table, chanting: "What? What? What?"

Jackie told her, "Give us some privacy, babe."

Claire stubbed out her cigarette. She pulled another from the pack, offered it to Jackie, was surprised when Jackie shook her head.

Annie grabbed on to Claire's skirt. "What are you reading? Tell me. Tell me."

Claire was too numb to talk.

Annie needed the reassurance of Mommy's attention. Mommy, however, was a thousand miles away, and almost two decades.

Mommy was twenty-three now. A One-L at Yale Law School. Probably one of the smartest students in her class, but she didn't actually feel like it. Most of the time she felt like crying, and very often she did. Most of the spring semester she'd been flying back and forth between Pittsburgh and La Guardia. Renting cars at the Pittsburgh airport and driving to Franklin. Taking buses from La Guardia to New Haven. Sitting by her mother's hospital bed and watching her succumb to liver cancer.

There were a dozen excuses. She was barely in New Haven that semester, the second term of her first year. She was distracted. She should have taken a leave but didn't. She was frightened. Even for a full-time student, law school was a challenge, and she barely saw the inside of the law library.

She meant to use the obscure law-review article only for inspiration. She had no interest, really, in civil procedures. The draft she handed in she'd meant to rework extensively, but she had a plane to catch. She'd just gotten the phone call from the attending telling her that her mother had just died. Anyone else would have taken a leave of absence, but she wanted to maintain a semblance of normalcy.

It was a bad break, really. A lousy coincidence.

Her professor was quite familiar with the obscure law-review article she'd all but rewritten under her name. The law-review article had been written by a former student of his, who'd proudly sent a signed reprint of it to his old professor.

A bad break.

He called her into his office and confronted her. Not for a moment did she try to deny it or make excuses. He was an acerb and bitter man, not inclined to grant clemency.

Plagiarism, pure and simple. The dean was more understanding than the professor. She'd been under stress. Her mother was dying. She should have requested a leave. At least she should have requested an extension. She'd been irresponsible, not criminal.

The charge was buried. She was given the chance to resubmit the paper. Only the understanding dean, and the aggrieved professor (whose later nomination to the Supreme Court was acrimoniously rejected), would ever know.

In the background the phone rang repeatedly, but no one rose from the kitchen table to answer it. Claire reread the article for the hundredth time. Substantially it was accurate. Here and there a detail was off, but it was a good job of reporting. The *Post* reporter could even say, truthfully, that repeated calls to Ms. Chapman's home were not returned.

The headline burned her insides like a red-hot poker.

A HARVARD PROFESSOR'S TAINTED PAST
*Celebrated Lawyer Plagiarized
While a Student at Yale Law School*

Annie clung to the hem of her skirt as if afraid her mother would leave her.

"What happens to you now?" Jackie said.

"I don't know," she said thickly. "I may lose my position at the Law School. I'm pretty sure that's what happens."

"But you have tenure."

"Tenure doesn't cover this sort of thing."

"There were mitigating circumstances."

"I could make the argument. Harvard might even listen. But more likely they'll quietly ask me to leave the faculty. I know how they work."

"The general warned you," Jackie said ruefully. " 'You have a career to be concerned about,' he said. 'You don't want to ruin it.' "

"Yeah," Claire agreed. "He warned me. But a threat like that wasn't going to stop me."

Finally Claire and Jackie began to take turns answering the phone. At least two dozen reporters, wire-service, newspaper, radio, and television, called to follow up on the *Post* story. To all of them she either refused to comment or declined to come to the phone. A few friends from Cambridge called, wonderfully full of understanding; loyal friends. Abe Margolis, her Law School colleague, called, and though he wasn't exactly the touchy-feely type, he too expressed his anger at the intrusion by the *Post* into a part of her personal life that was no one's business, and he talked strategy. He said he'd talk to the dean of the Law School. He thought this thing could be beat.

Claire was less sanguine.

Work had to go on.

Grimes and Embry interviewed witnesses, took depositions, pored over transcripts. Late that afternoon they all gathered in her library for a conference call with Mark Fahey of Pepper Pike, Ohio. Former Special Forces, now a realtor. Stranger things had happened.

"I heard Kubik slaughtered them all," came Fahey's resonant baritone over the speaker phone.

"But you didn't see it," Claire said.

"No. But everyone was talking about it afterward. They were really spooked."

"You gave a statement to the CID," Grimes said. "It said something totally different."

"Yeah, it was bullshit," Fahey said. "Canned. A total put-up job."

Grimes nodded, smiled.

"How so?" Claire asked.

Fahey's voice rose, both in pitch and in volume. "They fuckin wrote it out for me and told me to sign it."

"The CID agent."

"Fuckin-A right."

"Did Colonel Marks prep you for the interview?"

"He prepped everyone. Called us in before our

interviews, said, 'Now, let me get my facts straight here.' "

"Why was he so concerned with having everyone pin it on Kubik?" Embry asked.

"He was covering his ass."

"You mean Kubik didn't do it?" Claire asked. She felt herself holding her breath, waiting for his response.

"I told you, I didn't see the massacre. But everyone said the Six gave the order."

"The Six?" Claire asked.

"The colonel—O-6. He ordered Kubik to do it. And Kubik, fucking wacko that he was, mowed 'em down happily."

"But Marks wasn't there," Grimes said.

"He gave the order over the field radio. He said, You got 'em rounded up? And Hernandez, the XO, he goes, Yeah, we got 'em. And he says, Wax 'em. And Hernandez goes, But, sir—and Marks says, Wax 'em. And wacko Kubik does it happily. Knowing they're all innocent."

"So you were told," Claire corrected. "You didn't see that."

"Right. But those guys had no reason to lie to me."

"But isn't it possible," Claire persisted, "that the cover-up was already beginning by then? That a number of the men had carried out the murders and they were already planning to blame it on Kubik?"

After a long silence came Fahey's voice: "Anything's possible, I guess."

"If you're asked to testify," Claire said, "you can't talk about what you *heard* about Kubik. Or, for that matter, what you heard about Marks. That's all hearsay, and it's not admissible. But you can testify about how Marks called you in to prep you for your CID interview, and about how the CID wrote it out for you."

There was a short laugh. "What makes you think I'm going to testify?"

Grimes asked, "Did anyone come talk to you about testifying?"

"Yeah, some guys from Army CID came to see me, ask me to take the stand. I told them what I told you. Told them I'm not going to lie to cover Marks's ass. I don't care if he's the fucking President of the United States. So they said they were going to use my sworn statement from 1985, and I'd better come in and testify the same way."

"Or?" Claire prompted.

"They muttered something about my veteran's benefits, shit like that. I knew they were bullshitting. They can't take that away. I told 'em to go fuck themselves. They got no power over me anymore. I gave a fake statement, what more do you want? I'm not going to go in there and perjure myself."

"Excellent," Claire said. "You're right, they have no power over you."

"That it?"

"Would you be willing to testify?" Grimes asked.

"That I lied to the CID? What, are you crazy?"

"To clear the record. Clear your conscience," Grimes said.

"I got no interest in visiting that nightmare again."

"We'll fly you out here first class," Grimes said with a weak smile at Claire and a shrug.

"Hey, first-class trip to Quantico," Fahey said. "What's second prize? All-expenses-paid vacation in Leavenworth?"

"If you'd rather do it the hard way, we can subpoena you," Claire said.

"Military courts can't subpoena people," Fahey said. "Don't bullshit me."

"I'm not talking military courts," she said. "I'm talking about issuing a subpoena through the U.S. attorney."

A long silence. "Who says I'm going to cooperate once I get there?"

"The law," Claire said. "You won't have a choice."

"Hey, you do what you gotta do," Fahey said.

There was a click, and the line was dead.

37

❖

In the middle of the night, the phone rang again.

Claire awoke with a hammering heart and pounding temples.

She let it ring. The answering machine would get it.

After five rings, the machine switched on, played her outgoing message, beeped. There was silence, then a click. She reached over, fumbled with the phone, and finally managed to turn off the ringer.

Her heartbeat slowing, she finally fell back asleep.

It didn't ring again for three hours.

At five-fifty-six Monday morning, she awoke, glanced at the digital alarm clock, knew she should get up and start preparing for court. Then she realized that the phone had been ringing, somewhere distant, somewhere in another room in the house. She remembered she'd turned off the ringer. She lay there in bed, her heart thumping again, and waited for the machine to get it.

This time a male voice came on over the answering machine. It was a youngish-sounding voice, crisp and authoritative. "Claire Heller," he said.

She waited.

"Pick up the phone, it's important."

She reached over and picked it up. "Yes?"

"I have information for you," the voice said.

"What kind of information?" She sat up slowly.

"For your trial."

"Who's this?"

"Information on Marks."

"Who *is* this?"

Silence. Had he hung up?

"Lentini. You recognize the name?"

"Yes."

"I need complete secrecy, and let me tell you right now, I won't testify. I'm not testifying against him."

"Can we meet?"

"Not at your house."

"Where?"

"And with you only. Not with either of the other attorneys. Not your private eye either. I see anyone else, I take off."

"How do you know I'm working with two attorneys?"

"I know people."

"Is that how you got my number?"

"I can only meet at night. I have a job, and it's not easy for me to get out of town."

"I'll meet you wherever it's convenient for you."

"Not near me. I won't take that chance. Write this down."

He gave her precise directions.

"Just you alone," he said.

Annie was already at the breakfast table, wearing her feet pajamas and eating Cocoa Puffs. Claire, dressed in a handsome olive twill suit, kissed her and gave her a quick squeeze. "How's my baby?"

"Goob," Annie said through an immense mouthful.

"You going to paint with Jackie today?"

Annie nodded enthusiastically, eyes sparkling, and kept chewing. Claire made a large pot of coffee.

"Are you going to get Daddy out today?" Annie asked when she'd finally swallowed.

"I'm working on it. Might not be today, sweetie."

"Can you and I play today?"

Claire hesitated. "I'm going to do my very, very best." Then she said, "Yes, honey, we are, when I get home from work. We'll play together. You, me, and Jackie—or just you and me, if you want."

"Who's taking my name in vain?" rasped Jackie as she dragged herself, dazed, into the kitchen. She leaned against the doorframe and massaged her forehead. "Morning, snookums."

Claire took in Jackie's long black Grateful Dead T-shirt and black sweatpants. She raised both hands and snapped her fingers in beatnik applause. "Dig those crazy threads, man."

"It's too early, Claire," Jackie groaned, watching the coffee gurgle and hiss into the glass pot. "I need to mainline some of that caffeine."

The phone rang.

"Not again," Claire said. "Can you get it?"

"No," Jackie said. "I can barely talk."

It rang again. "Oh, God," Claire said, and picked up the wall phone.

"Claire, it's Winthrop."

Winthrop Englander, the dean of Harvard Law School. Three guesses, she thought, what's on his mind.

"Win, good morning," she said.

"Claire, this is not a call I ever wanted to make," he said.

"Win—"

"Is the report true?"

"Largely yes."

"This puts me in an extremely difficult position."

"I understand. I'll make only one excuse, which is to say that it happened a long time ago, and it was very bad judgment made at a time when my mother had just died."

"I understand."

"That doesn't excuse it, Win, but—"

"It's still going to be very difficult, Claire. You've been a valuable member of the faculty, an outstanding teacher, a real asset to the Law School." She heard the verb tense; this was his version of the gold-watch retirement speech.

She wanted to ask him: If I told you about the incident, and no one else knew, would you still stick by your lofty principles? Or is it the *Washington Post*—and probably by now *The New York Times* and, by wire service, every other newspaper and broadcast medium in the country—that's stiffening your sense of morality?

But she said, "I understand."

"There will be all sorts of meetings and consultations. I'll be in touch."

She arrived at Quantico just in time to see the white van from the brig pull up to the building that housed the secure facility. From a distance she saw Tom step out, in full chains. He seemed small. She made a quick calculation: Did she want to catch his eye? To give him a hug? Increasingly she found it painful to make human contact with him before and after trial. Easier to treat him as just another client, one she rarely saw.

But he saw her first. "Claire," he called out hoarsely.

She smiled, though smiling was the last thing she felt like doing this morning. Why burden him with her two hundred worries?

"Claire," he said again, putting both cuffed arms out to her as if displaying them. An odd gesture.

She approached. His eyes glistened with tears. Puzzled, she hugged him. He couldn't hug back, and it stabbed her heart. "It's show time," she said with false good humor.

"Those bastards." His voice was muffled.

She pulled away to see his face. He was crying now.

"Tom?"

"God*damn* them. I saw CNN this morning. They actually let me watch."

"Oh," she said.

"They want to go after me, that's one thing. Now they're trying to destroy you." The guards stood by, eyeing them with hostility, though they knew enough by now not to interrupt.

"It's true, Tom. I did it."

"I don't give a damn. It's the past, it's your private business. . . ." Now he clenched both his hands into fists, and punched the air like a hobbled pugilist. His chains jingled. "God*damn* them, Claire. Come here, please. Will you hug me? These damned handcuffs."

She hugged him, felt his face warm against hers.

"I want you to know something," he said very quietly. "I know what you've been going through for me. What they're trying to do to you. And I'm here for you, the way you've been here for me. I'm in these fucking chains, I'm locked up all day, but I'm your rock, too, okay? I think about you all the time. You're suffering as much as me, maybe more.

You don't have time to be with Annie, you're cut off from all your friends, you can't tell anyone what you're going through, except maybe Jackie, right? And now this. We're going to get through all this shit. I promise you."

38

"*The government* calls Frank La Pierre," Waldron announced.

The prosecution was beginning its case with the Criminal Investigation Division agent who was in charge of the case against Ronald Kubik. Frank La Pierre was escorted by the bailiff into the courtroom. He walked with a slow shuffle, as if he'd been injured long ago. He wore a cheap-looking dark suit that flapped open; he'd clearly been unable to button it over his pot belly. He had owlish horn-rimmed glasses, a pinched nose, and a small downturned mouth. His receding hairline came down in a widow's peak.

Waldron stood with his hands clasped behind his back. "Mr. La Pierre, is it correct that you are a special agent for the CID?"

"That is correct," La Pierre boomed in a sonorous, assured baritone.

"You are in fact the CID agent in charge of this investigation, is that correct?" As if there might be another reason he was here.

"That is correct."

"Now, Mr. La Pierre, how long have you been a CID agent?"

"Eight years."

"And what office are you attached to?"

"CID headquarters at Fort Belvoir."

"Do you have a specialty as a CID agent?"

"Yes, I do."

"And what is that specialty?"

"Personal crimes, particularly homicide."

"I see. Mr. La Pierre, how many murder cases would you say you've worked in your career?"

"I don't know, maybe forty."

"Forty? Well, that's quite a few." He took La Pierre through his credentials and his involvement in the Kubik case. It was all matter-of-fact, often quite dry, but thorough.

After lunch, Claire stood to cross-examine the witness. She looked momentarily lost. "Mr. La Pierre, you say eighty-seven civilians were killed at La Colina, El Salvador, on 22 June 1985, is that right?"

"That's correct." La Pierre's certitude was almost defiant.

"Well, can you identify, please, for the investigating officer the individuals who are dead?"

La Pierre hesitated. "Identify how?"

"Well, how many, say, were male?" Claire gave a sudden little open-palmed shrug, as if the thought had just occurred to her.

He paused again, furtively glanced at Waldron, then looked down. "I don't know that."

"How many were female?"

With annoyance: "There's no way of knowing—"

"Well, what were the *ages* of the eighty-seven victims?"

"Look, this was thirteen years—"

"Answer the question, please. What were the ages of the victims?"

Firmly: "I don't know."

"Well, where are they buried?"

"I'm sure I can get that for you—"

"Who buried them?"

"Your Honor," Waldron burst in angrily, "counsel is engaging in a completely specious line of questioning, completely improper, inadmissible—"

"Sustained," Judge Farrell replied blandly. "Let's move this along, counsel."

"Thank you. Mr. La Pierre, do you have any photographs of the dead bodies?"

"No," he said testily.

"No? What about death certificates? Surely you have those?"

"No."

"*No?* Autopsy reports, no doubt. You must have those."

"No, but—"

"Mr. La Pierre, can you tell me the name of *one individual* that my client is accused of killing?"

La Pierre stared at her venomously. "No, I cannot."

"Not even one?"

"No."

"If you can't tell me one, I know you can't tell me two. Let alone twenty-two. Yet you're accusing Sergeant Kubik of murdering *eighty-seven* people, is that your testimony here today, sir?"

But Frank La Pierre had had his fill of badgering. He came back at her with high moral indignation: "Ronald Kubik murdered eighty-seven innocent people in—"

"Yet you can't testify that you've seen even a single one of the bodies of the eighty-seven people that my client is alleged to have killed. You can't, can you?"

"But—"

"And you haven't seen an autopsy report for a single person that my client is alleged to have killed?"

"No, I have not," he said, this time almost proudly.

"And you haven't seen a death certificate for a single person that my client is alleged to have killed?"

"No, I have not."

"In point of fact, sir, you don't have a single document, except for the"—she paused for emphasis, lifted her eyebrows—"'sworn' statements that the government has introduced, to prove that eighty-seven people were killed at La Colina on 22 June 1985. Is that correct?"

"Yes."

"Or who these eighty-seven people were."

"Yes."

"So we're to take this on your word?"

"Based on seven identical sworn statements," La Pierre managed to get in.

"Oh, I see. The seven"—she held up two fingers on each hand and flicked them in the universal quotation-mark sign—"'sworn' statements. Which are, as you correctly point out, identical. Yet you have no autopsy reports. You have no death certificates. In fact, you have no hard evidence whatsoever, do you?"

A long pause. "Besides the statements, no."

"Now, Mr. La Pierre, we've had an opportunity to examine the service records of each of the members of Detachment 27 who made a statement to you. And, you know, it's funny, but we didn't discover any entry in those service records that would indicate temporary duty in El Salvador. Did we miss something?"

Now we were back on his turf. "No. Often top-secret missions aren't recorded in service records."

"So we didn't miss anything."

"I believe not."

"Good. There was no mention in *any* of those service records of the incursion into El Salvador in June 1985, right?"

"I believe that's correct."

"Mr. La Pierre, did you see my discovery request?"

"No, trial counsel didn't show it to me."

"Well, Mr. La Pierre, the defense made a discovery request for the *order* assigning these individuals to El Salvador. And the strange thing was, we never got any. And I'm thinking, you know, bureaucracies and everything, the way things fall between the cracks . . . Did you happen to see any order assigning the members of Detachment 27 to El Salvador in June 1985?"

"No, I did not."

"No record of any order?"

"That's correct."

"None at all."

Warily, he said, "Uh, that's right."

"That's a relief," Claire said, "because I didn't either." Scattered laughter in the courtroom. "It's good to hear I'm not the only one who hasn't had an easy time dealing with the Pentagon's paper-shufflers. And presumably you went to the supervisory headquarters for this particular Special Forces detachment."

"I believe we did, yes."

"Yet you got no records of any order assigning them to El Salvador?"

"Right."

She turned suddenly to the witness as if another thought had just occurred to her. "Did you attempt to locate in archived records copies of the temporary duty orders that every single military unit has to get before they're sent anywhere?"

"Uh, no."

"You didn't? What about travel claims? Did you attempt to locate in archived records the travel claims for Detachment 27's alleged incursion into El Salvador in June 1985?"

"Well, no, but—"

"You know, Mr. La Pierre, I'm not a member of the military—"

"I wouldn't have guessed," he said flatly.

Hearty laughter broke out among the spectators. Claire laughed along, sharing the joke at her own expense. "And, well, you know, I really don't know much about your world here, but it's my under-standing—and correct me if I'm wrong—that any-time any U.S. soldier goes *anywhere* where there's travel involved, there's got to be a travel claim sub-mitted. Am I right?"

"I believe so," La Pierre said, seemingly bored.

"You believe so. Hmm. Yet you didn't find any travel claim for this alleged operation in El Salvador in June 1985."

"Well, no, but—"

"So there's really no corroboration these individ-uals went anywhere."

La Pierre worked his open mouth a few times, and at last began, "I—"

"Presumably you've made some efforts," Claire

interrupted, "to corroborate whether or not this operation ever actually occurred."

With narrowed eyes, La Pierre shot back, "You're not denying this operation took place, are you?"

"Let me ask the questions, Mr. La Pierre. You've made some efforts to determine whether or not this operation actually occurred, haven't you?"

"It's obvious it occurred—"

"It's obvious? To whom? To you and Major Waldron over there? Or to me and Mr. Grimes and Ronald Kubik over here? Who is it obvious to?"

"*The operation occurred*," La Pierre hissed.

"But you have no records of any orders to corroborate that, do you?" She didn't wait for his reply. "Now, Mr. La Pierre, it's my understanding—and again, correct me if I'm wrong—that before the U.S. government, including the military, engages in a covert operation, there must be a presidential finding authorizing that covert operation. A classified order signed personally by the President of the United States. Is that right?"

"I believe so, yes."

"A presidential finding authorizing covert action is called an NSDD—a National Security Decision Directive—is that right?"

"Uh, yes."

"Which may be classified, right?"

"It can be."

"Sometimes an NSDD can have a classified and an unclassified version, correct?"

"I think so."

"And this operation was a covert operation, isn't that true?"

"Yes, it was."

"So there must exist an NSDD, presumably a clas-

sified one, authorizing Detachment 27's mission to
El Salvador in June 1985. Right?"

He attempted to sidestep the jaw trap. "I wouldn't
know."

"But you just said that every covert action must
be authorized by an NSDD. And this was a covert
action, you said yourself. So there must be an NSDD,
right?"

"I suppose so."

"Yet you didn't obtain the presidential finding authorizing the June 1985 covert operation and signed
by the President of the United States?"

"No, I did not."

"Well, gosh, Mr. La Pierre, as the chief investigator in this case, don't you think it's important to
know whether this operation was authorized by the
President?"

"In my job," he said ringingly, "I don't get into
foreign affairs. I do personal crimes, including hom-
icides."

"You don't get into foreign affairs," she repeated.

"No, I do not."

"Mr. La Pierre, if a full-bird colonel in the Special
Forces, who's now the chief of staff of the army, ran
an operation into El Salvador in June 1985 that was
illegal—because it wasn't authorized by a presidential finding—don't you think you'd want to advise
him of his rights?"

Frank La Pierre looked over at the judge. "I don't
know how to answer that," he said.

"Just answer the question," Farrell said with annoyance. "Did you read General Marks his rights?"

"No, I most certainly did not."

"Why not?" Claire asked.

"I had no reason to believe this was an illegal operation."

"Because you don't 'get into' foreign affairs. Well, sir, don't you think that, as the lead investigator in a mass-murder case that allegedly took place in a foreign country during a covert operation, you might want to educate yourself about foreign policy and the rules governing covert action?"

"I don't see why I need to."

"Really?" Claire said, amazed. "So it's not important to educate yourself as to whether a U.S. operation violated the laws of the United States in its inception?"

"That's not my job."

"So let me get all this straight. You can't identify a single person who was killed. In fact, you don't know who was killed, or, indeed, if *anyone* was killed. So much for element one of the charge—that is, that a 'certain named or described person is dead.' We don't know.

"And, secondly, we don't even know whether or not this operation took place. And if it *did* take place, we don't even know if the operation was authorized. So, heck, we don't even know whether any of these alleged killings—of which we have no proof—were unlawful. Because we don't know what was lawful in this case. We have no idea what the President of the United States ordered—assuming this mission even happened at all! So much for element two of the charge—that is, was the killing unlawful." She shook her head in disgust. "I have nothing further, Your Honor."

39

This time the call came at close to 4:00 A.M. She answered, said, "Keep it up. We'll trace you," then hung up.

Before she left the house that morning, Devereaux called. "The FBI's close," he said.

"What do you mean?"

"On those mysterious phone calls. They've narrowed it down to one of several public payphones within the Pentagon."

"The *Pentagon*?"

"Yeah," Devereaux replied. "Whoever's trying to scare you doesn't want to make them from his Pentagon office, I'll bet. That time of night, you can only get into the Pentagon if you're an employee or have a pass."

"That narrows it down to twenty-five thousand people," she said tartly.

The first day of testimony had been, all told, a good one for the defense. Claire's cross had been devastating. Waldron's attempt to rehabilitate the CID man in his redirect was perfunctory and not particularly effective.

But by the end of the second morning of testimony, things took a sudden bad turn for the defense.

Colonel James J. Hernandez was testifying for the government, and for the most part he was repeating the same charges he'd made before. Waldron had put him on in order to establish what the law calls the *corpus delicti*, the material evidence that a crime has been committed, the body of a murdered person. They had no photographs of bodies, no autopsies, so they would have to present eyewitness testimony that there were in fact bodies—which Hernandez did ably and without a hitch.

Until shortly before lunchtime, when Waldron guided Hernandez to the moment when the unit, in the dead of night, entered the town. Hernandez had approached alongside Ronald Kubik, he testified.

"And what did you proceed to do?" Waldron asked in a seemingly offhand way.

"We went around from hut to hut, rousting people out of there, waking them up, checking for weapons or any signs of the guerrillas."

"Did you find any weapons or any guerrillas?"

"No, we did not, sir."

"Did you use your weapons while you were forcing them out of their huts?"

"Only to point at them. Bayonets or rifles or carbines or machine guns, whatever we had on us."

"You didn't shoot at them, did you?"

"Didn't have to. They were scared. They were old men and women, and mothers with babies and little kids. They cooperated right away."

"Did you see what Sergeant Kubik was doing at that time?"

"Yes, I did."

"What was he doing?"

Hernandez drew himself up and turned toward

the jury. Claire's attention quickened. When a witness turned toward the jury, or the judge, he was often about to say something that he expected would elicit a reaction.

"He—well, he was doing sicko things."

"Would you use the term 'sadistic'?"

"Objection." Claire shot up. "The witness isn't a psychiatrist or a mental-health professional, to my knowledge. He's not qualified to render diagnoses."

"Your Honor," Waldron said, clearly annoyed that she had broken his rhythm, "the witness is permitted to characterize actions using words he's familiar with."

"Overruled," Farrell said.

"Go ahead," Waldron prompted Hernandez. "Did he do things you'd characterize as sadistic?"

"Yes, sir."

"Can you tell us about those things?"

"Well, one old man tried to escape through the back window of his hut, and Sergeant Kubik, he says, 'You want to flee? I told you to go out the front door.' And he hamstrung the guy."

"Hamstrung?"

"He cut the old man's Achilles tendon. One slash of his knife. He said, 'There, now you'll never walk again.'"

Claire turned to Tom, who shook his head, compressing his lips. "Did you hear any of this before?" she whispered.

He continued shaking his head. "It's a total fabrication, Claire."

Waldron continued: "And what did you do when you saw Sergeant Kubik do this?"

"I told him to stop it."

"And did he?"

"No, sir. He said, if I ever told anyone about it, he'd kill me."

"Did he do anything else?"

"Well, yes, sir. It was so horrible." Hernandez looked genuinely stricken. Either he was telling the truth, Claire thought, or he was a remarkable actor. "This boy—he couldn't have been much more than ten—this boy was throwing rocks at him. Shouting obscenities. And Kubik forced him to the ground and took out his knife and sliced his belly."

"Sliced how?"

"He made this quick Y shape on the boy's belly with his knife. Real quick. Not deep."

"What was the point of that?"

"Well, sir, it was so horrible." Hernandez's lips curled up on one side. His face was contorted as if he were about to be sick. "When you do that—well, the boy's insides came out. His—his intestines popped out. When that happens, the victim dies a slow, agonizing death. I shouted—screamed at Kubik—but it was like he was enjoying himself."

Claire whispered to Grimes, "Did this guy say any of this before?"

Grimes shook his head. "Nowhere I ever saw."

"What about his original CID statement?"

"No way. You think I'd forget it?"

"We gotta object."

"Ask for a 39(a) session, with the jury out," Grimes said.

Claire stood. "Your Honor, this is the first we've heard this testimony. We claim surprise. We request a 39(a) session."

"Is that really necessary?" Farrell asked.

"Sir, this is outrageous. The witness is introducing new material he never gave before, not in his CID interview, or his interviews with the prosecutor, or with us—"

"All right," Farrell said, cutting her off. "The members will be excused."

Everyone in the courtroom rose as the bailiff escorted the jurors out.

"Your Honor," Claire said when the jury was gone and the witness temporarily excused, "this witness has been interviewed countless times about the incident in question, by army investigators, by prosecutors, and by ourselves. Not once did he make mention of all this alleged sadism by my client. Now, if the government is going to try to tell us that the witness has been hypnotized, I want to hear it now. Because the courts have recently been taking a pretty dim view of hypnosis-induced prior recollection—"

"Your Honor," Waldron said, "this incident took place thirteen years ago, and, given the horrific nature of Sergeant Kubik's actions, it's only natural that the witness has tried to forget it."

Claire gave Waldron a look of astonishment. "Is trial counsel trying to say that the witness didn't recall these alleged actions immediately after they took place, when the CID interviewed him in 1985?" Claire snapped. "Your Honor, in light of the new testimony being presented, we request a reinterview of this witness, as well as time to confer with our client and among ourselves."

"Your request is granted," Farrell said. "We will resume after the lunch hour, at fourteen hundred hours."

Waldron brushed by Claire on his way out and remarked casually, "Saw your name in the paper."

She looked up, but before she could think of a response, he was gone.

* * *

They interviewed Jimmy Hernandez in a small conference room within the classified facility.

He sat uncomfortably at the conference table, his eyes hooded and darting uneasily.

"So," Grimes said. "Sudden rush of memory, huh?"

Hernandez scowled, twisted in his seat.

"Have you been hypnotized?" Grimes asked.

His scowl deepened. He rolled his eyes.

"Cat got your tongue? You got anything to tell us you forgot to tell us before?"

Hernandez said nothing. With his index finger he stroked the scar under his right eye.

"Lemme ask you something," Grimes went on. "You and Marks—how far back you guys go?"

Hernandez furrowed his brow, shrugged.

"Colonel, look," Claire said. "We have copies of the citation and the statements from when you got your first Bronze Star, at the end of the Vietnam War. One of the eyewitness statements that supported your citation was a William O. Marks. So you two obviously go back quite some time. What I want to know is, how many times did you serve with him?"

"A lot," Hernandez finally said. "Many operations."

"A lot," Claire echoed. "Care to be more specific?"

Hernandez shrugged again.

The reinterview went on for almost an hour.

When Claire, Embry, and Grimes entered the conference room where Tom had been sitting, his chasers standing post outside, Tom got to his feet. "Every time I think they can't sink any lower," he said, "there's a new low."

"I take it you deny it," Grimes said, handing him a cardboard-encased double cheeseburger and large fries.

"I hope you're kidding me," Tom said, taking them. He unwrapped the burger ravenously and took a large bite.

"I'm not. These are serious accusations, whether they come out of left field or not."

Tom chewed quickly, shaking his head. His reply was muffled. "Of course I deny it. I deny them all. How can you seriously ask?"

"It's my job, man."

"Claire, you don't believe that crap, do you?" He put down his burger.

"No, I don't believe it," she said. "The way it was introduced is totally suspicious. I don't believe he's suddenly an honest man."

"That isn't what I'm asking," Tom said. "I'm talking about me. Forget about the legal junk. You can't possibly believe that about me."

She felt her stomach tighten. "No, Tom," she said. "Of course I don't. Terry, do you think you can try to turn up Hernandez's medical records?"

"Sure," Embry said. "I mean, I think so."

"But quietly, okay? I don't want Waldron to know—he'll make us show relevance."

"No problem. But what are you looking for?"

"Well, correct me if I'm wrong, but isn't it true that psychiatric records aren't privileged in the military?"

"Man, nothing's privileged in the military," Grimes put in. "You don't think this creep ever saw a shrink, do you?"

"Not voluntarily, I'll bet. But maybe he was compelled to. I don't know. It's worth checking. See if we can find any interesting information about the guy."

"What are you thinking?" Tom asked.

"Something about him I don't get."

Tom's eyes narrowed. "What do you mean?"

"Just—is he covering for his boss, or is there something more going on?"

Tom shook his head. "He's just covering Marks's ass."

"Well, I hope you're right. I hope there's nothing we're missing."

When court resumed after lunch, the members were brought back in and Hernandez was back on the stand for the cross-examination. Claire paced in front of him for a few seconds before she began, trying to strike the right note.

"Mr. Hernandez, when you were interviewed by the Army Criminal Investigation Division in 1985—"

"Objection," Waldron called out. "The witness is a colonel and is fully entitled to all the respect that rank deserves. Ask that defense counsel refer to him as 'Colonel Hernandez.' "

"Fine, Your Honor," Claire said. "*Colonel* Hernandez, when you were interviewed by the CID in 1985, were you asked to give a complete version of the events at La Colina?"

"Yes—"

"Thank you. Did you do so?"

"No."

"I see," she said, moving hastily along. "Were you aware that when you gave that statement you were under oath to tell the *whole* truth and nothing but the truth, so help you God?"

"Yes," he conceded.

"When you testified at the Article 32 hearing, were you also aware that you were under oath to tell the whole truth, so help you God?"

"Yes."

"Well, then, I have to admit I'm puzzled, Colonel. Did you consciously think about these details, and then willfully and intentionally not give testimony about these alleged events at the Article 32 hearing?"

The question confused him. He had to think a moment. "Um, yes, but as I explained to you—"

"Just answer the question, please. Colonel, if you didn't tell the whole truth under oath to the CID investigators, and you didn't tell the whole truth at the 32 hearing, when you were also under oath—how can we believe what you're saying now?"

"I'm telling the truth!"

"The whole truth?"

"Right!"

"Because you're under oath?"

He hesitated. "Because I'm telling the truth."

"I see. Thank you for clearing that up for the members. You're telling the whole truth now because you *are*. Thank you."

"Objection, Your Honor," Waldron shouted. "Badgering the witness."

"Move on, Ms. Chapman," Farrell admonished.

"Colonel Hernandez, did you tell the prosecutor about this before the trial began?"

Hernandez looked uncomfortable again. Claire was learning to read him. "No," he said at last.

"May I remind you you're under oath?"

"Your Honor!" Waldron exclaimed.

"I said no," Hernandez said.

"Colonel Hernandez, did anyone else see the events you describe—the disemboweling of the young boy and so on?"

"Just me and Kubik."

"Nobody else can corroborate your testimony?"

"I guess not. But I saw it."

"So we have to rely on your memory from thirteen years ago—which we've just seen is seriously unreliable?"

"My memory is not unreliable!" Hernandez exploded. "I told you before, I—"

"Thank you, Colonel," Claire interrupted.

Hernandez looked plaintively at Waldron. "Can't I answer the question?" he asked.

"That's enough," Farrell boomed.

"Colonel," Claire said, "I have another question for you. What were you doing, exactly, when you say Sergeant Kubik was doing all these terrible things?"

"I was rousting people from their huts."

"That must have taken all of your concentration, right? After all, you never knew if the guerrillas might be hiding in one of the huts you were emptying out. Am I right?"

Hernandez looked suspicious. His eyes narrowed. "I could see what Kubik was doing."

"Really? Let me get this straight. You saw him giving orders to an old man and his family, you saw him going after the old man climbing out the window. You saw him slash the old man's Achilles tendon. You saw—and heard—him taunt the old man. Then you saw a young boy throw rocks at Kubik. You saw Kubik force the young boy to the ground and cut his stomach. You saw a great deal, didn't you?"

"I couldn't help but look. The people were screaming."

"After he hurt them?"

"And before, when they were afraid about what he was going to do."

"What span of time would you say these events took place over?"

"Five minutes, maybe. Maybe ten."

"Ten minutes! You were able to see all of this, in the space of ten minutes—while, at the same time, you were doing some highly dangerous work that required all of your attention—that required, in fact, that you not divert your eyes from what you were doing or you might be killed?"

Hernandez stared at her with sluggish hostility. He seemed defeated. He didn't reply.

"Unbelievable," she said, shaking her head, and returned to the table.

"Objection, Your Honor," Waldron shouted.

"Sustained."

"Withdrawn," Claire said as she sat. Tom reached around and squeezed her shoulder.

"Trial counsel, do you have redirect?"

"Yes, sir." Waldron rose and stood squarely in front of his witness. "Colonel Hernandez, when you came back from El Salvador after this mission was over, you were subjected to a long and rigorous interrogation by the CID, right?"

"Right," Hernandez said. He had the tone of a parched man who'd finally found a drinking fountain.

"Tell me about this investigation."

"Man, they were always in my face. They were hardasses."

"The investigators from the CID?"

"Right. They was doing all this good-cop/bad-cop stuff, and they wanted to polygraph me, and they looked like they was looking to hang me, too, along with Kubik. I figured, if I told them about the twisted stuff I saw Kubik do, they'd have thought I was part of it. Or, you know, why didn't I stop it?"

"Why didn't you?" Waldron asked reasonably.

"A crazy guy like that? No way you go near him. We're trained to stay out of the line of fire, that's our self-defense training. I knew he was losing it, and I wasn't going to get in his way."

"You thought they were going to charge *you* with the crime," Waldron suggested.

"They always shoot the survivor."

"But your thoughts weren't just about saving yourself, were they?"

"I figured if this came out it would just blacken the army's name even more. I didn't want to hand that to these CID guys. I was hoping this would just die its own death, you know what I mean."

"What about Kubik?" Waldron asked, leading egregiously. "I thought you didn't much like the guy?"

" 'Like' had nothing to do with it. We weren't exactly friends, yeah. But I did train with the guy, and he saved my life not two months before—he pulled me back when I almost stepped on a mine in Nicaragua. He saw the trip wire before I did."

"So you felt you owed it to him to, maybe, minimize his crimes," Waldron said.

"Yeah. Then, at the 32, I thought I might get in trouble if I brought it up—like, false swearing or whatever it's called. I mean, I've really been agonizing over this. But I finally decided I gotta tell the truth here."

"Thank you," Waldron said, satisfied.

"Defense counsel, do you have any re-cross?" Judge Farrell asked.

Claire cradled her chin in a cupped hand and thought a brief moment. "Uh, yes, Your Honor." She rose. "Colonel Hernandez, you love the army, don't you?"

He replied without hesitation: "Yes, I do."

"How many times have you served with General Marks?"

"Several times."

"Five tours of duty, is that correct?"

"Yes."

"Isn't it a fact that, every time you served with General Marks, he was your immediate supervisor, and you even socialized with him after hours?"

Hernandez hesitated but a moment. "Yes," he replied crisply.

"You'd follow General Marks anywhere, wouldn't you?"

He paused for a moment, then gave her a steely stare. "I have many times, and I would again. The general likes to surround himself with people he can trust, and I know he trusts me, and I know I trust—"

"Thank you, Colonel," Claire said.

"Your Honor," Waldron interrupted, "where's this going?"

"Yes," the judge said, "enlighten me, counsel."

"Bias, Your Honor."

"Fine," Farrell said. "Proceed."

"Now, Colonel, why is it that we cannot find a single After Action Report on the incident of 22 June 1985 at La Colina, even a classified one?"

Hernandez gave her a look at once imperious and vacant. "Maybe you haven't looked hard enough."

"Oh, we've looked high and low, Colonel," Claire said. "In fact, Major Waldron has assured me—has given us his word as an officer and, further, as an officer of this court—that no such report exists. Are you telling me that you did not do one?"

"That's correct. I did not do one."

"Do you know of anyone *else* who wrote an After Action Report on the incident of 22 June 1985?"

"No."

"Well, was there any *other* type of account you know of concerning this alleged massacre at La Colina on 22 June 1985?"

He paused. "I believed the CO did one, but I didn't see it."

"The CO being General Marks, then Colonel Marks?"

"Yes."

"Thank you," she said with a glint in her eyes. "I have nothing further."

40

◆

The three attorneys sat at a table in a coffee shop in Manassas.

"Well, that sucks," Grimes said, tucking into an outsized wedge of sour-cream coffee cake. The owners of the shop knew him and obviously liked him. "Panel members, they're going to eat up Hernandez's motive for holding back—helping out a buddy, *esprit de corps*, protecting the army's good name. Shit, only thing he left out was God."

Claire sipped a black coffee and looked balefully at the NO SMOKING sign posted on the wall directly above their table. "But it's a lie," she said. Embry nodded and took a sip of coffee.

"You think the guy just dreamed up that stuff to spice up his story? Sort of like icing on the cake? Or Waldron told him to suddenly 'remember' it?"

Embry put in: "Waldron must have had something to do with it. Hernandez had all the right reasons—it's not like he tried to claim he'd forgotten."

"Maybe so," Grimes said, "but the panel won't think that."

"So they're one up on us," she said. "You think I should have recrossed?"

Embry shook his head, puzzled. Grimes spoke first. "Maybe," he said at length. "I don't know what I would have done."

She nodded. "Fair enough. It was a tough call. A criminal trial is a psychodrama—and a crap shoot."

The owner, or owner's wife, appeared with a pot of coffee. She was an ample-bosomed, middle-aged black woman who smelled of sweat and Opium. She lay her free hand on Grimes's shoulders. "Refill, sugar?"

He held out his mug. "Thanks, babe."

"Anyone else?" she asked. Embry and Claire shook their heads no. "How's my coffee cake, honey?" she asked Grimes.

"Tastes just like my mamma used to make, before she got arrested."

The woman stopped short for an instant, baffled. Grimes laughed, ha-*ha*! "But it's not as sweet as you," he said.

"Not like you'd know," she said mock-sternly, and moved on.

"At least we've got Mark Fahey," Embry said.

"One witness to their ten," Claire said mordantly. "Has he been served with a subpoena yet?"

Embry nodded. "Prosecution's been notified. Fahey will be here in three days, ready to testify."

"Wonder what kind of rat hole the government puts him up at," Grimes said, and shoveled another immense forkload of coffee cake into his mouth.

"What's up with the transcription?" Claire asked.

"I've hired five different transcriptionists," Embry replied. "This is going to cost big-time."

"I need to read over Abbott. He done yet?" she asked.

"Close. Maybe by tonight; I'll call. These women

are working round the clock. That's why it's so expensive."

Grimes looked up. Crumbs had colonized the lines around his mouth. "You still getting spooky phone calls?"

Claire nodded. "Yeah, but if I let the answering machine get them, he hangs up. Funny, he doesn't seem to want to leave us a voice sample. Ray says the FBI's got nothing on the trap-and-trace: the caller moves around to different exchanges, he's only on for a few seconds."

"He'll stop," Grimes said. "He's made his point—trying to unnerve you—but it didn't work."

"You guys mind if I leave you here?" Embry asked. "I've got a boatload of ballistics stuff to go over, and I'm working on an idea."

"Share," Claire said.

"When I've checked it out," Embry said, standing up.

After Embry had left, Claire told Grimes about the call from Lentini.

"Jesus fucking Christ," he said. "So he turns up after all. Man, this guy must be in deep fucking cover."

"For good reason, I'd guess."

"I want to go with you. We know nothing about him, and I don't like mysteries."

"I can take care of myself."

Grimes seemed to consider this for a moment. "Can I ask you something?"

She looked at him.

"Was that all cooked up—that *Post* stuff?"

"No," she admitted.

He nodded slowly. He was silent for a moment. "Shit, Claire," he said at last, "we all make mistakes."

"Mistakes?" she said with a bitter laugh.

"We all got skeletons in our closet. Stuff we wish we'd never done."

She didn't say anything, embarrassed to be talking about this with Grimes, but he gamely forged ahead. "General Marks said pursuing this case could be hazardous to your career. Guess he meant it, huh?"

"Guess so."

"You think he, or one of his people, sent out people to dig stuff up?"

"My guess is it came up in the FBI background check. One of my professors at Yale." She gave his name. Grimes, recognizing the name, nodded. "All it takes is someone in CID who's friendly to the general."

"Like just about anyone with ambitions," Grimes said. "Suck up to the boss. You want to bring this up to the judge, get an investigation going?"

"For what? So he can say no, or, worse, he can order an investigation that goes nowhere? There won't be any fingerprints on this."

Robert Lentini had selected, as a rendezvous point, a hilltop restaurant some sixty miles northwest of D.C., in the Catoctin mountain range in Maryland. The first sign for MOUNTAIN CHALET was posted on Route 70 by the turnoff, in fake old-style Germanic lettering. She could see the restaurant from the highway, lit up, perched atop a hill like an Alpine ski resort. The approach was a long, narrow uphill road with barely enough room for two cars traveling in both directions. It wound up the hillside at such a steep grade that she could feel the rented car's engine strain, the automatic transmission shift into lower and lower gear.

She parked in the small lot. There were only three

other cars here, and it seemed to be the only parking area. She could see why he'd chosen this particular location. It wasn't for her convenience, certainly, or for the garish ersatz-Alpine decor, or, she guessed, for the food. It was instead the vantage point. From here you could see the countryside in all directions for miles.

Still sitting in the car, she checked the concealed Uher tape recorder Ray had taped to the small of her back. A wire came around to the front, taped to the side of her brassiere. With a quick motion she switched it on: the tiny on-off switch nestled beside her left breast. To anyone who might be watching, she'd simply appear to be scratching herself. She shuffled through the papers in her leather portfolio and, in another unseen gesture, switched on the miniature backup tape recorder concealed there, disguised as a pack of Marlboro cigarettes (not her brand, but she wasn't going to quibble). There was, of course, the risk that he'd check to see whether she was wearing a wire, but she was willing to take that risk.

She did not expect Lentini to make himself available to testify in court.

She got out of the car, holding the portfolio, and made her way to the main entrance. The decor inside set her teeth on edge: cobblestone-paved floor, low wood-beamed ceiling (the beams looked fake even at a distance), artificially weathered wooden table, kitschy imitation stained-glass windows, a large artificial fireplace with roaring gas flames licking phony logs even in the summer heat. She found a table by a window overlooking a valley, and waited.

Nine o'clock came and went, and still she waited. She ordered a Coke.

At twenty past nine she wondered whether he

would show up at all. She made a circuit of the almost empty restaurant and found only couples. No one who might possibly be Lentini. She asked the maître d', who said that no one had mentioned meeting anybody. She called home; Jackie said no one had left a message for her.

At nine-forty-five she decided to leave. It was extremely unlikely she'd gotten the place wrong, unless there was more than one imitation-Swiss mountainside chalet in this remote Maryland town, which seemed improbable. More likely was that he had changed his mind, or for some reason had been scared off.

She left a few dollars for her Coke and went out to the parking lot. Two other cars there now. No sign of anyone who might remotely resemble Lentini.

Annoyed, she got in the car, started it up, and pulled out of the lot, half expecting him to arrive in his car as she was leaving. But no. She'd been stood up.

She maneuvered the car down the narrow mountain road. It was dark, and she was concerned that a car approaching from the opposite direction might whip around a bend and smash into her. So she flashed her brights as she approached the first hairpin turn, and braked to slow down as well.

And the brake pedal sunk to the floor.

"Jesus," she exclaimed, trying the brakes again and finding only a dead pedal. The bend in the road loomed closer. She turned the steering wheel abruptly to avoid going off the road and into the ravine.

The car accelerated from the natural gravitational pull, faster and faster, and she swung the wheel over to the left, then the right, as the road shimmied ahead of her and rushed toward her. She tried the brakes one last time, and nothing. Not working.

Spinning the wheel first to one side, then to another, the car speeding faster and faster down the incline, she yanked the emergency-brake lever upward. It pulled up easily, too easily, and the lever jiggled up and down uselessly.

"Oh, God," she keened. Her eyes were frozen on the road ahead. The car careened, trees flying by in a blur, faster and faster and faster, and the thought suddenly leaped into her mind that any second another car might approach, and her stomach seized up.

"*No!*" she shouted. "No! God, *no!*"

Her eyes were blurry with tears, but they did not move from the headlong rush of the paved road ahead, her hands clenching the steering wheel with a death grip. The car hurtled forward wildly, now sixty, seventy miles an hour, accelerating madly. For a split second she felt herself at a remove, looking down calmly at this terrifying scene; then the next second she was screaming at the top of her lungs, petrified in her seat, immobilized while the car plummeted down the road. She shifted into neutral, but that made little difference.

Should I switch off the ignition? No, don't dare, that would shut off the steering!

She spun the wheel left, then right, then left, then right, as the road whipped by and the trees and boulders on either side were dark blurs.

And then she saw, parked in the dead center of the road just ahead, a green military jeep, two large gas cans at its rear.

There was no way to avoid crashing into it!

She made an instant decision and spun the wheel to the left, steering the car sharply up the steep embankment overgrown with brush. As the car ran over the low bushes, rocks and branches crunching loudly, it slowed considerably, just what she'd hoped would happen, and she forced her left hand from the wheel, reached down for the car door, couldn't find it, fumbled around, not daring to take her eyes off the road; then her hand touched steel, and she grabbed at the handle and pulled it, and the door flung open—

—and with a gasp of terror she leaned to her left, tucked her head in, and tumbled out onto the embankment, her head striking something hard among the brush, the taste of blood and fear metallic in her mouth, her eyes shut tight, a terrible crack of pain shooting up her neck, and then she heard the car lurch on forward, veering back onto the road, and strike something. There was a horrifying crunch of steel.

Crouched along the side of the road, half in the pine-needle-covered soft earth, half on the asphalt, her head throbbing, she opened her eyes and stared ahead and saw that her car had crashed into the jeep, and then there was a cataclysmic, deafening explosion, and she shut her eyes, and even through her eyelids she saw the brilliant flash of light that was a gasoline fire, and she scrambled to her feet and turned and ran up the road, screaming.

A few minutes later, though it seemed hours, stumbling and weaving up the pitch-dark road, she remembered she was wearing her cell phone.

PART FIVE

41

"*I'm moving* in," Devereaux said. "You got more rooms in here than the goddamn Hilton, and the roach motel's starting to wear on me. And you need protection."

Claire lay on a couch in one of the sitting rooms, both Jackie and Grimes hovering nearby with grave concern. It was close to one in the morning. She was considerably banged up, particularly along her side and her left hip, where she had landed on several small rocks. There were quite a few scrapes as well, including a long, ugly one along her neck and left cheek, by the ear. She also had a ferocious, thudding headache. She'd spent over an hour being questioned by Maryland state police, from which nothing, she knew, would ever come.

"I don't need protection, Ray," she said weakly.

"Naw, you don't need protection," he said sardonically. "Not you. Someone disables your braking system, intending for you to wipe out on a jeep that's conveniently left in your path, with two probably half-empty gas tanks on the back, and get blown up, but, naw, everything's fine."

"If you care about me—" Jackie said. "No, forget about me. If you care about Annie, you'll take him up on his offer."

Claire shrugged, unwilling to argue with such logic.

"So you never lost consciousness at all?" Devereaux asked.

"Nope."

"No vomiting, change in vision, none of that?"

"Nope."

"Your pupils look the same size, far as I can tell. So you don't have a concussion, but you really should get over to the ER and have 'em do a CAT scan."

"Suddenly you're a doctor, too?" Claire said.

"You're not disoriented."

"No more than usual," she replied.

"All right, now, Jackie," Devereaux said, "I want you to wake her up in a couple hours, make sure she can wake up."

"Don't bother," Claire said. "I've got my nightly harassing phone call to wake me up."

"You think it really was Lentini behind this, or just someone using his name for the set-up?" Grimes asked.

"Who cares?" Claire said.

"Nah," Devereaux said. "The call you got—arranging your little meeting in Maryland—I got a local phone-company source tells me it came from a payphone inside the Pentagon. I doubt it really came from Lentini—if he's lying low, hiding, he won't be calling from inside the belly of the beast."

"We gotta file a notice with the Quantico cops, the MPs," Grimes said.

"To what end?" Claire asked. "Until we can figure

out who did this to me, and prove it, we've got nothing."

"You know something," Devereaux said, looming over her, "you really piss me off royally. What the hell you think you were doing, arranging a meeting like that, asking me to wire you, and not telling me where you were going? I woulda gone with you."

"He insisted I go alone," Claire said feebly.

"They always do," Devereaux scowled. "You gotta stop being so casual about your safety. I got news for you." He turned around to the others. "For all of youse. You know your realtor from Pepper Pike?"

"Our witness? What's-his-name, Fahey?" Grimes said. "Don't tell me . . ."

"Yeah. He was killed in a car accident this morning."

Claire bolted upright. Her head almost exploded with a searing pain. "Oh my God."

"Whoever wanted him out of the way are the same folks who wanted *you* out of the way," Devereaux said. "Similar modus vivendi."

"Operandi," Grimes said.

"Right. It seems to be the modus operandi of *Kubik* v. *the United States*."

The phone rang at almost three-thirty in the morning.

Claire rolled over, remembered the pain she was in, and grabbed the phone before the machine could get it.

She didn't wait for the man's voice, or for the breathing.

"Missed, motherfucker," she said, and slammed it down.

*   *   *

She woke up late—ten after nine. Court was already in session. She felt the jolt of pain, and then a jolt of realization in her stomach. "Oh, *God*," she exclaimed, and leaped out of bed.

No, she remembered. This morning the armorer from Fort Bragg was taking the stand to testify for the government about the integrity of the computer armory records he supervised. Grimes was doing the cross. She never liked to miss a moment of testimony, but this wasn't a tragedy. And she'd needed the sleep.

Devereaux and Jackie were seated at the breakfast table, talking. Annie was in Devereaux's lap, sketching with a marker on a drawing pad. Claire could smell freshly brewed coffee.

"Hey, killah," Devereaux greeted her.

Annie stared at her scraped-up mother with wide, tear-filled eyes, and she started to cry.

42

❖

She was able to cover her scraped cheek fairly well with a concealer, but a large, garish purple-yellow bruise had emerged around her left eye that even the most industrial-strength cover-up she had wouldn't hide unless she troweled it on.

Tom noticed it immediately as he was brought to the defense table. "What the hell happened to you?" he said, gaping.

"I slipped and fell," she said. "Living in a strange house, you know. Happens."

He looked unpersuaded.

The fact was that they were losing the case. Despite Claire's powerful cross-examinations of both Hernandez and La Pierre, the two witnesses had still done the job the prosecution had called them to do. The jury no doubt believed not only that Tom had machine-gunned eighty-seven mothers, children, and old men, but that he had visited upon them acts of sadism that could only have been devised by a disturbed mind.

By the afternoon session of the third day of testimony, Henry Abbott, the next eyewitness, was ready for cross-examination. Claire looked around the courtroom, located Ray Devereaux sitting in a spectator seat with his hands folded over his great belly, and smiled. He was wearing one of what he called his courtroom suits, in case he had to take the stand, and looked ill-at-ease.

She got slowly to her feet and approached the witness stand. Henry Abbott, dressed in a navy-blue suit and crisp white shirt with silver-striped tie, looked relaxed and confident. He gazed at her with dead eyes. He exuded neither hatred nor contempt. He looked blankly through her, as if she were some invisible bag lady on the street.

"Mr. Abbott," she said, "I'm Claire Chapman. I'm the lead defense counsel."

He blinked and gave the barest nod.

"Mr. Abbott, did you see the accused shoot those eighty-seven people?"

"Yes, I did."

Claire turned her head slightly so that she was out of the line of sight of the jury, then gave Abbott a brief smile. "So you saw the victims react to the impact of the bullets?"

"Yes."

"Can you describe their reaction?"

"Their reaction? Some of them screamed and cried, some of them fell to the ground and tried to cover their heads. The mothers shielded their children with their bodies."

Very good. He was well prepared. "And you saw their reaction to the bullets' impact?"

"Yes."

"Which was—?"

"Some of them flew backward. They twitched, fell, crumpled in bizarre positions."

"And you believe the accused was the only one who could have fired those bullets?"

"He was the only one that did."

"But can you state positively that the bullets that struck those victims came from the accused's firearm?"

"As I say, he was the only one firing."

"But did you see the bullets exiting his machine gun?"

"I couldn't see the bullets in flight, if that's what you mean. I'm not Superman."

A few chuckles came from the jury box. Abbott was unshakable. He had been thoroughly briefed.

"Mr. Abbott, how many rounds are in an M-60's ammunition belt?"

"One hundred."

"If you're machine-gunning eighty-seven people, one hundred rounds isn't enough, is it?"

"No, it's not."

"So you must have seen him reload."

But Abbott was too well prepared. "He had two belts linked together," he said evenly. "He didn't have to reload." A brief twinkle of triumph seemed to enter his eyes.

"Mr. Abbott, did your unit have muzzle devices called distorters available for your M-60 machine guns?"

"Yes."

"Why?"

"Why did we have them?"

"Correct."

"To mask the location of the shooter," he said, one eyebrow cocked in a deft expression of contempt. "Sometimes it was very important that we not be located."

"And can you tell me whether Sergeant Kubik had

a distorter or a sound-suppressor on his weapon?"

Abbott hesitated. This detail they hadn't furnished him.

"I believe not."

"You believe not?" Claire echoed. "Well, isn't the sound of an M-60 machine gun extremely loud?"

"Yes," he conceded grudgingly.

"So there's nothing subtle about it, is there? It would be just about impossible not to know whether an M-60 had a sound-suppressor on it, isn't that right?"

He shrugged, wary of the trap he suspected she was laying for him. "Perhaps."

"So, then, is it your testimony that Sergeant Kubik did not use a sound-suppressor or distorter when he fired the rounds that killed the eighty-seven civilians?"

"Right."

Had he guessed? If so, he was lucky. Abbott was too sharp, or too well briefed, to be shaken from his prefabricated story. She decided it was time to pounce.

"Mr. Abbott, how much business does your company do with the Department of Defense?"

"I don't really know."

"Surely you have a fairly good idea."

"A couple billion, certainly."

"A couple of *billion dollars*," she marveled. "So a good relationship with the Pentagon, and the army in particular, must be important to you and your company."

He shrugged. "The customer's always right, I like to say."

"I'll bet. And are you currently involved in any contract negotiations with the Pentagon?"

"Yes."

"For what?"

"That's a classified matter."

"We're in a classified courtroom, Mr. Abbott. Everyone here is cleared, including the jurors and the spectators. You can speak freely."

"We're conducting negotiations with the army for the purchase of a new generation of attack helicopters."

"That must mean quite a lot of potential income for your firm."

"Yes, it does."

"And you're one of the point men in those negotiations, correct?"

"Yes."

"So that must make you inclined to be cooperative with the army."

"Is that a question?"

"The customer's always right, as you like to say." He shrugged.

"Mr. Abbott, do you remember the interview we had at the Madison Hotel four days ago?"

"Yes."

"We met for breakfast, did we not?"

"We did."

"Did I meet you along with my cocounsel, Mr. Grimes?"

"Yes, you did."

"How long was the interview?"

"I don't recall."

"Does twenty-six minutes sound about right?"

"It may be. I don't know."

"Mr. Abbott, at our interview with you at the Madison Hotel, did you tell us you were coached by Colonel Marks, and told what to say in your CID interview?"

Now his eyes were dead again, the flat eyes of a snake. "No."

"You don't remember saying that?"

He leaned forward. "I never said it."

"You never said you were coached before your CID interview?"

"No, I didn't, and no, I wasn't."

"Are you sure?"

"Yes."

"Are you positive?"

"Objection, Your Honor," Waldron shouted. "Asked and answered."

"Overruled," Farrell said, and took a sip of Pepsi as though he were watching a particularly exciting game on TV.

"I remind you you're under oath, Mr. Abbott. You never told me that your commanding officer told you what to say to the CID?"

"I never said that, and he never did."

"Are you aware, Mr. Abbott, that I can move to the witness stand and testify about what you told me?"

"Then it would be your word against mine," he said blandly. "And you're not exactly an unbiased witness, are you?"

Claire noticed several jurors watching this exchange with great interest. The foreman, or president of the court, the bespectacled black man, was busily taking notes. "If I told you that's exactly what I remember, would I be lying?" she said.

"Yes, you would."

"If I told you that's exactly what my cocounsel remembers, would he be lying?"

"He most certainly would."

"If I told you we were tape-recording that interview, would we be lying?" she asked casually and turned toward the defense table. The courtroom stirred. She saw Tom's eyes gleaming. He was doing all he could not to smile.

Grimes handed her a small stack of papers. She saw Abbott stiffen and clench both hands at his side. He glared at her fiercely.

"Your Honor," she said, "may I approach the witness?"

"You may."

She strolled over to the prosecution table and dropped a stapled sheaf of paper, then placed one on the judge's bench. Then she handed one to Abbott.

"Mr. Abbott," she said, "that's a verbatim transcript of your interview with us, certified by my colleague, Mr. Grimes, and my investigator, Mr. Devereaux, transcribed from a tape recording made by Mr. Devereaux." She didn't yet bother to explain that Devereaux had provided her with a transmitter in a dummy cellular phone and had taped the conversation in his car parked in front of the Madison. "Please turn to page thirty-four, Mr. Abbott, and begin reading where it's marked, seven lines down, beginning with, 'He says, "Didn't you see Kubik suddenly raise his weapon and begin to shoot?" I say, "No, sir, I didn't." ' And ending with 'they don't like snitches and turncoats.' "

Abbott's face was dark with fury. Under his breath, he said, "Cunt."

"Excuse me? What did you say?"

Abbott stared ferociously. A vein at his right temple throbbed.

"Did you just refer to me by a four-letter vulgarism, Mr. Abbott?"

Suddenly Abbott threw the transcript to the floor

of the witness box. "Goddamn you, that was off the record!"

"It *was* off the record back then," Claire said quietly. "But you led yourself into the perjury you just committed, not us, and we can't allow that to happen."

"Your Honor!" Waldron shot to his feet.

"That's it!" Judge Farrell exploded, hammering his gavel. "The members are excused."

43

"*Did you* really agree that conversation was off the record?" rasped Farrell.

"Yes, Your Honor, I did," Claire replied. "I tricked him. I had my investigator make a tape recording to ensure that we got accurate testimony at the trial."

"Does your investigator secretly tape-record all your witness interviews?"

"I'd rather not say. But it's legal, sir."

"Why'd you tape him?"

"I mean no disrespect to you or to this court, but I had my doubts about his veracity. This witness should not be permitted to come in here and tell barefaced lies to you, me, and the jury."

Waldron, who'd been pacing during this exchange, stopped suddenly and said, "Your Honor, this is a clear-cut violation of reciprocal discovery. We've got a discovery request for all statements by government witnesses in the hands of the defense. How come we never got this transcript?" He was smooth.

"It was nondisclosable," Claire said. "This is obviously not a statement of the witness. The witness hasn't read and signed the statement and sworn to the truth of it. We didn't put the guy under oath."

"But, Your Honor—"

"Well, I gotta go along with defense counsel on this one," Farrell said, draining his can of Pepsi and setting it down on the podium with a hollow *thock*. "It's no violation of discovery."

"Thank you, Your Honor," Claire said.

"But I'm going to grant prosecution a delay of one hour. I don't like this surprise stuff. I want the witness to have the chance to read through this transcript. I'm not interested in soliciting perjury in this case just to help you out, Ms. Chapman. Or you, Mr. Waldron. Really. Mr. Waldron, you put your poor excuse for a witness in a room, and I'm going to let the members take a break."

"But, Your Honor," Claire said, "this is right in the middle of my cross-examination. Can you instruct the government not to talk to the witness?"

"No, I will not."

Claire sputtered, "But, sir—"

"Now we're finished here," Farrell said.

"Have you read the transcript?" Claire asked when Henry Abbott was finally back on the stand. His hair was freshly combed, and he even appeared to have changed his shirt.

"Yes, I have."

"And are you satisfied it's a true and accurate transcription of our interview with you at the Madison?"

"Yes, I am, as far as I can tell, without my notes."

He probably was the sort of person who'd have taken notes on what was said at their twenty-six-minute breakfast, Claire reflected. "Then can you explain to this court why you lied under oath?"

"I didn't," Abbott said.

"You *didn't*? Would you like me to have the reporter read back your testimony before we took a break?"

"Not necessary," he said. "I didn't lie under oath."

"Excuse me? Would you like me to play the tape for you?"

"I said I didn't lie under oath. I was lying to you."

Claire's heart sank. Waldron had obviously coached him. "I told you what I thought you wanted to hear," he continued. "You were obviously on a conspiracy-theory jag, and that pissed me off. You seemed to think that nobody in the military could be trusted to tell the truth, and, frankly, I found that offensive. So I decided, well, this was off the record—I took your word of honor on that—and I decided I'd put you in your place, give you a load of bull, give you what you so desperately wanted to hear." And he gave her the barest wisp of a smile.

That evening Claire met Dennis, Tom's CIA source, at the same yuppie Georgetown bar he so loathed.

He wore a blue blazer with gaudy gold anchor buttons, a white shirt, and a red-and-blue rep tie. "Now, I should tell you," Dennis began, "that I may not contact you again. The situation's getting uncomfortable."

"I've got your number. I'll call only if it's important."

"That number's no longer in service."

"You moved?"

"Just changed phone numbers. I do that periodically."

"Why, you get a lot of crank calls?" she said. "I've been getting them myself recently."

He looked puzzled but went on, "We've got a little old lady who works for us. Got the memory of
an elephant."

"Does every spy agency have one of those?"

"She remembered seeing the MFR I told you
about. The memorandum for the record. Found it in
operational files."

"Really?" she exulted, but then she was troubled
by something. "Why would CIA have an internal
army document?"

He shrugged. "We're pack rats. We had a source
in the army's Southern Command, SOUTHCOM,
friendly to us. Found it in a safe full of classified
stuff down there in Panama. Figured it would be of
interest to us."

" 'Friendly' to you means he works for you?"

Dennis raised his heavy, Mephistophelian brows.
"You said it, not me." He slid a single photocopied
sheet across the table.

It was not a good photocopy. It bore the smudges
and detritus and vestigial chicken-scratchings of a
document copied many times over. Yet it was quite
readable. The general, fortunately, had had neat, if
minuscule, handwriting. It was no more than three
lines. She read it and looked up.

"He says here the peasants had weapons, so he
got on the radio to Hernandez and instructed his
men to fire." She looked up, astonished.

Dennis drank his bourbon.

"That's not in his statement to CID, or his interview with the government. That's not in *anyone's*
statements," she mused. "Nowhere else did he or
anyone else ever mention weapons. Or that he gave
the order. And to *Hernandez*!"

Dennis smiled. "That's why I never put anything
in writing," he said.

*   *   *

Ten minutes later, when Dennis left Claire, he did not notice the tall, bulky figure of Ray Devereaux get up from a table near the door and follow him out.

44

Claire and Tom met in the small private conference room within the secure courtroom complex. She showed him the photocopy of General Marks's memorandum for the record that Dennis had given her. He read it, betraying no expression, and looked up. "Nice," he said, and smiled.

" 'Nice'?" Claire said, aghast. "Is that all you can say? 'Nice'? This little piece of paper may have just won the case for us here!"

Tom cocked his head and said curiously, "You think so?"

"Well, who the hell knows what will happen in this kangaroo court. But now we've got proof that Marks gave Hernandez the order to have those people killed. This is hugely important." She looked at him for a moment. "Do you think it's possible Hernandez was one of the shooters?"

Tom shrugged. "I told you, I didn't see anything. I heard gunfire, and by the time I got there all I saw was the bodies."

"But did you see Hernandez holding his machine gun as if he'd just fired it, anything like that? You're not withholding anything from me, are you?"

"Claire," Tom said, raising his voice, "are you listening to me? I said I didn't see anything. Okay? You want me to repeat it? I didn't see anything."

She stared at him, taken aback by this sudden flash of anger. What in the world was he so mad about?

"I hear you," she replied tersely, and got up to enter the courtroom.

"The government calls Frederick W. Coultas." Coultas was the prosecution's ballistics man, a firearms-identification expert of national rank.

A tall, awkward man in a cheap brown suit, Coultas walked up the center aisle, settled himself in the witness chair, and was sworn in. He had a large oblong head, a tall forehead fringed by an ill-fitting hairpiece of beaver-pelt brown, wire-rim glasses framing beady brown eyes, and virtually no chin.

The jurors turned to look at him with curiosity. Most of the time they seemed to betray little emotion, but not once had Claire ever seen them look bored or distracted.

Coultas stated his credentials for the record, and Waldron helped him elaborate. Frederick Coultas was with the FBI's Firearms and Toolmarks Unit and an instructor in firearms identification at the FBI Academy at Quantico. Graduate of the U.S. Army Small Arms Repair School, Aberdeen Proving Grounds, in Maryland. Graduate of armorer school, of gunsmith courses, of the firearms-instructors course at the Smith & Wesson Academy. A dozen years with the FBI's Firearms Identification Section. Specialist in tool marks. On and on in overwhelming detail. Waldron made his point with wearying unsubtlety: Frederick Coultas knew his guns.

He went on to a methodical direct examination, Waldron at his merciless best.

"Tell me about the ammunition that was recovered," Waldron said sometime later.

"Thirty-nine projectiles, bullets, were recovered, and one hundred thirty-seven cartridge casings."

"Were they in good condition?"

"Yes."

"Is that number of bullets, thirty-nine, consistent in your opinion with testimony that two hundred rounds were fired?"

"Yes. Even if you use a metal detector at the scene of the crime, many tend to be lost. You can't help it."

"Was anything else found?"

"Yes. One hundred and seven links, the little serrated and notched metal pieces that connect cartridges to each other in the ammo belt."

"Were these links of use to you in identifying which gun was used?"

Coultas pushed the nosepiece of his glasses. "No. It's quite hard to identify links to a specific weapon, though I suppose it's theoretically possible."

"Mr. Coultas, does the El Salvador government report say whether any of the bullets were recovered from bodies?"

"No, it does not, but that doesn't mean anything. It's extremely hard to recover machine-gun projectiles from the body, since most of them pass right through."

Relentlessly, like a jackhammer, Waldron took him through the chain of custody. Coultas was satisfied with the way the evidence had been collected by the Salvadorans and sent to Army CID, marked with a metal scribe and put down on an evidence worksheet. Waldron left no stone unturned, right down to the head stamp at the base of each cartridge.

"Now, tell us, were these projectiles and cartridge casings all fired by the same exact weapon?"

"Yes, they were."

"And was it this one?" Waldron held up the plastic-wrapped machine gun. Coultas leaned forward to inspect it. Theatrics.

"Yes, it was."

"Mr. Coultas, can you tell us how you can connect a particular bullet to a particular weapon?"

Coultas settled back in his seat and pushed again with a long finger at the nosepiece of his glasses. His voice became high, nasal, and insufferably pompous. "Inside the barrel of every gun, spiral grooves are cut. This is called the 'rifling.' It causes the bullet to twist in a certain direction, to spin quickly and thus travel faster and with greater accuracy. Also, the spiral grooves of each type of weapon have a unique pattern. Between the grooves are raised areas called 'lands.' These lands and grooves make an imprint on the bullet, the gross markings that we can see under the microscope."

He had to be a deadly instructor, Claire reflected. No wonder the FBI lab was always in trouble.

"And did the rifling system on this particular weapon match the bullets you looked at?" Waldron asked.

"Absolutely. The rifling system on this particular M-60 machine gun is what we call 4-R, a four-right system, or four lands and grooves with a right twist. Also, there's one turn in twelve inches. Using comparison microscoping, I saw that the projectiles showed traces of this rifling. Also, I noticed that one of the lands in this barrel was narrower than the others. That was another distinguishing feature. The striations on the bullets caused by passage through a barrel were identical to the barrel of the weapon in question. That is, they all appeared to come from the same weapon."

Farrell popped open a can of Pepsi.

"What about the cartridge casings?" Waldron asked.

"I inspected the ejected casings, looking at the primer, the firing-pin impression, the chamber markings, and, on the bottom, the breech-face impression."

"So there's no doubt in your mind that these bullets were fired by the machine gun you examined?"

"None whatsoever."

"Thank you very much, Mr. Coultas. Nothing further."

"Defense, do you have cross-examination?" Farrell asked.

"Yes, sir," Claire said as she stood. For a few seconds she looked questioningly at the witness. Finally, she said, "Mr. Coultas, do you know if this was the gun used by Sergeant Kubik?"

"No," he admitted.

"Oh? Why not?"

"Well, I'm really not competent to testify to that. I understand the government has already had a witness from Fort Bragg up here, describing the computer armory records and how they're maintained. But that's outside of my area of competence."

"So you have no idea whose gun this was?"

"That's right."

"And, Mr. Coultas, you've already testified that you don't know whether any of these bullets were recovered from bodies, is that right?"

"That's right."

"So do you know whether these bullets killed anybody?"

"No."

"You don't."

"No. That's outside my area of expertise, strictly speaking. I suppose the eyewitnesses—"

"Thank you. Now, Mr. Coultas, based on your thorough examination of the evidence, can you tell the court when these rounds were fired?"

"Actually, no."

"You can't? Really? You have absolutely no idea?"

"Well, the attached records—"

"I said, based on your examination of the evidence. Were they fired on the date in question, June 22, 1985?"

"I really wouldn't know."

"Can you tell if they were fired that week?"

"No."

"Or that month?"

"No."

"Or even that year?"

"No, I can't."

"Interesting. And, Mr. Coultas, can you tell me something? When you fire a machine gun for a long time, what happens to the barrel?"

"Well, it gets hot."

A low chuckle from the jury box, and some titters from the spectators.

"And what do you do then? Do you keep using it?"

"Oh, no. After five hundred rounds have been fired, you change the barrel to avoid overheating. You remove it and replace it with another."

"Even when you're out in the field?"

"Oh, sure. The machine gun is usually issued with a spare barrel. Sometimes you might have a whole sack of barrels. They're interchangeable. They also deteriorate. After a while, you throw them away.''

"So this particular machine gun might have been issued with two separate barrels?"

"Correct."

"Possibly more."

"Possibly."

She gave Embry a sidelong glance. His eyes gleamed with, she thought, pride. "Mr. Coultas, are machine-gun barrels serialized the way guns usually are?"

"Sometimes. I've seen it."

"But is this one?"

"No."

"It's not marked."

"No."

"So do you know whether *this exact* barrel was issued along with *this exact* gun?"

Coultas shook his head in bafflement as he stroked his receding chin. "I'd have no way to know that."

"But you do know that they're easily switched?"

"That I do know."

"Mr. Coultas, granting for the sake of argument that this is the barrel that was used to fire the projectiles you've so carefully studied—isn't it possible that someone might have switched barrels?"

"Well, I suppose so, yes."

"You *suppose* so?"

"It's possible, yes."

"So someone might have taken this gun, with this particular serial number stamped on it, and actually put on it the barrel that was used to fire all those rounds?"

"I can't rule it out."

"It's possible?"

"Theoretically, yes, it is."

"It's not difficult to do?"

"No, it's not."

"It would, in fact, be quite an easy thing to do, wouldn't it, Mr. Coultas?"

"Yes, it would," he said. "It would be very easy."

"Thank you, Mr. Coultas. I have nothing further."

45

❖

The weekend, at last. Some much-needed time off. She tried to sleep late but couldn't. She awoke before seven and realized the phone hadn't rung in the middle of the night. Progress. Or maybe they took weekends off. She ran a very hot bath in the big old white porcelain tub in the master-suite bathroom, whose floor was tiled in tiny black-and-white octagons as in a grand hotel of old, and took a long soak. She was tempted to bring some work into the tub with her, maybe a transcript, but then forced herself not to. She needed a break. She needed to let her fevered brain rest a bit. She needed perspective on the case. So she closed her eyes and soaked away the bruises and the aches. She thought about Tom, wanted to visit him at the brig, but knew that Annie needed her even more right now.

Then she got into jeans, a sweatshirt, and sneakers, and took Annie out to breakfast in Georgetown, just the two of them. They left without notifying Devereaux, who was probably still sleeping.

"When can we go home?" Annie asked. She was making designs on her pancakes with the squeeze bottle of syrup.

"You mean Boston?"

"Yeah. I want to see my friends. I want to see Katie."

"Soon, honey."

"What's 'soon'?"

"A couple of weeks. Maybe sooner."

"With Daddy?"

She didn't know what to say now. No, she wanted to say. Not with Daddy. Daddy's kangaroo court will probably find him guilty and sentence him to life in Leavenworth, where you'll be able to visit him once in a while. It will tear your life apart. And that's if Mommy's able to get the sentence reduced from death. All the while, Mommy will be fighting uphill battles, writing and filing briefs like one of these half-crazed prison legal scholars, taking the case to the Army Court of Criminal Appeals, and higher and higher, all the way up to the Supreme Court. While the family's resources dwindled away, because Harvard would have fired her, which she was sure would happen any day now. Probably at some point, once they were out of the military system, the verdict would be overturned; it surely couldn't stand up, the government's case was a joke. But Daddy would certainly not survive prison, because too many people wanted him dead.

"Of course with Daddy," she said, and tousled Annie's miraculously soft, glossy brown hair. "Now, when you're done with your pancakes, we'll go to the zoo, okay?"

Annie shrugged as if the idea didn't appeal to her.

"You don't like the zoo?" Claire said.

Annie shook her head.

"You're still upset with me."

"No, Mommy. I'm *angry* with you."

"I know."

"No, you don't, Mommy. You always *say* you know, but you don't." Her eyes shone. "You said you were going to be home more, but you're still always gone."

"You wanted me to play with you last night, but I had to work with Mr. Grimes and Mr. Embry and Uncle Ray. I know."

"How come you're always working?"

"Because Daddy's on trial," she said. "They want to lock him up in the jail for a long, long time, and it's up to me and my friends to make sure they don't do that."

"But why does it take so long?"

A tough one. "Because the people who want to put him away are bad guys, and sometimes they lie."

"Why?"

Claire thought about that one for a long time. Finally she said, honestly, "I don't really know."

"So you have nothing on the general?" Claire asked, when they'd gathered that evening. Embry and Grimes sat in their usual chairs. Devereaux stood and paced, because he liked to loom over people. She sat behind the beautiful library-table-cum-desk, leaning back in the high leather-upholstered executive chair, and exhaled a cloud of cigarette smoke. "No wife-beating, no adultery, no child molestation, nothing?"

"He's clean as a whistle," Devereaux said. "Fastest-promoted general ever to serve in the army. Eagle Scout, kind to animals, good to his neighbors. Gives generously to charity, serves on the board of the United Way and the American Cancer Society. He doesn't even rent dirty videos."

" 'Even'?" Claire said. "Like everyone does?"

"Well, *you* don't," Devereaux said. "That I know."

"Thanks. Nice to know you respect my privacy."

"What about Robert Lentini?" Grimes asked. "Still can't turn that guy up?"

"Even assuming he wasn't behind that setup in the Catoctin mountains, and that they just used his name because they knew Claire would bite—no. The guy's disappeared without a trace. Either that, or he never existed."

"Well, we know he existed, from his service records," Embry said.

"Maybe," Devereaux said.

"And what about my CIA guy, Dennis?" Claire asked.

Devereaux broke out in a grin. "You gotta love this. These cloak-and-dagger boys can't even pick up on a tail if it's six four and three hundred pounds. I followed baldy home to Chevy Chase, right to his suburban manse. His name is Dennis T. Mackie. 'Course, I don't know what good that'll do you. Unless you have a CIA personnel directory. Now, you guys mind if I take my leave? I gotta get my beauty sleep."

"I wanted to say something," Embry ventured bashfully. "That was a really great cross you did of the ballistics guy."

"Thanks," she said. "But this was definitely a case of I-couldn't-have-done-it-without-you." Embry shrugged. "No, I really couldn't have," she insisted. "I'd never have thought of the barrels. What the hell do I know about guns?"

"*You* prepped her on that?" Grimes said.

Embry looked at Grimes uneasily.

"You're a smart dude," Grimes said.

Embry smiled in amazement. "Thanks."

"Even Coultas didn't remember about the barrels," Grimes said.

"I don't believe that," Claire said. "Not someone like Coultas. He's a national ballistics authority, and he doesn't overlook something obvious like that."

"It wasn't *that* obvious," Embry protested.

"It is to a guy like Coultas," she said. "I'm sure he was hoping he wouldn't be asked."

"Naw," Grimes said, "he's a neutral expert. He doesn't take sides. He was probably instructed, by Waldron, not to bring it up unless asked, not to point to it in any way."

"Is there anything else?" Embry asked after a while. "Because I want to get to work on the General Marks stuff, see if I can come up with any angles. Actually, I'd kind of like to go home and get some shut-eye."

"Go ahead, Terry," she said. "Thanks for coming over."

When Embry had left, Grimes said, "You want a drink?"

"I don't think so, no. Thanks anyway."

"You look tired."

"I'm always tired these days."

"Then I'll head home myself." He stood up, collected his papers, and put them in his briefcase. Standing near her desk, he said, "Can I tell you something kind of personal?"

"Yeah?" she said warily.

"I just—what I mean is, you're this big hotshot lawyer, and I've been, like, a fan of yours for a hell of a long time, and I thought it was kind of cool you wanted to hire me."

She nodded, smiled. "You came highly recommended."

"Forget that shit. I'm saying, even though I was,

like, totally intimidated when you came into my office that first time, I still couldn't help think it was a joke, you wanting to try this case, a totally high-pressure military court-martial, and not knowing shit about military law. But you know what?"

"What?"

"Now I get it. Now I see why you're the hotshot you are. You're just fucking *good* at whatever you do."

Tears came into her eyes. It was late, she was exhausted, and she was emotionally a wreck. She smiled and shrugged and shook her head. She stood up and came around to where he was standing. "Grimes—Charlie—Charles—oh, fuck it." And she hugged him long and hard.

The phone rang again, at two-thirty Monday morning.

She fumbled for it, picked up the handset.

"Ask yourself who really wants him locked away," the electronically altered voice said.

"Thanks," Claire said. "We've almost got you, asshole."

46

"*They're putting* the general on the stand today?" Devereaux asked. Claire sat in the front
seat of Devereaux's rented car, a Lincoln Town Car
even larger and more luxurious than the one he
drove back in Boston. Corinthian leather was everywhere.

"Apparently." Distracted, she sipped from a take-
out cup of coffee.

"So he's going to sit there in his general's costume
with the four stars and the fruit salad on the front
and say Sergeant Ronald Kubik did it? And that's
going to sway the jury because he's a four-star general? Even though he wasn't even on the scene?"

"That's Waldron's theory, and it's not a bad one."

"And you're going to do what?" He pulled into
the back gate of Quantico and waved at the sentry,
who by now recognized them.

"I'm going to look for the soft spots," she said,
"and plunge in the knife."

Devereaux looked at her for a moment and turned
back to the road. He gave a crooked smile. "Why do
I get a feeling you're gonna plunge in the knife even

336

if there isn't a soft spot? You get a call this morning, around two-thirty?"

She nodded. "The FBI boys got something?"

"Nope. Me. See, there's only two entrances to the Pentagon that're open twenty-four hours a day. There's the Mall entrance, and there's the River entrance. I gambled, and staked out the Mall entrance. At around twenty after two in the morning—ten minutes before you received a call—guess who's striding into the Pentagon, all bright-eyed and bushy-tailed?"

"I can't guess," she said.

"The good soldier. Colonel James Hernandez. He's your caller. And probably behind that car 'accident' in Maryland. Nice guy, huh?"

Waldron's direct examination of the general was crisp, professional, and respectful. It lasted most of the morning, and the court recessed for an early lunch.

When Claire, Grimes, and Embry returned from lunch they noticed that the prosecution table was empty, which was unusual. Waldron and Hogan were punctual men who liked to confer at their table with plenty of time to spare before Judge Farrell returned.

The two men returned with just seconds to spare, talking in low voices with evident excitement. Waldron was accompanied by a CID investigator Claire had seen from time to time, whose name she'd forgotten.

"What's going on?" Tom whispered, grasping her shoulder.

She shook her head.

"Something's up," Grimes muttered under his

breath. "Waldron looks like the cat that ate the canary."

Claire introduced herself to the general with extravagant graciousness, emphasizing for the jury something she might, at another time, be inclined to downplay: General William Marks's august rank.

Another attorney might well have chosen to treat the general as just another witness, silently communicating to the panel members, This witness is really no different from any others, and don't you forget it. And that wouldn't have been an incorrect strategy.

But she noticed that the jurors seemed on their best behavior while the general was in the courtroom. They sat up straight, they refrained from chewing pencils or cradling their chins on their hands or any of the little gestures of inattention or boredom. Even Judge Farrell, she noticed, hadn't brought a can of Pepsi to the stand. So she slathered on the deference, knowing that in a matter of seconds she'd be treating him with all the disrespect he actually deserved.

"General Marks," she said once the dull preliminaries were out of the way, "you have been granted immunity in exchange for your testimony here today, is that correct?"

"Yes, it is." His response was frank and confident. With his silver hair and his aquiline nose, he looked resplendent in his dress uniform.

"There are two types of immunity, general. One covers just your testimony here in the courtroom. Another kind covers the events you've been testifying about—specifically, the events in El Salvador in June of 1985. Which kind of immunity have you been given, sir?"

"The latter. Transactional immunity," he said with a nod.

"And why is that, sir?"

"War is sloppy, counselor. Mistakes are inevitably made, and often the commander is held responsible for them."

"Oh? And were we at war with El Salvador in 1985, General?"

Judge Farrell interrupted. "Madame Defense Counsel, I'm not going to countenance your taking that tone with the general. I don't like that disrespect."

Claire dipped her head agreeably, not inclined to quarrel just yet. "Certainly, Your Honor. General, when you use the word 'war,' do you mean to say that we were at war in 1985? I wasn't under the impression that Congress had declared war against El Salvador at the time."

General Marks gave a wry smile. "Any time a unit of the army, including the Special Forces, conducts operations downrange against a potentially hostile force, we operate under the conditions of war."

"Ah," she said. "Now I see. That certainly makes sense. And do you agree with the notion that the commander is responsible for the actions of the men under him?"

"It's not just a notion, counselor. It's the way the army operates."

"So you have no quibble with it?"

He gave a small snort of amusement. "No, I have no 'quibble,' as you say, with the way the army operates."

"So, as the commanding officer of Detachment 27, you were ultimately responsible for all of the actions of your men?"

"Yes, indeed," he said, nodding his head vigorously. "Even actions over which I had no control—"

"Thank you, General—"

"—which is why I've been granted immunity to explore the tragic actions of your client."

"Thank you, General. Now, sir, Detachment 27 was sent down to El Salvador to take reprisals for the Zona Rosa bombing, isn't that correct?"

A rueful smile. "No, counselor, that's not correct. We were sent to locate the murderers, the so-called urban guerrillas who murdered four marines. Not to take revenge."

"Thank you for that distinction, General. And would it be correct to point out, sir, that you had a personal stake in that mission?"

"Absolutely not."

"Really? You weren't a close friend of one of the marines killed in the Zona Rosa bombing on 19 June 1985, a Marine Force Recon, Lieutenant Colonel Arlen Ross?"

"Well, there's another important distinction to make," he said, quite reasonably. "I was indeed an acquaintance of Arlen Ross—"

"No, sir," she interrupted. "Not an 'acquaintance.' A friend."

The general shrugged. "If you wish. A friend. I have no quarrel with that. Lieutenant Colonel Ross was, sadly, among those killed in the Zona Rosa. But make no mistake, counselor. I was there at the direction of the President of the United States. I most certainly did not use the might of the United States Army Special Forces to carry out my own personal vendetta."

"I certainly never implied such a thing, General," Claire said, feigning astonishment. "Merely that you might have had a personal stake in the mission, as anyone might have who'd had a close friend killed a few days before by antigovernment rebels."

But the general was too shrewd for that. Not for nothing had he advanced as high as he had, and as quickly. "That's very generous of you, counselor," he said brusquely, "but I operate at the behest of my commander-in-chief. Not as some Mafioso out for blood."

Never lose control of the witness, Claire reminded herself, and here she was doing just that. This line of cross-examination was clearly a mistake.

"General," she said, "when we met for a pretrial interview at your office in the Pentagon, did you warn me not to pursue this matter because it might be damaging to my career?"

General Marks regarded her for a few seconds with an indecipherable stare. He had been briefed. He knew about the secret tape recording of Henry Abbott. "Yes, I did," he replied at length. "I was quite frankly concerned that you were on some sort of self-destructive kamikaze mission, counselor, because the client is your husband."

There, it was finally out. She had no doubt that all of the panel members already knew that Tom was her husband. But now the fact, in all its complexity and ambiguity, lay out there on official display.

"I was concerned," he went on, "that if you continued to pursue this case without knowing all the facts, you'd end up looking foolish in the extreme. You are, after all, married to a man who may be a murderer. You're not exactly objective." He smiled sadly. "You are the same age as my daughter. I can't help but take a fatherly concern."

"Well, that's very kind of you, General," she said without irony. "I certainly appreciate your concern and your solicitude." And she decided to move right in for the kill. "General Marks, when my client allegedly fired upon the civilians, how far away were you standing?"

"I wasn't there," he said. "The unit was being led by my XO, Major James Hernandez. I was issuing commands over the radio."

"Major James Hernandez, who is still your XO, is that correct?"

"Yes."

"Now, General, it is alleged that my client killed eighty-seven people, and it occurs to me that killing eighty-seven people must take some time, isn't that right?"

"Alas, no," the general replied. "It can be done in a surprisingly short time, counselor, I am sorry to say."

"Really?"

"It would surprise you," he said, and gave another sad smile. "Sergeant Kubik fired two hundred rounds. The M-60 machine gun fires at a rate of five hundred fifty rounds per minute. So firing two hundred rounds takes not much more than twenty seconds, counselor."

Ordinarily, the general's reply would have been devastating. But Claire knew where this was going. "Twenty seconds," she mused.

"A little bit more."

"But I thought there are only one hundred rounds in a belt," she said, playing the ingenue.

"That's true," the general replied, "but he had apparently linked two belts together, using a technique he said he'd learned from a squad leader in Vietnam. That way, the second belt pulls evenly."

"If the ammo belt gets twisted, what happens?"

"The weapon will jam."

Claire nodded, and began to pace in front of the

witness rail, thinking. "So, if one of your men had grabbed Sergeant Kubik's ammo belt and twisted it, his weapon would have jammed, and he'd have been unable to fire."

"Only if someone could get close enough to grab the belt."

"And no one could?"

"Seriously? A man firing a machine gun?"

"None of your men could have bounded up to him in a few steps and grabbed the weapon out of his hands? Or twisted the ammo belt so that the gun jammed?"

"The man had an M-60 in his hands, counselor. I was told that his head was pivoting all around, looking, and he would most certainly have sensed anyone moving toward him."

"But your men must have had weapons, too, general."

"Indeed."

"What weapons did they have?"

"They had .45s. And I certainly wasn't going to have them go up against an M-60 machine gun with a .45. He could have hit them much more easily than they could have hit him."

"Did you order him to stop?"

"Yes, I did. Through Major Hernandez."

"And?"

"Hernandez said, 'He's wacko, we can't stop him.' "

She fell silent for a moment. He was good, and well briefed. And she knew this was going nowhere. He would continue to insist that he couldn't have stopped Kubik, and he would be unshakable in his certainty. "General, in your opinion, would you have been within your rights as an officer to order your men to shoot Sergeant Kubik dead, if, as you claim, he was in fact massacring those eighty-seven civilians?"

"In fact, yes," Marks said. "The Uniform Code of Military Justice permits the use of lethal force to save your life or the life of another."

Claire winced inwardly. That was the right answer. He had just foreclosed the line of cross-examination she'd prepared designed to show that he'd been negligent as an officer and a commander—which could at least have damaged his credibility. So she tried again, coming back to the question of whether he could have killed Kubik. As she questioned the witness about this fictitious Sergeant Kubik that the prosecution was creating, she didn't think of him as Tom. "General, isn't it true that any of your men could have waited for the instant that Sergeant Kubik's eyes were trained on his civilian targets, and simply aimed a Colt .45 and fired?"

The general exhaled noisily. "Counselor, I don't know whether you've ever fired a gun—whether you've ever even *picked up* a gun—and I *know* you've never served in a war—"

"Move to strike as nonresponsive, Your Honor," Claire interrupted.

"I'm afraid you opened the door to that with your theoretical question," Judge Farrell said. "Continue, sir."

"Thank you," General Marks said. "Counselor, sitting in your comfy office at Harvard thirteen years after the fact, I suppose you could make that argument. But when you're commanding a ten-man unit in conditions of war, it's a different matter. There are chances you have to take, so there are chances you *will not* take. Perhaps you would have exercised superior judgment. I used the best I had." He bowed his head. "We lost a number of Americans in El Salvador, counselor, for what the President of the United States, my commander-in-chief, deemed our strategic interests. Covert operations aren't always pretty. But there's a difference between the price of covert ops and what that evil man did. It sickens me what happened in that village—sickens me as an army man and as a human being."

This was, Claire realized, one of the worst crosses she'd ever conducted, and not for want of preparation. She could see how moved the jury was. General Marks was a terrific witness, and an extremely well prepared one. It should not have surprised her.

But it was not over yet.

"General, a few moments ago you referred to the unarmed civilians. But is it possible that Sergeant Kubik believed they were in fact armed combatants?"

"No," he replied flatly.

"Why not?"

"They weren't in uniform, for one. They were lined up peacefully, and not making any hostile or antagonistic movements. And there were no weapons."

"But isn't it possible he might have *thought* he saw weapons?"

The question, she knew, would perplex the general. It seemed to point to a new theory of defense— that Tom had fired because he saw weapons. Whereas they had all along insisted that the entire incident was made up, implying that someone else must have done the shooting. She could see the general hesitating, and glancing furtively at Waldron. She stepped to the side deftly, placing her body in his line of sight.

So the general reverted to his customary arrogance. "No," he finally said. "There were no weapons."

"How can you be so sure?"

"Because, counselor, I had my XO inspect the bodies, and he found no weapons."

"So you knew objectively, after the fact, that there were no weapons. But *at the time*, General, did you have any reason to believe the villagers had weapons?"

"None."

"Your men saw no weapons."

"Correct."

"They saw nothing, no glint of metal, nothing that might make them even the slightest bit apprehensive that the villagers had weapons."

"Nothing."

"So they saw no weapons pointed at Sergeant Kubik, or any of your men."

Waldron called out, "Asked and answered, Your Honor."

"Sustained. Move on, counselor."

"My apologies, Your Honor. Just wanted to be absolutely sure we were on the same page. General Marks, early on the morning of June 22, 1985, you sat down and wrote out an MFR, a memorandum for the record, isn't that correct?"

"That's correct."

"Isn't that unusual?"

"How so?"

"Well, sir, isn't the usual thing to do to file an After Action Report?"

"Yes, it is. But this wasn't a 'usual' incident, counselor. One of my men had just waxed an entire village full of innocent civilians."

"In fact, unarmed civilians."

"As I've said, counselor."

"So why file an MFR? What's the point in doing that?"

"Because I wanted to get the event on the record. I was sure that Sergeant Kubik would be prosecuted for this, and I wanted to begin preserving records."

"You mean, *creating* records."

"Your Honor!" Waldron shouted.

"I said preserving records, counselor," the general said crisply.

"General, do you have a copy of the memorandum you wrote that morning?"

"Unfortunately, I do not. It appears to have been lost."

"How could that have happened?"

He smiled. "Papers are lost all the time, counselor, especially in wartime. Believe me, I wish I had it. Even general officers can be victimized by a large and at times unwieldy bureaucracy."

She returned the smile. "General, in the memorandum you wrote that morning, did you state that the villagers had weapons, and that was why you ordered your men to shoot?"

"Absolutely not," Marks said, his eyes flashing.

"You didn't write that?"

"No, I didn't, because it wasn't the case. I didn't order anyone to kill those civilians, and the civilians didn't have weapons."

"Thank you, General." She stepped back to the defense table, where Embry handed her several sheets of paper. Smoothly she came around to the prosecution table and dropped one in front of Waldron, then handed one to Judge Farrell. "Your Honor, may I approach the witness with what has been previously marked Defense Exhibit C for identification?"

"You may," Farrell said, looking down confusedly at the document he'd just been given.

She gave the paper to the general. "General Marks, do you recognize this form?"

The general said nothing. For the first time, he appeared to have lost his composure. His face seemed to be going white.

"Is this your signature, General?"

Nothing.

"Is this your handwriting?"

The courtroom was silent, absolutely still, but she could feel all hell breaking loose. Waldron was scribbling something furiously, a note he was showing to Hogan. Out of the corner of her eye she saw a motion at the back of the room, and realized it was the general's lawyer, Jerome Fine, making some sort of hand signal.

"We can take a recess if you like," Claire said gently. "We can have a continuance. I have a handwriting expert standing by. We can ask you to copy this document and have it analyzed on the spot." It was a bluff; she had no such handwriting expert. "I think you know this is your handwriting. Let me remind you, sir, that your immunity does not cover lying under oath, perjury, or false swearing."

"Yes," he said at last, staring at her with hatred. His tone, however, was even. "I believe it is my handwriting."

"Your Honor," she said, turning pleasantly toward Farrell, "at this time I'd like to offer Defense Exhibit C for identification, and ask permission to publish it to the jury."

"It is admitted," Farrell said, "and the words 'for identification' will be stricken. You may publish it to the jury now."

She handed six copies of the document to the president of the court, who took one and passed the others out. Turning back to the general, she said, "Please read that to the court."

He hesitated, turned to the judge. Annoyed, he asked: "Do I have to?"

"Yes," Farrell said, "I'm afraid you do."

Marks compressed his lips into a thin line, then turned back to Claire and gave her a poisonous look. Donning a pair of reading glasses, he began to read: " 'In the early-morning hours of 22 June 1985, I was informed by Major James Hernandez that armed villagers in La Colina, El Salvador, had been observed acting with apparent hostile intent toward Detachment 27.' " He cleared his throat. His face was flushed. " 'I ordered free fire based on presence of armed hostiles. My orders were executed, and eighty-seven aggressors were terminated with prejudice. The detachment retired from the scene of aggressor contact and returned to Ilopango. Signed, Colonel William O. Marks, Commanding Officer, Detachment 27. Ilopango, El Salvador.' " He looked up slowly, his eyes flashing with anger.

"General Marks," Claire said, "is every word of what you just read the truth as you remembered it on 22 June 1985? Or is there anything you want to change?"

For several seconds they glared at each other.

Then General Marks turned to the judge. "Your Honor," he said, "I'd like to speak with my attorney before I answer that question."

"Your Honor," Waldron said, standing, "we need a recess for the witness to consult his attorney."

"Members," Farrell said, "will you excuse us?"

As the members were escorted out by the bailiff, the courtroom exploded in a maelstrom of voices.

47

"*Your Honor*," Waldron demanded, "I'd like to have the defense counsel state for the record, as an officer of the court, how long she's had this memorandum, and where she got it."

"No, Your Honor," Claire said before Farrell had a chance to respond. "I don't have to do that, and I'm not going to. The prosecution isn't entitled to a preview of my cross-examination. For God's sake, we put this exact MFR in our discovery request— we named it specifically!—and the government, in effect, made a written denial that it even existed! I got this after their written denial; this document is a photocopy from the CIA operational files, fully marked with a complete chain of custody, and that's all I'm going to say."

"The *CIA!*" Waldron stammered, looking at Claire. Why was he so astonished, she wondered?

Farrell was clearly taken aback by the whole business, by how quickly the tables had turned, by the spectacle of an entire courtroom watching a four-star general lie under oath. Everything the judge said on the record was going to be scrutinized minutely. He had to tiptoe, and he knew it. He popped open a Pepsi and swigged long and hard.

"Mr. Trial Counsel," Farrell said, "it's your witness, and it was your job to find that document, so I'm not inclined to help you out here."

In the meantime, Jerome Fine, the general's counsel, had moved a chair right next to the general's on the witness stand, and the two of them were conferring in whispers.

"General," Claire said, approaching him, "is that your attorney there?"

Marks seemed vaguely amused. "Yes, it is."

"And what's his name?"

"Jerome R. Fine. He's the army general counsel."

"Hmm. Interesting, General, that you have your attorney sitting right next to you. Do you feel you have something to hide?"

He smiled and said with a low chuckle, "Not at all."

"Now, General, prior to your testifying here today, did you review the testimony you gave before Congress when you were confirmed as chief of staff of the army?"

Marks hesitated but a moment. "Yes."

"Your attorney advised you to do that, didn't he?"

"Ms. Chapman," the general said hotly, "I don't have to tell you anything that my attorney and I discussed."

"Ah, but I'm afraid you do." She glanced at Jerome Fine, who looked uneasy. "You see, General, we can call Mr. Fine to the stand right after you—nothing you two have talked about is privileged, since he works for the United States of America. Not for you."

The general looked at his lawyer, who gave a tiny nod.

"So perhaps you can answer my question, General. Did your attorney advise you to review your congressional testimony?"

A pause. The lawyer nodded again. "Yes, he did."

"Now, General Marks, did you tell your attorney that the memorandum for the record you wrote immediately after the incident at La Colina had been destroyed, as far as you knew, and that you didn't remember its contents?"

Marks turned again to Judge Farrell. "Do I have to answer that, Your Honor?"

"Yes, you do," Farrell replied.

"Yes, I did tell him that," Marks replied, "but that was my recollection—"

"Thank you," Claire interrupted. "General, did you ever tell your wife about the alleged massacre at La Colina?"

"My wife?" Incredulous, he turned back to the judge. "Your Honor, I don't have to answer questions about my *personal* life, do I?"

"Yes, General, you do," the judge said evenly.

Raising his voice a few decibels, Marks said tartly, "My wife and I never discuss this sort of thing."

"Oh? And what sort of thing is that?"

"Covert actions—"

"And was the incident at La Colina a 'covert action'?"

"Don't twist my words," Marks snapped. "That massacre was the most godawful tragic thing that ever happened during my—"

"And you mean to tell us you didn't tell your wife about this most godawful tragic thing?"

He hesitated.

"Or did you lie to her, too?"

"*I have never lied about La Colina!*" Marks thundered.

"Oh no? You lied to Congress, didn't you? Isn't it a fact that, when you were asked about this incident by the Senate during your confirmation, you gave a version entirely contradicted by the MFR you wrote? You lied to Congress, did you not?"

"I do not have to take this!" Marks shouted. "I have dedicated over thirty years of my life to serving the Constitution of the United States and the people of this country—"

"General," said his attorney, grabbing his arm.

"But you lied to Congress, General, did you not?" Claire persisted.

"I do not have to take that from someone like you!" Marks shouted, half rising from his seat. His face was crimson. "You're out of line!"

"General, please!" his attorney said, tugging at Marks's arm to pull him back into his seat.

"What does that mean, someone like me?" Claire asked with a faint smile. "A defense attorney doing her job? Protecting a client falsely accused of murders he did not commit? That you might have had a hand in as an accomplice—?"

"Objection!" shouted Waldron.

"This is an *obscenity*!" thundered Marks.

"Move on," Judge Farrell said.

"General," Claire said in a ringing voice, "you lied to Congress, did you not?"

There was a moment of silence.

The general's lawyer cupped a hand in front of his mouth and whispered something to his client. General Marks, his composure regained, looked up and said blithely, "Upon advice of counsel, I decline to comment."

"Wait a second," Claire said. "Are you taking the Fifth?"

"Yes, I am."

"Well, what—what are you taking the Fifth *about*?"

"About my testimony," Marks replied evenly. "My lawyer has just advised me that I may have committed false swearing." He turned toward Judge Farrell. "Your Honor, I haven't seen that document in thirteen years. I testified here as to what I remembered of that document. And, frankly, I was ambushed."

"Your Honor," Claire said, "I move to strike the direct testimony of this witness, since we're being denied the Sixth Amendment right to cross-examination."

Farrell squinted at the general, then shook his head in disbelief. "Your motion is granted. The witness's direct testimony is stricken."

"Thank you, Your Honor. At this time, defense moves for a mistrial on the grounds that this witness's testimony can't be taken back. You can't unring that bell."

"Denied," Farrell snapped with a red-faced scowl.

"In that case, Your Honor, we ask that you instruct the members that the chief of staff of the army is no longer a witness before this court, and the members may not consider any testimony he has given. I also ask that Your Honor inform the members that you, the military judge, believe that the chief of staff may have perjured himself, and that the members should put his testimony out of their minds, and that the military judge has advised the chief of his rights against self-incrimination under Article 31 of the Uniform Code of Military Justice, and the chief of staff has decided he will give no further testimony here before this court-martial."

"All right," Farrell said. He knew he had little choice. "You got it. I will so instruct the members.

And, General, you're excused, with our deepest apologies."

Claire stared in disbelief as the general got to his feet, shrugged his uniform back into place, and strode off, attorney in tow.

"Uh, Your Honor," Waldron said. "While we're in this 39(a) session, I'd like to introduce our next exhibit, Prosecution Exhibit 4, for identification, which is a tape recording of the accused speaking on a tactical field radio on 22 June 1985, referring to the events he's on trial for, as well as a verbatim transcript of that conversation."

Claire looked at Grimes, then Embry, then Tom. All of them looked as astonished as she did.

"Your Honor, I don't *believe* this!" she said.

"And the worm turns," Farrell said. "What is this, Surprise Evidence Day? Give the Judge an Ulcer Day? Trial counsel, you got the tape right here?"

"Yes, we do, sir," Waldron said. He handed the black cassette to the judge, along with a small tape player.

"Well, let's hear it," Farrell said.

Grimes said aloud, "The hits just keep on coming."

The tape sounded as if it had been enhanced, the static filtered out, and so Tom's voice was crystal-clear.

And it was Tom's voice, there was no question about it.

"It was unbelievable. Just fucking unbelievable. I mean, I was just so fucking sick and tired of those peasants lying to us, you know? I just picked up my M-60 and blew 'em away, and it was just fucking great. Fuckin-A right I did."

There was silence, and then the judge clicked off the tape recorder.

"That's not me," Tom said to Claire in a low voice.

"Where's this from?" Judge Farrell asked.

"Defense Intelligence Agency made the original recording, Your Honor," Waldron said. "Their signals-intelligence section. The copy was provided by CIA after a search of their SIGINT archives."

"When did you get this?"

"Just today, Your Honor. At lunch."

"How long you know about its existence?" Farrell asked.

"I was called this morning, but I didn't believe it until I actually heard the tape at lunch today."

"Whadda we got here, CIA versus DIA?" Farrell said. "Civilian spooks versus military spooks?"

Waldron replied, "This conversation was overheard by signals intercept, 123rd Signals Battalion, down in El Salvador, on 22 June 1985. Their communications receivers were automatically sweeping between certain frequency ranges, between four and five hundred megahertz. The accused's conversation was made in the clear on a tactical field radio with a range of up to twenty miles."

Claire's mind raced. This could be no coincidence, the surprise memorandum immediately followed by a surprise tape. What was going on here? She turned to Tom. "You never said those words?" she whispered. Her stomach ached.

"Claire, that's not me," he said.

"It's your voice."

"That's *not me*," he repeated.

She rose. "Your Honor," she said, her voice loud and emphatic, "this is trial by ambush. That tape was covered in our discovery request, and we should have gotten it long ago."

"Your Honor," Waldron said, "defense counsel just heard me say we just received the tape today, at lunch."

"The question," she replied tartly, "is not when did trial counsel get it. The question is when did the United States *government* get it. This is covered by our discovery request, and trial counsel had a duty to cover the government and find out if *any* part of the U.S. government possessed any relevant information. I planned my case based on what the government disclosed—and now here we are, halfway through this case, and suddenly we have some seriously prejudicial evidence we haven't had an opportunity to test! This is outrageous!"

"Sir," said Waldron, "as defense counsel well knows, these things do happen. Evidence turns up at the eleventh hour—just as happened with this memorandum for the record."

"Well, it's true, Madame Defense Counsel, you can't exactly complain, given you just pulled the same thing."

"What we 'pulled,' Your Honor, was a rectification of prosecutorial misconduct. We were fortunate to have turned up, through our sources, a document that the prosecution should have given us quite some time ago. Now they're trying the same trick again. 'Suddenly' they 'happen' to find a key piece of evidence, and now they're attempting to introduce it into the court so late that they hope we won't have a chance to have our experts examine it. If the Defense Intelligence Agency made this recording thirteen years ago, why has it taken so long to see the light?"

"Sir," Waldron said, "it's not impossible that this court-martial has provoked persons within the gov-

ernment to comb old files for things they might have
otherwise assumed were lost."

Tom said aloud, indignantly: "I don't believe
they're trying this!" Then he raised his voice: "You
check the tape, Claire! That's not me!"

"Sergeant," Farrell said, "you will refrain from
talking. Counsel, you are advised that you are to
keep your client under control. No further outbursts
will be permitted. Now, counsel, I assume you want
a continuance."

"Absolutely, sir. We request one month in order
to conduct a full and thorough examination."

"This is a goddamned frame-up!" Tom shouted, rising.

"Sergeant," Farrell thundered, "I told you to keep
quiet. Now, you were advised that you have a right
to attend this court-martial. However, if you're going to disrupt this court-martial, we will arrange for
you to watch the proceedings by closed-circuit television, do you hear me? You will not sit in my courtroom and disrupt it further, you understand?"

"That's not me!" he shouted. "It's not true. *That's
not my voice!"*

"MPs, take this man away!" Farrell bellowed. The
brig guards immediately surrounded Tom and wres-
tled him to the ground as they clamped the handcuffs on him.

"This is a goddamned frame-up!" Tom shouted.

"I want him out of here *now!"*

The guards yanked at Tom's elbow and led him
away.

"All right," Farrell said to Claire, when the courtroom was finally quiet. "You've got forty-eight
hours."

48

Late at night, Claire and Jackie sat at the kitchen table, drinking and smoking. The tape had already been flown out to one of the world's foremost forensic voice-and-tape analysts, in Boulder, Colorado. Claire had chosen the expert carefully: the woman had done extensive voice-identification work for the military, and had even done cases with Waldron. She was virtually a Pentagon insider, and her word would be unquestioned.

"Of course he denies it," Jackie said carefully. "He's denied everything about this case, Claire. I mean, he denies it's his gun, right?"

"Yeah, well, it's probably not his gun!" Claire said, furious. "Or else they switched the barrel!"

"Of course they could have. These guys can do whatever the fuck they want to. But don't you believe—deep down—that it's his gun? That he fired it? That maybe Colonel Marks gave the order over the radio, maybe he didn't, but *Tom did it*?" She poured more Famous Grouse into both of their glasses.

"No, I don't."

Jackie took a long sip of straight scotch, and shuddered. "Claire, if a man can lie to you about his entire *life*, why can't he lie to you about the one horrible incident he's spent his life evading?"

Claire shook her head. The exhaustion had defeated her. Tears flooded her eyes, and one of them splashed on the table. "I need to talk to him."

The phone rang.

"It's only midnight," Jackie said. "A bit early for the breather."

Claire picked it up, expecting Grimes or Embry.

"Professor Heller?" said a deep female voice. "This is Leonore Eitel, in Boulder."

"Yes?"

"I hope I'm not calling too late—you asked me to call as soon as I had the first results—"

"That's fine." Her heart beat so loud she could barely hear the woman's voice.

"Well, I'm afraid—I'm afraid it may not be what you want to hear."

"It's him, isn't it?" Claire said thickly.

"I want you to know exactly what tests I've run. I used a really quite sophisticated system from Kay Elemetrics, a Computer Speech Lab Model 4300B, to run the oral and spectrographic analysis of the voice, and I matched it against the samples your husband gave me over the phone."

"It's him, isn't it?"

"I looked at things like frequency on the vertical axis, and, in the time domain, the trajectory of formant structure, the consonant-vowel couplings. Pitch, which reflects vocal-fold oscillation and is represented by the vertical striations in the spectrograms—"

"*Damn it, is it Tom's voice?*"

"Yes, it is," the expert said quietly. "I used

twenty-two different words, and I got nineteen very good matches based on the number of formant structures."

"How certain are you?"

"Ninety-nine percent, I'd say. But I'm still not done with my tests, and there's one more thing I need to check."

Eight o'clock the next morning. In the long sterile conference room at the brig, the only one where there wasn't a camera.

"I need the truth now," she said.

He grimaced. "Come on, Claire—"

"No. Tell me the truth. Did you say that?"

"Of course not. We weren't out in the field the day after the massacre, we were back at the hooch. And I never carried the radio—that wasn't my job." He smiled and sandwiched her right hand between his. "Come on, honey."

"That's your voice."

"They faked it somehow."

"You can't fake that, Tom. That's your voice."

"Well, I didn't say all that stuff."

"And you're telling me the truth?"

He withdrew his hands. "I'm telling you the truth," he said softly.

"Promise me."

His eyes expressed hurt. "My God, you think I did it, don't you? They've turned you around, haven't they? They've gotten to you—my own wife!"

"Come on, Tom!" she shouted. "I don't *know* what I think! What about the gun?"

"We're not still talking about that, are we? You proved how easily they could have—"

"Forget what I did and said in there. Forget my courtroom tricks. It's just you and me now."

"You showed how they could have substituted the barrel."

"Don't get legalistic on me. Did you kill those people?"

"Claire—"

"Were you ordered to do it? Is that why everyone's covering up, to protect the general?"

"Claire—"

"If you were ordered to do it—well, that's not really a defense, but we could argue mitigating factors, and—"

"And you think I massacred eighty-seven people?"

She looked at him, not knowing what to say. "Promise me that's not you on the tape."

For a long moment he looked at her, his eyes at once wounded and furious. *"I am not a monster, Claire,"* he said.

There was a loud knock on the door. She opened it to find Embry standing there, out of breath, holding a sheet of paper.

"What have you got there?" Claire asked.

"You asked about Hernandez's medical records a couple of days ago," Embry panted. "I had a buddy of mine check around—they were at the Pentagon dispensary, like I thought. He just faxed this over."

"You got his shrink records?"

"No," Embry said. "Better." He grinned, then broke out into laughter. "Much, much better."

The forensic tape expert, Leonore Eitel, was a petite and dignified-looking woman, slight to the point of tiny, silver-haired, with oversized round black spectacles. She wore a perfect dove-gray suit.

"If you would please stand in front of the witness chair, raise your right hand, and turn and face me,"

Waldron said. The attorneys and the judge were meeting in a separate evidentiary hearing, a 39(a) session. "Do you swear that the evidence you shall give in the case now in hearing shall be the truth, the whole truth, and nothing but the truth, so help you God?"

"I do."

Claire then took Leonore Eitel through her credentials, which were extensive and impressive. Then Eitel stated her findings: that the voice on the tape was indeed that of Ronald M. Kubik, a.k.a. Thomas Chapman.

"And what else, Ms. Eitel, can you tell us about this tape recording?" Claire asked.

"Well, to begin with, using a spectrum analyzer, I detected a sixty-cycle hum on the recording."

"What's the significance of that?"

"That's the sound made by line power. That tells us that the voice was recorded on an electrical, plugged-in tape recorder, as opposed to a battery-operated one."

"But couldn't that hum have come from the tape recorder used by the Signal Corps, the people who allegedly taped the broadcast off the air?"

"No. If the speaker's voice had been broadcast over a field radio and then recorded off the air, I wouldn't have picked up that hum where I did. I can demonstrate precisely what I mean."

"Thank you, but for now, let's move on. Could this hum have been caused by copying the original?"

"No. I'll explain—"

"In a few moments. What else did you observe?"

"The band width was different from what you'd expect to see from a voice broadcast over the air. The range of speech and microphone characteristics was markedly different, in terms of frequency response, from what you'd see in a radio transmission."

"Is that it?"

"Oh, no. There were things missing that should have been there."

"Such as?"

"Such as the keying of the microphone on the field radio, the button you push to transmit or receive. That sound was missing."

"Anything else?"

"There were digital artifacts that shouldn't have been there in an analog tape. That's a real red flag. There were inverted V-shape figures in the upper frequencies, unexplained spikes in there, half an inch apart. Acoustic marks that aren't associated with either speech or an analog tape recorder, but with a computer."

"A computer?"

"That's correct."

"So what are you telling us?"

"That this tape was created on a computer, using editing software to splice together words and phrases. I would speculate that the subject did in fact speak all these words, but in a different order. Perhaps in an interrogation or an interview. My conclusion, and I state it with ninety-nine-percent certainty, is that this tape is a fake. A very, very skillful one—really, a beautiful job—but a fake all the same."

The courtroom exploded. Farrell pounded his gavel. "Order!" he bellowed. "I want order! Trial counsel?"

Waldron's eyes flashed with anger and shame. Both his hands flew up, palms out. "Your Honor," he said, "we had no idea this tape was a forgery, we submitted it in good faith, and we hereby withdraw it—"

"You had a duty," Farrell thundered, "to ascertain if it was real before throwing it into this court."

"Sir, no one is as surprised as we are," Waldron protested. "We had no reason to believe—"

"Sit down, trial counsel! I am appalled. I warned you there'd be no prosecutorial misconduct, and here you've had a general officer lie to this court, then he takes the Fifth like some drug dealer. Now you introduce this tape, and you didn't even *ask* for the time to have it tested! You leave me no choice. Ms. Chapman, do you have a motion for a finding of not guilty on these charges?"

Claire stared at the judge, momentarily speechless. She got slowly to her feet. "Uh—yes, Your Honor, yes, I do."

"Your request is granted," Farrell said. "I find Sergeant First Class Ronald Kubik not guilty of all charges and specifications." He gave a loud wallop of the gavel. "Trial counsel is instructed to prepare the results of the trial, after which the accused is to be returned to the brig for processing out of confinement. This court is adjourned." And with another slam of the gavel, he rose.

Time slowed virtually to a standstill.

All around her was turmoil, yet everything seemed slow, quiet, muffled. The light seemed to have been refracted through a clouded lens. Her suit was soaked through with sweat. She moved slowly, as if underwater. She hugged Tom, then Grimes, then Devereaux. She smiled, laughed, then wept. Devereaux almost crushed her in his immense embrace, then shook Tom's hand, too. Tom was also weeping. Embarrassed, he tried to shield his tear-strewn face from the gaze of others with a splayed hand. As she hugged Tom again, she saw Waldron storm past, then stop, then circle back to her. He stood and waited while Tom patted her on the back and said, "You saved my life, Claire. You saved my life." She felt strange: relieved, of course, and mortally exhausted; but more—mildly depressed, and oddly tense.

"Counselor," Waldron said sharply. He held out his hand, but his countenance was unsmiling. "Congratulations."

She extricated herself from Tom's embrace, held out her hand. "Thank you," she said. She feigned geniality. "You did an impressive job. Apart from all the discovery stuff, which I'd like to believe wasn't your fault."

"It wasn't. Can I call you Claire?"

She shrugged.

"You were a fearsome adversary, Claire, and one I hope I never have to face again."

"Believe me," she said, "I hope I never have to face *you* again, either. Let's talk in private for a minute, okay?"

Waldron hesitated, puzzled. "Sure."

They found a quiet corner of the courtroom where they could talk undisturbed.

"I hope you don't believe I was behind that forged tape," Waldron said.

She avoided his eyes. "Let me put it this way," she said. "I don't think it was necessarily your idea to put bugs in my rented house, but you didn't exactly shy away from using whatever information you were given, right?" Waldron's face was a mask, neutral and inexpressive. His eyes narrowed. "I just think there are a lot of people behind you who wanted to see you succeed. Such as General Marks." She gave him a saccharine smile.

Anger flashed in his hawklike face. "The tape was

given to me," he said. "Believe me, I would never have used it if I had the slightest inkling it was fake. And by the way: he killed himself, did you hear?"

"Who?"

"General Marks. About two hours ago. Bullet through his head with his service revolver. Dressed in his Class A's. In his office at the Pentagon."

She felt the blood drain from her face. *"What?"*

"He knew his career was destroyed, and he'd be facing criminal charges," Waldron said. "He didn't want to go down that way."

"I'm sorry he's not around to see the acquittal," Claire said.

"It wasn't his decision to court-martial your husband."

"Then whose decision was it?"

"Officially, the secretary of the army's—the only one senior to the general. Who never much liked Marks. But I'll bet there were others who persuaded the secretary to convene the court-martial. Rivals of the general's. We'll see who they are when we see who succeeds Marks as chief of staff of the army. He had some powerful enemies."

"So his enemies wanted a court-martial," Claire said, staring into the middle distance, "in order to bring out, even within limited circles, the fact that General Marks probably gave the order to massacre the entire village, even though he didn't know—not being there—that they really were innocent. A horrible mistake. And his enemies knew that a court-martial would bring out the fact that he lied to Congress about it, even had his memorandum destroyed. Lied about the massacre for thirteen years. They knew they'd expose his high crimes." Now she faced Waldron directly. "And yet, at the same time, the court-martial had to be secret, closed to all but military observers. . . ."

"Because, if the word got out that the U.S. military had massacred eighty-seven innocent civilians and covered it up for thirteen years, the worldwide ramifications would be incalculable."

She nodded. "And now the pieces begin to fall into place." She handed him a sheet of paper.

"What?" Waldron said, looking it over. "This is a medical record of some sort. . . . What's the point?"

"Read it," she said.

"It's Hernandez's—what, it's about some eye injury or something?"

"You know that scar under his eye? He got it in 1985. At La Colina."

"Okay," Waldron said, still baffled. "He had it treated at the infirmary at Fort Bragg—"

"Right after the massacre. There's a note there from an ophthalmologist and surgeon."

" 'Burn and laceration to soft tissue inferiolateral to right eye not involving lid margin' . . ." Waldron read. "Why is this important? He got wounded at La Colina. So?"

"In his sworn statements he says he never fired a gun in the village," Claire said. "Now read what the army surgeon wrote there. He recorded exactly what Hernandez told him. We've contacted the surgeon, and he's prepared to back that up."

Waldron read the sheet closely, and looked up after a minute. His eyes were wide with astonishment. "Hernandez was hit just below his right eye by a red-hot ejected shell casing while firing over two hundred rounds with his M-60. His barrel may have overheated, or he swung it a little too wildly. . . . Jesus fucking Christ. Your husband really *is* innocent."

Claire nodded.

"My God," Waldron breathed. He gestured to Hogan to come over at once. "Contact CID," he called. "They've got an arrest to make." He turned back toward Claire. "I—I don't really know what to say."

"Just get the guy who did it," she said, and headed back toward Tom.

They walked out of the courtroom in a daze. The early-summer sunshine was blinding. They blinked owlishly, Tom and she. Tom was still in his chains, but that was how the military worked. They sat on the steps of the building, near the white van, the guards standing by at a discreet distance. Tom was weeping again.

Grimes approached. "Hey, you guys," he said softly. "I guess this is where I say goodbye."

Claire and Tom got to their feet. Claire put her arms around Grimes and pulled him close to her. She hugged him hard, the way a man saved from drowning might hug his rescuer. "I'm going to miss you," she said softly. "Thank you."

"Hey," Grimes said, "I ought to thank *you*. I finally got the fuckers." He noticed Claire crying, and added: "Don't get so emotional. You'll be getting my bill soon. Then you'll *really* cry." And he gave one of his unique, trademarked cackles.

Once Waldron had returned with the document they needed, the report of results of trial, she and Tom got into the white van and were taken to the brig. The next hour was a blur of bureaucratic procedures. The release order was prepared. Tom was escorted to his cell to pack his items. He was sent to sick bay to get his medical records, then to the mail room to fill out a change-of-address card—the mundane things that had to be done!—and then to the control-center supervisor to hand in the checkout sheet. She sat in the confinement-release area and waited. She tried to think clearly, but her mind continued to reel. Then Tom was brought in. His brig uniform was removed, his brig items were taken from him, and his civilian clothes—including a good, freshly pressed suit that Jackie had brought up from Cambridge—were handed to him.

In about an hour, handsome in his charcoal Armani suit and a green tie, Tom was free.

They walked out together hand in hand. She felt the sunshine warm her face. The air was sweet and heavy with the chlorophyll scent of new-mown grass.

"Hey, honey," he said.

"Hey." She turned her face upward and kissed him.

His voice was low and sultry. "You saved my life."

"Aw, it was nothing." She smiled. "And I'll tell you something else. Even better than being acquitted. We've got proof that Hernandez was the shooter." She explained.

For a moment he seemed not to understand. Then his face lit up. "I'll bet Waldron wants to bury it."

She shook her head. "He's already in touch with CID. They're going to bring Hernandez in for questioning, but I'd say he's headed for Leavenworth in six months."

"Or less, if Farrell's on the bench. I love you." He leaned over and kissed her again, this time a serious kiss. "We're going to be a family again."

She squeezed his hand. "We've got some packing to do," she said. "And some celebrating."

For the first time, she dared to believe that they might finally have their life back.

49

"Who's for more paella?" Tom called out, looking around the crowded dinner table. He brandished a large silver ladle over an immense crockery bowl heaped with lobster, mussels, littleneck clams, chicken, shrimp, and innumerable other kinds of seafood mixed with rice, onions, garlic, and about a dozen other things. He made the finest, most delicately seasoned paella Claire had ever tasted. Of all Tom's specialties, this was the one he most liked to prepare for guests.

Around their dining table in Cambridge sat Ray Devereaux and his on-again, off-again girlfriend; Tom's chief trader, the darkly handsome Jeff Rosenthal, and his latest bimbo girlfriend; Claire's closest friend on the Law School faculty, Abe Margolis, gray-bearded, pudgy, around sixty, and Abe's wife; and Claire's good friend Jennifer Evans, very thin, deeply tanned, mid-forties, straight dark hair cut in a highly stylized bob like the silent-film star Louise Brooks. She was unaccompanied, because she was in one of her frequent antimale phases. Next to Claire sat Jackie, who seemed tired, moody, and remote.

Annie, in a white sailor dress already stained with saffron-yellow paella drippings, sat on Tom's lap while he sang to her. She looked little and achingly pretty.

"No more for me," Ray said. "This is my fourth bowl."

"I'll take some," Jeff said, reaching for the ladle to serve himself.

They were all gathered to celebrate Tom's return from an extended business trip to the Canary Islands to explore a potentially enormous venture-capital project, a cover story that none of them seemed to question.

"Wanna switch to red?" Claire said to Abe Margolis's wife, Julia, a large and still very beautiful brunette in her late fifties, who was just finishing a glass of white wine. "Or are you still working on that?" She gave Tom a quick, undetected wink.

"Fill 'er up," Julia said, extending her glass. "If they mix, what the hell, it's rosé." Claire, who'd had a lot to drink, poured unsteadily. "In the glass, if you don't mind," Julia Margolis said.

"I'll have some of that," Devereaux said. "That Chablis?"

"It's merlot," Claire said. "Close enough."

"Wine is wine to me," Devereaux said. "Either it has a cork or a screw-top."

Tom bounced Annie up and down as he continued singing the song he was improvising: "If you're happy and you know it, pick your nose. . . ."

"No!" squealed Annie. "That's not how it goes. It's clap your hands!"

"If you're happy and you know it, pick your nose!" Tom sang in a booming, pleasant baritone.

"No!" she shrieked with delight. "You don't know the words!"

He hoisted her way up in the air. "I love you so much, Annie-Banannie!" he exulted.

"Hey, Tom," called Jen Evans. "In your absence, you missed the grand opening of yet another new restaurant in the South End."

"Another one?" groaned Jeff Rosenthal. "Remember when the South End used to be a scuzzy hellhole? Now you can't walk down Columbus Avenue without tripping over an arugula bush."

"Arugula doesn't come in bushes," his bimbo girlfriend, the stunningly beautiful blonde Candy, objected with great earnestness.

"Oh, really?" Jeff said. A look of embarrassment passed briefly over his face. He was clearly in the terminal stages of infatuation with Candy. "Well, then, it must be a weed or something. Like, Italians are yanking it up from their flower gardens and tossing it in burlap sacks and shipping it off to America, laughing at us the whole time."

Candy shook her head, eyes wide. "It's not a weed, Jeff!" she exclaimed. "You can buy it in supermarkets! I've seen it!"

Jackie, silent and distant, rolled her eyes.

"This restaurant's so loud," Jen went on, "that you practically have to wear earmuffs—you know, those things airport workers have to wear to keep from going deaf when they're working on the jets? Plus they won't give you water or bread unless you specifically request it. Like it might drive them into bankruptcy or something."

"If you're happy and you know it," Tom sang, "then you never better show it—"

"No! No!" Annie screamed, thrilled. "That's wrong!"

"Boy, how do you like that story about the general who offed himself," said Abe Margolis. General William Marks's suicide was the lead news story every-where. "General what's-his-name. I'll bet you we don't have the real story yet. It'll turn out he was facing some big sexual-harassment suit or some-thing."

"Blackmail, maybe," Jeff Rosenthal suggested.

"God, there's just *something* about a man in uni-form," vamped the buxom Julia Margolis breathily, then smiled lasciviously. "Those guys can't keep it in their pants."

For an instant Claire caught Tom's eye. Devereaux inspected his half-finished bowl of paella. There was a brief silence around the table.

"Well," Claire said, getting up, "I could sure use some fizzy water. Any takers?"

Several hands went up. Claire went to the kitchen. Tom set Annie down, and she scampered off. "I'll help you with the glasses," he said, following Claire.

Tom put his arms around Claire's waist as she stood at the refrigerator gathering up cobalt-blue bottles of enormously overpriced Welsh sparkling water. "Hey, hon," he said.

"Hey." She raised her face and kissed him.

Then she said, "You know, Abe says he thinks Harvard's going to keep me on after all. He says Dean Englander told him he fought like hell for me, and he won."

"Of course Englander's going to say that. He's a politician."

The phone rang. Neither one of them made a move to get it.

But Jackie got up from the dining table and an-swered the wall phone at the entrance to the kitchen. "Uh, sure," she said into the receiver. "One second. It's for you, Claire. It's Terry Embry."

"Terry Embry?" she said. Tom shrugged as he

took the cobalt-blue seltzer bottles from her.

She picked up the phone. "Terry?"

"Gosh, I'm really sorry to bother you, um, Claire. Sounds like you guys are having a party, I'm really sorry—"

"Don't worry about it, Terry. What's up?"

"I got that stuff you asked me to get, the logs and all that, and I was going to FedEx it to you."

"To my office, okay?" She gave the address. "And thanks."

"You know Hernandez has gone missing. They want him for questioning, but no one can find him."

"He'll turn up," she said.

She hung up and began gathering water glasses.

50

There was a knock at Claire's office door, then it opened. Connie, her secretary, tilted her head and asked, "Is this a good time to go over some more mail and messages?"

Claire looked up from a law-review article that a student had asked her to read. Distracted, she smiled, nodded.

"We got a real logjam here." Connie sat next to Claire's desk, set down a pile of mail. "I figure if we do an hour in the morning and an hour in the afternoon we'll get caught up on your mail and phone calls by . . . Oh, early next year sometime." She shook her head.

Claire noticed the large white cardboard envelope with the Federal Express logo on it in blue and orange. "That FedEx for me?"

"Oh, right. Just came in." Connie handed it to her.

The sender was Terry Embry. Claire opened the envelope and slid out its contents.

She drew a breath. "Connie," she said, "maybe now's not such a good time after all."

Connie looked at her curiously. "Okay," she said.

"Let me know when." She left slowly, glancing back before she closed the door.

Claire held up the small square black-and-white photograph and examined it. It was an enlistment photograph of a young soldier with dark eyes and dark curly hair. She read the name: LENTINI, ROBERT.

A week or so ago, Ray Devereaux had put in a request with Army Personnel Records to locate the photograph in the archives. Then, at her request, Embry had sent for it.

She knew where she had seen Robert Lentini before, even though Robert Lentini had since lost his head of hair.

Robert Lentini had become a CIA operations officer named Dennis T. Mackie.

Her "deep throat." He had shed his previous identity like a rattlesnake.

Maybe he had always been Dennis T. Mackie. Maybe he was a CIA officer even before he joined Detachment 27 and became Robert Lentini. These things happened. Stranger things, in fact, happened. The CIA liked to plant its people wherever it could.

Her source.

The man who had "somehow" turned up General Marks's memorandum and effectively ended the general's career.

She was beginning to understand. She pulled out a small square of paper, the routing slip that had accompanied the forged tape recording. It was headed CENTRAL INTELLIGENCE AGENCY.

The scrawled initials said "DTM."

DTM was, had to be, Dennis T. Mackie.

Her deep throat.

The man who had "somehow" turned up a tape recording of Tom speaking over a field radio down in El Salvador, and had gotten it to the Defense In-

telligence Agency, the tape that was not just a fake
but provably so—good enough to pass prosecution
scrutiny but not so good that a defense expert
couldn't prove it a fake. The piece of manufactured
evidence that had jettisoned the trial and sprung
Tom.

She felt faint. A splash of stomach acid washed up
into her mouth, brackish and corrosive.

As she thought, she ran her fingers back and forth
inside the FedEx envelope and realized there was
something else in there, a stapled sheaf of papers.
She pulled it out.

The photocopies she'd asked Embry to make from
the Quantico brig visitors' log of the last several
weeks. The logbook that all visitors must sign.

It took her only a few seconds to locate Dennis T.
Mackie's signature in the VISITOR'S NAME column
(REPRESENTING: "Self," he had written); then she
found it twice more. Dennis T. Mackie had visited
Tom three times in the last two weeks of his con-
finement.

Perhaps there was an explanation.

She called Jackie and asked her to pick up Annie
immediately, take her for the night.

Then she called Ray Devereaux and asked his advice.

And then she drove home as quickly as she could,
her heart thudding.

Tom was already there.

The house smelled of garlic, wonderful and invit-
ing.

"Guess we're not having leftover paella," Claire
tried to joke, setting down her briefcase and removing her jacket.

"Linguine with clam sauce," he said. He came

over, gave her a kiss. "Your favorite. Ready to eat? I'm starved."

"Let's eat." Claire smiled. She had no appetite. Her stomach was a small hard ball.

"Where's my little doll?" he asked, dishing out pasta and salad.

"She wanted to sleep over at Jackie's."

"She's really gotten attached to Jackie, hasn't she?" He dug into the pasta. "Sorry. Mind if I start?"

"Go ahead."

"Aren't you going to eat?"

She toyed with her napkin. "Tom, we need to talk."

"Uh-oh," he said through a mouthful of linguine. He chewed, swallowed. "That's not an auspicious opening line." He smiled, took a sip of sparkling water, took another forkful of pasta.

"Who's Lentini?"

Tom's chewing slowed a moment, then resumed. After he'd swallowed, he said casually, "Another member of the unit."

"What's his real name? Lentini or Mackie?"

Tom took a long sip of his fizzy water. His eyes watched her steadily over the curve of the glass. He set down the glass. "What's with the cross-ex, Claire? Trial's over."

She replied very quietly. "Not to me. Not yet."

He shook his head slowly.

She said very quietly, almost in a whisper: "Do you love me, Tom?"

"You know I do."

"Then I need you to tell me the truth now."

He nodded, and with a sad smile, he said: "Lentini—his true name's Mackie, but I always knew him as Lentini—well, he's really a CIA guy. CIA's secretly been his employer ever since he was assigned to the detachment. So, anyway, he tells me that CIA considers—*considered*—Marks a real enemy, a bureaucratic opponent, and they all wanted to undermine his candidacy for the Joint Chiefs job. But I really think that with Lentini it was personal. He despised Marks as much as I did."

"Is that why he gave Waldron the forged tape? To set up the prosecution, sabotage their case?"

"Does it make any difference now?" Tom took another forkful of pasta.

The room was utterly quiet.

"I'd like to know. Was it your idea or his?"

He shook his head as he chewed. He swallowed, said, "Claire, I haven't seen the guy in years. Like thirteen years."

Claire felt herself go numb.

"I have copies of the brig visitors' log," she said. "Right here. He visited you three times."

He regarded her quizzically; then another expression took over, one of calm realization.

Slowly he set down his knife and fork. He breathed a long, soulful sigh. "Claire," he said wearily. "Claire, Claire, Claire. This was all a very long time ago."

She whispered: "You killed those people."

He looked at her pensively. "I don't think Marks knew the peasants were unarmed and innocent, but he was so riled up about his buddy Arlen Ross being killed at the Zona Rosa that he wasn't thinking clearly. Later, when the shit hit the fan back at Fort Bragg and they needed a scapegoat, Marks sure wasn't going to take the fall, and he wasn't going to point the finger at his XO. Even though he gave Hernandez the fire order. So I realized it was my word against a major's, and Marks was on his XO's side, of course. And I knew I had to disappear. Because they were going to pin it on me. And they did, sure enough. And Hernandez and Marks have been blackmailing each other ever since. Partners in crime, so to speak."

"But you fired, too, didn't you?" Claire said. "You helped Hernandez massacre those people."

Tom's eyes became moist. "Marks knew he could count on me. Everyone in the unit refused except me and, of course, Hernandez."

He reached out his hand and placed it over hers. It was warm and damp. She withdrew her hand suddenly, as though she'd been burned. She felt her stomach flip over. Suddenly she felt very tired. "You did it," she said. "You helped Hernandez kill eighty-seven people."

"You have to understand things in their proper context, Claire. These villagers, they were laughing at us. Totally uncooperative. I had to be a little coercive with them."

"Torture them."

"A few of them. Had to. But I couldn't just torture some of them and then leave them there to report human-rights violations, understand? You don't do that. You gotta mop up your own work. I didn't have any choice."

She felt very cold. She crossed her arms over her chest, hugged herself. She shivered.

"Marks knew he could count on me," Tom said again, almost conversationally. "You know, before I went to Vietnam they put me through a whole battery of tests. And . . . and they concluded that I was— what was the expression?—'morally impaired.' Which was their way of saying I was just the kind of guy they needed. For the assassination squads, and later for Detachment 27. I could kill without feeling any guilt or remorse."

She stared at him. The room seemed to be revolving slowly.

"The government *needed* people like me," he said. "Always does. People who can do the job others won't. Then, when they're done with you, it's, 'Oh, we're shocked, *shocked* at what you've done. Here, spend the rest of your life in Leavenworth. Here's your thanks.' I do what they tell me, and suddenly I'm a criminal when they don't need me."

Claire nodded. "I don't get it, Tom," she said. "The ballistics guy—there was evidence of only one shooter. All the bullets came from the same barrel."

"All the bullets he examined. I told you those weren't my bullets."

She needed to make sense of this, even as her head was swimming. "I don't understand."

He shrugged. "I cleared the scene. I always liked to do my own mop-up. Always used my own ammo—German .308 rounds, full metal jacket, steel-cased. Easy to pick up with a magnetic wand. Unlike the standard brass shit Hernandez was using that won't stick to a magnet. I went over the scene pretty carefully, got all the projectiles and cartridge casings. I never like to leave behind my calling card."

Again she nodded. She swallowed hard. She got up from the table, made her way to the wall phone.

"What are you doing, Claire?" he said. He got up, came close. He smiled. "It's over, you know. Remember? I've been found not guilty."

She nodded again. "Of course," she said blandly. She felt queasy. Her stomach boiled like a cauldron. She wanted to vomit. She picked up the receiver, punched out a seven-digit number.

"This is all between you and me, Claire," he said. A note of harshness entered his voice. "You're my lawyer. You're bound by attorney-client privilege."

She could hear ringing on the line.

"It's over, Claire. Double jeopardy, remember? I can't be tried again."

Ringing. Where was Devereaux?

"Don't do it, Claire." He reached over and depressed the plungers, on the top of the phone to break the connection.

She replaced the handset carefully. She looked around the kitchen, furnished so beautifully. So homey. How many breakfasts had they had there, she and Tom and Annie? How many times had Tom cooked dinner for his wife and stepdaughter? And all this time it had been a carefully sustained lie. How safe he had made her feel, when in fact she and her daughter had been living with a dangerous, sick man. "You need to turn yourself in, Tom," she whispered.

"It's not going to happen that way, Claire."

She reached again for the phone.

He moved closer, his body between her and the phone.

"I mean it, babe. Don't do it. Look how much we've gone through together. Look how much we've *got* together, you and me."

She withdrew her hand slowly. "You're sick, Tom," she said, very quietly.

"We're a family," he said. "You and me and Annie. We're a family."

Claire nodded, head spinning, and once again picked up the phone.

"I mean it, Claire. Put down that phone. Think of Annie. There's no reason to do this, Claire. We can be a family again."

She shook her head, tears blurring her eyes, listening to the phone ring.

With a sudden motion he slammed the phone out

of her hand, causing her to lose her balance, knocking her to the floor. He depressed the plunger, reached down to retrieve the handset, and replaced it in the cradle.

"I *need* you, Claire!" he shouted suddenly.

Sprawled on the kitchen floor, she looked up at him, saw his flushed face. She winced. Tears streamed down her cheeks. She reached over to her suit jacket, which hung on the back of one of the kitchen chairs, and retrieved the cell phone. She flipped it open, pulled out the little antenna.

"Claire, babe," he said. His eyes were sad, his face anguished. "I shouldn't have done that. I'm sorry. I just need you to listen to me."

She punched out a few numbers, realized she hadn't pressed the power button.

"Sweetie," he said, and leaned over toward her. He swatted the cell phone out of her hands. It clattered against the tile floor. "Listen. We can be a family again. Put the past behind you. Put it behind you. Think of Annie."

Weeping, unable to focus her eyes, she slunk across the kitchen floor and grabbed the cell phone; he came at her again, kicked it out of her hand.

Pain knifed up her arm. She scrambled to her feet, tried to stumble toward the door, but he blocked her way.

"Understand, Claire, that if you force me to, I'll just disappear again. I've done it before, I can do it again. You know it." His tone was reasonable, calm, in control. The way he reassured her about problems around the house he'd take care of, a toilet that wouldn't stop flushing, a lamp that had burned out, a mouse in the kitchen. "I want you to think of Annie. Think of what's best for her."

"Let me go," she said. "You son of a bitch."

"I know you'll do the right thing. I'd never, *ever* do anything to harm my little dolly if I didn't absolutely have to. Never. But I want you to keep in mind that everything in the world that's precious to you—your sister, your daughter . . . You can never be sure. I'll disappear, and you might not even recognize me, and you and your sister and your daughter will never be safe."   She stared at him in horror, realizing that this was no idle threat, that he meant this. That he would indeed take from her the most precious thing in the world if he had to. Because he was incapable of feeling guilt or remorse. He could do it easily. She shivered again.

"That's a special kind of hell, always having to worry like that," he said. "You don't want that. Believe me."

The doorbell rang, two chimes that echoed like carillon bells. She squeezed past him and ran to open the door.

Behind her, she could hear the chuff of his pants as he came after her. She opened the door, only then realizing how fast her heart was beating.

The pistol looked tiny in Devereaux's massive hand.

"Didn't I tell you to block your caller ID?" Devereaux said. "I get a call, a hangup, and it's your number. I hate hangups. What's going on?"

"Everything's fine," Tom said. "Everything's under control."

Devereaux looked at Claire questioningly. "What's up, Claire?"

Claire stared at him, her eyes desperate. "Ray," she said.

And suddenly there was a series of explosions, from somewhere behind Devereaux, *one-two-three-four*, and the front of his white shirt was stained blood-red. Claire screamed. Tom's body coiled, his eyes alert. Devereaux groaned, grabbed his immense gut, then toppled forward and hit the floor. A great whoosh of air escaped his lungs, like an anguished sigh.

Screaming, she threw herself to the floor next to him, cradled his head. Saw he was alive but feeble with pain. Bright-red blood seeped down the front of his shirt.

Now she saw, entering the front door, Colonel James Hernandez, holding a large pistol. Hernandez was dressed in jeans and a sweatshirt.

"Hey, Ronny, buddy," Hernandez said. "Just like old times, huh?'"

Tom's stance relaxed. "Fuck *you*, old times," he said. "What did you have to go and testify about that dog stuff for, Jimbo. And that torture shit."

Hernandez entered the foyer. "Come on, bud," he said. "You knew Lentini's fake tape would get the case thrown out. You never had anything to worry about, no matter what I said. I just didn't want them going after *me*. And where's my thank you? I just saved your life." He held up his left palm and Tom gave him a "high five."

"Like I saved yours in Nicaragua, Jimmy," Tom said, with a grin.

Claire looked up, watched them in disbelief.

"Jimmy, you deal with the fat fuck here. Get this mess cleaned up. Claire and I have some business to discuss. Then you better get out of here. You've got a lot of people looking for you." He put an arm around Hernandez. "That stunt with the jeep out in Maryland—you almost got my wife here killed. That was stupid. I needed her."

"That wasn't me," Hernandez said. "Maybe some other Special Forces guys, but not—"

A sudden movement. A glint of light off Devereaux's gun as his hand suddenly moved and a bullet exploded in Hernandez's head. Hernandez sagged to his feet, quite obviously dead.

Tom spun around, startled by the gunfire, and, when he saw what had happened, he lunged toward his dead comrade.

At that moment, Claire felt something cold and hard nudge her, and realized that Devereaux was pressing his pistol into her right hand.

Tom saw the gun in her hand. He shook his head in disgust. "Sorry, Claire," he said. His voice was flat, taunting. "No one's here to help you now."

She hesitated, looked back at him as if through fog. Her mouth moved but she could not speak.

She raised the pistol, getting to her feet as she did so. She could barely get her fingers around the grip to reach the trigger. Using both hands to steady it, she aimed at Tom's chest.

Suddenly Tom reached down, grabbed Hernandez's pistol, swept it upward until it was pointing at her. He smiled sweetly. His face transformed back into that of the wonderful man she had loved. "You don't want to hurt me," he said.

She shuddered. Her eyes would not focus.

His smile slowly faded. He was his old self—his new self? "You don't know how to use that thing," he said.

"We'll see," she said.

He watched her intently, then pulled the trigger.

There was a click.

She saw the realization in his eyes that the gun was out of bullets, that Hernandez had fired the last four rounds. He dropped the gun to the foyer floor and looked around, obviously searching for something to use in its place.

"Stop right there, Tom," she said.

"You're not going to fire that," he said, his eyes still roaming the foyer. "You're a lawyer. You work within the system. You play by the rules." His body seemed to be coiling again. "I know you'll do the right thing. For Annie."

She saw his snake eyes light on something. She followed his line-of-sight, saw it was a small marble sculpture on the hall table, and as he suddenly darted forward toward the table, she inhaled, then breathed out noisily. She shuddered. "You're right," she said, and she pulled the trigger. The gun recoiled backward, almost flew from her hand. A bright strawberry of blood appeared on his white shirt at the center of his chest. He sagged to the floor and emitted a horrible, low, animallike sound. She aimed again, and fired. The bullet exploded in his chest. His eyes stared, unseeing, and she knew he was dead.

Her hands began to tremble first, then her shoulders. Her entire body shook violently. She too slumped to the floor.

A great sob welled up in the back of her throat. The floodgates had opened, and the sobs had broken loose and were coming in powerful waves.

She saw that she was kneeling in a pool of Tom's blood, seeping from the wounds in his chest. The fine gray wool of her skirt darkened as the stain spread.

In the distance the wail of sirens grew steadily louder. She caught a sulfurous waft of cordite, then the smell of blood, pungent and metallic, and as she cried she thought of Annie, who'd been no less trusting than she, whose life would never be the same, and yet, at the same moment, for the first time, she felt at peace.